New~ ~stl~ ⚜

Newcastle Librari   **e**

☎ D1586267

Due for return	Due for return	Due for return
17/11/16 ~3.BP		

Please return this item to any of Newcastle's Libraries by the last
date shown above. If not requested by another customer the loan
can be renewed, you can do this by phone, post or in person.
Charges may be made for late returns.

cyberabad days

Ian McDonald

The Little Goddess: Asimov's Science Fiction. Copyright © Ian McDonald 2005
The Djinn's Wife: Asimov's Science Fiction. Copyright © Ian McDonald 2006
Kyle Meets the River: Forbidden Planets, ed. Peter Crowther, Daw Books Ltd.
Copyright © Ian McDonald 2006
Sanjeev and Robotwallah: Fast Forward 1, ed. Lou Anders, Pyr.
Copyright © Ian McDonald 2007
The Dust Assassin: The Starry Rift, ed. Jonathan Strahan, Viking.
Copyright © Ian McDonald 2008

The right of Ian McDonald to be identified as the author of this work has
been asserted by him in accordance with the
Copyright, Designs and Patents Act 1988.

First published in Great Britain in 2009 by Gollancz
An imprint of the Orion Publishing Group
Orion House, 5 Upper St Martin's Lane, London WC2H 9EA
An Hachette UK Company

This edition published in Great Britain in 2009 by Gollancz

1 3 5 7 9 10 8 6 4 2

A CIP catalogue record for this book is available
from the British Library.

ISBN 978 0 575 08406 3

Typeset by Input Data Services Ltd, Bridgwater, Somerset

Printed in Great Britain by CPI Mackays, Chatham ME5 8TD

www.orionbooks.co.uk

The Orion Publishing Group's policy is to use papers that are
natural, renewable and recyclable products and made from wood
grown in sustainable forests. The logging and manufacturing
processes are expected to conform to the environmental
regulations of the country of origin.

contents

be used his stupidity for anyone with eyes

Sanjeev and Robotwallah

Every boy in the class ran at the cry. *Robotwar robotwar!* The teacher called after them, *Come here come here bad wicked things* but she was only a Business-English aeai and by the time old Mrs Mawji hobbled in from the juniors only the girls remained, sitting primly on the floor, eyes wide in disdain and hands up to tell tales and name names.

Sanjeev was not a fast runner, the other boys pulled ahead from him as he stopped among the dhal bushes for puffs from his inhalers. He had to fight for position on the ridge that was the village's high point, popular with chaperoned couples for its views over the river and the water plant at Murad. This day it was the inland view over the dhal fields that held the attention. The men from the fields had been first up to the ridge; they stood, tools in hands, commanding all the best places. Sanjeev pushed between Mahesh and Ayanjit to the front.

'Where are they what's happening what's happening?'

'Soldiers over there by the trees.'

Sanjeev squinted where Ayanjit was pointing but he could see nothing but yellow dust and heat shiver.

'Are they coming to Ahraura?'

'Delhi wouldn't bother with a piss-hole like Ahraura,' said another man whose face Sanjeev knew – as he knew every face in Ahraura – if not his name. 'It's Murad they're after. If they take that out, Varanasi will have to make a deal.'

'Where are the robots? I want to see the robots.'

Then he cursed himself for his stupidity for anyone with eyes could see where the robots were. A great cloud of dust was moving down the north road and over it a flock of birds milled in eerie silence. Through the dust Sanjeev caught sunlight flashes of armour, clawed booted feet lifting, antennae bouncing, insect heads bobbing, weapon pods glinting. Then he and everyone else up on the high place felt the ridge begin to tremble to the march of the robots.

A cry from down the line. Four, six, ten, twelve flashes of light from the copse; streaks of white smoke. The flock of birds whirled up into an arrowhead and aimed itself at trees. *Airdrones*, Sanjeev realised and, in the same thought, *missiles!* As the missiles reached their targets the cloud of dust exploded in a hammer of gunfire and firecracker flashes. It was all over before the sound reached the watchers. The robots burst unscathed from their cocoon of dust in a thundering run. *Cavalry charge!* Sanjeev shouted, his voice joining with the cheering of the men of Ahraura. Now hill and village quaked to the running iron feet. The wood broke into a fury of gunfire, the airdrones rose up and circled the copse like a storm. Missiles smoked away from the charging robots; Sanjeev watched weapon housings open and gunpods swing into position.

The cheered died as the edge of the wood exploded in a wall of flame. Then the robots opened up with their guns and the hush became awed silence. The burning woodland was swept away in the storm of gunfire; leaves, branches, trunks shredded into splinters. The robots stalked around the perimeter of the small copse for ten minutes, firing constantly as the drones circled over their heads. Nothing came out.

A voice down the line started shouting *Jai Bharat! Jai Bharat!* but no one took it up and the man soon stopped. But there was another voice, hectoring and badgering, the voice of school-mistress Mawji labouring up the path with a lathi cane.

'Get down from there you stupid stupid men! Get to your families, you'll kill yourselves.'

Everyone looked for the story on the evening news but bigger flashier things were happening in Allahabad and Mirzapur; a handful of contras eliminated in an unplace like Ahraura did not rate a line. But that night Sanjeev became Number One Robot Fan. He cut out pictures from the papers and those pro-Bharat propaganda mags that survived Ahraura's omnivorous cows. He avidly watched J- and C-anime where andro-sexy kids crewed titanic battle droids until sister Priya rolled her eyes and his mother whispered to the priest that she was worried about her son's sexuality. He pulled gigabytes of pictures from the world web and memorised manufacturers and models and serial numbers, weapon loads and options mounts, rates of fire and maximum speeds. He saved up the pin-money he made from helping old men with the computers the self-proclaimed Bharati government thought every village should have to buy a Japanese trump game but no one would play him at it because he had learned all the details. When he tired of flat pictures, he cut up old cans with tin-snips and brazed them together into model fighting machines; MIRACLE GHEE fast pursuit drones, TITAN DRENCH perimeter defence bots, RED COLA riot-control robot.

Those same old men, when he came round to set up their accounts and assign their passwords, would ask him, 'Hey! You know a bit about these things; what's going on with all this Bharat and Awadh stuff? What was wrong with plain old India anyway? And when are we going to get cricket back on the satellite?'

For all his robot-wisdom, Sanjeev did not know. The news breathlessly raced on with the movements of politicians and breakaway leaders but everyone had long ago lost all clear memory of how the conflict had begun. Naxalites in Bihar, an over-mighty Delhi, those bloody Muslims demanding their own laws again? The old men did not expect him to answer, they just liked to complain and took a withered pleasure in showing the smart boy that he did not know everything.

'Well, as long as that's the last we see of them,' they would say when Sanjeev replied with the spec of a Raytheon 380 *Rudra* I-war airdrone, or an *Akhu* scout mecha and how much much better they were than any human fighter. Their general opinion was that the Battle of Vora's Wood – already growing back – was all the War of Separation Ahraura would see.

It was not. The men did return. They came by night, walking slowly through the fields, their weapons easily sloped in their hands. Those that met them said they had offered them no hostility, merely raised their assault rifles and shooed them away. They walked through the entire village, through every field and garden, up every gali and yard, past every byre and corral. In the morning their bootprints covered every centimetre of Ahraura. Nothing taken, nothing touched. *What was that about?* the people asked. *What did they want?*

They learned two days later when the crops began to blacken and wither in the fields and the animals, down to the last pi-dog, sickened and died.

Sanjeev would start running when their car turned into Umbrella Street. It was an easy car to spot, a big military hummer that they had pimped Kali-black and red with after-FX flames that seemed to flicker as it drove past you. But it was an easier car to hear: everyone knew the thud thud thud of Desi-metal that grew guitars and screaming vocals when they wound down the window to order food, food to go. And Sanjeev would be there, *What can I get you sirs?* He had become a good runner since coming to Varanasi. Everything had changed since Ahraura died.

The last thing Ahraura ever did was make that line in the news. It had been the first to suffer a new attack. *Plaguewalkers* was the popular name; the popular image was dark men in chameleon camouflage walking slowly through the crops, hands outstretched as if to bless, but sowing disease and blight. It was a strategy of desperation – deny the separatists as much as they could – and only ever partially effective; after the few first attacks plaguewalkers were shot on sight.

But they killed Ahraura, and when the last cow died and the wind whipped the crumbled leaves and the dust into yellow clouds the people could put it off no longer. By car and pick-up, phatphat and country bus they went to the city, and though they had all sworn to hold together, family by family they drifted apart in Varanasi's ten million and Ahraura finally died.

Sanjeev's father rented an apartment on the top floor of a block on Umbrella Street and put his savings into a beer-and-pizza stall. Pizza pizza, that is what they want in the city, not samosas or tiddy-hoppers or rasgullahs. And beer, Kingfisher and Godfather and Bangla. Sanjeev's mother did light sewing and gave lessons in deportment and Sanskrit, for she had learned that language as part of her devotions. Grandmother Bharti and little sister Priya cleaned offices in the new shining Varanasi that rose in glass and chrome beyond the huddled peeling houses of old Kashi. Sanjeev helped out at the stall under the rows of tall neon umbrellas that gave the street its name, useless against rain and sun both but magnetic to the party-people, the night-people, the badmashes and fashion-girlis. It was there that he had first seen the robotwallahs.

It had been love at first sight the night that Sanjeev saw them stepping down Umbrella Street in their slashy Ts and bare sexy arms with Krishna bangles and henna tats, cool cool boots with metal in all the hot places and hair spiked and gelled like one of those J-anime shows. The merchants of Umbrella Street edged away from them, turned a shoulder. They had a cruel reputation. Later Sanjeev was to see them overturn the stall of a pakora man who had irritated them, eve-tease a woman in a business sari who had looked askance at them, smash up the phatphat of a taxi-driver who had thrown them out for drunkenness, but that first night they were stardust and he wanted to be them with a want so pure and aching and impossible it was tearful joy. They were soldiers, teen warriors, robotwallahs. Only the dumbest and cheapest machines could be trusted to run themselves; the big fighting bots carried human jockeys behind their aeai systems. Teenage boys possessed the best combination of reflex speed and viciousness, amped up with fistfuls of combat drugs.

'Pizza pizza pizza!' Sanjeev shouted, running up to them. 'We got pizza every kind of pizza and beer, Kingfisher beer, Godfather beer, Bangla beer, all kinds of beer.'

They stopped. They turned. They looked. Then they turned away. One looked back as his brothers moved. He was tall and very thin from the drugs, fidgety and scratchy, his bad skin ill-concealed with make-up. Sanjeev thought him a street-god.

'What kind of pizza?'

'Tikka tandoori murgh beef lamb kebab kofta tomato spinach.'

'Let's see your kofta.'

Sanjeev presented the drooping wedge of meatball-studded pizza in both hands. The robotwallah took a kofta between thumb and forefinger. It drew a sagging string of cheese to his mouth, which he deftly snapped.

'Yeah, that's all right. Give me four of those.'

'We got beer we got Kingfisher beer we got Godfather beer we got Bangla beer ...'

'Don't push it.'

Now he ran up alongside the big slow-moving car they had bought as soon as they were old enough to drive. Sanjeev had never thought it incongruous that they could send battle robots racing across the country on scouting expeditions or marching behind heavy tanks, but the law would not permit them so much as a moped on the public streets of Varanasi.

'Do did you kill anyone today?' he called in through the open window, clinging on to the door handle as he jogged through the choked street.

'Kunda Khadar, down by the river, chasing out spies and surveyors,' said bad-skin boy, the one who had first spoken to Sanjeev. He called himself Rai. They all had made-up J-anime names. 'Someone's got to keep those bastard Awadhi damwallahs uncomfortable.'

A black plastic Kali swung from the rear-view mirror, red-tongued, yellow-eyed. The skulls garlanded around her neck had costume-sapphires for eyes. Sanjeev took the order, sprinted back through the press to his father's clay tandoor oven. The order was ready by the time the Kali-hummer made its second cruise. Sanjeev slid the boxes to Rai. He slid back the filthy, wadded Government of Bharat scrip-rupees and, as Sanjeev fished out his change from his belt-bag, the tip: a little plastic zip-bag of battle-drugs. Sanjeev sold them in the galis and courtyards behind Umbrella Street. Schoolkids were his best customers, they went through them by the fistful when they were cramming for exams. Ahraura had been all the school Sanjeev ever wanted to see. Who needed it when you had the world and the web in your palmer? The little shining capsules in black and yellow, purple and sky blue, were the Rajghatta's respectability. The pills held them above the slum.

But this night Rai's hand shot out to seize Sanjeev's hand as it closed around the plastic bag.

'Hey, we've been thinking.' The other robotwallahs, Suni and Ravana and Godspeed! and Big Baba nodded. 'We're thinking we could use someone around the place, do oddjobs, clean a bit, keep stuff sweet, get us things. Would you like to do it? We'd pay – it'd be government scrip not dollars or euro. Do you want to work for us?'

He lied about it to his family: the glamour, the tech, the sexy spun-diamond headquarters and the chrome he brought up to dazzling dazzling shine by the old village trick of polishing it with toothpaste. Sanjeev lied from disappointment, but also from his own naive over-expectation: too many nights filled with androgynous teenagers in spandex suits being clamshelled up inside block-killing battle machines. The robotwallahs of the 15th Light Armoured and Recon Cavalry – sowars properly – worked out of a cheap pressed-aluminium go-down on a dusty commercial road at the back of the new railway station. They sent their wills over provinces and countries to fight for Bharat. Their talents were too rare to risk in Raytheon assault bots or Aiwa scout mecha. No robotwallah ever came back in a bodybag.

Sanjeev had scratched and kicked in the dust, squatting outside the shutter door squinting in the early light. Surely the phatphat had brought him to the wrong address? Then Rai and Godspeed! had brought him inside and shown him how they made war inside a cheap go-down. Motion-capture harnesses hung from steadi-rigs like puppets from a hand. Black mirror-visored insect helmets – real J-anime helmets – trailed plaited cables. One wall of the go-down was racked up with the translucent blue domes of processor cores, the adjoining wall a massive video-silk screen flickering with the ten thousand dataflashes of the ongoing war: skirmishes, reconnaissances, air-strikes, infantry positions, minefields and slow-missile movements, heavy armour, and the mecha divisions. Orders came in on this screen from a woman jemadar at Divisional Headquarters. Sanjeev never saw her flesh. None of the robotwallahs had ever seen her flesh, though they joked about it every time she came on the screen to order them to a reconnaissance or a skirmish or a raid. Along the facing wall, behind the battle-harnesses, were cracked leather sofas, sling chairs, a water cooler (full), a coke machine (three quarters empty). Gaming and girli mags were scattered like dead birds across the sneaker-scuffed concrete floor. A door led to a rec-room, with more sofas, a couple of folding beds and a game console with three VR sets. Off the rec-room were a small kitchen area and a shower unit.

'Man, this place stinks,' said Sanjeev.

By noon he had cleaned it front to back top to bottom magazines stacked in date of publication shoes set together in pairs lost clothes in a black plastic sack for the dhobiwallah to launder. He lit incense. He threw out the old bad milk and turning food in the refrigerator, returned the empty Coke bottles for their deposits – made chai and sneaked out to get samosas which he passed off as his own. He nervously watched Big Baba and Ravana step into their battle-harnesses for a three-hour combat mission. So much he learned in that first morning. It was not one boy one bot; Level 1.2 aeais controlled most of the autonomous processes like motion and perception, the pilots were more like officers, each commanding a bot platoon, their point-of-view switching from scout machine to assault bot to I-war drone. And they did not have their favourite old faithful combat machine, scarred with bullet holes and lovingly customised with hand-sprayed graffiti and Desi-metal demons. Machines went to war because they could take damage human flesh and families could not. The Kali Cavalry rotated between a dozen units a month as attrition and the jemadar dictated. It was not not not Japanese anime, but the Kali boys did look sexy dangerous cool in their gear even if they went home to their parents every night, and working for them cleaning for them getting towels for them when they went sweating and stinking to the shower after a tour in the combat rig was the maximum thing in Sanjeev's small life. They were his children, they were his boys; no girls allowed.

'Hanging round with those badmashes all day, never seeing a wink of sun, that's not good for you,' his mother said, sweeping round the tiny top-floor living room before her next lesson. 'Your dad needs the help more; he may have to hire a boy in, what kind of sense does that make, when he has a son of his own? They do not have a good reputation, those robot-boys.'

Then Sanjeev showed her the money he had got for one day.

'Your mother worries about people taking advantage of you,' Sanjeev's dad said, loading up the handcart with wood for the pizza oven. 'You weren't born to this city. All I'd say is, don't love it too much, soldiers will let you down, they can't help it. All wars eventually end.'

With what remained from his money when he had divided it between his mother and father and put some away in the credit union for Priya, Sanjeev went down to Tea Lane and stuck down the deposit and first payment on a pair of big metally leathery black and red and flame-pattern boots. He wore them proudly to work the next day, stuck out beside the driver of the phatphat so everyone could see them, and paid the owner of the Bata Boot and Shoe store assiduously every Friday. At the end of twelve weeks they were Sanjeev's entirely. In that time he had also bought the Ts, the fake-latex pants (real latex hot hot far too hot and sweaty for Varanasi, baba), the Kali bangles and necklaces, the hair gel and the eye kohl but the boots first, the boots before all. Boots make the robotwallah.

'Do you fancy a go?'

It was one of those questions so simple and unexpected that Sanjeev's brain rolled straight over it and it was only when he was gathering up the fast-food wrappers (messy messy boys) that it crept up and hit him over the head.

'What, you mean, that?' A nod of the head toward the harnesses hanging like flayed hides from the feedback rig.

'If you want; there's not much on.'

There hadn't been much on for the better part of a month. The last excitement had been when some cracker in a similar go-down in Delhi had broken through the Kali Cav's aeai firewall with a spike of burnware. Big Baba had suddenly leaped up in his rig like a million billion volts had just shot through (which, Sanjeev discovered later, it kind of had) and next thing the biocontrol interlocks had blown (indoor fireworks, woo) and he was kicking on the floor like epilepsy. Sanjeev had been first to the red button and a crash team had whisked him to the rich people's private hospital. The aeais had evolved a patch against the new burnware by the time Sanjeev went to get the lunch tins from the dhabawallah and Big Baba was back on his corner of the sofa within three days suffering nothing more than a lingering migraine. Jemadar-woman sent a get well e-card.

So it was with excitement and wariness that Sanjeev let Rai help him into the rig. He knew all the snaps and grips, he had tightened the straps and pulled snug the motion sensors a hundred times, but Rai doing it made it special, made Sanjeev a robotwallah.

'You might find this a little freaky,' Rai said as he settled the helmet over Sanjeev's head. For an instant it was black-out, deafness as the phonobuds sought out his eardrums. 'They're working on this new thing, some kind of bone induction thing so they can send the pictures and sounds straight into your brain,' he heard Rai's voice say on the com. 'But I don't think we'll get it in time. Now, just stand there and don't shoot anything.'

The warning was still echoing in Sanjeev's inner ear as he blinked and found himself standing outside a school compound in a village so like Ahraura that he instinctively looked for Mrs Mawji and Shree the holy red calf. Then he saw that the school was deserted, its roof gone, replaced with military camouflage sheeting. The walls were pocked with bullets down to the brickwork. Siva and Krishna with his flute had been hastily painted on the intact mud plaster, and the words, *13th Mechanised Sowar: Section Headquarters*. There were men in smart, tightly belted uniforms with moustaches and bamboo lathis. Women with brass water pots and men on bicycles passed the open gate. By stretching Sanjeev found he could elevate his sensory rig to crane over the wall. A village, an Ahraura, but too poor to even avoid war. On his left a robot stood under a dusty neem tree. *I must be one of those*, Sanjeev thought; a General Dynamics A8330 *Syce;* a mean, skeletal desert-rat of a thing on two vicious clawed feet, a heavy sensory crown and two gatling arms – fully interchangeable with gas shells or slime guns for policing work, he remembered from *War Mecha*'s October 2023 edition.

Sanjeev glanced down at his own feet. Icons opened across his field of vision like blossoming flowers: location elevation temperature, ammunition load-out, the level of methane in his fuel tanks, tactical and strategic satmaps – he seemed to be in south-west Bihar – but what fascinated Sanjeev was that if he formed a mental picture of lifting his Sanjeev-foot, his *Syce-claw* would lift from the dust.

Go on try it it's a quiet day you're on sentry duty in some cow-shit Bihar village.

Forward, he willed. The bot took one step, two. *Walk*, Sanjeev commanded. *There*. The robot walked jauntily toward the gate. No one in the street of shattered houses looked twice as he stepped among them. *This is great!* Sanjeev thought as he strolled down the street, then, *This is like a game*. Doubt then: *So how do I even know this war is happening?* A step too far; the *Syce* froze a hundred metres from the Ganesh temple, turned and headed back to its sentry post. *What what what what what?* he yelled in his head.

'The onboard aeai took over,' Rai said, his voice startling as a firecracker inside his helmet. Then the village went black and silent and Sanjeev was blinking in the ugly low-energy neons of the Kali Cavalry battle room, Rai gently unfastening the clips and snaps and strappings.

That evening, as he went home through the rush of people with his fist of rupees, Sanjeev realised two things; that most of war was boring, and that this boring war was over.

The war was over. The jemadar visited the video-silk wall three times, twice, once a week where in the heat and glory she would have given orders that many times a day. The Kali Cav lolled around on their sofas playing games, lying to their online fans about the cool exciting sexy things they were doing, though the fans never believed they ever really were robotwallahs, but mostly doing battle-drug combos that left them fidgety and aggressive. Fights flared over a cigarette, a look, how a door was closed or left open. Sanjeev threw himself into the middle of a dozen robotwallah wars. But when the American peacekeepers arrived Sanjeev knew it truly was over because they only came in when there was absolutely no chance any of them would get killed. There was a flurry of car-bombings and I-war attacks and even a few suicide blasts but everyone knew that that was just everyone who had a grudge against America and Americans in sacred Bharat. No, the war was over.

'What will you do?' Sanjeev's father asked, meaning, *What will I do when Umbrella Street becomes just another Asian ginza?*

'I've saved some money,' Sanjeev said.

With the money he had saved, Godspeed! had bought a robot. It was a Tata Industries D55, a small but nimble anti-personnel bot with detachable free-roaming sub-mechas, Level 0.8s, about as smart as a chicken, which they resembled. Even second-hand it must have cost much more than a teenage robotwallah heavily consuming games, online time, porn and Sanjeev's dad's kofta pizza could ever save. 'I got backers,' Godspeed! said. 'Funding. Hey, what do you think of this? I'm getting her pimped, this is the skin-job.' When the paint dried the robot would be road-freighted up to Varanasi.

'But what are you going to do with it?' Sajeev asked.

'Private security. They're always going to need security drones.'

Tidying the tiny living room that night for his mother's nine o'clock lesson, opening the windows to let out the smell of hot ghee though the stink of the street was little better, Sanjeev heard a new chord in the ceaseless song of Umbrella Street. He threw open the window shutters in time to see an object, close, fast as a dashing bird, dart past his face, swing along the powerline and down the festooned pylon. Glint of anodised alu-plastic: a boy raised on *Battlebots Top Trumps* could not fail to recognise a Tata surveillance mecha. Now the commotion at the end of the Umbrella Street became clear: the hunched back of a battlebot was pushing between the cycle rickshaws and phatphats. Even before he could fully make out the customised god-demons of Mountain Buddhism on its carapace, Sanjeev knew the machine's make and model and who was flying it.

A badmash on an alco moto rode slowly in front of the ponderously stepping machine, relishing the way the street opened in front of him and the electric scent of heavy firepower at his back. Sanjeev saw the mech step up and squat down on its hydraulics before Jagmohan's greasy little pakora stand. The badmash skidded his moped to a stand and pushed up his shades.

They will always need security drones.

Sanjeev rattled down the many many flights of stairs of the patriotically-renamed Diljit Rana Apartments, yelling and pushing and beating at the women and young men in very white shirts. The robot had already taken up its position in front of his father's big clay pizza oven. The carapace unfolded like insect wings into weapon mounts. Badmash was all teeth and grin in the anticipation of another commission. Sanjeev dashed between his father and the prying, insect sensory rig of the robot. Red demons and Sivas with fiery tridents looked down on him.

'Leave him alone, this is my dad, leave him be.'

It seemed to Sanjeev that the whole of Umbrella Street, every vehicle upon it, every balcony and window that overlooked it, stopped to watch. With a whir the weapon pods retracted, the carapace clicked shut. The battle machine reared up on its legs as the surveillance drones came skittering between people's legs and over counter-tops, scurried up the machine and took their places on its shell mounts, like egrets on the back of a buffalo. Sanjeev stared the badmash down. He sneered, snapped down his cool sexy dangerous shades and spun his moped away.

Two hours later, when all was safe and secure, a Peacekeeper unit had passed up the street asking for information. Sanjeev shook his head and sucked on his asthma inhalers.

'Some machine, like.'

Suni left the go-down. No word no note no clue, his family had called and called and called but no one knew. There had always been rumours of a man with money and prospects, who liked the robotwallah thing, but you do not tell those sorts of stories to mothers. Not at first asking. A week passed without the jemadar calling. It was over. So over. Rai had taken to squatting outside, squinting up through his cool sexy dangerous shades at the sun, watching for its burn on his pale arms, chain-smoking street-rolled bidis.

'Sanj.' He smoked the cheap cigarette down to his gloved fingers and ground the stub out beneath the steel heel of his boot. 'When it happens, when we can't use you any more, have you something sorted? I was thinking, maybe you and I could do something together, go somewhere. Just have it like it was, just us. An idea, that's all.'

The message came at three a.m. *I'm outside.* Sanjeev tiptoed around the sleeping bodies to open the window. Umbrella Street was still busy, Umbrella Street had not slept for a thousand years.

The big black Kali Cav hummer was like a funeral moving through the late night people of the new Varanasi. The door locks made too much noise so Sanjeev exited through the window, climbing down the pipes like a Raytheon Double- eight thousand I-war infiltration bot. In Ahraura he would never have been able to do that.

'You drive,' Rai said. From the moment the message came through, Sanjeev had known it would be him, and him alone.

'I can't drive.'

'It drives itself. All you have to do it steer. It's not that different from the game. Swap over there.'

Steering wheel pedal drive windshield display all suddenly looked very big to Sanjeev in the driver's seat. He touched his foot to the gas. Engines answered, the hummer rolled, Umbrella Street parted before him. He steered around a wandering cow.

'Where do you want me to go?'

'Somewhere, away. Out of Varanasi. Somewhere no one else would go.' Rai bounced and fidgeted on the passenger seat. His hands were busy busy, his eyes were huge. He had done a lot of battle drugs. 'They sent them back to school, man. To school, can you imagine that? Big Baba and Ravana. Said they needed real-world skills. I'm not going back, not never. Look!'

Sanjeev dared a glance at the treasure in Rai's palm: a curl of sculpted translucent pink plastic. Sanjeev thought of aborted goat foetuses, and the sex toys the girls had used in their favourite pornos. Rai tossed his head to sweep back his long, gelled hair and slid the device behind his ear. Sanjeev thought he saw something move against Rai's skin, seeking.

'I saved it all up and bought it. Remember, I said? It's new, no one else has one. All that gear, that's old, you can do everything with this, just in your head, in the pictures and words in your head.' He gave a stoned grin and moved his hands in a dancer's mudra. 'There.'

'What?'

'You'll see.'

The hummer was easy to drive: the in-car aeai had a flocking reflex that enabled it to navigate Varanasi's ever-swelling morning traffic, leaving little for Sanjeev to do other than blare the triple horns, which he enjoyed a lot. Somewhere he knew he should be afraid, should feel guilty at stealing away in the night without word or note, should say stop, whatever it is you are doing, it can come to nothing, it's just silliness, the war is over and we must think properly about what to do next. But the brass sun was rising above the glass towers and spilling into the streets and men in sharp white shirts and women in smart saris were going busy to their work, and he was free, driving a big smug car through them all and it was so good, even if just for a day.

He took the new bridge at Ramnagar, hooting in derision at the gaudy, lumbering trucks. The drivers blared back, shouting vile curses at the girli-looking robotwallahs. Off A roads on to B roads, then to tracks and then bare dirt, the dust flying up behind the hummer's fat wheels. Rai itched in the passenger seat, grinning away to himself and moving his hands like butterflies, muttering small words and occasionally leaning out of the window. His gelled hair was stiff with dust.

'What are you looking for?' Sanjeev demanded.

'It's coming,' Rai said, bouncing on his seat. 'Then we can go and do whatever we like.'

From the word *drive*, Sanjeev had known where he must go. Satnav and aeai did his remembering for him but he still knew every turn and side road. Vora's Wood there, still stunted and grey; the ridge between the river and the fields from which all the men of the village had watched the battle and he had fallen in love with the robots. The robots had always been pure, had always been true. It was the boys who flew them who hurt and failed and disappointed. The fields were all dust, drifted and heaped against the lines of thorn fence. Nothing would grow here for a generation. The mud walls of the houses were crumbling, the school a roofless shell, the temple and tanks clogged with windblown dust. Dust, all dust. Bones cracked and went to powder beneath his all-wheeli drive. A few too desperate even for Varanasi were trying to scratch an existence in the ruins. Sanjeev saw wire-thin men and tired women, dust-smeared children crouched in front of their brick-and-plastic shelters. The poison deep within Ahraura would defeat them in the end.

Sanjeev brought the hummer to a halt on the ridge top. The light was yellow, the heat appalling. Rai stepped out to survey the terrain.

'What a shit-hole.'

Sanjeev sat in the shade of the rear cabin watching Rai pace up and down, up and down, kicking up the dust of Ahraura with his big Desi-metal boots. *You didn't stop them, did you?* Sanjeev thought. *You didn't save us from the Plaguewalkers.* Rai suddenly leaped and punched the air.

'There, there, look!'

A storm of dust moved across the dead land. The high sun caught glints and gleams at its heart. Moving against the wind, the tornado bore down on Ahraura.

The robot came to a halt at the foot of the ridge where Sanjeev and Rai stood waiting. A Raytheon ACR, a heavy line-of-battle bot, it out-topped them by some metres. The wind carried away its cloak of dust. It stood silent, potential, heat shimmering from its armour. Sanjeev had never seen a thing so beautiful.

Rai raised his hand. The bot spun on its steel hooves. More guns than Sanjeev had ever seen in his life unfolded from its carapace. Rai clapped his hands and the bot opened up with all its armaments on Vora's Wood. Gatlings sent dry dead silvery wood flying up into powder, missiles streaked from its back-silos; the line of the wood erupted in a wall of flame. Rai separated his hands and the roar of sustained fire ceased.

'I got it all in here, everything that the old grai had, in here Sanj, everyone will want us, we can go wherever we want, we can do whatever we want, we can be real anime heroes.'

'You stole it.'

'I had all the protocols. That's the system.'

'You stole that robot.'

Rai balled his fists, shook his head in exasperation.

'Sanj, it was always mine.'

He opened his clenched fist. And the robot danced. Arms, feet, all the steps and the moves, the bends and head-nods, a proper Bollywood item-song dance. The dust flew up around the battle-bot's feet. Sanjeev could feel the eyes of the squatters, wide and terrified in their hovels. *I am sorry we scared you.*

Rai brought the dance to an end.

'Anything I want, Sanj. Are you coming with us?'

Sanjeev's answer never came, for a sudden, shattering roar of engines and jet-blast from the river side of the ridge sent them reeling and choking in the swirling dust. Sanjeev fought out his inhalers: two puffs blue one puff brown and by the time they had worked their sweet way down into his lungs a tilt-jet with the Bharati air force's green white and orange roundels on its engine pods stood on the settling dust. The cargo ramp lowered, a woman in dust-war camou and a mirror-visored helmet came up the ridge toward them.

With a wordless shriek Rai slashed his hand through the air like a sword. The bot crouched, its carapace slid open in a dozen places, extruding weapons. Without breaking her purposeful stride the woman lifted her left hand. The weapons retracted, the hull ports closed, the war machine staggered as if confused and then sat down heavily in the dead field, head sagging, hands trailing in the dust. The woman removed her helmet. The cameras made the jemadar look five kilos heavier, but she had big hips. She tucked her helmet under her left arm, and with her right swept back her hair to show the control unit coiled behind her ear.

'Come on now, Rai. It's over. Come on, we'll go back. Don't make a fuss. There's not really anything you can do. We all have to think what to do next, you know? We'll take you back in the plane, you'll like that.' She looked Sanjeev up and down. 'I suppose you could take the car back. Someone has to and it'll be cheaper than sending someone down from Divisional, it's cost enough already. I'll retask the aeai. And then we have to get that thing ...' She shook her head, then beckoned to Rai. He went like a calf, quiet and meek down to the tilt-jet. Black hopping crows settled on the robot, trying its crevices with their curious shiny-hungry beaks.

The hummer ran out of gas twenty kays from Ramnagar. Sanjeev hitched home to Varanasi. The army never collected it and as the new peace built, the local people took it away bit by bit.

With his war dividend Sanjeev bought a little alco-buggy and added a delivery service to his father's pizza business, specialising in the gap-year hostels that blossomed after the peacekeepers left. He wore a polo-shirt with a logo and a baseball cap and got a sensible haircut. He could not bring himself to sell his robotwallah gear, but it was a long time before he could look at it in the box without feeling embarrassed. The business grew fast and fat.

He often saw Rai down at the ghats or around the old town. They worked the same crowd: Rai dealt Nepalese ganja to tourists. Robotwallah was his street name. He kept the old look and everyone knew him for it. It became first a novelty and then retro. It even became fashionable again, the spiked hair, the andro make-up, the slashed Ts and the latex and most of all the boots. It sold well and everyone wore it, for a season.

Kyle Meets the River

Kyle was the first to see the exploding cat. He was coming back from the compound HFBR-Mart with the slush cone – his reward for scoring a goal in the under elevens – squinted up at the sound of a construction helicopter (they were still big and marvellous and exciting) and saw it leap the narrow gap between the med centre and Tinneman's coffee bar. He pointed to it one fragment of a second before the security men picked it up on their visors and started yelling. In an instant the compound was full of fleeing people; men and women running, parents sweeping up kids, guards sweeping their weapons this way and that as the cat, sensing it had been spotted, leaped from the roof in two bounds onto the roof of an armoured Landcruiser, then dived to ground and hunted for targets. A security guard raised his gun. He must be new. Even Kyle knew not to do that. They were not really cats at all, but smart missiles that behaved like them, and if you tried to catch them or threatened them with a weapon, they would attack and blow themselves up. From the shade of the arcade he could see the look on the guard's face as he tried to get a fix on the dashing, dodging robot. Machine-gun rattle. Kyle had never heard it so close. It was very exciting. Bullets cracked all over the place, flying wild. Kyle thought that perhaps he should hide himself behind something solid. But he wanted to see. He had heard it so many times before and now here it was, on the main streets in front of him. That cat-missile was getting really really close. Then the guard let loose a lucky burst; the steel cat went spinning up into the air and blew itself up.

Kyle reeled back. He had never heard anything so loud. Shrapnel cracked the case of the Coke machine beside him into red and white stars. The security man was down but moving, scrabbling away on his back from the blast site and real soldiers were arriving, and a med Hummer, and RAV airdrones. Kyle stood and stared. It was wonderful wonderful wonderful and all for him, and there was Mom, running towards him in her flappy-hands, flappy-feet run, coming to take it all away, snatching him up in front of everyone and crying, 'Oh, what were you doing what were you thinking are you all right all right all right?'

'Mom,' he said. 'I saw the cat explode.'

His name is Kyle Rubin and he's here to build a nation. Well, his father is. Kyle doesn't have much of an idea of nations and nationhood, just that he's not where he used to live but it's OK because it's not really all that different from the gated community, there are a lot of folk like him, though he's not allowed to leave the compound. In here is Cantonment. Out there is the nation that's being built. That's where his dad goes in the armoured cars, where he directs the construction helicopters and commands the cranes that Kyle can just see from the balcony around the top floor of the International School. You're not allowed to go there because there are still some snipers working but everyone does and Kyle can watch the booms of the tower cranes swing across the growing towers of the new capital.

It all fell apart, and it takes us to put it back together again, his father explained. Once there was a big country called India, with a billion and a half people in it, but they just couldn't live together, so they fell to squabbling and fighting. *Like you and Kelis's mom*, Kyle said, which made his father raise his eyebrows and look embarrassed and mom – his mom, not Kelis's – laugh to herself. Whatever, it all fell apart and these poor people, they need us and our know-how to put it all back together for them. And that's why we're all here, because it's families that make us strong and hopeful. And that's how you, Kyle Rubin, are building a nation. But some people don't think we should be doing that. They think it's their nation so they should build it. Some people think we're part of the problem and not part of the solution. And some people are just plain ungrateful.

Or, as Clinton in class said, the Rana's control is still weak and there are a lot of under-represented parties out there with big grievances and arsenals of left-over weaponry from the Sundering. Western interests are always first in the firing line. But Clinton was a smart-mouth who just repeated what he heard from his dad who had been in Military Intelligence since before there was even a Cantonment, let alone an International Reconstruction Alliance.

The nation Kyle Rubin is building is Bharat, formerly the states of Bihar, Jharkand and half of Utter Pradesh on the Indo Gangetic plain, and the cranes swing and the helicopters fly over the rising towers of its new capital, Ranapur.

When there weren't cats exploding, after practice Kyle would visit Salim's planet.

Before Kyle, Striker Salim had been the best forward on Team Cantonment U-11. Really he shouldn't have been playing at all because he didn't actually live within the compound. His father was the Bharati government's man in Cantonment, so he could pretty much do whatever he liked.

At first they had been enemies. On his second game Kyle had headed home a sweet cross from Ryan from Australia and after that every cross floated his way. In the dressing room Striker Salim had complained to Coach Joe that the *new boy* had got all the best balls because he was a Westerner and not Bharati. The wraths of dads were invoked. Coach Joe said nothing and put them on together for the game against the army kids, who imagined that being army kids was like an extra man for them. Salim on wing, Kyle in centre: three three four. Cantonment beat US Army two one, one goal by Salim, the decider from a run by Salim and a rebound from the goalkeeper by Kyle, in the forty-third minute. Now, six weeks in another country later, they were inseparable.

Salim's planet was very close and easy to visit. It lived in the palmer-glove on his brown hand and could manifest itself in all manner of convenient locations: the school system, Tinneman's coffeehouse, Kyle's e-paper workscreen, but the best was the full proprioception so-new-it's-scary lighthoek (trademark) that you could put behind you ear so, fiddle it so, and it would get inside your head and open up a whole new world of sights and sounds and smells and sensations. They were so new not even the Americans had them, but Varanasi civil servants engaged on the grand task of nation building needed to use and show off the latest Bharati technology. And their sons too. The safety instructions said you weren't supposed to use it in full sensory outside because of the risk of accidents, crime or terror but it was safe enough in Guy's Place up on the roof under the solar farm that was out of shot of any sniper, no matter how good or young she was.

Kyle plugged the buddy-lead into Salim's lighthoek and slipped the curl of plastic behind his ear. It had taken a while to work out the sweet spot but now he got it first time every time. He was not supposed to use lighthoek tech; Mom's line was that it hadn't been proved safe yet but Kyle suspected it was his father: it was opening yourself up to evil influences to let things inside your head like that. That was before you even got to what he thought of the artificial evolution game itself. Maybe if he could experience the lift out of the Cantonment, up through the solar arrays, past the cranes and helicopters, and see Salim's world there in front of him; Alterre, as it was properly called, and feel yourself falling towards it, through the clouds faster than anything could possibly go, to stop light as a feather with your feet brushing the wave tops, maybe he would change his mind. He could smell the salt. He could feel the wind. He could see the lifted jelly sails of a kronkaeur fleet above the white-edged swell.

'Aw not these jellyfish guys again,' said Kyle.

'No no no, this is different.' Salim stood beside him above the waves. 'Look, this is really cool.' He folded his hands and leaned forward and flew across the ocean, Kyle a heartbeat behind him. He always thought of those Hindu gods you saw on the prayer cards that blew into the compound from the street shrines. His dad didn't like those either. They arrived over the kronkaeur armada, beating through a rising ocean on a steady breeze, topsails inflated. When the huge, sail-powered jellyfish had appeared, Kyle had been so excited at his first experience of a newly evolved species that the vast, inflatable monsters had sailed like translucent galleons through his dreams. But all they did was raise their triangular sails and weave their tentacles together into huge raft-fleets and bud off little jellies that looked like see-through paper boats. Once the initial thrill of being part of the global game-experiment to start life on earth all over again and see how it evolved differently had worn off, Kyle found himself wishing that Salim had been given somewhere a bit more exciting than a huge square of ocean. An island would have been good. A bit of continent would have been better. Somewhere things could attack each other.

'Every bit of water on Alterre was land, and every bit of land was water,' Salim had said. 'And they will be again. And anyway, everything eats everything out on the open ocean.'

But not in a cool way, Kyle thought.

Apart from his teach and his skill at football, nothing about Salim was cool. At home he would never have been Kyle's friend.

Kyle would probably have beat him about a bit: he was geeky, had a big nose, couldn't get clothes right – all the wrong labels – and had no idea how to wear a beanie. He went to a weird religious school for an hour every afternoon and Fridays to the mosque down by the river steps where they burned the dead people. Really, they should not be friends at all. Ozzie Ryan, who'd been the team big one before Kyle, said it was unnatural and disloyal and you couldn't trust them; one moment they'd be giving you presents and the next they'd be setting you up for people out there to shoot you. Kyle knew Ozzie Ryan was just jealous.

'Now, isn't this so cool?' Salim said, his toes brushing the wave-tops. The sculpted upper surfaces of the great ocean-going jellies between the inflatable booms that held out the sails were bloated with bubbles, visibly swelling and bulging as Kyle floated around to a closer angle. Bigger, bigger, now the size of footballs, now the size of beach balls, stretching the skin until it split with a gush and acid-smelling liquid and a host of balloon dashed into the air. They rose in a mass, tethered to their parents by woven strands of tentacles, rubbing and bouncing and rebounding from each other in the wind; higher than the sail-tops now, and Kyle could make out detail: each balloon carried a cluster of stingers and translucent claspers beneath its domed canopy. Blue eyes were grouped in threes and fours. One by one their tethers parted and the balloon-jellies sprang up into the air and were whisked away on the sea breeze. All around him the flotilla was bubbling and bursting into spasms of balloons; they soared up around him, some still tangled together by the tentacles. Kyle found himself laughing as he watched them stream up into the sky until they vanished against the fast-moving clouds. It was definitely undeniably way way way cool.

'It's a completely new way of reproducing,' Salim said. 'It's a new species!' Kyle knew what that meant. By the rules of Alterre, played out on eleven million computers around the globe, whoever found a new species gave it his or her name. 'They're not krankaris any more. I went and registered them, they're mansooris!'

Gunfire on Monday Tuesday Wednesday. They were working up to something; that was the pattern of it. (*Dad Dad who are they this time, is it the Hindus?* but his father had eyes and ears and arms only for Mom, full of thanks and praise to have him safe home from that fearsome city.) The Cantonment went to orange alert but security was still unprepared for the ferocity of the attack. Bombers simultaneously attacked twelve Western-owned targets across Old and New Varanasi. The twelfth and final device was a car-bomb driven at full speed across the Green Zone, impervious to automatic fire, its driver dead or ecstatic to die. Close-defence robots uncoiled from their silos and leaped, nanodiamond blades unsheathed, but the bombers had recced Cantonment's weaknesses well. Slashed, gashed, leaking oil and fuel, engine dead but still rolling under a heaving cancer of robots trying to cocoon it in impact-foam, the car rammed the inner gate and blew up.

On the soccer pitch the referee had heard the general alert siren, judged the distance to the changing room and ordered everyone to lie flat in the goal. Kyle had just wrapped his arms around his head – Day One Lesson One – when the boom lifted him off the ground by the belly and punched every breath of wind out of him. For a moment he thought he had gone deaf, then the sounds of sirens and RAV airdrones pushed through the numb until he was sitting on the grass beside Salim seemingly at the centre of a vast spiral of roar. It was much bigger than the exploding cat. A column of smoke leaned over toward the south. Hummers were rushing past, security men on foot dodging between them. The football net was full of chunks of blast-foam and scraps of wire and fragments of shattered plastic robot shell and warning signs in three languages that this was a restricted area with security authorised in the use of deadly force. A shard of nanodiamond anti-personnel blade was embedded in the left upright. The referee stood up, took off his shirt and wrapped it around the shard wedged under the crossbar.

'Would you look at that?' Kyle said.

There was a long green smear down the front of his fresh-laundered soccer shirt.

'Salim's always welcome here,' Mom called from the kitchen where she was blitzing smoothies. 'Just make sure he calls home to let them know he's all right the moment the network comes back up. Now promise you'll do that.'

Of course they did and of course they didn't and the smoothies stood there forgotten and warming on the worktop while Mom edged about folding underwear and pillowcases but really keeping an eye on the rolling news. She was worried. Kyle knew that. Cantonment was locked down and would be until Coalition and Bharati forces had re-secured the Green Zone: that was the way it was, Kyle had learned that. Locked-down was locked-out for Dad, and the SKYIndia hovercams were still showing towers of black plastic-smoke and ambulances being walked through the crowds of lost people and burned-out cars by Bharati police-men. The reporters were saying there were casualties but they were also saying that the network wasn't fully restored and that was why he couldn't call; if there had been Western casualties they would have said straight away because dead Bharatis didn't count and anyway, it was inconceivable that anything could happen to Kyle's dad. No, in situations like this you kept your head down and got on with things while you waited for the call, so he didn't trouble Mom and fetched the smoothies himself from the kitchen and took them to join Salim in his world.

On the house smartsilk screen you couldn't get that full-sensory drop from orbit or the sense of walking like God over the water but in the house, even with Mom in her distracted fold-laundry state, it wasn't smart to use the buddy-lead. Anyway, Kyle didn't want to give her more to worry about. Three days in Alterre was more like three million years: still water water water whichever way he turned the point of view, but the Mansooris had evolved. High above the blue Atlantic, fleets of airships battled.

'Whoa,' said Kyle Rubin and Salim Mansoori.

In three days the jelly-fish balloons had become vast sky-going gasbags, blimp-creatures, translucent airships the size of the Boeing troop transports that brought supplies and workers in to the secure end of Varanasi airport. Their bodies were ridged like the condom Kyle had been shown at the back of the bike rack behind the school; light rippled over them and broke into rainbows as the air-jellies manoeuvred. For this was battle, no doubt about it. This was hot war. The sky-jellyfish trailed long clusters of tentacles beneath them, many hanging in the water, their last connection with their old world. But some ended in purple stingers, some in long stabbing spines, some in barbs, and these the airships wielded as weapons. The air-medusas raised or lowered sail-flaps to tack and manoeuvre into striking positions. Kyle saw one blimp, body blotched with black sting-weals, vent gas from nose and tail and drop out of combat. In a tangle of slashing and parrying tentacles Kyle watched a fighting blimp tear a gash the length of an army hummer down an opponent's flank with its scimitar-hook. The mortally wounded blimp vented glittering dust, crumpled, folded in half in the middle and plunged into the sea where it split like a thrown water-balloon. The sea instantly boiled with almkvists, spear-fast scavengers all jaw and speed.

'Cool,' both boys said together.

'Hey now, didn't you promise you'd let your folks know as soon as the network was up?' said Mom, standing behind them. 'And Kyle, you know your dad doesn't like you playing that game.'

But she wasn't mad. She couldn't be mad. Dad was safe, Dad had called in, Dad would be home soon. It was all in the little tremble in her voice, the way she leaned over between them to look at the screen, the smell of perfume just dabbed on. You know these things.

It had been close. Kyle's Dad called Kyle in to show him the rolling news and point out where his company car had been when the bombers hit the escort hummers.

'There's next to no protection in those things,' he said over jerky, swooping flash-cut images of black smoke boiling out of yellow flames and people standing and shouting and not knowing what to do; pictures taken from a passer-by's palmer. 'They used a drone RAV; I saw something go past the window just before it hit. They were aiming for the soldiers, not for us.'

'It was a suicide attack here,' Kyle said.

'Some karsevak group claimed responsibility; some group no one's ever heard of before. Fired everything off in one shooting match.'

'Don't they go straight into a state of *moksha* if they blow themselves up in Varanasi?'

'That's what they believe, son. Your soul is released from the wheel of reincarnation. But I still can't help feeling that this was the final throw. Things are getting better. The Ranas are taking control. People can see the difference we're making. I do feel we've turned the corner on this.'

Kyle loved it when his dad talked military, though he was really a structural engineer.

'So Salim got home safe.'

Kyle nodded.

'That's good.' Kyle heard his father sigh in the way that men do when they're supposed to talk about things they don't want to. 'Salim's a good kid, a good friend.' Another intake of breath. Kyle waited for it to shape into a *but*.

'Kyle, you know, that game. Well . . .'

Not a *but*, a *well*.

'Well, I know it's real educational and a lot of people play it and enjoy it and get a lot out of it, but, it's not really right. I mean, it's not accurate. It claims it's an evolution simulation, and it is as far as it goes. But if you think about it, really, it's just following rules laid down by someone else. All that code was programmed by someone else; so really, it's evolution inside a bigger framework that's been deliberately designed. But they don't tell you, Kyle, and that's dishonest; it's pretending to be something it's not. And that's why I don't like it; because it isn't honest about the truth, and I know that whatever I say, what you do with Salim is your thing, but I do think you're not to play it here, in the house. And it's good you've got a good friend here – I remember when Kelis was your age when we were in the Gulf, she had a really good friend, a Canadian girl – but it would be good if you had a few more friends from your own background. OK? Now, how about "Wrestle Smackdown" on cable?'

The referee had gone down with a head-butt to the nuts in the first thirty seconds so it was only when the decibel count exceeded the mundane Varanasi traffic roar that security heads-upped, guns-downed and came running. A guard-woman in full colour-smear combats and smart-visor locked her arms around Kyle and hauled him out of the steel-cage match into which the under-eleven practice had collapsed.

'I'll sue you I'll sue the ass of you your children will end up living in a cardboard box, let go of me,' Kyle yelled. The security woman hauled.

It was full fight, boys, girls, supporters, cheerleaders. At the bottom of the dog-pile, Striker Salim and Ozzie Ryan. Security hauled them off each other and returned the snoopy RAV drones that flocked to any unusual action to their stand-by roosts. Parameds rushed to the scene. There was blood, there were bruisings and grazings, there were torn clothes and black eyes. There were lots and lots of tears but no contusions, no concussions, no breaks.

Then the gitmoisation.

Coach Joe: OK, so want to tell me what that was about?

Ozzie Ryan: He started it

Striker Salim: Liar! You started it.

Coach Joe: I don't care who started it; I want to know what all that was about.

Ozzie Ryan: He's the liar. His people just lie all the time; they don't have a word for the truth.

Striker Salim: Ah! Ah! That's such a lie too.

Ozzie Ryan: See? You can't trust them: he's a spy for them, it's true; before he came here they never got in, since he came there's been things happening almost every day. He's a spy and he's telling them all ways to get in and kill us because he thinks we're all animals and going to hell anyway.

Coach Joe: Jesus. Kyle; what happened?

Kyle Rubin: I don't know, I didn't see anything, I just heard this noise like and when I looked over they were on the ground tearing lumps out of each other.

Striker Salim: That is so not true . . . I cannot believe you said that. You were there, you heard what he said.

Kyle Rubin: I didn't hear everything, I just heard like shouting . . .

Gitmoisation part two.

Kyle's dad: Coach Joe called me, but I'm not going to bawl you out, I think there's been enough of that already. I'm disappointed, but I'm not going to bawl you out. Just one thing: did Ryan call Salim something?

Kyle Rubin: (inaudible.)

Kyle's dad: Son, did Ryan use a racist term to Salim?

Kyle Rubin: (twisting foot.)

Kyle's dad: I thought Salim was your friend. Your best friend. I think if someone had done something to my best friend, doesn't matter who he is, what he is, I'd stand up for him.

Kyle Rubin: He said Salim was a diaper-head curry-nigger and they were all spies and Salim was just standing there so I went in there and popped him, Ryan I mean, and he just went for Salim, not me, and then everyone was piling on with Ryan and Salim at the bottom and they were all shouting curry-nigger-lover curry-nigger-lover at me and trying to get me too and then the security came in.

At the end of it two things were certain: soccer was suspended for one month, and when it did come back, Salim would not be playing, never would be again. Cantonment was not safe for Bharatis.

He was trapped, a traffic island castaway. Marooned on an oval of concrete in Varanasi's never-ebbing torrent of traffic by the phatphat driver when he saw Kyle fiddling in his lap with pogs.

'Ey, you, out here, get out, trying to cheat, damn gora.'

'What here, but?'

Out onto this tiny, traffic island twenty centimetres in front of him twenty centimetres behind him, on one side a tall man in a white shirt and black pants, on the other a fat woman in a purple sari who smelled of dead rose, and the phatphat, the little yellow-and-black plastic bubble, looked/sounded like a hornet as it throbbed away into the terrifying traffic.

'You can't do this, my dad's building this country!'

The man and the woman turned to stare. Stares everywhere,

every instant from the moment he slipped out of the back of the Hi-Lux at the phatphat stand. They had been eager for his money then, *Hey sir, hey sahib, good clean cab, fast fast, straight there no detours, very safe safest phatphat in Varanasi.* How was he to know that the cheap, light cardboard pogs were only money inside the Cantonment? And now here he was on his traffic island, no way forward, no way back, no way through the constant movement of trucks, buses, cream-coloured Marutis, mopeds, phatphats, cycle-rickshaws, cows, everything roaring ringing hooting yelling as it tried to find its true way while avoiding everything else. People were walking through that, just stepping out in the belief that the traffic would steer around them; the man in the white shirt, there he went, the woman in the purple sari, *Come on boy, come with me*, he couldn't, he daren't, and there she went and now there were people piling up behind him, pushing him pushing pushing pushing him closer to the kerb, out in that killing traffic . . .

Then the phatphat came through the mayhem, klaxon buzzing, weaving a course of grace and chaos, sweeping in to the traffic island. The plastic door swivelled up and there, there, was Salim.

'Come on come on.'

Kyle bounded in, the door scissored down and the driver hooted off into Varanasi's storm of wheels.

'Good thing I was looking for you,' Salim said, tapping the lighthoek coiled behind his ear. 'You can find anyone with these. What happened?' Kyle showed him the Cantonment pogs. Salim's eyes went wide. 'You really haven't ever been outside, have you?'

Escaping from Cantonment was easier than anything. Everyone knew they were only looking for people coming in, not going out, so all Kyle had to do was slip into the back of the pick-up while the driver bought a mochaccino to go at

Tinneman's. He even peeked out from under the tarpaulin as the inner gate closed because he wanted to see what the bomb damage was like. The robots had taken away all the broken masonry and metal spaghetti but he could see the steel reinforcing rods through the shattered concrete block work and the black scorch marks over the inner wall. It was so interesting and Kyle was staring so hard that he only realised he was out of Cantonment entirely, in the street, the alien street, when he saw the trucks, buses, cream-coloured Marutis, mopeds, phatphats, cycle-rickshaws, cows close behind the pick-up and felt the city roar surge over him.

'So, where do you want to go then?' Salim asked. His face was bright and eager to show Kyle his wonderful wonderful city. This was a Salim Kyle had never seen before; Salim not-in-Cantonment, Salim in-his-own-place, Salim-among-his-own-people. This Mansoori seemed alien to Kyle. He was not sure he liked him. 'There's theNewBharatSabhaholydeerofSarnath DoctorSampunananandcricketgroundBuddhiststupaRamnagar FortVishwanathTempleJantarMantar . . .'

Too much too much, Kyle's head was going round all the people, all the people, the one thing he never saw, never noticed from the roof-top look-out, under all the helicopters and cranes and military RAV drones, there were people.

'River,' he gasped. 'The river, the big steps.'

'The ghats. The best thing. They're cool.' Salim spoke to the driver in a language Kyle had never heard from his mouth before. It did not sound like Salim at all. The driver waggled his head in that way that you thought was *no* until you learned better, threw the phatphat around a big traffic circle with a huge pink concrete statue of Ganesh to head away from the glass towers of Ranapur into the old city. Flowers. There were garlands of yellow flowers at the elephant god's feet, little smoking smudges of incense; strange strings of chillies and limes; and a man with big dirty ash-grey dreadlocks, a man with his lips locked shut with fishing hooks.

'The man, look at the man . . .' Kyle wanted to shout but that wonder/horror was behind him, a dozen more unfolding on every side as the phatphat hooted down ever narrower, ever darker, ever busier streets. 'An elephant, there's an elephant and that's a robot and those people, what are they carrying, that's a body, that's like a dead man on a stretcher oh man . . .' He turned to Salim. He wasn't scared now. There were no bodies behind him, squeezing him, pushing him into fear and danger. It was just people, everywhere just people, working out how to live. 'Why didn't they let me see this?'

The phatphat bounced to a stop.

'This is where we get out, come on, come on.'

The phatphat was wedged in an alley between a clot of cycle rickshaws and a Japanese delivery truck. Nothing on wheels could pass but still the people pressed by on either side. Another dead man passed, handed high on his stretcher over the heads of the crowd. Kyle ducked instinctively as the shadow of the corpse passed over the dome of the phatphat, then the doors flew up and he stepped out into the side of a cow. Kyle almost punched the stupid, baggy thing, but Salim grabbed him, shouted, 'Don't touch the cow, the cow is special, like sacred.' Shout was the only possible conversation here. Grab the only way not to get separated. Salim dragged Kyle by the wrist to a booth in a row of plastic-canopied market stalls where a bank of chill-cabinets chugged. Salim bought two Limkas and showed the stallholder a Cantonment pog, which he accepted for novelty value. Again the hand on the arm restrained Kyle.

'You have to drink it here, there's a deposit.'

So they leaned their backs against the tin bar and watched the city pass and drank their Limkas from the bottle which would have had Kyle's mom screaming germs bacteria viruses infections and felt like two very very proper gentlemen. In a moment's lull in the street racket Kyle heard his palmer call. He hauled it out of his pants pocket, a little ashamed because everyone had a newer better brighter cleverer smaller one than him, and saw, as if she knew what dirty thing he had done, it was his mom calling. He stared at the number, the jingly tune, the little smiley animation. Then he thumbed the off button and sent them all to darkness.

'Come on.' He banged his empty bottle down on the counter. 'Let's see this river then.'

In twenty steps, he was there, so suddenly, so huge and bright Kyle forgot to breathe. The narrow alley, the throng of people opened up into painful light, light in the polluted yellow sky light from the tiers of marble steps that descended to the river and light from the river itself, wider and more dazzling than he had ever imagined, white as a river of milk. And people: the world could not hold so many people, crowding down the steps to the river in their coloured clothes and coloured shoes, jammed together under the tilted wicker umbrellas to talk and deal and pray, people in the river itself, waist deep in the water, holding up handfuls of the water and the water glittering as it fell through their fingers, praying, washing – washing themselves, washing their clothes, washing their children and their sins. Then the boats: the big hydrofoil seeking its way to dock through the little darting rowboats, the pilgrim boats making the crossing from Ramnagar, rowers standing on their sterns pushing at their oars, the tourist boats with their canopies, the lids in inflated tractor tyres paddling around scavenging for river-scraps, down to the bobbing saucers of butter-light woven from mango leaves that the people set adrift on the flow. Vision by vision the Ganga revealed itself to Kyle: next he became aware of the buildings; the guesthouses and hotels and havelis shouldering up to the steps, the ridiculous pink water towers, the many domes of the mosque and the golden spires of the temples and little temple down at the river leaning into the silt; the arcades and jetties and galleries and across the river, beyond the yellow sand and the black, ragged tents of the holy men, the chimneys and tanks and pipes of the chemical and oil plants, all flying the green white and orange wheel-banners of Bharat.

'Oh,' Kyle said. 'Oh man.' And: 'Cool.'

Salim was already halfway down the steps.

'Come on.'

'Is it all right? Am I allowed?'

'Everyone is allowed. Come on, let's get a boat.'

A boat. People didn't do things like that but here they were settling on the seat as the boatman pushed out, a kid not that much older than Kyle himself with teeth that would never be allowed inside Cantonment yet Kyle felt jealous of him, with his boat and his river and the people all around and a life without laws or needs or duties. He sculled them through floating butter-candles – *diyas*, Salim explained to Kyle – past the ghat of the sadhus, all bare-ass naked and skinny as famine, and the ghat where people beat their clothes against rock washing-platforms and the ghat where the pilgrims landed, pushing each other into the water in their eagerness to touch the holy ground of Varanasi, and the ghat of the buffalos – *where where?* Kyle asked and Salim pointed out their nostrils and black, black-curved horns just sticking up out of the water. Kyle trailed his hand in the water and when he pulled it in it was covered in golden flower peals. He lay back on the seat and watched the marble steps flow past, and beyond them the crumbling, mould-stained waterfront buildings and beyond them the tops of the highest towers of New Varanasi and beyond them the yellow clouds, and he knew that even when he was a very old man, maybe forty or even more, he would always remember this day and the colour of this light and the sound of the water against the hull.

'You got to see this!' Salim shouted. The boat was heading in to shore now through the tourists and the souvenir-boats and a slick of floating flower garlands. Fires burned on the steps, the marble was blackened with trodden ashes, half-burned wood lapped at the water's edge. There were other things among the coals: burned bones. Men stood thigh deep in the water, panning it with wide wicker baskets.

'They're Doms, they run the burning ghats. They're actually untouchable but they're very rich and powerful because they're the only ones who can handle the funerals,' said Salim. 'They're sifting the ashes for gold.'

The burning ghats. The dead place. These fires, these piles of wood and ash, were dead people, Kyle thought. This water beneath the boat was full of dead people. A funeral procession descended the steps to the river. The bearers pushed the stretcher out into the water, a man with a red cord around his shoulder poured water over the white shroud. He was very thorough and methodical about it, he gave the dead body a good washing. The river-boy touched his oars, holding his boat in position. The bearers took the body up to a big bed of wood and set the whole thing on top. A very thin man in a white robe and with a head so freshly shaved it looked pale and sick piled wood on top of it.

'That's the oldest son,' Salim said. 'It's his job. These are rich people. It's real expensive to get a proper pyre. Most people use the electric ovens. Of course, we get properly buried like you do.'

It was all very quick and casual. The man in white poured oil over the wood and the body, picked up a piece of lit wood and almost carelessly touched it to the side. The flame guttered in the river wind, almost went out, then smoke rose up and out of the smoke, flame. Kyle watched the fire take hold. The people stood back, no one seemed very concerned, even when the pile of burning wood collapsed and a man's head and shoulders lolled out of the fire.

That is a burning man, Kyle thought. He had to tell himself that. It was hard to believe, all of it was hard to believe; there was nothing that connected to any part of his world, his life. It was fascinating, it was like a wildlife show on the sat; he was close enough to smell the burning flesh but it was too strange, too alien. It did not touch him. He could not believe. Kyle thought, *This is the first time Salim has seen this too.* But it was very very cool.

A sudden crack, a pop a little louder than the gunfire Kyle heard in the streets every day, but not much.

'That is the man's skull bursting,' Salim said. 'It's supposed to mean his spirit is free.'

Then a noise that had been in the back of Kyle's head moved to the front of his perception: engines, aircraft engines. Tilt-jet engines. Loud, louder than he had ever heard them before, even when he watched them lifting off from the field in Cantonment. The mourners were staring, the Doms turned from their ash-panning to stare too. The boat-boy stopped rowing; his eyes were round. Kyle turned in his seat and saw something wonderful and terrible and strange: a tilt-jet in Coalition markings, moving across the river towards him, yes *him*, so low, so slow, it was as if it were tiptoeing over the water. For a moment he saw himself, toes scraping the stormy waters of Alterre. River-traffic fled from it, its down-turned engines sent flaws of white across the green water. The boat-boy scrabbled for his oars to get away but there was now a second roar from the ghats. Kyle turned back to see Coalition troopers in full combat armour and visors pouring down the marble steps, pushing mourners out of their way, scattering wood and bones and ash. Mourners and Doms shouted their outrage; fists were raised; the soldiers lifted their weapons in answer. The boat-boy looked around him in terror as the thunder of the jet engines grew louder and louder until Kyle felt it become part of him and when he looked round he saw the big machine, morphing between city and river camouflage, turn, unfold landing gear and settle into the water. The boat rocked violently, Kyle would have been over the side had not Salim hauled him back. Jet-wash blew human ash along the ghats. A single oar floated lost down the stream. The tilt-jet stood knee-deep in the shallow water. It unfolded its rear ramp. Helmets. Guns. Between them, a face Kyle recognised, his dad, shouting wordlessly through the engine roar. The soldiers on the shore were shouting, the people were shouting, everything was shout shout roar. Kyle's dad beckoned, to me to me. Shivering with fear, the boat-boy stood up, thrust his sole remaining oar into the water like a punt pole and pushed toward the ramp. Gloved hands seized him, dragged him out of the rocking boat up the ramp. Everyone was shouting, shouting. Now the soldiers on the shore were beckoning to the boat-boy and Salim, this way this way, the thing is going to take off, get out of there.

His dad buckled Kyle into the seat as the engine roar peaked again. He felt the world turn, then the river was dropping away beneath him. The tilt-jet banked. Kyle looked out the window. There was the boat, being pulled in to shore by the soldiers, and Salim standing in the stern staring up at the aircraft, a hand raised: goodbye.

Gitmoisation part three.

Dad did the don't-you-know-the-danger-you-were-in/ trouble-you-caused/expense-you-cost bit.

'It was a full-scale security alert. Full-scale alert. We thought you'd been kidnapped. We honestly thought you'd been kidnapped. Everyone thought that, everyone was praying for you. You'll write them, of course. Proper apologies, handwritten. Why did you turn your palmer off? One call, one simple call, and it would have been all right, we wouldn't have minded. Lucky we can track them even when they're switched off. Salim's in big trouble too. You know, this is a major incident, it's in all the papers, and not just here in Cantonment. It's even made SKYIndia News. You've embarrassed us all, made us look very very stupid. Sledgehammer to crack a nut. Salim's father has had to resign. Yes, he's that ashamed.'

But Kyle knew his dad was burning with joy and relief to have him back.

Mom was different. Mom was the torturer.

'It's obvious we can't trust you; well, of course you're grounded, but really, I thought you knew what it was like here, I thought you understood that this is not like anywhere else, that if we can't trust each other, we can really put one another in danger. Well, I can't trust you here and your dad, well, he'll have to give it up. We'll have to quit and go back home and the Lord knows, he won't get a job anything closer to what we have here. We'll have to move to a smaller house in a less good area, I'll have to go out to work again. And you can forget about that Salim boy, yes, forget all about him. You won't be seeing him again.'

Kyle cried himself out that night in bed, cried himself into great shivering, shuddering sobs empty of everything except the end of the world. Way way late he heard the door open.

'Kyle?' Mom's voice. He froze in his bed. 'I'm sorry. I was upset. I said things I shouldn't have said. You did bad, but all the same, your dad and I think you should have this.'

A something was laid beside his cheek. When the door had closed, Kyle put on the light. The world could turn again. It would get better. He tore open the plastic bubble-case. Coiled inside, like a beckoning finger, like an Arabic letter, was a lighthoek. And in the morning, before school, before breakfast, before anything but the pilgrims going to the river, he went up on to the roof at Guy's Place, slipped the 'hoek behind his ear, pulled his palmer-glove over his fingers and went soaring up through the solar farm and the water tanks, the cranes and the construction helicopters and the clouds, up towards Salim's world.

The Dust Assassin

When I was small a steel monkey would come into my room. My ayah put me to bed early, because a growing girl needed sleep, big sleep. I hated sleep. The world I heard beyond the carved stone jali screens of my verandah was too full of things for sleep. My ayah would set the wards, but the steel monkey was one of my own security robots and invisible to them. As I lay on my side in the warmth and perfume of dusk, I would see first its little head, then one hand, then two appear over the lip of my balcony, then all of it. It would crouch there for a whole minute, then slip down into the night shadows filling up my room. As my eyes grew accustomed to the dark I would see it watching me, turning its head from one side to the other. It was a handsome thing; metal shell burnished as soft as skin (for in time it came close enough for me to slip a hand through my mosquito nets to stroke it) and adorned with the symbol of my family and make and serial number. It was not very intelligent, less smart than the real monkeys that squabbled and fought on the rooftops, but clever enough to climb and hunt the assassin robots of the Azads along the ledges and turrets and carvings of the Jodhra Palace. And in the morning I would see them lining the ledges and rooftops with their solar cowls raised and then they did not seem to me like monkeys at all, but cousins of the sculpted gods and demons among which they sheltered, giving salutation to the sun.

You never think your life is special. Your life is just your life, your world is just your world, even lived in a Rajput palace defended by machine monkeys against an implacable rival family. Even when you are a weapon.

Those four words are my memory of my father: his face filling my sight like the Marwar moon, his lips, full as pomegranates, saying down to me, *You are a weapon, Padmini, our revenge against the Azads*. I never see my mother's face there: I never knew her. She lived in seclusion in the zenana, the women's quarters. The only woman I ever saw was my ayah, mad Harpal, who every morning drank a steaming glass of her own piss. Otherwise, only men. And Heer, the khidmutgar, our steward. Not man, not woman: other. A nute. As I said, you always think your life is normal.

Every night, the monkey-robot watched me, turning its head this way, that way. Then one night it slipped away on its little plastic paws and I slid out of my nets in my silk pyjamas after it. It jumped up on the balcony, then in two leaps it was up the vine that climbed around my window. Its eyes glittered in the full moon. I seized two handfuls of tough, twisted vine, thick as my thigh, and was up after it. Why did I follow that steel monkey? Maybe because of that moon on its titanium shell. Maybe because that was the moon of the great kite festival, which we always observed by flying a huge kite in the shape of man with a bird's tail and outstretched wings for arms. My father kept all the festivals and rituals, the feasts of the gods. It was what made us different from, better than, the Azads. That man with wings for arms, flying up out of the courtyard in front of my apartment with the sun in his face, could see higher and further than I, the only daughter of the Jodhras, ever could. By the moonlight in the palace courtyard I climbed the vine, like something from one of ayah's fairytales of gods and demons. The steel monkey led on, over balconies, along ledges, over carvings of heroes from legends and full-breasted apsara women. I never thought how high I was: I was as light and luminous as the bird-man. Now the steel monkey beckoned me, squatting on the parapet with only the stars above it. I dragged myself up on to the roof. Instantly an army of machine monkeys reared up before me like Hanuman's host. Metal gleamed, they bared their antipersonnel weapons: needle throwers tipped with lethal neurotoxins. My family has always favoured poison. I raised my hand and they melted away at the taste of my body chemistry, all but my guide. It skipped and bounded before me. I walked barefoot through a moonlit world of domes and turrets, with every step drawn closer to the amber sky-glow of the city outside. Our palace presented a false front of bays and windows and jharokas to the rude people in the street: I climbed the steps behind the façade until I stood on the very top, the highest balcony. A gasp went out of me. Great Jaipur lay before me, a hive of streetlights and pulsing neons, the reds and whites and blinking yellows of vehicles swarming along the Johan Bazaar, the trees hung with thousands of fairylights, like stars fallen from the night, the hard fluorescent shine of the open shop fronts, the glowing waver of the tivi screens, the floodlight pools all along the walls of the old city: all reflected in the black water of the moat my father had built around his palace. A moat, in the middle of a drought.

The noise swirled up from the street: traffic, a hundred musics, a thousand voices. I swayed on my high perch but I was not afraid. Softness brushed against my leg, my steel monkey pressed close, clinging to the warm pink stone with plastic fingers. I searched the web of light for the sharp edges of the Jantar Mantar, the observatory my ancestors had built three hundred years before. I made out the great wedge of the Samrat Yantra, seven storeys tall, the sundial accurate to two seconds; the floodlit bowls of the Jai Prakash Yantra, mapping out the heavens on strips of white marble. The hot night wind tugged at my pyjamas; I smelled biodiesel, dust, hot fat, spices carried up from the thronged bazaar. The steel monkey fretted against my leg, making a strange keening sound, and I saw out on the edge of the city a slash of light down the night, curved like a sail filled with darkness. A tower, higher than any of the others of the new industrial city on the western edges of Jaipur. The glass tower of the Azads, our enemies, as different as could be from our old-fashioned, Rajput-style palace: glowing from within with blue light. And I thought, *I am to bring that tower to the ground.*

Then, voices. Shouts. *Hey, you. Up there. Where? There. See that? What is it? Is it a man? I don't know. Hey, you, show yourself.* I leaned forward, peered carefully down. Light blinded me. At the end of the flashlight beams were two palace guards in combat armour, weapons trained on me. *It's all right, it's all right, don't shoot, for gods' sake, it's the girl.*

'Memsahib,' a soldier called up. 'Memsahib, stay exactly where you are, don't move a muscle, we're coming to get you.'

I was still staring at the glowing scimitar of the Azad tower when the roof door opened and the squad of guards came to bring me down.

Next morning I was taken to my father in his audience diwan. Climate-mod fields held back the heat and the pollution; the open, stone-pillared hall was cool and still. My father sat on his throne of cushions between the two huge silver jars, taller than two of me, that were always filled with water from the holy River Ganga. My father drank a glass at dawn every morning. He was a very traditional Rajput. I saw the plastic coil of his lighthoek behind his ear. To him his diwan was full of attendants; his virtual aeai staff, beamed through his skull into his visual centres, busy busy busy on the affairs of Jodhra Water.

My brothers had been summoned and sat uncomfortably on the floor, pulling at their unfamiliar, chafing old-fashioned costumes. This was to be a formal occasion. Heer knelt behind him, hands folded in yts sleeves. I could not read yts eyes behind yts polarized black lenses. I could never read anything about

Heer. Not man, not woman – yt – yts muscles lay in unfamiliar patterns under yts peach-smooth skin. I always felt that yt did not like me.

The robot lay on its back, deactivated, limbs curled like the dry dead spiders I found in the corners of my room where ayah Harpal was too lazy to dust.

'That was a stupid, dangerous thing to do,' my father said. 'What would have happened if our jawans had not found you?'

I set my jaw and flared my nostrils and rocked on my cushions.

'I just wanted to see. That's my right, isn't it? It's what you're educating me for, that world out there, so it's my right to see it.'

'When you are older. When you are a . . . woman. The world is not safe, for you, for any of us.'

'I saw no danger.'

'You don't need to. All danger has to do is see you. The Azad assassins . . .'

'But I'm a weapon. That's what you always tell me, I'm a weapon, so how can the Azads harm me? How can I be a weapon if I'm not allowed to see what I'm to be used against?'

But the truth was I didn't know what that meant, what I was meant to do to bring that tower of blue glass collapsing down into the pink streets of Jaipur.

'Enough. This unit is defective.'

My father made a gesture with his fingers and the steel monkey sprang up, released. It turned its head in its this-way, that-way gesture I knew so well, confused. In the same instant, the walls glittered with light reflecting from moving metal as the machines streamed down the carved stonework and across the pink marble courtyard. The steel monkey gave a strange, robot cry and made to flee but the reaching plastic paws seized it and pulled it down and turned it on its back and, circuit by circuit, chip by chip, wire by wire, took it to pieces. When they had finished there was no part of my steel monkey left big enough to see. I felt the tightness in my chest, my throat, my head of about-to-cry but I would not, I would never, not in front of these men. I glanced again at Heer. Yts black lenses gave nothing, as ever. But the way the sun glinted from those insect eyes told me yt was looking at me.

My life changed that day. My father knew that something between us had been taken apart like the artificial life of the steel monkey. But I had seen beyond the walls of my life so I was allowed out from the palace a little way into the world. With Heer, and guards, in armoured German cars to bazaars and malls; by tilt-jet to family relatives in Jaisalmer and Delhi; to festivals and melas and pujas in the Govind temple. I was still schooled in the palace by tutors and aeai artificial intelligences, but I was presented with my new friends, all the daughters of high-ranking, high-caste company executives, carefully vetted and groomed. They wore all the latest fashions and make-up and jewellery and shoes and tech. They dressed me and styled me and wove brass and amber beads into my hair; they took me to shops and pool parties – in the heart of a drought – and cool summer houses up the mountains but they were never comfortable like friends, never free, never friends at all. They were afraid of me. But there were clothes and trips and Star Asia tunes and celebrity gupshup and so I forgot about the steel monkey that I once pretended was my friend and was taken to pieces by its brothers.

Others had not forgotten

They remembered the night after my fourteenth birthday. There had been a puja by the Govind priest in the diwan. It was a special age, fourteen, the age I became a woman. I was blessed with fire and ash and light and water and given a sari, the dress of a woman. My friends wound it around me and decorated my hands with mehndi, intricate patterns in dark henna. They set the red bindi of the kshatriya caste over my third eye and led me out through the rows of applauding company executives and then to a great party. There were gifts and kisses, the food was laid out the length of the courtyard and there were press reporters and proper French champagne that I was allowed to drink because I was now a woman. My father had arranged a music set by MTV-star Anila – real, not artificial intelligence – and in my new woman's finery I jumped and down and screamed like any other of my teenage girlfriends. At the very end of the night, when the staff took the empty silver plates away and Anila's roadies folded up the sound system, my father's jawans brought out the great kite of the Jodhras, the winged man-bird the colour of fire, and sent him up, shining, into the night above Jaipur, up towards the hazy stars. Then I went to my new room, in the zenana, the women's quarter, and old disgusting ayah Harpal locked the carved wooden door to my nursery.

It was that that saved me, when the Azads struck.

I woke an instant before Heer burst through the door but in that split-second was all the confusion of waking in an unfamiliar bed, in a strange room, in an alien house, in a body you do not fully know as your own.

Heer. Here. Not Heer. Dressed in street clothes. Men's clothes. Heer, with a gun in yts hand. The big gun with the two barrels, the one that killed people and the one that killed machines.

'Memsahib, get up and come with me. You must come with me.'

'Heer ...'

Now, memsahib.'

Mouth working for words, I reached for clothes, bag, shoes, things. Heer threw me across the room to crash painfully against the Rajput chest.

'How dare ...' I started and, as if in slow motion, I saw the gun fly up. A flash, like lightning in the room. A metallic squeal, a stench of burning and the smoking steel shell of a defence robot went spinning across the marble floor like a burning spider. Its tail was raised, its stinger erect. Not knowing if this was some mad reality or I was still in a dream, I reached my hand toward the dead machine. Heer snatched me away.

'Do you want to die? It may still be operational.'

Yt pushed me roughly into the corridor, then turned to fire a final e-m charge into the room. I heard a long keening wail like a cork being turned in a bottle that faded into silence. In that silence I heard for the first time the sounds. Gunfire, men shouting, men roaring, engines revving, aircraft overhead, women crying. Women wailing. And everywhere, above and below, the clicking scamper of small plastic feet.

'What's going on?' Suddenly I was chilled and trembling with dread. 'What's happened?'

'The House of Jodhra is under attack,' Heer said.

I pulled away from yts soft grip.

'Then I have to go, I have to fight, I have to defend us. I am a weapon.'

Heer shook yts head in exasperation and with yts gun hand struck me a ringing blow on the side of my head.

'Stupid stupid! Understand! The Azads, they are killing everything! Your father, your brothers, they are killing everyone. They would have killed you, but they forgot you moved to a new room.'

'Dadaji? Arvind, Kiran?'

Heer tugged me along, still reeling, still dizzy from the blow but more dazed, more stunned by what the nute had told me. My father, my brothers . . .

'Mamaji?' My voice was three years old.

'Only the gene-line.'

We rounded a corner. Two things happened at the same time. Heer shouted 'Down!' and as I dived for the smooth marble I glimpsed a swarm of monkey-machines bounding towards me, clinging to walls and ceiling. I covered my head and cried out with every shot as Heer fired and fired and fired until the gas-cell canister clanged to the floor.

'They hacked into them and reprogrammed them. Faithless, betraying things. Come *on*.' The smooth, manicured hand reached for me and I remember only shards of noise and light and dark and bodies until I found myself in the back seat of a fast German car, Heer beside me, gun cradled like a baby. I could smell hot electricity from the warm weapon. Doors slammed. Locks sealed. Engine roared.

'Where to?'

'The Hijra Mahal.'

As we accelerated through the gate more monkey-robots dropped from the naqqar khana. I heard their steel lives crack and burst beneath our wheels. One clung to the door, clawing at the window frame until the driver veered and scraped it off on a streetlight.

'Heer ...'

Inside it was all starting to burst, to disintegrate into the colours and visions and sounds and glances of the night. My father my head my brothers my head my mother my family my head my head my head.

'It's all right,' the nute said, taking my hand in yts. 'You're safe. You're with us now.'

The house of Jodhra, which had endured for a thousand years, fell, and I came to the house of the nutes. It was pink, as all the great buildings of Jaipur were pink, and very discreet. In my life *before*, as I now thought of it, I must have driven past its alleyway a hundred times without ever knowing the secret it concealed; cool marble rooms and corridors behind a façade of orioles and turrets and intricately carved windows, courts and tanks and water-gardens open only to the sky and the birds. But then the

Hijra Mahal had always been a building apart. In another age it had been the palace of the hijras, the eunuchs. The un-men, shunned yet essential to the ritual life of Rajput Jaipur, living in the very heart of the old city, yet apart.

There were six of them: Sul the janampatri seer, astrologer to celebs as far away as the movie boulevards of Mumbai; Dahin the plastic surgeon, who worked on faces on the far side of the planet through remote machines accurate to the width of an atom; Leel the ritual dancer, who performed the ancient Nautch traditions and festival dances; Janda the writer, whom half of India knew as Queen Bitch of gupshup columnists; Suleyra, whose parties and events were the talk of society from Srinagar to Madurai; and Heer, once khidmutgar to the House of Jodhra. My six guardians bundled me from the car wrapped in a heavy chador like a Muslim woman and took me to a domed room of a hundred thousand mirror fragments. Their warm, dry hands gently held me on the divan – I was thrashing, raving as the shock hit me – and Dahin the face surgeon deftly pressed an efuser to my arm.

'Hush. Sleep now.'

I woke among the stars. For an instant I wondered if I was dead, stabbed in my sleep by the poison needle of an Azad assassin robot that had scaled the hundred windows of the Jodhra Mahal. Then I saw that they were the mirror shards of the roof, shattering the light of a single candle into a hundred thousand pieces. Heer sat cross-legged on a dhuri by my low bedside.

'How long . . .'

'Two days, child.'

'Are they . . .'

'Dead. Yes. I cannot lie. Every one.'

But even as the House of Jodhra fell, it struck back like a cobra, its back broken by a stick. Homing missiles, concealed for years, clinging like bats under shop eaves and bus shelters, unfolded their wings and lit their engines and sought out the pheromone profiles of Azad vehicles. Armoured Lexuses went up in fireballs in the middle of Jaipur's insane traffic as they hooted their ways towards the safety of the airport. No safety even there, a Jodhra missile locked on to the company tilt-jet as it lifted off, hooked into the engine intake with its titanium claws until the aircraft reached an altitude at which no one could survive. The blast cast momentary shadows across the sundials of the Jantar Mantar, marking the moment of Jodhra revenge. Burning debris set fires all across the slums.

'Are they . . .'

'Jahangir and the Begum Azad died in the tilt-jet attack and our missiles took out much of their board, but their counter-measures held off our attack on their headquarters.'

'Who survived?'

'Their youngest son Salim. The line is intact.'

I sat up in my low bed that smelled of sandalwood. The stars were jewels around my head.

'It's up to me then.'

'Memsahib . . .'

'Don't you remember what he said, Heer? My father? *You are a weapon, never forget that.* Now I know what I am a weapon for.'

'Memsahib . . . Padmini.' The first time yt had ever spoken my name. 'You are still shocked, you don't know what you're saying. Rest. You need rest. We'll talk in the morning.' Yt touched yts forefinger to yts full lips, then left. When I could no longer hear soft footfalls on cool marble, I went to the door. Righteousness, rage and revenge were one song inside me. Locked. I heaved, I beat, I screamed. The Hijra Mahal did not listen. I went to the balcony that hung over the alley. Even if I could have shattered the intricate stone jali, it was a ten-metre drop to street level where the late night hum of phatphat autorickshaws and taxis was giving way to the delivery drays and cycle-vans of the spice merchants. Light slowly filled up the alley and crept across the floor of my bedroom: by its gathering strength I could read the headlines of the morning editions. WATER WARS: DOZENS DEAD IN CLASH OF THE RAJAS. JAIPUR REELS AS JODHRAS ANNIHILATED. POLICE POWERLESS AGAINST BLOODY VENDETTA.

In Rajputana, now as always, water is life, water is power. The police, the judges, the courts: we owned them. Us, and the Azads. In that we were alike. When gods fight, what mortal would presume to judge?

'A ride in triumph, a fall through a window into love, a marriage and a mourning?' I asked. 'That's it?'

Sul the astrologer nodded slowly. I sat on the floor of yts observatory. Incense rose on all sides of me from perforated brass censors. At first glance the room was so simple and bare that even a sadhu would have been uncomfortable, but as my eyes grew accustomed to the shadow in which it must be kept to work as a prediction machine, I saw that every centimetre of the bare pink marble was covered in curving lines and Hindi inscriptions, so small and precise they might be the work of tiny gods. The only light came from a star-shaped hole in the domed ceiling: Sul's star chamber was in the topmost turret of the Hijra Mahal, closest to heaven. As yt worked with its palmer and made the gestures in the air of the janampatri calculations, I watched a star of dazzling sunlight crawl along an arc etched in the floor, measuring out the phases of the House of Meena. Sul caught me staring at it, but I had only been curious to see what another nute looked like, close up. I had only ever known Heer. I had not known there could be as many as six nutes in the whole of India, let alone Jaipur. Sul was fat and had unhealthy yellow skin and eyes and shivered a lot as it pulled yts shawl around yt, though the turret room directly under the sun was stifling hot. I looked for clues to what yt had been before: woman, man. *Woman*, I thought. I had always thought of Heer as a man – an ex-man, though yt never mentioned the subject. I had always known it was taboo. When you stepped away, you never looked back.

'No revenge, no justice?'

'If you don't believe me, see for yourself.'

Fingers slipped the lighthoek behind my ear and the curving lines on the floor leaped up into mythical creatures studded with stars. Makara the crocodile, Vrishaba the Bull, the twin fishes of Meena: the twelve rashi. Kanya the dutiful daughter. Between them the twenty-seven nakshatars looped and arced, each of them subdivided into four padas; wheels within wheels within wheels, spinning around my head like blades as I sat on Sul's marble floor.

'You know I can't make any sense out of this,' I said, defeated by the whirling numbers. Sul leaned forward and gently touched my hand.

'A ride in triumph, a fall through a window into love, a marriage and a mourning. Window to widow. Trust me.'

'Young girls are truly beautiful on the inside.' Dahin the dream doctor's voice came from beyond the bank of glaring surgical lights as the bed on which I lay tilted back. 'No pollution, no nasty dirty hormones. Everything clean and fresh and lovely. Most of the women who come here, I never see any deeper than their skin. It is a rare privilege to be allowed to look inside someone.'

It was midnight in the chrome and plastic surgery in the basement of the Hijra Mahal, a snatched half-hour between the last of the consultations (society ladies swathed in veils and chadors to hide their identities) and Dahin hooking into the global web, settling the lighthoek over the visual centre in yts brain and pulling on the manipulator gloves connected to surgical robots in theatres half a world away. So gentle, so deft; too agile for any man's. Dahin of the dancing hands.

'Have you found it yet?' I asked. My eyes were watering from the lights. Something in them, something beyond them, was looking into my body and displaying it section by section, organ by organ, on Dahin's inner vision. Traditionally, the hijras were the only ones allowed to examine the bodies of the zenana women and reported their findings to the doctors outside.

'Found what? Finger lasers? Retractable steel claws? A table-top nuke wired into your tummy?'

'My father said over and over, I'm a weapon, I'm special ... I will destroy the house of Azad.'

'Cho chweet, if there's anything there, this would have shown it to me.'

My eyes were watering. I pretended it was the brightness of the light.

'Maybe there's something ... smaller, something you can't see, like ... bugs. Like a disease.'

I heard Dahin sigh and imagined the waggle of yts head.

'It'll take a day or two but I can run a diagnostic.' Tippy-tapping by the side of my head. I turned my head and froze as I saw a spider robot no bigger than my thumb walking towards my throat. It was a month since *the night*, but still I was distrustful of robots. I imagined I always would be. I felt a little flicking needle pain in the side of my neck, then the robot moved over my belly. I cringed at the soft spiking of its sharp, precise feet. I said, 'Dahin, do you mind me asking; did you do this?'

A short jab of pain in my belly.

'Oh yes, baba. All this, and more. Much much more. I only work on the outside, the externals. To be like me – to become one of us – you have to go deep, right down into the cells.'

Now the robot was creeping over my face. I battled the urge to sweep it away and crush it on the floor. I was a weapon, I was special. This machine would show me how.

'Woman, man, that's not a thing easily undone. They take you apart, baba. Everything, hanging there in a tank of fluid. Then they put you back together again. Different. Neither. Better.'

Why, I wanted to ask, *why do this thing to yourself?* But then I felt a tiny scratch in the corner of my eye as the robot took a scrape from my optic nerve.

'Three days for the test results, baba.'

Three days, and Dahin brought the results to me as I sat in the Peacock Pavilion overlooking the bazaar. The wind was warm and smelled of ashes of roses as it blew through the jali and turned the delicately handwritten sheets. No implants. No special powers or abilities. No abnormal neural structures, no tailored combat viruses. I was a completely normal fourteen-year-old Kshatriya girl.

I leaped over the swinging stick. While still in the air, I brought my own staff up in a low arc, catching the Azad's weapon between his hands. It flew from his grasp, clattered across the wooden floor of the hall. He threw a kick at me, rolled to pick up his pole, but my swinging tip caught him hard against the temple, sending him down to the floor like dropped laundry. I vaulted over him, swung my staff high to punch its brass-shod tip into the nerve cluster under the ear. Instant death.

'And finish.'

I held the staff millimetres away from my enemy's brain. Then I slipped the lighthoek from behind my ear and the Azad vanished like a djinn. Across the practice floor, Leel set down yts staff and unhooked yts 'hoek. In yts inner vision yts representation of me – enemy, sparring partner, pupil – likewise vanished. As ever at these practice sessions, I wondered what shape Leel's avatar took. Yt never said. Perhaps yt saw me.

'All fighting is dance, all dance is fighting.' That was Leel's first lesson to me on the day yt agreed to train me in silambam. For weeks I had watched yt from a high balcony practise the stampings and head movements and delicate hand gestures of the ritual dances. Then one night after yt had dismissed yts last class something told me, *stay on*, and I saw yt strip down to a simple dhoti and take out the bamboo staff from the cupboard and leap and whirl and stamp across the floor in the attacks and defences of the ancient Keralan martial art.

'Since it seems I was not born a weapon, then I must become a weapon.'

Leel had the dark skin of a southerner and I always felt that yt was very much older than yt appeared. I also felt – again with no evidence – that yt was the oldest inhabitant of the Hijra Mahal, that yt had been there long before any of the others came. I felt that yt might once have been a hijra and that the dance moves it practised and taught were from the days when no festival or wedding was complete without the outrageous, outcast eunuchs.

'Weapon, so? Cut anyone who tries to get close you, then when you've cut everyone, you cut yourself. Better things for you to be than a weapon.'

I asked Leel that same question every day until one evening thick with smog and incense from the great Govind festival yt came to me as I sat in my window reading the chati channels on my lighthoek.

'So. The stick fighting.'

That first day, as I stood barefoot on the practice floor in my Adidas baggies and stretchy sports top trying to feel the weight and heft of the fighting staff in my hands, I had been surprised when Leel fitted the lighthoek behind my ear. I had assumed I would spar against the guru ytself.

'Vain child. With what I teach you, you can kill. With one blow. Much safer to fight your image, in here.' Yt tapped yts forehead. 'As you fight mine. Or whatever you make me.'

All that season I learned the dance and ritual of Silambam; the leaps and the timings and the sweeps and the stabs. The sharp blows and the cries. I blazed across the practice floor yelling Kerala battle hymns, my staff a blur of thrusts and parries and killing strokes.

'Heavy child, heavy. Gravity has no hold on you, you must fly. Beauty is everything. See?' And Leel would vault on yts staff and time seemed to freeze around yt, leaving yt suspended there, like breath, in midair. And I began to understand about Leel, about all the nutes in this house of hijras. Beauty was everything, a beauty not male, not female; something else. A third beauty.

The hard, dry winter ended and so did my training. I went down in my Adidas gear and Leel was in yts dance costume, bells ringing at yts ankles. The staffs were locked away.

'This is so unfair.'

'You can fight with the stick, you can kill with a single blow, how much more do you need to become this weapon you so want to be?'

'But it takes years to become a master.'

'You don't need to become a master. And that is why I have finished your training today, because you should have learned enough to understand the perfect uselessness of what you want to do. If you can get close, if you ever learn to fly, perhaps you might kill Salim Azad, but his soldiers will cut you apart. Realise this, Padmini Jodhra. It's over. They've won.'

In the morning when the sun cast pools of light in the shapes of birds on to the floor of the little balcony, Janda would drink coffee laced with paan and, lazily lifting a finger to twirl away another page in yts inner vision, survey the papers the length and breadth of India, from the Rann of Kutch to the Sundarbans of Bengal.

'Darling, how can you be a bitch if you don't *read*?'

In the afternoon over tiffin, Janda would compose yts scandalous gossip columns: who was doing what with whom where and why, how often and how much and what all good people should think. Yt never did interviews. Reality got in the way of creativity.

'They love it, sweetie. Gives them an excuse to get excited and run to their lawyers. First real emotion some of them have felt in years.'

At first I had been scared of tiny, monkey-like Janda, always looking, checking, analysing from yts heavily kohled eyes, seeking weaknesses for yts acid tongue. Then I saw the power that lay in yts cuttings and clippings and entries, taking a rumour here, a whisper there, a suspicion yonder and putting them together into a picture of the world. I began to see how I could use it as a weapon. Knowledge was power. So dry winter gave way to thirsty spring and the headlines in the streets clamoured MONSOON SOON? and RAJPUTANA DEHY-DRATES, and Janda helped me build a picture of Salim Azad and his company. Looking beyond those sensationalist headlines to the business sections I grew to recognise his face beneath the headlines: AZAD PLUNDERS CORPSE OF RIVALS. SALIM AZAD: REBUILDER OF A DYNASTY. AZAD WATER IN FIVE RIVERS PROJECT. In the society section I saw him at weddings and parties and premiers. I saw him skiing in Nepal and shopping in New York and at the races in Paris. In the stockmarket feeds I watched the value of Azad Water climb as deals were struck, new investments announced, take-overs and buy-outs made public. I learned Salim Azad's taste in pop music, restaurants, tailors, designers, filmi stars, fast fast cars. I could tell you the names of the people who hand-sewed his shoes, who wrote the novel on his bedside table, who massaged his head and lit cones of incense along his spine, who flew his private tilt-jets and programmed his bodyguard robots.

One smoggy, stifling evening as Janda cleared away the thalis of sweetmeats yt gave me while I worked ('Eat, darling, eat and act') I noticed the lowlight illuminate two ridges of shallow bumps along the inside of yts forearm. I remembered them on Heer all my life and had always known they were as much part of a nute as the absence of any sexual organs, as the delicate bones and the long hands and the bare skull. In the low, late light they startled me because I had never asked, *What are they for?*

'For? Dear girl.' Janda clapped yts soft hands together. 'For love. For making love. Why else would we bear these nasty, ugly little goose-bumps? Each one generates a different chemical response in our brains. We touch, darling. We play each other like instruments. We feel ... things you cannot. Emotions for which you have no name, for which the only name is to experience them. We step away to somewhere not woman, not man; to the nute place.'

Yt turned yts arm wrist-upward to me so that yts wide sleeve fell away. The two rows of mosquito-bite mounds were clear and sharp in the yellow light. I thought of the harmonium the musicians would play in the old Jodhra Palace, fingers running up and down the buttons, the other hand squeezing the bellows. Play any tune on it. I shuddered. Janda saw the look on my face and snatched yts arm back into yts sleeve. And then, laid on in the newspaper in front of me, was an emotion for which I had no name, which I could only know by experiencing it. I thought no one knew more than I about Salim Azad, but here was a double-page spread of him pushing open the brass-studded gates of the Jodhra Mahal, my old home, where his family annihilated mine, under the screaming headline: AZAD BURIES PAST, BUYS PALACE OF RIVALS. Below that, Salim Azad standing by the pillars of the diwan, shading his eyes against the sun, as his staff ran our burning sun-man-bird kite up above the turrets and battlements into the hot yellow sky.

In the costume and make-up of Radha, divine wife of Krishna, I rode the painted elephant through the pink streets of Jaipur. Before me the band swung and swayed, its clarinets and horns rebounding from the buildings. Around and through the players danced Leel and the male dancer in red, swords flashing and clashing, skirts whirling, bells ringing. Behind me came another twenty elephants, foreheads patterned with the colours of Holi, howdahs streaming pennons and gold umbrellas. Above me robot aircraft trailed vast, gossamer-light banners bearing portraits of the Holy Pair and divine blessings. Youths and children in red wove crimson patterns with smoke-sticks and threw handfuls of coloured powder into the crowd. *Holi hai! Holi hai!* Reclining beside me on the golden howdah, Suleyra waved yts flute to the crowd. Jaipur was an endless tunnel of sound; people cheering, holiday shouts, the hooting of phatphat horns.

'Didn't I tell you you needed to get out of that place, cho chweet?'

In the blur of days inside the Hijra Mahal, I had not known that a year had passed without me setting foot outside its walls. Then Suleyra, the fixer, the jester, the party-maker, had come skipping into my room, pointed yts flute at me and said, 'Darling, you simply must be my wife,' and I had realised that it was Holi, the Elephant Festival. I had always loved Holi, the brightest, maddest of festivals.

'But someone might see me ...'

'Baba, you'll be blue all over. And anyway, no one can touch the bride of a god on her wedding day.'

And so, blue from head to toe, I reclined on gilded cushions beside Suleyra, who had been planning this public festival for six months, equally blue and not remotely recognisable as anything human, man, woman or nute. The city was clogged with people, the streets stifling hot, the air was so thick with hydrocarbon fumes the elephants wore smog goggles and I loved every bit of it. I was set free from the Hijra Mahal.

A wave of Suleyra/Krishna's blue hand activated the chips in the elephant's skull and turned it left through the arched gateway to the Old City, behind the boogieing band and the leaping, sword-wielding dancers. The crowds spilled off the arcades onto the street, ten, twenty deep. Every balcony was lined; women and children threw handfuls of colour down on us. Ahead I could see a platform and a canopy. The band was already marching in place while Leel and yts partner traded mock blows.

'Who is up there?' I asked, suddenly apprehensive.

'A most important dignitary,' said Suleyra, taking the praise of the spectators. 'A very rich and powerful man.'

'Who is he, Suleyra?' I asked. Suddenly, I was cold in the stinking heat of Jaipur. '*Who is he?*'

But the dancers and the band had moved on and now our elephant took its place in front of the podium. A tap from Suleyra's Krishna-flute: the elephant wheeled to face the dais and bent its front knees in a curtsey. A tall, young man in a Rajput costume with a flame-red turban stood up to applaud, face bright with delight.

I knew that man's shoe size and star sign. I knew the tailor who had cut his suit and the servant who wound his turban. I knew everything about him, except that he would be here, reviewing the Holi parade. I tensed myself to leap. One blow; Suleyra's Krishna-flute would suffice as a weapon. But I did nothing, for I saw a thing more incredible. Behind Salim Azad, bending forward, whispering in his ear, eyes black as obsidian behind polarising lenses, was Heer.

Salim Azad clapped his hands in delight.

'Yes, yes, this is the one! Bring her to me. Bring her to my palace.'

So I returned from the Palace of the Hijras to the Palace of the Jodhras, that was now the Palace of the Azads. I came through the brass gates under the high tower from which I had first looked out across Jaipur on the night of the steel monkey, across the great courtyard. The silver jars of holy Ganga water still stood on either side of the diwan where my father had managed his water empire. Beneath the gaze of the gods and the monkeys on the walls, I was dragged out of the car by Azad jawans and carried, screaming and kicking up the stairs to the zenana. 'My brother lay there, my mother died there, my father died there,' I shouted at them as they dragged me along that same corridor down which I had fled a year before. The marble floors were pristine, polished. I could not remember where the blood had been. Women retainers waited for me at the entrance to the zenana, for men could not enter the women's palace, but I flew and kicked and punched at them with all the skills Leel had taught me. They fled shrieking but all that happened was the soldiers held me at gunpoint until house robots arrived. I could kick and punch all I liked and never lay a scratch on their spun-diamond carapaces.

In the evening I was brought to the Hall of Conversations, an old and lovely room where women could talk and gossip with men across the delicate stone jali that ran the length of the hall. Salim Azad walked the foot-polished marble. He was dressed as a Rajput, in the traditional costume. I thought he looked like a joke. Behind him was Heer. Salim Azad paced up and down for

65

five minutes, studying me. I pressed myself to the jali and tried to stare him down. Finally he said,

'Do you have everything you want? Is there anything you need?'

'Your heart on a thali,' I shouted. Salim Azad took a step back.

'I'm sorry about the necessity of this ... But please understand, you're not my prisoner. Both of us are the last. There has been enough death. The only way I can see to finish this feud is to unite our two houses. But I won't force you, that would be ... impolite. Meaningless. I have to ask and you have to answer me.' He came as close to the stonework as was safe to avoid my Silambam punch. 'Padmini Jodhra, will you marry me?'

It was so ridiculous, so stupid and vain and so impossible that, in my shock, I felt the word *yes* in the back of my throat. I swallowed it down, drew back my head and spat long and full at him. The spit struck a moulding and ran down the carved sandstone.

'Understand I have nothing but death for you, murderer.'

'Even so, I shall ask every day, until you say yes,' Salim Azad said. With a whisk of robes, he turned and walked away. Heer, hands folded in yts sleeves, eyes pebbles of black, followed.

'And you, hijra,' I yelled, reaching a clawing hand through the stone jali to seize, to rip. 'You're next, traitor.'

That night I thought about starving myself to death, like the great Gandhiji when he battled the British to make India free and their Empire had stepped aside for one old, frail, thin, starving man. I forced my fingers down my throat and puked up the small amount of food I had forced myself to eat that evening. Then I realised that starved and dead I was no weapon. The House of Azad would sail undisturbed into the future. It was the one thing kept me alive, kept me sane in those first days in the zenana; my father's words: *You are a weapon.* All I had to discover was what kind.

In the night a small sweeper came and cleaned away my puke. It was as he said. Every evening as the sun touched the battlements of the Nahargarh Fort on the hill above Jaipur, Salim Azad came to the Hall of the Conversations. He would talk to me about the history of his family; back twenty generations to central Asia, from where they had swept down into the great river plains of Hindustan to build an empire of unparalleled wealth and elegance and beauty. They had not been warriors or rulers. They had been craftsmen and poets, makers of exquisite fine miniatures and jewel-like verses in Urdu, the language of poets. As the great Mughals erected their forts and palaces and fought their bloody civil wars, they had advanced from court painters and poets to court advisers, then to viziers and khid-mutgars, not just to the Mughals, but to the Rajputs, the Mara-thas and later to the East India Company and the British Raj. He told me tales of illustrious ancestors and stirring deeds; of Aslam who rode out between the armies of rival father and son Emperors and saved the Panjab; of Farhan who carried love notes between the English Resident of Hyderabad and the daughter of the Nizam and almost destroyed three kingdoms; of Shah Hussain who had struggled with Gandhi against the British for India, who had been approached by Jinnah to support partition and the creation of Pakistan but who had refused, though his family had been all but annihilated in the ethnic holocaust fol-lowing Independence. He told me of Elder Salim, his grand-father, founder of the dynasty, who had come to Jaipur when the monsoon failed the first terrible time in 2008 and set up village water reclamation schemes that over the decades became the great water empire of the Azads. Strong men, testing times, thrilling stories. And every night he said as the sun dipped behind Nahargarh fort, 'Will you marry me?' Every night I turned away from him without a word. But night by night, story by story, ancestor by ancestor, he chipped away at my silence. These were people as real, as vital as my own family. Now their stories had all ended. We were both the last.

I tried to call Janda at the Hijra Mahal, to seek wisdom and comfort from my sister/brothers, to find out if they knew why Heer had turned and betrayed me but mostly to hear another voice than the sat channels or Salim Azad. My calls bounced. White noise: Salim had my apartments shielded with a jamming field. I flung the useless palmer against the painted wall and ground it under the heel of my jewelled slipper. I saw endless evenings reaching out before me. Salim would keep coming, night after night, until he had his answer. He had all the time in the world. Did he mean to drive me mad to marry him?

Marry him. This time I did not push the thought away. I turned it this way, studied it, felt out its implications. Marry him. It was the way out of this marble cage.

In the heat of the midday, a figure in voluminous robes came hurrying down the cool corridor to the zenana. Heer. I had summoned yt. Because yt was not a man yt could enter the *zenana*, like the eunuchs of the Rajput days. Yt did not fear the skills Leel had taught me. Yt knew. Yt namasted.

'Why have you done this to me?'

'Memsahib, I have always been, and remain, a loyal servant of the House of Jodhra.'

'You've given me into the hands of my enemies.'

'I have saved you from the hands of your enemies, Padmini. It would not just be the end of this stupid, pointless bloody vendetta. He would make you a partner. Padmini, listen to what I am saying; you would be more than just a wife. Azad Jodhra. A name all India would learn.'

'Jodhra Azad.'

Heer pursed yts rosebud lips.

'Padmini Padmini, always, this pride.'

And yt left without my dismissal.

That night in the blue of the magic hour Salim Azad came again to the zenana, a pattern of shadows beyond the jali. I saw him open his lips. I put a finger up to mine.

'Ssh. Don't speak. Now it's time for me to tell you a story, my story, the story of the House of Jodhra.'

So I did, for one hundred and one nights, like an old Muslim fairytale, seated on cushions leaning up against the jali, whispering to Salim Azad in his Rajput finery wonderful tales of dashing Kshatriya cavalry charges and thousand cannon sieges of great fortresses, of handsome princes with bold moustaches and daring escapes with princesses in disguise in baskets over battlements, of princedoms lost over the fall of a chessman and Sandhurst-trained sowar officers more British than the British themselves and air-cav raids against Kashmiri insurgents and bold anti-terrorist strikes; of great polo matches and spectacular durbars with a hundred elephants and the man-bird-sun kite of the Jodhras sailing up into the sky over Jaipur; for a thousand years our city. For one hundred nights I bound him with spells taught to me by the nutes of the Hijra Mahal, then on the one hundred and first night I said, 'One thing you've forgotten.'

'What?'

'To ask me to marry you.'

He gave a little start, then waggled his head in disbelief and smiled. He had very good teeth.

'So, will you marry me?'

'Yes,' I said. 'Yes.'

The day was set three weeks hence. Sul had judged it the most propitious for a wedding of dynasties. Suleyra had been commissioned to stage the ceremony: Muslim first, then Hindu. Janda had been asked to draw on yts celebrity inside knowledge to invite all India to the union of the houses of Azad and Jodhra.

This is the wedding of the decade, yt cried in yts gupshup columns, *come or I will bad-mouth you.* Schedules of the great and glorious were rearranged, aeai soapi stars prepared avatars to attend, as did those human celebs who were unavoidably out of the subcontinent. From the shuttered jharokas of the zenana I watched Salim order his staff and machines around the great court, sending architects here, fabric designers there, pyrotechnicians yonder. Marquees and pavilions went up, seating was laid out, row upon row, carpet laid, patterns drawn in sand to be obliterated by the feet of the processional elephants. Security robots circled among the carrion-eating black kites over the palace, camera drones flitted like bats around the great court, seeking angles. Feeling my eyes on him, Salim would glance up at me, smile, lift his hand in the smallest greeting. I glanced away, suddenly shy, a girl-bride. This was to be a traditional, Rajputana wedding. I would emerge from purdah only to meet my husband. For those three weeks, the zenana was not a marble cage but an egg from which I would hatch. Into what? Power, unimaginable wealth, marriage to a man who had been my enemy. I still did not know if I loved him or not. I still saw the ghost shadows on the marble where his family had destroyed mine. He still came every night to read me Urdu poetry I could not understand. I smiled and laughed but I still did not know if what I felt was love, or just my desperation to be free. I still doubted it on the morning of my wedding.

Women came at dawn to bathe and dress me in wedding yellow and make up my hair and face and anoint me with turmeric paste. They decked me with jewels and necklaces, rings and bangles. They dabbed me with expensive perfume from France and gave me good luck charms and advice. Then they threw open the brass-studded doors of the zenana and, with the palace guard of robots, escorted me along the corridors and down the stairs to the great court. Leel danced and somersaulted before me; no wedding could be lucky without a hijra, a nute.

All of India had been invited and all of India had come, in flesh and in avatar. People rose, applauding. Cameras swooped on ducted fans. My nutes, my family from the Hijra Mahal, had been given seats at row ends.

'How could I improve on perfection?' said Dahin the face doctor as my bare feet trod rose petals towards the dais.

'The window, the wedding!' said Sul. 'And, pray the gods, many many decades from now, a very old and wise widow.'

'The setting is nothing without the jewel,' exclaimed Suleyra Party Arranger, throwing pink petals into the air.

I waited with my attendants under the awning as Salim's retainers crossed the courtyard from the men's quarters. Behind them came the groom on his pure white horse, kicking up the rose petals from its hooves. A low, broad ooh went up from the guests, then more applause. The maulvi welcomed Salim onto the platform. Cameras flocked for angles. I noticed that every parapet and carving was crowded with monkeys – flesh and machine – watching. The maulvi asked me most solemnly if I wished to be Salim Azad's bride.

'Yes,' I said, as I had said the night when I first accepted his offer. 'I do, yes.'

He asked Salim the same question, then read from the Holy Quran. We exchanged contracts, our assistants witnessed. The maulvi brought the silver plate of sweetmeats. Salim took one, lifted my gauze veil and placed it on my tongue. Then the maulvi placed the rings upon our fingers and proclaimed us husband and wife. And so were our two warring houses united, as the guests rose from their seats cheering and festival crackers and fireworks burst over Jaipur and the city returned a roaring wall of vehicle horns.

Peace in the streets at least. As we moved towards the long, cool pavilions for the wedding feast, I tried to catch Heer's eye as yt paced behind Salim. Yts hands were folded in the sleeves of yts robes, yts head thrust forward, lips pursed. I thought of a perching vulture.

We sat side by side on golden cushions at the head of the long, low table. Guests great and good took their places, slipping off their Italian shoes, folding their legs and tucking up their expensive Delhi frocks as waiters brought vast thalis of festival food. In their balcony overlooking the diwan, musicians struck up a Rajput piece older than Jaipur itself. I clapped my hands. I had grown up to this tune. Salim leaned back on his bolster.

'And look.'

Where he pointed, men were running up the great sun-bird-man kite of the Jodhras. As I watched, it skipped and dipped on the erratic winds in the court, then a stronger draught took it soaring up into the blue sky. The guests went oooh again.

'You have made me the happiest man in the world,' Salim said.

I lifted my veil, bent to him and kissed his lips. Every eye down the long table turned to me. Everyone smiled. Some clapped.

Salim's eyes went wide. Tears suddenly streamed from them. He rubbed them away and when he put his hands down, his eyelids were two puffy, blistered boils of flesh, swollen shut. He tried to speak but his lips were bloated, cracked, seeping blood and pus. Salim tried to stand, push himself away from me. He could not see, could not speak, could not breath. His hands fluttered at the collar of his gold-embroidered sherwani.

'Salim!' I cried. Leel was already on yts feet, ahead of all the guest doctors and surgeons as they rose around the table. Salim let out a thin, high-pitched wail, the only scream that would form in his swollen throat. Then he went down onto the feast table.

The pavilion was full of screaming guests and doctors shouting into palmers and security staff locking the area down. I stood useless as a butterfly in my make-up and wedding jewels and finery as doctors crowded around Salim. His face was like a cracked melon, a tight bulb of red flesh. I swatted away an intrusive hovercam. It was the best I could do. Then I remember Leel and the other nutes taking me out into the courtyard where a tilt-jet was settling, engines sending the rose petals up in a perfumed blizzard. Paramedics carried Salim out from the pavilion on a gurney. He wore an oxygen rebreather. There were tubes in his arms. Security guards in light-scatter armour pushed the great and the celebrated aside. I struggled with Leel as the medics slid Salim into the tilt-jet but yt held me with strange, withered strength.

'Let me go, let me go, that's my husband . . .'

'Padmini, Padmini, there is nothing you can do.'

'What do you mean?'

'Padmini, he is dead. Salim your husband is dead.'

Yt might have said that the moon was a great mouse in the sky.

'Anaphylactic shock. Do you know what that is?'

'Dead?' I said simply, quietly. Then I was flying across the court toward the tilt-jet as it powered up. I wanted to dive under its engines. I wanted to be scattered like the rose petals. Security guards ran to cut me off but Leel caught me first and brought me down. I felt the nip of an efuser on my arm and everything went soft as the tranquilizer took me.

After three weeks I called Heer to me. For the first week the security robots had kept me locked back in the zenana while the lawyers argued. I spent much of that time out of my head, part grief-stricken, part insane at what had happened. Just one kiss. A widow no sooner than I was wed. Leel tended to me, the lawyers and judges reached their legal conclusions. I was the sole and lawful heir of Azad-Jodhra Water. The second week I came to terms with my inheritance: the biggest water company in Rajputana, the third largest in the whole of India. There were contracts to be signed, managers and executives to meet, deals to be set up. I waved them away, for the third week was my week, the week in which I understood what I had lost. And I understood what I had done, and how, and what I was. Then I was ready to talk to Heer.

We met in the diwan, between the great silver jars that Salim, dedicated to his new tradition, had kept topped up with holy Ganga water. Guard-monkeys kept watch from the rooftops. My monkeys. My diwan. My palace. My company, now. Heer's hands were folded in yts sleeves. Yts eyes were black marble. I wore widow's white – a widow, at age fifteen.

'How long had you planned it?'

'From before you were born. From before you were even conceived.'

'I was always to marry Salim Azad.'

'Yes.'

'And kill him.'

'You could not do anything but. You were designed that way.'

Always remember, my father had said, here among these cool, shady pillars, *you are a weapon*. A weapon deeper, subtler than I had ever imagined, deeper even than Leel's medical machines could look. A weapon down in the DNA: designed from conception to cause a fatal allergic reaction in any member of the Azad family. An assassin in my every cell, in every pore and hair, in every fleck of dust shed from my deadly skin.

I killed my beloved with a kiss.

I felt a huge, shuddering sigh inside me, a sigh I could never, must never utter.

'I called you a traitor when you said you had always been a loyal servant of the House of Jodhra.'

'I was, am and will remain so, please God.' Heer dipped yts hairless head in a shallow bow. Then yt said, 'When you become one of us, when you step away, you step away from so much; from your own family, from the hope of ever having children … You are my family, my children. All of you, but most of all you, Padmini. I did what I had to for my family, and now you survive, now you have all that is yours by right. We don't live long, Padmini. Ours lives are too intense, too bright, too brilliant. There's been too much done to us. We burn out early. I had to see my family safe, my daughter triumph.'

'Heer …'

Yt held up a hand, glanced away, I though I saw silver in the corners of those black eyes.

'Take your palace, your company, it is all yours.'

That evening I slipped away from my staff and guards. I went up the marble stairs to the long corridor where my room had been before I became a woman, and a wife, and a widow, and the owner of a great company. The door opened to my thumbprint, I swung it open into dust-hazy golden sunlight. The bed was still made, mosquito nets neatly knotted up. I crossed to the balcony. I expected the vines and creepers to have grown to a jungle; with a start I realised it was just over a year since I had slept here. I could still pick out the hand-holds and foot-holds where I had followed the steel monkey up onto the roof. I had an easier way to that now. A door at the end of the corridor, previously locked to me, now opened onto a staircase. Sentry robots immediately bounced up as I stepped out onto the roof, crests raised, dart-throwers armed. A mudra from my hand sent them back into watching mode.

Once again I walked between the domes and turrets to the balcony at the very top of the palace façade. Again, great Jaipur at my bare feet took my breath away. The pink city kindled and burned in the low evening light. The streets still roared with traffic, I could smell the hot oil and spices of the bazaar. I now knew how to find the domes of the Hijra Mahal among the confusion of streets and apartment buildings. The dials and half-domes and buttresses of the Jantar Mantar threw huge shadows over each other, a confusion of clocks. Then I turned towards the glass scimitar of the Azad Headquarters – my headquarters now, my palace as much as this dead old Rajput pile. I had brought that house crashing down, but not in any way I had imagined. I wanted to apologise to Salim as he had apologised to me, every night when he came to me in the zenana, for what his family had done. *They made me into a weapon and I did not even know.*

How easy to step out over the traffic, step away from it all. Let it all end, Azad and Jodhra. Cheat Heer of yts victory. Then I saw my toes with their rings curl over the edge and I knew I could not, must not. I looked up and there, at the edge of vision, along the bottom of the red horizon, was a line of dark. The monsoon, coming at last. My family had made me one kind of weapon, but my other family, the kind, mad, sad, talented family of the nutes had taught me, in their various ways, to be another weapon. The streets were dry but the rains were coming. I had reservoirs and canals and pumps and pipes in my power. I was Maharani of the Monsoon. Soon the people would need me. I took a deep breath and imagined I could smell the rain. Then I turned and walked back through the waiting robots to my kingdom.

An Eligible Boy

A robot is giving Jasbir the whitest teeth in Delhi. It is a precise, terrifying procedure involving chromed steel and spinning, shrieking abrasion heads. Jasbir's eyes go wide as the spidery machine-arms flourish their weapons in his face, a demon of radical dentistry. He read about the *Glinting Life!* Cosmetic Dentistry Clinic, (Hygienic, Quick and Modern) in the February edition of *Shaadi! for Eligible Boys*. In a double-page spread it looked nothing like these insect-mandibles twitching inside his mouth. He'd like to ask the precise and demure dental nurse (married, of course) if it's meant to be like this but his mouth is full of clamps and anyway an Eligible Boy never shows fear. But he closes his eyes as the robot reaches in and spinning steel hits enamel.

Now the whitest teeth in Delhi dart through the milling traffic in a rattling phatphat. He feels as if he is beaming out over an entire city. The whitest teeth, the blackest hair, the most flawless skin and perfectly plucked eyebrows. Jasbir's nails are beautiful. There's a visiting manicurist at the Ministry of Waters, so many are the civil servants on the shaadi circuit. Jasbir notices the driver glancing at his blinding smile. He knows; the people on Mathura Road know, all Delhi knows that every night is great game night.

On the platform of Cashmere Café metro station, chip-implanted police-monkeys canter, shrieking, between the legs of passengers, driving away the begging, tugging, thieving macaques that infest the subway system. They pour over the

77

edge of the platform to their holes and hides in a wave of brown fur as the robot train slides in to the stop. Jasbir always stands next to the Women Only section. There is always a chance one of them might be scared of the monkeys – they bite – and he could then perform an act of Spontaneous Gallantry. The women studiously avoid any glance, any word, any sign of interest but a true Eligible Boy never passes up a chance for contact. But that woman in the business suit, the one with the fashionable wasp-waist jacket and the low-cut hip-riding pants, was she momentarily dazzled by the glint of his white white teeth?

'A robot, madam,' Jasbir calls as the packer wedges him into the 18:08 to Barwala. 'Dentistry of the future.' The doors close. But Jasbir Dayal knows he is a white-toothed Love God and this, this will be the shaadi night he finally finds the wife of his dreams.

Economists teach India's demographic crisis as an elegant example of market failure. Its seed germinated in the last century, before India became Tiger of Tiger economies, before political jealousies and rivalries split her into twelve competing states. A *lovely boy*, was how it began. *A fine, strong, handsome, educated, successful son, to marry and raise children and to look after us when we are old.* Every mother's dream, every father's pride. Multiply by the three hundred million of India's emergent middle class. Divide by the ability to determine sex in the womb. Add selective abortion. Run twenty-five years down the x-axis, factoring in refined, twenty-first century techniques such as cheap, powerful pharma patches that ensure lovely boys will be conceived and you arrive at great Awadh, its ancient capital Delhi of twenty million and a middle class with four times as many males as females. Market failure. Individual pursuit of self-interest damages larger society. Elegant to economists; to fine, strong, handsome, educated, successful young men like Jasbir caught in a wife-drought, catastrophic.

There's a ritual to shaadi nights. The first part of it involves Jasbir in the bathroom for hours playing pop music too loud and using too much expensive water while Sujay knocks and leaves copious cups of tea at the door and runs an iron over Jasbir's collars and cuffs and carefully removes the hairs of previous shaadis from Jasbir's suit jacket. Sujay is Jasbir's housemate in the government house at Acacia Bungalow Colony. He's a character designer on the Awadh version of *Town and Country*, neighbour-and-rival Bharat's all-conquering artificial intelligence generated soap opera. He works with the extras, designing new character skins and dropping them over raw code from Varanasi. Jahzay Productions is a new model company, meaning that Sujay seems to do most of his work from the verandah on his newfangled lighthoek device, his hands drawing pretty, invisible patterns on air. To office-bound Jasbir, with a ninety-minute commute on three modes of transport each way each day, it looks pretty close to nothing. Sujay is uncommunicative and hairy and neither shaves nor washes his too-long hair enough but his is a sensitive soul and he compensates for the luxury of being able to sit in the cool cool shade all day waving his hands by doing housework. He cleans, he tidies, he launders. He is a fabulous cook. He is so good that Jasbir does not need a maid, a saving much to be desired in pricey Acacia Bungalow Colony. This is a source of gossip to the other residents of Acacia Bungalow Colony. Most of the goings-on in Number 27 are the subject of gossip over the lawn sprinklers. Acacia Bungalow Colony is a professional, family gated community.

The second part of the ritual is the dressing. Like a syce preparing a Mughal lord for battle, Sujay dresses Jasbir. He fits the cufflinks and adjusts them to the proper angle. He adjusts the set of Jasbir's collar just so. He examines Jasbir from every angle as if he is looking at one of his own freshly-fleshed characters. Brush off a little dandruff here, correct a desk-slumped posture there. Smell his breath and check teeth for lunch-time spinach and other dental crimes.

'So what do you think of them then?' Jasbir says.

'They're white,' grunts Sujay.

The third part of the ritual is the briefing. While they wait for the phatphat, Sujay fills Jasbir in on upcoming plot-lines on *Town and Country*. It's Jasbir's major conversational ploy and advantage over his deadly rivals; soap-opera gossip. In his experience, what the women really want is gupshup from the meta-soap, the no-less-fictitious lives and loves and marriages and rows of the aeai actors that believe they are playing the roles in *Town and Country*. 'Auh,' Sujay will say. 'Different department.'

There's the tootle of phatphat horns. Curtains will twitch, there will be complaints about waking up children on a school night. But Jasbir is glimmed and glammed and shaadi-fit. And armed with soapi gupshup. How can he fail?

'Oh, I almost forgot,' Sujay says as he opens the door for the God of Love. 'Your father left a message. He wants to see you.'

'You've hired a what?' Jasbir's retort is smothered by the cheers of his brothers from the living room as a cricket ball rolls and skips over the boundary rope at Jawaharlal Nehru Stadium. His father bends closer, confidentially, across the tiny tin-topped kitchen table. Anant whisks the kettle off the boil so she can overhear. She is the slowest, most awkward maid in Delhi but to fire her would be to condemn an old woman to the streets. She lumbers around the Dayal kitchen like a buffalo, feigning disinterest.

'A matchmaker. Not my idea, not my idea at all; it was hers.' Jasbir's father inclines his head toward the open living-room door. Beyond it, enthroned on her sofa amidst her non-eligible boys, Jasbir's mother watches the test match on the smart-silk wallscreen Jasbir had bought her with his first civil service pay-check. When Jasbir left the tiny, ghee-stinky apartment on Nabi Karim Road for the distant graces of Acacia Bungalow Colony, Mrs Dayal delegated all negotiations with her wayward son to her husband. 'She's found this special matchmaker.'

'Wait wait wait. Explain to me *special*.'

Jasbir's father squirms. Anant is taking a long time to dry a tea-cup.

'Well, you know in the old days people would maybe have gone to a hijra ... Well, she's updated it a bit, this being the twenty-first century and everything, so she's, ah, found a nute.'

A clatter of a cup hitting a stainless-steel draining-board.

'A *nute*?' Jasbir hisses

'He knows contracts. He knows deportment and proper eti-quette. He knows what women want. I think he may have been one, once.'

Anant lets out an *aie!*, soft and involuntary as a fart.

'I think the word you're looking for is "yt",' Jasbir says. "And they're not hijras the way you knew them. They're not men become women or women become men. They're neither.'

'Nutes, neithers, hijras, yts, hes, shes; whatever; it's not as if I even get to take tea with the parents let alone see an announce-ment in the shaadi section in the *Times of Awadh*.' Mrs Dayal shouts over the burbling commentary to the second Awadh-China Test. Jasbir winces. Like papercuts, the criticisms of parents are the finest and the most painful.

Inside the Haryana Polo and Country Club the weather was raining men snowing men hailing men. Well-dressed men, moneyed men, charming men, groomed and glinted men, men with prospects all laid out in their marriage résumés. Jasbir knew most of them by face. Some he knew by name, a few had passed beyond being rivals into becoming friends.

'Teeth!' A cry, a nod, a two-six-gun showbiz point from the bar. There leant Kishore, a casual lank of a man draped like a skein of silk against the Raj-era mahogany. 'Where did you get those, badmash?' He was an old university colleague of Jasbir's, much given to high-profile activities like horse racing at the Delhi Jockey Club or skiing, where there was snow left on the Himalayas. Now he was In Finance and claimed to have been to five hundred shaadis and made a hundred proposals. But when they were on the hook, wriggling, he let them go. *Oh, the tears, the threats, the phone calls from fuming fathers and boiling brothers. It's the game, isn't it?* Kishore rolls on, 'Here, have you heard? Tonight is Deependra's night. Oh yes. An astrology aeai has predicted it. It's all in the stars, and on your palmer.'

Deependra was a clenched wee man. Like Jasbir he was a civil servant, heading up a different glass-partitioned workcluster in the Ministry of Waters: Streams and Watercourses to Jasbir's Ponds and Dams. For three shaadis now he had been nurturing a fantasy about a woman who exchanged palmer addresses with him. First it was a call, then a date. Now it's a proposal.

'Rahu is in the fourth house, Saturn in the seventh,' Deependra said lugubriously. 'Our eyes will meet, she will nod – just a nod. The next morning she will call me and that will be it, done, dusted. I'd ask you to be one of my groomsmen, but I've already promised them all to my brothers and cousins. It's written. Trust me.'

It was a perpetual bafflement to Jasbir how a man wedded by day to robust fluid accounting by night stakes love and life on an off-the-shelf janampatri artificial intelligence.

A Nepali khidmutgar banged a staff on the hardwood dance-floor of the exclusive Haryana Polo and Country Club. The Eligible Boys straightened their collars, adjusted the hang of their jackets, aligned their cufflinks. This side of the mahogany double doors to the garden they were friends and colleagues. Beyond it they were rivals.

'Gentlemen, valued clients of the Lovely Girl Shaadi Agency, please welcome, honour and cherish the Begum Rezzak and her Lovely Girls!'

Two attendants slid open the folding windows onto the polo ground. There waited the lovely girls in their saris and jewels and gold and henna (for the Lovely Girl Agency is a most traditional and respectable agency). Jasbir checked his schedule – five minutes per client, maybe less, never more. He took a deep breath and unleashed his thousand-rupee smile. It was time to find a wife.

'Don't think I don't know what you're muttering about in there,' Mrs Dayal calls over the mantra commentary of Harsha Bhogle. 'I've had the talk. The nute will arrange the thing for much less than you are wasting on all those shaadi agencies and databases and nonsense. No, nute will make the match that is it stick stop stay.' There is a spatter of applause from the Test Match.

'I tell you your problem: a girl sees two men sharing a house together, she gets ideas about them,' Dadaji whispers. Anant finally sets down two cups of tea and rolls her eyes. 'She's had the talk. Yt'll start making the match. There's nothing to be done about it. There are worse things.'

The women may think what they want, but Sujay has it right, Jasbir thinks. *Best never to buy into the game at all.*

Another cheer, another boundary. Haresh and Sohan jeer at the Chinese devils. *Think you can buy it in and beat the world, well, the Awadhi boys are here to tell you it takes years, decades, centuries upon centuries to master the way of cricket.* And there's too much milk in the tea.

*

A dream wind like the hot gusts that forerun the monsoon sends a spray of pixels through the cool white spacious rooms of 27 Acacia Avenue Bungalows. Jasbir ducks and laughs as they blow around him. He expects them to be cold and sharp as wind-whipped powder snow but they are only digits, patterns of electrical charge swept through his visual cortex by the clever little device hooked behind his right ear. They chime as they swirl past, like glissandis of silver sitar notes. Shaking his head in wonder, Jasbir slips the lighthoek from behind his ear. The vision evaporates.

'Very clever, very pretty but I think I'll wait until the price comes down.'

'It's, um, not the 'hoek,' Sujay mutters. 'You know, well, the matchmaker your mother hired. Well, I thought, maybe you don't need someone arranging you a marriage.' Some days Sujay's inability to talk to the point exasperates Jasbir. Those days tend to come after another fruitless and expensive shaadi night and the threat of a matchmaker but particularly after Deependra of the non-white teeth announces he has a date. With the girl. The one written in the fourth house of Rahu by his pocket astrology aeai. 'Well, you see I thought, with the right help you could arrange it yourself.' Some days, debate with Sujay is pointless. He follows his own calendar. 'You, ah, need to put the 'hoek back on again.'

Silver notes spray through Jasbir's inner ears as the little curl of smart plastic seeks out the sweet spot in his skull. Pixel birds swoop and swarm like starlings on a winter evening. It is inordinately pretty. Then Jasbir gasps aloud as the motes of light and sound sparklingly coalesce into a dapper man in an old-fashioned high-collar sherwani and wrinkle-bottom pyjamas. His shoes are polished to mirror-brightness. The dapper man bows.

'Good morning, sir. I am Ram Tarun Das, Master of Grooming, Grace and Gentlemanliness.'

'What is this doing in my house?' Jasbir unhooks the device beaming data into his brain.

'Er, please don't do that,' Sujay says. 'It's not aeai etiquette.'

Jasbir slips the device back on and there he is, that charming man.

'I have been designed with the express purpose of helping you marry a suitable girl,' says Ram Tarun Das.

'Designed?'

'I, ah, made him for you,' says Sujay. 'I thought that if anyone knows about relationships and marriages, it's soap stars.'

'A soap star. You've made me a, a marriage life-coach out of a soap star?'

'Not a soap star exactly, more a conflation of a number of sub-systems from the central character register,' Sujay says. 'Sorry Ram.'

'Do you usually do that?'

'Do what?'

'Apologise to aeais.'

'They have feelings too.'

Jasbir rolls his eyes. 'I'm being taught husbandcraft by a mash-up.'

'Ah, that is out of order. Now you apologise.'

'Now then, sir, if I am to rescue you from a marriage forged in hell, we had better start with manners,' says Ram Tarun Das. 'Manners maketh the man. It is the bedrock of all relationships because true manners come from what he is, not what he does. Do not argue with me, women see this at once. Respect for all things, sir, is the key to etiquette. Maybe I only imagine I feel as you feel, but that does not make my feelings any less real to me. So this once, I accept your apology as read. Now, we'll begin. We have so much to do before tonight's shaadi.'

Why, Jasbir thinks, *why can I never get my shoes like that?*

*

The lazy crescent moon lolls low above the out-flarings of Tughluk's thousand stacks; a cradle to rock an infant nation. Around its rippling reflection in the infinity pool bob mango-leaf diyas. No polo grounds and country clubs for Begum Jaitly. This is 2045, not 1945. Modern style for a modern nation, that is philosophy of the Jaitly Shaadi Agency. But gossip and want are eternal and in the mood lighting of the penthouse the men are blacker-than-black shadows against greater Delhi's galaxy of lights and traffic.

'Eyebrows!' Kishore greets Jasbir with TV-host pistol-fingers two-shot bam bam. 'No seriously, what did you do to them?' Then his own eyes widen as he scans down from the eyebrows to the total product. His mouth opens, just a crack, but wide enough for Jasbir to savour an inner fist-clench of triumph.

He'd felt self-conscious taking Ram Tarun Das to the mall. He had no difficulty accepting that the figure in its stubbornly atavistic costume was invisible to everyone but him (though he did marvel at how the aeai avoided colliding with any other shopper in the thronged Centrestage Mall). He did feel stupid talking to thin air.

'What is this delicacy?' Ram Tarun Das said in Jasbir's inner ear. 'People talk to thin air on the cellphone all the time. Now this suit, sir.'

It was bright, it was brocade, it was a fashionable retro cut that Jasbir would have gone naked rather than worn.

'It's very ... bold.'

'It's very you. Try it. Buy it. You will seem confident and stylish without being flashy. Women cannot bear flashy.'

The robot cutters and stitchers were at work even as Jasbir completed the card transaction. It was expensive. *Not as expensive as all the shaadi memberships*, he consoled himself. *And something to top it off*. But Ram Tarun Das manifested himself right in the jeweller's window over the display.

'Never jewellery on a man. One small brooch at the shirt collar to hold it together, that is permissible. Do you want the lovely girls to think you are a Mumbai pimp? No, sir, you do not. No to jewels. Yes to shoes. Come.'

He had paraded his finery before a slightly embarrassed Sujay. 'You look, er, good. Very dashing. Yes.'

Ram Tarun Das, leaning on his cane and peering intensely, said, 'You move like a buffalo. Ugh, sir. Here is what I prescribe for you. Tango lessons. Passion and discipline. Latin fire, yet the strictest of tempos. Do not argue, it is the tango for you. There is nothing like it for deportment.'

The tango, the manicures, the pedicures, the briefings in popular culture and Delhi gossip ('Soap opera insults both the intelligence and imagination, I should know, sir'), the conversational ploys, the body language games of when to turn so, when to make or break eye-contact, when to dare the lightest, engaging touch. Sujay mooched around the house, even more lumbering and lost than usual, as Jasbir chatted with air and practised Latin turns and drops with invisible partners. Last of all, on the morning of the Jaitly shaadi.

'Eyebrows sir. You will never get a bride with brows like a hairy sadhu. There is a girl not five kilometres from here, she has a moped service. I've ordered her, she will be here within ten minutes.'

As ever, Kishore won't let Jasbir wedge an answer in, but rattles on, 'So, Deependra then?'

Jasbir has noticed that Deependra is not occupying his customary place in Kishore's shadows; in fact he does not seem to be anywhere in this penthouse.

'Third date,' Kishore says, then mouths it again silently for emphasis. 'That janampatri aeai must be doing something right. You know, wouldn't it be funny if someone took her off him? Just as a joke, you know?'

Kishore chews his bottom lip. Jasbir knows the gesture of old. Then bells chime, lights dim and a wind from nowhere sends the butter-flames flickering and the little diyas flocking across the infinity pool. The walls have opened, the women enter the room.

She stands by the glass wall looking down into the cube of light that is the car park. She clutches her cocktail between her hands as if in prayer or concern. It is a new cocktail designed for the international cricket test, served in an egg-shaped goblet made from a new spin-glass that will always self-right, no matter how it is set down or dropped. A Test of Dragons is the name of the cocktail. Good Awadhi whisky over a gilded syrup with a six-hit of Chinese Kao Liang liqueur. A tiny red gel dragon dissolves like a sunset.

'Now, sir,' whispers Ram Tarun Das standing at Jasbir's shoulder. 'Faint heart, as they say.'

Jasbir's mouth is dry. A secondary application Sujay pasted onto the Ram Tarun Das aeai tells him his precise heart rate, respiration, temperature and the degree of sweat in his palm. He's surprised he's still alive.

You've got the entry lines, you've got the exit lines and the stuff in the middle Ram Tarun Das will provide.

He follows her glance down into the car park. A moment's pause, a slight inclination of his body towards hers. That is *the line.*

So, are you a Tata, a Mercedes, a Li Fan or a Lexus? Ram Tarun Das whispers in Jasbir's skull. He casually repeats the line. He has been rehearsed and rehearsed and rehearsed in how to make it sound natural. He's as good as any newsreader, better than those few human actors left on television.

She turns to him, lips parted a fraction in surprise.

'I beg your pardon?'

She will say this, Ram Tarun Das hints. *Again, offer the line.*

'Are you a Tata, a Mercedes, a Li Fan or a Lexus?'

'What do you mean?'

'Just pick one. Whatever you feel, that's the right answer.'

A pause, a purse of the lips. Jasbir subtly links his hands behind his back, the better to hide the sweat.

'Lexus,' she says. Shulka, her name is Shulka. She is a twenty-two-year-old marketing graduate from Delhi U working in men's fashion, a Mathur – only a couple of caste steps away from Jasbir's folk. The Demographic Crisis has done more to shake up the tiers of varna and jati than a century of the slow drip of democracy. And she has answered his question.

'Now, that's very interesting,' says Jasbir.

She turns, plucked crescent-moon eyebrows arched. Behind Jasbir, Ram Tarun Das whispers, *Now, the fetch.*

'Delhi, Mumbai, Kolkata, Chennai?'

A small frown now. Lord Vishnu, she is beautiful.

'I was born in Delhi . . .'

'That's not what I mean.'

The frown becomes a nano-smile of recognition.

'Mumbai then. Yes, Mumbai definitely. Kolkata's hot and dirty and nasty. And Chennai – no, I'm definitely Mumbai.'

Jasbir does the sucked-in-lip nod of concentration Ram Tarun Das made him practise in front of the mirror.

'Red, green, yellow, blue?'

'Red.' No hesitation.

'Cat, dog, bird, monkey?'

She cocks her head to one side. Jasbir notices that she, too, is wearing a 'hoek. Tech girl. The cocktail bot is on its rounds, doing industrial magic with the self-righting glasses and its little spider-fingers.

'Bird . . . no.' A sly smile. 'No no no. Monkey.'

He is going to die he is going to die.

'But what does it mean?'

Jasbir holds up a finger.

'One more. Ved Prakash, Begum Vora, Dr Chatterji, Ritu Parvaaz.'

She laughs. She laughs like bells from the hem of a wedding skirt. She laughs like the stars of a Himalaya night.

What do you think you're doing? Ram Tarun Das hisses. He flips through Jasbir's perceptions to appear behind Shulka, hands thrown up in despair. With a gesture he encompasses the horizon wreathed in gas flares. *Look, tonight the sky burns for you, sir, and you would talk about soap opera! The script, stick to the script! Improvisation is death.* Jasbir almost tells his matchmaker, *Away djinn, away.* He repeats the question.

'I'm not really a *Town and Country* fan,' Shulka says. 'My sister now, she knows every last detail about every last one of the characters and that's before she gets started on the actors. It's one of those things I suppose you can be ludicrously well informed about without ever watching. So if you had to press me, I would have to say Ritu. So what does it all mean, Mr Dayal?'

His heart turns over in his chest. Ram Tarun Das eyes him coldly. *The* finesse: *make it. Do it just as I instructed you. Otherwise your money and my bandwidth are thrown to the wild wind.* ·

The cocktail bot dances in to perform its cybernetic circus. A flip of Shulka's glass and it comes down spinning, glinting, on the precise needle-point of its forefinger. Like magic, if you know nothing about gyros and spin-glasses. But that moment of prestidigitation is cover enough for Jasbir to make the ordained move. By the time she looks up, cocktail refilled, he is half a room away.

He wants to apologise as he sees her eyes widen. He needs to apologise as her gaze searches the room for him. Then her eyes catch his. It is across a crowded room just like the song that

Sujay mumbles around the house when he thinks Jasbir can't hear. Sujay loves that song. It is the most romantic, heart-felt, innocent song he has ever heard. Big awkward Sujay has always been a sucker for veteran Hollywood musicals. *South Pacific, Carousel, Moulin Rouge*, he watches them on the big screen in the living room, singing shamelessly along and getting moist-eyed at the impossible loves. Across a crowded room, Shulka frowns. Of course. It's in the script.

But what does it mean? she mouths. And, as Ram Tarun Das has directed, he shouts back, 'Call me and I'll tell you.' Then he turns on his heel and walks away. And that, he knows without any prompt from Ram Tarun Das, is the *finesse*.

The apartment is grossly over-heated and smells of singeing cooking ghee but the nute is swaddled in a crocheted shawl, hunched as if against a persistent hard wind. Plastic tea-cups stand on the low brass table, Jasbir's mother's conspicuously untouched. Jasbir sits on the sofa with his father on his right and his mother on his left, as if between arresting policemen. Nahin the nute mutters and shivers and rubs yts fingers.

Jasbir has never been in the physical presence of a third-gendered. He knows all about them — as he knows all about most things – from the single-professional-male general interest magazines to which he subscribes. Those pages, between the ads for designer watches and robot tooth-whitening, portray them as fantastical, Arabian Nights creatures equally blessed and cursed with glamour. Nahin the matchmaker seems old and tired as a god, knotting and unknotting yts fingers over the papers on the coffee table – 'The bloody drugs, darlings' – occasionally breaking into great spasmodic shudders. *It's one way of avoiding the Wife Game*, Jasbir thinks.

Nahin slides sheets of paper around on the tabletop. The documents are patterned as rich as damask with convoluted chartings of circles and spirals annotated in inscrutable alphabets. There is a photograph of a woman in each top right corner. The women are young and handsome but have the wide-eyed expressions of being photographed for the first time.

'Now, I've performed all the calculations and these five are both compatible and auspicious,' Nahin says. Yt clears a large gobbet of phlegm from yts throat.

'I notice they're all from the country,' says Jasbir's father.

'Country ways are good ways,' says Jasbir's mother.

Wedged between them on the short sofa, Jasbir looks over Nahin's shawled shoulder to where Ram Tarun Das stands in the doorway. He raises his eyebrows, shakes his head.

'Country girls are better breeders,' Nahin says. 'You said dynasty was a concern. You'll also find a closer match in jati and in general they settle for a much more reasonable dowry than a city girl. City girls want it all. Me me me. No good ever comes of selfishness.'

The nute's long fingers stir the country girls around the coffee table, then slide three toward Jasbir and his family. Dadaji and Mamaji sit forward. Jasbir slumps back. Ram Tarun Das folds his arms, rolls his eyes.

'These three are the best starred,' Nahin says. 'I can arrange a meeting with their parents almost immediately. There would be some small expenditure in their coming up to Delhi to meet with you; this would be in addition to my fee.'

In a flicker, Ram Tarun Das is behind Jasbir, his whisper a startle in his ear.

'There is a line in the Western wedding vows: speak now or forever hold your peace.'

'How much is my mother paying you?' Jasbir says into the moment of silence.

'I couldn't possibly betray client confidentiality.' Nahin has eyes small and dark as currants.

'I'll disengage you for an additional fifty per cent.'

Nahin's hands hesitate over the pretty hand drawn spirals and wheels. *You were a man before*, Jasbir thinks. *That's a man's gesture. See, I've learned how to read people.*

'I double,' shrills Mrs Dayal.

'Wait wait wait,' Jasbir's father protests but Jasbir is already shouting over him. He has to kill this idiocy here, before his family in their wedding fever fall into strategies they cannot afford.

'You're wasting your time and my parents' money,' Jasbir says. 'You see, I've already met a suitable girl.'

Goggle eyes, open mouths around the coffee table, but none so astounded and gaping as Ram Tarun Das's.

The Prasads at Number 25 Acacia Colony Bungalows have already sent over a pre-emptive complaint about the tango music but Jasbir flicks up the volume fit to rattle the brilliants on the chandelier. At first he scorned the dance, the stiffness, the formality, the strictness of the tempo. So very un-Indian. No one's uncle would ever dance this at a wedding. But he has persisted – never say that Jasbir Dayal is not a trier – and the personality of the tango has subtly permeated him, like rain into a dry riverbed. He has found the discipline and begun to understand the passion. He walks tall in the Dams and Water-courses. He no longer slouches at the watercooler.

'When I advised to you speak or forever hold your peace, sir, I did not actually mean, lie through your teeth to your parents,' Ram Tarun Das says. In tango he takes the woman's part. The lighthoek can generate an illusion of weight and heft so the aeai feels solid as Jasbir's partner. *If it can do all that, surely it could make him look like a woman?* Jasbir thinks. In his dedication to detail Sujay often overlooks the obvious. 'Especially in matters where they can rather easily find you out.'

'I had to stop them wasting their money on that nute.'

'They would have kept outbidding you.'

'Then, even more, I had to stop them wasting my money as well.'

Jasbir knocks Ram Tarun Das's foot across the floor in a sweetly executed *barrida*. He glides past the open verandah door where Sujay glances up from soap-opera building. He has become accustomed to seeing his landlord tango cheek to cheek with an elderly Rajput gentleman. *Yours is a weird world of ghosts and djinns and half-realities*, Jasbir thinks.

'So how many times has your father called asking about Shulka?' Ram Tarun Das's free leg traces a curve on the floor in a well-executed *volcada*. Tango is all about seeing the music. It is making the unseen visible.

You know, Jasbir thinks. *You're woven through every part of this house like a pattern in silk.*

'Eight,' he says weakly. 'Maybe if I called her ...'

'Absolutely not,' Ram Tarun Das insists, pulling in breath-to-breath close in the *embreza*. 'Any minuscule advantage you might have enjoyed, any atom of hope you might have entertained, would be forfeit. I forbid it.'

'Well, can you at least give me a probability? Surely knowing everything you know about the art of shaadi, you could at least let me know if I've any chance?'

'Sir,' says Ram Tarun Das, 'I am a Master of Grooming, Grace and Gentlemanliness. I can direct you to any number of simple and unsophisticated bookie-aeais; they will give you a price on anything though you may not fancy their odds. One thing I will say: Miss Shulka's responses were very – suitable.'

Ram Tarun Das hooks his leg around Jasbir's waist in a final *gancho*. The music comes to its strictly appointed conclusion. From behind it come two sounds. One is Mrs Prasad weeping. She must be leaning against the party wall to make her upset so clearly audible. The other is a call tone, a very specific call tone, a deplorable but insanely hummable filmi hit *My Back, My Crack, My Sack* that Jasbir set on the house system to identify one caller, and one caller only.

Sujay looks up, startled.

'Hello?' Jasbir sends frantic, pleading hand signals to Ram Tarun Das, now seated across the room, his hands resting on the top of his cane.

'Lexus Mumbai red monkey Ritu Parvaaz,' says Shulka Mathur. 'So what do they mean?'

'No, my mind is made up, I'm hiring a private detective,' Deependra says, rinsing his hands. On the twelfth floor of the Ministry of Waters all the dating gossip happens at the wash-hand basins in the Number 16 Gentlemen's WC. Urinals: too obviously competitive. Cubicles: a violation of privacy. Truths are best washed with the hands at the basins, and secrets and revelations can always be concealed by judicious use of the hot-air hand-drier.

'Deependra, this is paranoia. What's she done?' Jasbir whispers. A level 0.3 aeai chip in the tap admonishes him not to waste precious water.

'It's not what's she's done, it's what she's not done,' Deependra hisses. 'There's a big difference between someone not being available and someone deliberately not taking your calls. Oh yes. You'll learn this, mark my words. You're at the first stage, when it's all new and fresh and exciting and you are blinded by the amazing fact that someone, someone at last, at long last! thinks you are a catch. It is all rose petals and sweets and cho chweet and you think nothing can possibly go wrong. But you pass through that stage, oh yes. All too soon the scales fall from your eyes. You see ... and you hear.'

'Deependra.' Jasbir moves to the battery of driers. 'You've

been on five dates.' But every word Deependra has spoken has chimed true. He is a cauldron of clashing emotions. He feels light and elastic, as if he bestrode the world like a god, yet at the same time the world is pale and insubstantial as muslin around him. He feels light-headed with hunger though he cannot eat a thing. He pushes away Sujay's lovingly prepared dhals and roti. Garlic might taint his breath, saag might stick to his teeth, onions might give him wind, bread might inelegantly bloat him. He chews a few cleansing cardamoms, in the hope of spiced kisses to come. Jasbir Dayal is blissfully, gloriously love-sick.

Date one. The Qutb Minar. Jasbir had immediately protested. 'Tourists go there. And families on Saturdays.'

'It's history.'

'Shulka isn't interested in history.'

'Oh, you know her so well after three phone conversations and two evenings chatting on shaadinet – which I scripted for you? It is roots, it is who you are and where you come from. It's family and dynasty. Your Shulka is interested in that, I assure you, sir. Now, here's what you will wear.'

There were tour buses great and small. There were hawkers and souvenir peddlers. There were parties of frowning Chinese. There were schoolchildren with backpacks so huge they looked like upright tortoises. But wandering beneath the domes and along the colonnades of the Quwwat Mosque in his Casual Urban Explorer clothes, they seemed as remote and ephemeral as clouds. There was only Shulka and him. And Ram Tarun Das strolling at his side, hands clasped behind his back.

To cue, Jasbir paused to trace out the time-muted contours of a disembodied tirthankar's head, a ghost in the stone.

'Qutb-ud-din Aibak, the first Sultan of Delhi, destroyed twenty Jain temples and reused the stone to build his mosque. You can still find the old carvings if you know where to look.'

'I like that,' Shulka said. 'The old gods are still here.' Every word that fell from her lips was pearl-perfect. Jasbir tried to read her eyes but her BlueBoo! cat-eye shades betrayed nothing. 'Not enough people care about their history any more. It's all modern this modern that, if it's not up-to-the-minute it's irrelevant. I think that to know where you're going you need to know where you've come from.'

Very good, Ram Tarun Das whispered. *Now, the iron pillar.*

They waited for a tour group of Germans to move away from the railed-off enclosure. Jasbir and Shulka stood in the moment of silence gazing at the black pillar.

'Sixteen hundred years old, but never a speck of rust on it,' Jasbir said.

Ninety-eight per cent pure iron, Ram Tarun Das prompted. *There are things Mittal Steel can learn from the Gupta kings.*

'"He who, having the name of Chandra, carried a beauty of countenance like the full moon, having in faith fixed his mind upon Vishnu, had this lofty standard of the divine Vishnu set up on the hill Vishnupada".' Shulka's frown of concentration as she focused on the inscription around the pillar's waist was as beautiful to Jasbir as that of any god or Gupta king.

'You speak Sanskrit?'

'It's a sort of personal spiritual development path I'm following.'

You have about thirty seconds before the next tour group arrives, Ram Tarun Das cuts in. *Now sir; that line I gave you.*

'They say that if you stand with your back to the pillar and close your arms around it, your wish will be granted.'

The Chinese were coming the Chinese were coming.

'And if you could do that, what would you wish for?'

Perfect. She was perfect.

'Dinner?'

She smiled that small and secret smile that set a garden of

97

thorns in Jasbir's heart and walked away. At the centre of the gatehouse arch she turned and called back,

'Dinner would be good.'

Then the Chinese with their shopping bags and sun visors and plastic leisure shoes came bustling around the stainless iron pillar of Chandra Gupta.

Jasbir smiles at the sunny memory of Date One. Deependra waggles his fingers under the stream of hot air.

'I've heard about this. It was on a documentary, oh yes. White widows, they call them. They dress up and go to the shaadis and have their résumés all twinkling and perfect but they have no intention of marrying, oh no no no, not a chance. Why should they, when there is a never-ending stream of men to wine them and dine them and take them out to lovely places and buy them lovely presents and shoes and jewels, and even cars? So it said on the documentary. They are just in it for what can get; they are playing games with our hearts. And when they get tired or bored or if the man is making too many demands or his presents aren't as expensive as they were or they can do better somewhere else, then whoosh! Dumped flat and on to the next one. It's a game to them.'

'Deependra,' says Jasbir. 'Let it go. Documentaries on the Shaadi Channel are not the kind of model you want for married life. Really.' Ram Tarun Das would be proud of that one. 'Now, I have to get back to work.' Faucets that warn about water crime can also report excessive toilet breaks to line managers. But the doubt-seeds are sown, and Jasbir now remembers the restaurant.

Date Two. Jasbir had practised with the chopsticks for every meal for a week. He swore at rice, he cursed dhal. Sujay effort-lessly scooped rice, dhal, everything from bowl to lips in a flurry of stickwork.

'It's easy for you, you've got that code-wallah Asian culture thing.'

'Um, we are Asian.'

'You know what I mean. And I don't even like Chinese food, it's so bland.'

The restaurant was expensive, half a week's wage. He'd make it up on overtime; there were fresh worries in Dams and Water-courses about a drought.

'Oh,' Shulka said, the nightglow of Delhi a vast, diffuse halo behind her. She is a goddess, Jasbir thought, a devi of the night city with ten million lights descending from her hair. 'Chopsticks.' She picked up the antique porcelain chopsticks, one in each hand like drum sticks. 'I never know what to do with chopsticks. I'm always afraid of snapping them.'

'Oh, they're quite easy once you get the hang of them.' Jasbir rose from his seat and came round behind Shulka. Leaning over her shoulder he laid one stick along the fold of her thumb, the other between ball of thumb and tip of index finger. Still wearing her lighthoek. It's the city girl look. Jasbir shivered in anticipation as he slipped the tip of her middle finger between the two chopsticks. 'Your finger acts like a pivot, see? Keep relaxed, that's the key. And hold your bowl close to your lips.' Her fingers were warm, soft, electric with possibility as he moved them. Did he imagine her skin scented with musk?

Now, said Ram Tarun Das from over Shulka's other shoulder. *Now do you see? And by the way, you must tell her that they make the food taste better.*

They did make the food taste better. Jasbir found subtleties and piquancies he had not known before. Words flowed easily across the table. Everything Jasbir said seemed to earn her star-light laughter. Though Ram Tarun Das was as ubiquitous and unobtrusive as the waiting staff, they were all his own words and witticisms. *See, you can do this*, Jasbir said to himself. *What women want, it's no mystery; stop talking about yourself, listen to them, make them laugh.*

Over green tea Shulka began talking about that new novel everyone but everyone was reading, the one about the Delhi girl on the husband-hunt and her many suitors, the scandalous one, *An Eligible Boy*. Everyone but everyone but Jasbir.

Help! he subvocalized into his inner ear.

Scanning it now, Ram Tarun Das said. *Do you want a thematic digest, popular opinions or character breakdowns?*

Just be there, Jasbir silently whispered, covering the tiny movement of his jaw by setting the tea-pot lid ajar, a sign for a refill.

'Well, it's not really a book a man should be seen reading . . .'

'But . . .'

'But isn't everyone?' Ram Tarun Das dropped him the line. 'I mean, I'm only two thirds of the way in, but . . . how far are you? Spoiler alert spoiler alert.' It's one of Sujay's *Town and Country* expressions. Finally he understands what it means. Shulka just smiles and turns her tea-bowl in its little saucer.

'Say what you were going to say.'

'I mean, can't she see that Nishok is the one? The man is clearly, obviously, one thousand per cent doting on her. But then that would be too easy, wouldn't it?'

'But Pran, it would always be fire with him. He's the baddest of badmashes but you'd never be complacent with Pran. She'll never be able to completely trust him and that's what makes it exciting. Don't you think you feel that sometimes it needs that little edge, that little fear that maybe, just maybe you could lose it all to keep it alive?'

Careful, sir, murmured Ram Tarun Das.

'Yes, but we've known ever since the party at the Chatterjis where she pushed Jyoti into the pool in front of the Russian ambassador that she's been jealous of her sister because she was the one got to marry Mr Panse. It's the eternal glamour versus security. Passion versus stability. Town versus country.'

'Ajit?'

'Convenient plot device. Never a contender. Every woman he dates is just a mirror to his own sweet self.'

Not one sentence, not one word had he read of the hit trash novel of the season. It had flown around his head like clatter-winged pigeons. He's been too busy being that Eligible Boy.

Shulka held up a piece of sweet, salt, melting fatty duck breast between her porcelain forceps. Juice dripped on to the tablecloth.

'So, who will Bani marry, then? Guess correctly and you shall have a prize.'

Jasbir heard Ram Tarun Das's answer begin to form inside his head. *No*, he gritted on his molars.

'I think I know.'

'Go on.'

'Pran.'

Shulka stabbed forward, like the darting bill of a winter crane. There was hot, fatty soya duck in his mouth.

'Isn't there always a twist in the tale?' Shulka said.

In the Number 16 Gentlemen's WC Deependra checks his hair in the mirror and smooths it down.

'Dowry thievery; that's what it is. They string you along, get their claws into your money, then they disappear and you never see a paisa again.'

Now Jasbir really really wants to get back to his little work cluster.

'Deep, this is fantasy. You've read this in the news feeds. Come on.'

'Where there's smoke there's fire. My stars say that I should be careful in things of the heart and beware false friends. Jupiter is in the third house. Dark omens surround me. No, I have hired a private investigation aeai. It will conduct a discreet surveillance. One way or the other, I shall know.'

*

Jasbir grips the stanchion, knuckles white, as the phatphat swings through the great mill of traffic around Indira Chowk. Deependra's aftershave oppresses him.

'Exactly where are we going?'

Deependra had set up the assignation on a coded palmer account. All he would say was that it required two hours of an evening, good clothes, a trustworthy friend and absolute discretion. For two days his mood had been grey and thundery as an approaching monsoon. His PI Aeai had returned a result but Deependra revealed nothing, not even a whisper in the clubbish privacy of the Number 16 Gentlemen's WC.

The phatphat, driven by a teenager with gelled hair that falls in sharp spikes over his eyes – an obvious impediment to navigation – takes them out past the airport. At Gurgaon the geography falls into place around Jasbir. He starts to feel nauseous from more than spike-hair's driving and Deependra's shopping mall aftershave. Five minutes later the phatphat crunches up the curve of raked gravel outside the pillared portico of the Haryana Polo and Country Club.

'What are we doing here? If Shulka finds out I've been to shaadi when I'm supposed to be dating her it's all over.'

'I need a witness.'

Help me, Ram Tarun Das, Jasbir hisses into his molars but there is no reassuring spritz of silvery music through his skull to herald the advent of the Master of Grooming, Grace and Gentlemanliness. The two immense Sikhs on the door nod them through.

Kishore is sloped against his customary angle of the bar, surveying the territory. Deependra strides through the throng of Eligible Boys like a god going to war. Every head turns. Every conversation, every gossip falls silent.

'You . . . you . . . you,' Deependra stammers with rage. His face shakes. 'Shaadi stealer!' The whole club bar winces as the slap cracks across Kishore's face. Then two fists descend on Deependra, one on each shoulder. The man-mountain Sikhs turn him around and arm-lock him, frothing and raging, from the bar of the Haryana Polo and Country Club. 'You, you chuutya!' Deependra flings back at his enemy. 'I will take it out of you, every last paisa, so help me God. I will have satisfaction!'

Jasbir scurries behind the struggling, swearing Deependra, cowed with embarrassment.

'I'm only here to witness,' he says to the Sikhs' you're-next glares. They hold Deependra upright a moment to slap his face and bar him forever from Begum Rezzak's Lovely Girl Shaadi Agency. Then they throw him cleanly over the hood of a new model Li Fan G8 into the carriage drive. He lies dreadfully still and snapped on the gravel for a few moments, then with fetching dignity draws himself up, bats away the dust and straightens his clothes.

'I will see him at the river about this,' Deependra shouts at the impassive Sikhs. 'At the river.'

Jasbir is already out on the avenue, trying to see if the phatphat driver's gone.

The sun is a bowl of brass rolling along the indigo edge of the world. Lights twinkle in the dawn haze. There is never a time when there are not people at the river. Wire-thin men push handcarts over the trash-strewn sand, picking like birds. Two boys have set a small fire in a ring of stones. A distant procession of women, soft bundles on their heads, file over the grassy sand. By the shrivelled thread of the Yamuna an old brahmin consecrates himself, pouring water over his head. Despite the early heat, Jasbir shivers. He knows what goes into that water. He can smell the sewage on the air, mingled with wood smoke.

'Birds,' says Sujay, looking around him with simple wonder.

'I can actually hear birds singing. So this is what mornings are like. Tell me again what I'm doing here?'

'You're here because I'm not being here on my own.'

'And, ah, what exactly are you doing here?'

Deependra squats on his heels by the gym bag, arms wrapped around him. He wears a sharp white shirt and pleated slacks. His shoes are very good. Apart from grunted greetings he has not said a word to Jasbir or Sujay. He stares a lot. Deependra picks up a fistful of sand and lets it trickle through his fingers. Jasbir wouldn't advise that either.

'I could be at home coding,' says Sujay. 'Hey ho. Show time.'

Kishore marches across the scabby river-grass. Even as a well-dressed distant speck it is obvious to all that he is furiously angry. His shouts carry far on the still morning air.

'I am going to kick your head into the river,' he bellows at Deependra, still squatting on the riverbank.

'I'm only here as a witness,' Jasbir says hurriedly, needing to be believed. Kishore must forget and Deependra must never know that he was also the witness that night Kishore made the joke in the Tughluk tower.

Deependra looks up. His face is bland, his eyes are mild.

'You just had to, didn't you? It would have killed you to let me have something you didn't.'

'Yeah, well. I let you get away with that in the Polo Club. I could have taken you then, it would have been the easiest thing. I could have driven your nose right into your skull, but I didn't. You cost me my dignity, in front of all my friends, people I work with, business colleagues, but most of all, in front of the women.'

'Well then let me help you find your honour again.'

Deependra thrusts his hand into the gym bag and pulls out a gun.

'Oh my god it's a gun he's got a gun,' Jasbir jabbers. He feels his knees turn liquid. He thought that only happened in soaps and popular trash novels. Deependra gets to his feet, the gun never wavering from its aim in the centre of Kishore's forehead, the precise spot a bindi would sit. 'There's another one in the bag.' Deependra waggles the barrel, nods with his head. 'Take it. Let's sort this right, the man's way. Let's sort it honourably. Take the gun.' His voice has gained an octave. A vein beats in his neck and at his temple. Deependra kicks the gym bag towards Kishore. Jasbir can see the anger, the mad, suicidal anger rising in the banker to match the civil servant's. He can hear himself mumbling *Oh my god oh my god oh my god*. 'Take the gun. You will have a honourable chance. Otherwise I will shoot you like a pi-dog right here.' Deependra levels the gun and takes a sudden, stabbing step towards Kishore. He is panting like a dying cat. Sweat has soaked his good white shirt through and through. The gun muzzle is a finger's breadth from Kishore's forehead.

Then there is a blur of movement, a body against the sun, a cry of pain and the next Jasbir knows Sujay has the gun swinging by its trigger guard from his finger. Deependra is on the sand, clenching and unclenching his right hand. The old brahmin stares, dripping.

'It's OK now, it's all OK, it's over,' Sujay says. 'I'm going to put this in the bag with the other and I'm going to take them and get rid of them and no one will ever talk about this, OK? I'm taking the bag now. Now, shall we all get out of here before someone calls the police, hm?'

Sujay swings the gym bag over his sloping shoulder and strides out for the streetlights, leaving Deependra hunched and crying among the shredded plastic scraps.

'How, what, that was, where did you learn to do that?' Jasbir asks, tagging behind, feet sinking into the soft sand.

'I've coded the move enough times; I thought it might work in meat life.'

'You don't mean?'

'From the soaps. Doesn't everyone?'

There's solace in soap opera. Its predictable tiny screaming rows, its scripted swooping melodramas draw the poison from the chaotic, unscripted world where a civil servant in the water service can challenge a rival to a shooting duel over a woman he met at a shaadi. Little effigies of true dramas, sculpted in soap.

When he blinks, Jasbir can see the gun. He sees Deependra's hand draw it out of the gym bag in martial-arts-movie slow motion. He thinks he sees the other gun, nestled among balled sports socks. Or maybe he imagines it, a cut-away close-up. Already he is editing his memory.

Soothing to watch Nilesh Vora and Dr Chatterji's wife, their love eternally foiled and frustrated, and Deepti; will she ever realise that to the Brahmpur social set she is eternally that Dalit girl from the village pump?

You work on the other side of a glass partition from someone for years. You go with him to shaadis, you share the hopes and fears of your life and love with him. And loves turns him into a homicidal madman. Sujay took the gun off him. Big, clumsy Sujay took the loaded gun out of his hand. He would have shot Kishore. Brave, mad Sujay. He's coding, that's his renormalizing process. Make soap, watch soap. Jasbir will make him tea. For once. Yes, that would be a nice gesture. Sujay is always always getting tea. Jasbir gets up. It's a boring bit, Mahesh and Rajani. He doesn't like them. Those rich-boys-pretending-they-are-car-valets-so-they-can-marry-for-love-not-money characters stretch his disbelief too far. Rajani is hot, though. She's asked Mahesh to bring her car round to the front of the hotel.

'When you work out here you have lots of time to make up theories. One of my theories is that people's cars are their characters,' Mahesh is saying. *Only in a soap would anyone ever imagine that a pick-up line like that would work*, Jasbir thinks. 'So, are you a Tata, a Mercedes, a Li Fan or a Lexus?'

Jasbir freezes in the door.

'Oh, a Lexus.'

He turns slowly. Everything is dropping, everything is falling, leaving him suspended. Now Mahesh is saying,

'You know, I have another theory. It's that everyone's a city. Are you Delhi, Mumbai, Kolkata, Chennai?'

Jasbir sits on the arm of the sofa. *The fetch*, he whispers. *And she will say . . .*

'I was born in Delhi . . .'

'That's not what I mean.'

Mumbai, murmurs Jasbir.

'Mumbai then. Yes, Mumbai definitely. Kolkata's hot and dirty and nasty. And Chennai – no, I'm definitely Mumbai.'

'Red, green, yellow, blue,' Jasbir says.

'Red.' Without a moment's hesitation.

'Cat, dog, bird, monkey?'

She even cocks her head to one side. That was how he noticed Shulka was wearing the lighthoek.

'Bird . . . no.'

'No no no,' says Jasbir. She'll smile slyly here.

'Monkey.' And there is the smile. The *finesse*.

'Sujay!' Jasbir yells. 'Sujay! Get me Das!'

'How can an aeai be in love?' Jasbir demands.

Ram Tarun Das sits in his customary wicker chair, his legs casually crossed. *Soon, very soon,* Jasbir thinks, *voices will be raised and Mrs Prasad next door will begin to thump and weep.*

'Now sir, do not most religions maintain that love is the fundament of the universe? In which case, perhaps it's not so strange that a distributed entity, such as myself, should find – and be surprised by, oh, so surprised, sir – love? As a distributed entity, it's different in nature from the surge of neurochemicals and waveform of electrical activity you experience as love. With us it's a more … rarefied experience, judging solely by what I know from my subroutines on *Town and Country*. Yet, at the same time, it's intensely communal. How can I describe it? You don't have the concepts, let alone the words. I am a specific incarnation of aspects of a number of aeais and sub-programmes, as those aeais are also iterations of sub-programmes, many of them marginally sentient. I am many, I am legion. And so is she – though of course gender is purely arbitrary for us, and, sir, largely irrelevant. It's very likely that at many levels we share components. So ours is not so much a marriage of minds as a league of nations. Here we are different from humans in that, for you, it seems to us that groups are divisive and antipathetical. Politics, religion, sport, but especially your history, seem to teach that. For us folk, groups are what bring us together. They are mutually attractive. Perhaps the closest analogy might be the merger of large corporations. One thing I do know is that for humans and aeais, we both need to tell people about it.'

'When did you find out she was using an aeai assistant?'

'Oh, at once, sir. These things are obvious to us. And if you'll forgive the parlance, we don't waste time. Fascination at the first nanosecond. Thereafter, well, as you saw on the unfortunate scene from *Town and Country*, we scripted you.'

'So we thought you were guiding us …'

'When it was you who were our go-betweens, yes.'

'So what happens now?' Jasbir slaps his hands on his thighs.

'We are meshing at a very high level. I can only catch hints and shadows of it, but I feel a new aeai is being born, on a level far beyond either of us, or any of our co-characters. Is this a birth? I don't know, but how can I convey to you the tremendous, rushing excitement I feel?'

'I meant me.'

'I'm sorry, sir. Of course you did. I am quite, quite dizzy with it all. If I might make one observation, there's truth in what your parents say. First the marriage, then the love. Love grows in the thing you see every day.'

Thieving macaques dart around Jasbir's legs and pluck at the creases of his pants. Midnight metro, the last train home. The few late-night passengers observe a quarantine of mutual solitude. The djinns of unexplained wind that haunt subway systems send litter spiralling across the platform. The tunnel focuses distant shunts and clanks, uncanny at this zero hour. There should be someone around at the phatphat stand. If not he'll walk. It doesn't matter.

He met her at a fashionable bar, all leather and darkened glass, in an international downtown hotel. She looked wonderful. The simple act of her stirring sugar into coffee tore his heart in two.

'When did you find out?'

'Devashri Didi told me.'

'Devashri Didi.'

'And yours?

'Ram Tarun Das, Master of Grooming, Grace and Gentlemanliness. A very proper, old fashioned Rajput gent. He always called me sir; right up to the end. My house-mate made him. He works in character design on *Town and Country*.'

'My older sister works in PR in the meta-soap department at Jazhay. She got one of the actor designers to put Devashri Didi together.' Jasbir has always found the idea of artificial actors believing they played equally artificial roles head-frying. Then he found aeai love.

'Is she married? Your older sister, I mean.'

'Blissfully. And children.'

'Well, I hope our aeais are very happy together.' Jasbir raised a glass. Shulka lifted her coffee cup. She wasn't a drinker. She didn't like alcohol. Devashri Didi had told her it looked good for the Begum Jaitly's modern shaadi.

'My little quiz?' Jasbir asked.

'Devashri Didi gave me the answers you were expecting. She'd told me it was a standard ploy, personality quizzes and psychic tests.'

'And the Sanskrit?'

'Can't speak a word.'

Jasbir laughed honestly.

'The personal spiritual journey?'

'I'm a strictly material girl. Devashri Didi said . . .'

'. . . I'd be impressed if I thought you had a deep spiritual dimension. I'm not a history buff either. And *An Eligible Boy*?'

'That unreadable tripe?'

'Me neither.'

'Is there anything true about either of us?'

'One thing,' Jasbir said. 'I can tango.'

Her surprise, breaking into a delighted smile, was also true. Then she folded it away.

'Was there ever any chance?' Jasbir asked.

'Why did you have to ask that? We could have just admitted that we were both playing games and shaken hands and laughed and left it at that. Jasbir, would it help if I told you that I wasn't even looking? I was trying the system out. It's different for suitable girls. I've got a plan.'

'Oh,' said Jasbir.

'You did ask and we agreed, right at the start tonight, no more pretence.' She turned her coffee cup so that the handle faced right and laid her spoon neatly in the saucer. 'I have to go now.' She snapped her bag shut and stood up. *Don't walk away*, Jasbir said in his silent Master of Grooming, Grace and Gentle-manliness voice. She walked away.

'And Jasbir.'

'What?'

'You're a lovely man, but this was not a date.'

A monkey takes a liberty too far, plucking at Jasbir's shin. Jasbir's kick connects and sends it shrieking and cursing across the platform. *Sorry, monkey. It wasn't you.* Booms rattle up the subway tube; gusting hot air and the smell of electricity herald the arrival of the last metro. As the lights swing around the curve in the tunnel, Jasbir imagines how it would be to step out and drop in front of it. The game would be over. Deependra has it easy. Indefinite sick leave, civil service counselling and pharma. But for Jasbir there is no end to it and he is so so tired of playing. Then the train slams past him in a shout of blue and silver and yellow light, slams him back into himself. He sees his face reflected in the glass, his teeth still divinely white. Jasbir shakes his head and smiles and instead steps through the opening door.

It is as he suspected. The last phatphat has gone home for the night from the rank at Barwala metro station. It's four kays along the pitted, flaking roads to Acacia Bungalow Colony behind its gates and walls. Under an hour's walk. Why not? The night is warm, he's nothing better to do and he might yet pull a passing cab. Jasbir steps out. After half an hour a last, patrolling phatphat passes on the other side of the road. It flashes its light and pulls around to come in beside him. Jasbir waves it on. He is enjoying the night and the melancholy. There are stars up there, beyond the golden airglow of great Delhi.

Light spills through the French windows from the verandah into the dark living room. Sujay is at work still. In four kilometres Jasbir has generated a sweat. He ducks into the shower, closes his eyes in bliss as the jets of water hit him. Let it run let it run let it run. He doesn't care how much he wastes, how much it costs, how badly the villagers need it for their crops. *Wash the old tired dirt from me.*

A scratch at the door. Does Jasbir hear the mumble of a voice? He shuts off the shower.

'Sujay?'

'I've, ah, left you tea.'

'Oh, thank you.'

There's silence but Jasbir knows Sujay hasn't gone.

'Ahm, just to say that I have always . . . I will . . . always. Always . . .' Jasbir holds his breath, water running down his body and dripping on to the shower tray. 'I'll always be here for you.'

Jasbir wraps a towel around his waist, opens the bathroom door and lifts the tea.

Presently Latin music thunders out from the brightly lit windows of Number 27 Acacia Bungalows. Lights go on up and down the close. Mrs Prasad beats her shoe on the wall and begins to wail. The tango begins.

The Little Goddess

I remember the night I became a goddess.

The men collected me from the hotel at sunset. I was light-headed with hunger, for the child-assessors said I must not eat on the day of the test. I had been up since dawn, the washing and dressing and making-up was a long and tiring business. My parents bathed my feet in the bidet. We had never seen such a thing before and that seemed the natural use for it. None of us had ever stayed in a hotel. We thought it most grand, though I see now that it was a budget tourist chain. I remember the smell of onions cooking in ghee as I came down in the elevator. It smelled like the best food in the world.

I know the men must have been priests but I cannot remember if they wore formal dress. My mother cried in the lobby; my father's mouth was pulled in and he held his eyes wide, in that way that grown-ups do when they want to cry but cannot let tears be seen. There were two other girls for the test staying in the same hotel. I did not know them; they were from other villages where the devi could live. Their parents wept unashamedly. I could not understand it; their daughters might be goddesses.

On the street, rickshaw drivers and pedestrians hooted and waved at us with our red robes and third eyes on our foreheads. The devi, the devi, look! Best of all fortune! The other girls held on tight to the men's hands. I lifted my skirts and stepped into the car with the darkened windows.

They took us to the Hanumandhoka. Police and machines

kept the people out of Durbar Square. I remember staring long at the machines, with their legs like steel chickens and naked blades in their hands. The President's Own fighting machines. Then I saw the temple and its great roofs sweeping up and up and up into the red sunset and I thought for one instant its upturned eaves were bleeding.

The room was long and dim and stuffily warm. Low evening light shone in dusty rays through cracks and slits in the carved wood; so bright it almost burned. Outside, you could hear the traffic and the bustle of tourists. The walls seemed thin but at the same time kilometres thick. Durbar Square was a world away. The room smelled of brassy metal. I did not recognise it then but I know it now, it is the smell of blood. Beneath the blood was another smell, of time piled thick as dust. One of the two women who would be my guardians if I passed the test told me the temple was five hundred years old. She was a short, round woman with a face that always seemed to be smiling but when you looked closely you saw it was not. She made us sit on the floor on red cushions while the men brought the rest of the girls. Some of them were crying already. When there were ten of us the two women left and the door was closed. We sat for a long time in the heat of the long room. Some of the girls fidgeted and chattered but I gave all my attention to the wall carvings and soon I was lost. It has always been easy for me to lose myself; in Shakya I could disappear for hours in the movement of clouds across the mountain, in the ripple of the grey river far below and the flap of the prayer banner in the wind. My parents saw it as a sign of my inborn divinity, one of thirty-two that mark girls in whom the goddess could dwell.

In the failing light I read the story of Jayaprakash Malla playing dice with the devi Taleju Bhawani who came to him in the shape of a red snake and left with the vow that she would only return to the rulers of Kathmandu as a virgin girl of low caste, to spite their haughtiness. I could not read its end in the darkness, but I did not need to. I was its end, or one of the other nine girls in the god-house of the devi.

Then the doors burst open wide and firecrackers exploded and, through the rattle and smoke, red demons leaped into the hall. Behind them, men in crimson beat pans and clappers and bells. At once two of the girls began to cry and the two women came and took them away. But I knew the monsters were just silly men. In masks. These were not even close to demons. I have seen demons, after the rain clouds when the light comes low down the valley and all the mountains leap up as one. Stone demons, kilometres high. I have heard their voices, and their breath does not smell like onions. The silly men danced close to me, shaking their red manes and red tongues but I could see their eyes behind the painted holes and they were afraid of me.

Then the door banged open again with another crash of fireworks and more men came through the smoke. They carried baskets draped with red sheets. They set them in front of us and whipped away the coverings. Buffalo heads, so freshly struck off the blood was bright and glossy. Eyes rolled up, lolling tongues still warm, noses still wet. And the flies, swarming around the severed neck. A man pushed a basket towards me on my cushion as if it were a dish of holy food. The crashing and beating outside rose to a roar, so loud and metallic it hurt. The girl from my own Shakya village started to wail; the cry spread to another and then another, then a fourth. The other woman, the old, tall, pinched one with a skin like an old purse, came in to take them out, carefully lifting her gown so as not to trail it in the blood. The dancers whirled around like flame and the kneeling man lifted the buffalo head from the basket. He held it up in my face, eye to eye, but all I thought was that it must weigh a lot; his muscles stood out like vines, his arm shook. The flies looked like black jewels. Then there was a clap from outside and the men set down the heads and covered them up with their cloths and they left with the silly demon men whirling and leaping around them. There was one other girl left on her cushion now. I did not know her. She was of a Vajryana family from Niwar down the valley. We sat a long time, wanting to talk but not knowing if that too was part of the trial. Then the door opened a third time and two men led a white goat into the devi hall. They brought it right between me and the Niwari girl. I saw its wicked, slotted eye roll. One held the goat's tether, the other took a big ceremonial kukri from a leather sheath. He blessed it and with one fast strong stroke sent the goat's head leaping from its body.

I almost laughed, for the goat looked so funny, its body not knowing where its head was, the head looking around for the body and then the body realising that it had no head and going down with a kick, and why was the Niwari girl screaming, couldn't she see how funny it was, or was she screaming because I saw the joke and she was jealous of that? Whatever her reason, smiling woman and weathered woman came and took her very gently away and the two men went down on their knees in the spreading blood and kissed the wooden floor. They lifted away the two parts of the goat. I wished they hadn't done that. I would have liked someone with me in the big wooden hall. But I was on my own in the heat and the dark and over the traffic I could hear the deep-voiced bells of Kathmandu start to swing and ring. Then for the last time the doors opened and there were the women, in the light.

'Why have you left me all alone?' I cried. 'What have I done wrong?'

'How could you do anything wrong, goddess?' said the old, wrinkled woman who, with her colleague, would become my mother and father and teacher and sister. 'Now come along with us and hurry. The President is waiting.'

Smiling Kumarima and Tall Kumarima (as I would now have

to think of them) took a hand each and led me, skipping, from the great looming Hanuman temple. I saw that a road of white silk had been laid from the foot of the temple to a wooden palace close by. The people had been let back into the square and they pressed in on either side of the processional way, held back by the police and the robots. The machines held burning torches in their grasping hands. Fire glinted from their killing blades. There was great silence in the dark square.

'Your home, goddess,' said Smiling Kumarima, bending low to whisper in my ear. 'Walk the silk, devi. Do not stray off it. I have your hand, you will be safe with me.'

I walked between my Kumarimas, humming a pop tune I had heard on the radio at the hotel. When I looked back I saw that I had left two sets of bloody footprints.

You have no caste, no village, no home. This palace is your home, and who would wish for any other? We have made it lovely for you, for you will only leave it six times a year. Everything you need is here within these walls.

You have no mother or father. A goddess has no parents. You have no brothers or sisters. The President is your brother, Nepal your sister. The priests who attend on you, they are nothing. We your Kumarimas are less than nothing. Dust, dirt, a tool. You may say anything, and we must obey it.

As we have said, you will leave the palace only six times a year. You will be carried in a palanquin. Oh, it is a beautiful thing, carved wood and silk. Outside this palace you shall not touch the ground. The moment you touch the ground, you cease to be divine.

You will wear red, with your hair in a topknot and your toe- and fingernails painted. You will carry the red tilak of Siva on your forehead. We will help you with your preparations until they become second nature.

You will speak only within the confines of your palace, and little even then. Silence becomes the Kumari. You will not smile or show any emotion.

You will not bleed. Not a scrape, not a scratch. The power is in the blood and when the blood leaves, the devi leaves. On the day of your first blood, even one single drop, we will tell the priest and he will inform the President that the goddess has left. You will no longer be divine and you will leave this palace and return to your family. You will not bleed.

You have no name. You are Taleju, you are Kumari. You are the goddess.

These instructions my two Kumarimas whispered to me as we walked between priests to the President. He wore a western suit but a proper hat. He knew that though there were no longer any kings in Nepal, I was still royal. He namasted and we sat side by side on old royal lion thrones and the long hall throbbed to the bells and drums of Durbar Square. I remember thinking that a ruler must bow to me but there are rules even for goddesses.

Smiling Kumarima and Tall Kumarima. I draw Tall Kumarima in my memory first, for it is right to give pre-eminence to age. She was almost as tall as a Westerner and thin as a stick in a drought. At first I was scared of her. Then I heard her voice and could never be scared of her again; her voice was kind as a singing bird. When she spoke you felt you now knew everything. Tall Kumarima lived in a small apartment above a tourist shop on the edge of Durbar Square. From her window she could see my Kumari Ghar, among the stepped towers of the dhokas. Her husband had died of lung cancer from pollution and cheap Indian cigarettes. Her two tall sons were grown and married with children of their own, older than me. In that time she had mothered five Kumari Devis before me.

Now I remember Smiling Kumarima. She was short and round and had breathing problems for which she used inhalers, blue and brown. I would hear the snake hiss of them on days when Durbar Square was golden with smog. She lived out in the new suburbs up on the western hills, a long journey even by the official car at her service. Her children were twelve, ten, nine and seven. She was jolly and treated me like her fifth baby, the young favourite, but I felt even then that, like the demon-dancing men, she was scared of me. Oh, it was the highest honour any woman could hope for, to be the mother of the goddess – so to speak – though you wouldn't think it to hear her neighbours in the unit, *shutting yourself away in that dreadful wooden box, and all the blood, medieval, medieval,* but they couldn't understand. Somebody had to keep the nation safe against those who would turn us into another India or, worse, China; someone had to preserve the old ways of the divine kingdom. I understood early that difference between them. Smiling Kumarima was my mother out of duty. Tall Kumarima from love.

I never learned their true names. Their rhythms and cycles of shifts waxed and waned through the days and nights like the faces of the moon. Smiling Kumarima once found me looking up through the lattice of a jali screen at the fat moon on a rare night when the sky was clear and healthy, and she shouted me away, *Don't be looking at that thing, it will call the blood out of you, little devi, and you will be the devi no more.*

Within the wooden walls and iron rules of my Kumari Ghar, years become indistinguishable, indistinct. I think now I was five when I became Taleju Devi. The year, I believe, was 2034. But some memories break the surface, like flowers through snow.

Monsoon rain on the steep-sloped roofs, water rushing and gurgling through the gutters, and the shutter that every year blew loose and rattled in the wind. We had monsoons, then. Thunder demons in the mountains around the city, my room flash lit with lightning. Tall Kumarima came to see if I needed singing to sleep but I was not afraid. A goddess cannot fear a storm.

The day I went walking in the little garden, when Smiling Kumarima let out a cry and fell at my feet on the grass and the words to tell her to get up, not to worship me were on my lips when she held up, between thumb and forefinger, twisting and writhing and trying to find a place for its mouth to seize: a green leech.

The morning Tall Kumarima came to tell me people had asked me to show myself. At first I had thought it wonderful that people would want to come and look at me on my little jharoka balcony in my clothes and paint and jewels. Now I found it tiresome; all those round eyes and gaping mouths. It was a week after my tenth birthday. I remember Tall Kumarima smiled but tried not to let me see. She took me to the jharoka to wave to the people in the court and I saw a hundred Chinese faces upturned to me, then the high, excited voices. I waited and waited but two tourists would not go away. They were an ordinary couple, dark local faces, country clothes.

'Why are they keeping us waiting?' I asked.

'Wave to them,' Tall Kumarima urged. 'That is all they want.' The woman saw my lifted hand first. She went weak and grabbed her husband by the arm. The man bent to her, then looked up at me. I read many emotions on that face; shock, confusion, recognition, revulsion, wonder, hope. Fear. I waved and the man tugged at his wife, *look, look up*. I remember that, against all the laws, I smiled. The woman burst into tears. The man made to call out but Tall Kumarima hastened me away.

'Who were those funny people?' I asked. 'They were both wearing very white shoes.'

'Your mother and father,' Tall Kumarima said. As she led me along the Durga corridor with the usual order not to brush my free hand along the wooden walls for fear of splinters, I felt her grip tremble.

That night I dreamed the dream of my life, that is not a dream but one of my earliest experiences, knocking and knocking and knocking at the door of my remembering. This was a memory I would not admit in daylight, so it must come by night, to the secret door.

I am in the cage over a ravine. A river runs far below, milky with mud and silt, foaming cream over the boulders and slabs sheared from the mountainsides. The cable spans the river from my home to the summer grazing and I sit in the wire cage used to carry the goats across the river. At my back is the main road, always loud with trucks, the prayer banners and Kinley bottled water sign of my family's roadside teahouse. My cage still sways from my uncle's last kick. I see him, arms and legs wrapped around the wire, grinning his gap-toothed grin. His face is summer-burned brown, his hands cracked and brown from the trucks he services. Oil engrained in the creases. He wrinkles up his nose at me and unhooks a leg to kick my cage forward on its pulley-wheel. Pulley sways cable sways mountains, sky and river sway but I am safe in my little goat-cage. I have been kicked across this ravine many times. My uncle inches forwards. Thus we cross the river, by kicks and inches.

I never see what strikes him – some thing of the brain perhaps, like the sickness Lowlanders get when they go up to the high country. But the next time I look my uncle is clinging to the wire by his right arm and leg. His left arm and leg hang down, shaking like a cow with its throat cut, shaking the wire and my little cage. I am three years old and I think this is funny, a trick my uncle is doing just for me, so I shake back, bouncing my cage, bouncing my uncle up and down, up and down. Half his body will not obey him and he tries to move forward by sliding his leg along, like this, jerk his hand forward *quick* so he never loses grip of the wire, and all the while bouncing up and down, up and down. Now my uncle tries to shout but his words are noise and slobber because half his face is paralysed. Now I see his fingers lose their grip on the wire. Now I see him spin round and his hooked leg come free. Now he falls away, half his body reaching, half his mouth screaming. I see him fall, I see him bounce from the rocks and cartwheel, a thing I have always wished I could do. I see him go into the river and the brown water swallow him.

My older brother came out with a hook and a line and hauled me in. When my parents found I was not shrieking, not a sob or a tear or even a pout, that was when they knew I was destined to become the goddess. I was smiling in my wire cage.

I remember best the festivals, for it was only then that I left the Kumari Ghar. Dasain, at the end of summer, was the greatest. For eight days the city ran red. On the final night I lay awake listening to the voices in the square flow together into one roar, like I imagined the sea would sound, the voices of the men gambling for the luck of Lakshmi, devi of wealth. My father and uncles had gambled on the last night of Dasain. I remember I came down and demanded to know what all the laughing was about and they turned away from their cards and really laughed. I had not thought there could be so many coins in the world as there were on that table but it was nothing compared to Kathmandu on the eighth of Dasain. Smiling Kumarima told me it took some of the priests all year to earn back what they lost. Then came the ninth day, the great day and I sailed out from my palace for the city would worship me.

I travelled on a litter carried by forty men strapped to bamboo poles as thick as my body. They went gingerly, testing every step for the streets were slippery. Surrounded by gods and priests and sadhus mad with holiness, I rode on my golden throne. Closer to me than any were my Kumarimas, my two mothers, so splendid and ornate in their red robes and headdresses and make-up that they did not look like humans at all. But Tall Kumarima's voice and Smiling Kumarima's smile assured me as I rode with Hanuman and Taleju through the cheering and the music and the banners bright against the blue sky and the smell I now recognised from the night I became a goddess, the smell of blood.

That Dasain the city received me as never before. The roar of the night of Lakshmi continued into the day. As Taleju Devi I was not supposed to notice anything as low as humans but out of the corners of my painted eyes I could see beyond the security robots stepping in time with my bearers, and the streets radiating out from the stupa of Chhetrapati were solid with bodies. They threw jets and gushes of water from plastic bottles up into the air, glittering, breaking into little rainbows, raining down on them, soaking them, but they did not care. Their faces were crazy with devotion.

Tall Kumarima saw my puzzlement and bent to whisper.

'They do puja for the rain. The monsoon has failed a second time, devi.'

As I spoke, Smiling Kumarima fanned me so no one would see my lips move. 'We don't like the rain,' I said firmly.

'A goddess cannot do only what she likes,' Tall Kumarima said. 'It is a serious matter. The people have no water. The rivers are running dry.'

I thought of the river that ran far down deep below the house where I was born, the water creamy and gushing and flecked with yellow foam. I saw it swallow my uncle and could not imagine it ever becoming thin, weak, hungry.

'So why do they throw water then?' I asked.

'So the devi will give them more,' Smiling Kumarima explained. But I could not see the sense in that even for goddesses and I frowned, trying to understand how humans were, and so I was looking right at him when he came at me.

He had city pale skin and hair parted on the left that flopped as he dived out of the crowd. He moved his fists to the collar of his diagonally striped shirt and people surged away from him. I saw him hook his thumbs into two loops of black string. I saw his mouth open in a great cry. Then the machine swooped and I saw a flash of silver. The young man's head flew up into the air. His mouth and eyes went round: from a cry to an oh! The President's machine had sheathed its blade, like a boy folding a knife, before the body, like that funny goat in the Hanumandhoka, realised it was dead and fell to the ground. The crowd screamed and tried to get away from the headless thing. My bearers rocked, swayed, uncertain where to go, what to do. For a moment I thought they might drop me.

Smiling Kumarima let out little shrieks of horror, 'Oh! Oh! Oh!' My face was spotted with blood.

'It's not hers,' Tall Kumarima shouted. 'It's not hers!' She moistened a handkerchief with a lick of saliva. She was gently wiping the young man's blood from my face when security in their dark suits and glasses arrived, beating through the crowd. They lifted me, stepped over the body and carried me to the waiting car.

'You smudged my make-up,' I said to the guard as the car swept away. Worshippers barely made it out of our way in the narrow alleys.

Tall Kumarima came to my room that night. The air was loud with helicopters, quartering the city for the plotters. Helicopters, and machines like the President's Own robots, that could fly and look down on Kathmandu with the eyes of a hawk. She sat on my bed and laid a little transparent blue box on the red and gold embroidered coverlet. In it were two pale pills.

'To help you sleep.'

I shook my head. Tall Kumarima folded the blue box into the sleeve of her robe.

'Who was he?'

'A fundamentalist. A karsevak. A foolish, sad young man.'

'A Hindu, but he wanted to hurt us.'

'That is the madness of it, devi. He and his kind think our nation has grown too Western, too far from its roots and religious truths.'

'And he attacks us, the Taleju Devi. He would have blown up his own goddess, but the machine took his head. That is almost as strange as people throwing water to the rain.'

Tall Kumarima bowed her head. She reached inside the sash of her robe and took out a second object, which she set on my heavy cover with the same precise care as she had the sleeping pills. It was a light, fingerless glove, for the right hand; clinging to its back was a curl of plastic shaped like a very very tiny goat foetus.

'Do you know what this is?'

I nodded. Every devotee doing puja in the streets seemed to own one, right hands held up to snatch my image. A palmer.

'It sends messages into your head,' I whispered.

'That is the least of what it can do, devi. Think of it like your jharoka, but this window opens onto the world beyond Durbar Square, beyond Kathmandu and Nepal. It is an aeai, an artificial intelligence, a thinking-thing, like the machines up there, but much cleverer than them. They are clever enough to fly and hunt and not much else, but this aeai can tell you anything you want to know. All you have to do is ask. And there are things you need to know, devi. You will not be Kumari forever. The day will come when you will leave your palace and go back to the world. I have seen them before you.' She reached out to take my face between her hands, then drew back. 'You are special, my devi, but the kind of special it takes to be Kumari means you will find it hard in the world. People will call it a sickness. Worse than that, even ...'

She banished the emotion by gently fitting the foetus-shaped receiver behind my ear. I felt the plastic move against my skin, then Tall Kumarima slipped on the glove, waved her hand in a mudra and I heard her voice inside my head. Glowing words appeared in the air between us, words I had been painstakingly taught to read by Tall Kumarima.

Don't let anyone find it, her dancing hand said. *Tell no one, not even Smiling Kumarima. I know you call her that, but she would not understand. She would think it was unclean, a pollution. In some ways, she is not so different from that man who tried to harm you. Let this be our secret, just you and me.*

Soon after, Smiling Kumarima came to look in on me and check for fleas but I pretended to be asleep. The glove and the foetus-thing were hidden under my pillow. I imagined them talking to me through the goose down and soft soft cotton, sending dreams while the helicopters and hunting robots wheeled in the night above me. When the latch on her door clicked too, I put on the glove and earhook and went looking for the lost rain. I found it one hundred and fifty kilometres up, through the eye of a weather aeai spinning over east India. I saw the monsoon, a coil of cloud like a cat's claw hooking up across the sea. There had been cats in the village; suspicious things, lean on mice and barley. No cat was permitted in the Kumari Ghar. I looked down on my Kingdom but I could not see a city or a palace or me down here at all. I saw mountains, white mountains ridged with grey and blue ice. I was goddess of this. And the heart went out of me, because it was nothing, a tiny crust of stone on top of that huge world that hung beneath it like the full teat of a cow, rich and heavy with people and their brilliant cities and their bright nations. India, where our gods and names were born.

Within three days the police had caught the plotters and it was raining. The clouds were low over Kathmandu. The colour ran from the temples in Durbar Square but people beat tins and metal cups in the muddy streets calling praise on the Taleju Devi.

'What will happen to them?' I asked Tall Kumarima. 'The bad men.'

'They will likely be hanged,' she said.

That autumn after the executions of the traitors, the dissatisfaction finally poured onto the streets like sacrificial blood. Both sides claimed me: police and demonstrators. Others yet held me up as both the symbol of all that was good with our land and also everything wrong with it. Tall Kumarima tried to explain it to me but with my world mad and dangerous my attention was turned elsewhere, to the huge, old land to the south, spread out like a jewelled skirt. In such a time it was easy to be seduced by the terrifying depth of its history, by the gods and warriors who swept across it, empire after empire after empire. My land had always been fierce and free but I met the men who liberated India from the Last Empire – men like gods – and saw that liberty broken up by rivalry and intrigue and corruption into feuding states; Awadh and Bharat, the United States of Bengal, Maratha, Karnataka.

Legendary names and places. Shining cities as old as history. There aeais haunted the crowded streets like gandhavas. There men outnumbered women four to one. There the old distinctions were abandoned and women married as far up and men as few steps down the tree of caste as they could. I became as enthralled by their leaders and parties and politics as any of their citizens by the aeai-generated soaps they loved so dearly. My spirit was down in India in that early, hard winter when the police and government machines restored the old order to the city beyond Durbar Square. Unrest in earth and the three heavens. One day I woke to find snow in the wooden court; the roofs of the temple of Durbar Square heavy with it, like frowning, freezing old men. I knew now that the strange weather was not my doing but the result of huge, slow changes in the climate. Smiling Kumarima came to me in my jharoka as I watched flakes thick and soft as ash sift down from the white sky. She knelt before me, rubbed her hands together inside the cuffs of her wide sleeves. She suffered badly in the cold and damp.

'Devi, are you not one of my own children to me?'

I waggled my head, not wanting to say yes.

'Devi, have I ever, ever given you anything but my best?'

Like her counterpart a season before, she drew a plastic pillbox from her sleeve, set it on her palm. I sat back on my chair, afraid of it as I had never been afraid of anything Tall Kumarima offered me.

'I know how happy we all are here, but change must always happen. Change in the world, like this snow – unnatural, devi, not right – change in our city. And we are not immune to it in here, my flower. Change will come to you, devi. To you, to your body. You will become a woman. If I could, I would stop it happening to you, devi. But I can't. No one can. What I can offer is … a delay. A stay. Take these. They will slow down the changes. For years, hopefully. Then we can all stay here together, devi.' She looked up from her deferential half-bow, into my eyes. She smiled. 'Have I ever wanted anything but the best for you?'

I held out my hand. Smiling Kumarima tipped the pills into my palm. I closed my fist and slipped from my carved throne. As I went to my room I could hear Smiling Kumarima chanting prayers of thanksgiving to the goddesses in the carvings. I looked at the pills in my hand. Blue seemed such a wrong colour. Then I filled my cup in my little washroom and washed them down, two gulps, down, down.

After that they came every day, two pills, blue as the Lord Krishna, appearing as miraculously on my bedside table. For some reason I never told Tall Kumarima, even when she commented on how fractious I was becoming, how strangely inattentive and absent-minded at ceremonies. I told her it was the devis

128

in the walls, whispering to me. I knew enough of my specialness, that others have called my *disorder*, that that would be unquestioned. I was tired and lethargic that winter. My sense of smell grew keen to the least odour and the people in my courtyard with their stupid, beaming upturned faces infuriated me. I went for weeks without showing myself. The wooden corridors grew sharp and brassy with old blood. With the insight of demons, I can see now that my body was a chemical battlefield between my own hormones and Smiling Kumarima's puberty suppressants. It was a heavy, humid spring that year and I felt huge and bloated in the heat, a waddling bulb of fluids under my robes and waxy make-up. I started to drop the little blue pills down the commode. I had been Kumari for seven Dasains.

I had thought I would feel like I used to, but I did not. It was not unwell, like the pills had made me feel, it was sensitive, acutely conscious of my body. I would lie in my wooden bed and feel my legs growing longer. I became very very aware of my tiny nipples. The heat and humidity got worse, or so it seemed to me.

At any time I could have opened my palmer and asked it what was happening to me, but I didn't. I was scared that it might tell me it was the end of my divinity.

Tall Kumarima must have noticed that the hem of my gown no longer brushed the floorboards but it was Smiling Kumarima who drew back in the corridor as we hurried towards the darshan hall, hesitated a moment, said, softly, smiling as always,

'How you're growing, devi. Are you still ... ? No, forgive me, of course ... Must be this warm weather we're having, makes children shoot up like weeds. My own are bursting out of everything they own, nothing will fit them.'

The next morning, as I was dressing, a tap came on my door, like the scratch of a mouse or the click of an insect.

'Devi?'

No insect, no mouse. I froze, palmer in hand, earhook babbling the early morning news reports from Awadh and Bharat into my head.

'We are dressing.'

'Yes, devi, that is why I would like to come in.'

I just managed to peel off the palmer and stuff it under my mattress before the heavy door swung open on its pivot.

'We have been able to dress ourselves since we were six,' I retorted.

'Yes, indeed,' said Smiling Kumarima, smiling. 'But some of the priests have mentioned to me a little laxness in the ritual dress.'

I stood in my red and gold night-robe, stretched out my arms and turned, like one of the trance-dancers I saw in the streets from my litter. Smiling Kumarima sighed.

'Devi, you know as well as I ...'

I pulled my gown up over my head and stood unclothed, daring her to look, to search my body for signs of womanhood.

'See?' I challenged.

'Yes,' Smiling Kumarima said, 'but what is that behind your ear?'

She reached to pluck the hook. It was in my fist in a flick.

'Is that what I think it is?' Smiling Kumarima said, soft smiling bulk filling the space between the door and me. 'Who gave you that?'

'It is ours,' I declared in my most commanding voice but I was a naked twelve-year-old caught in wrongdoing and that commands less than dust.

'Give it to me.'

I clenched my fist tighter.

'We are a goddess, you cannot command us.'

'A goddess is as a goddess acts and right now, you are acting like a brat. Show me.'

She was a mother, I was her child. My fingers unfolded. Smiling Kumarima recoiled as if I held a poisonous snake. To the eyes of her faith, I did.

'Tulullah,' she said faintly. 'Spoiled, all spoiled.' Her voice rose. 'I know who gave you this!' Before my fingers could snap shut, she snatched the coil of plastic from my palm. She threw the earhook to the floor as if it burned her. I saw the hem of her skirt raise, I saw the heel come down, but it was my world, my oracle, my window on the beautiful. I dived to rescue the tiny plastic foetus. I remember no pain, no shock, not even Smiling Kumarima's shriek of horror and fear as her heel came down, but I will always see the tip of my right index finger burst in a spray of red blood.

The pallav of my yellow sari flapped in the wind as I darted through the Delhi evening crush-hour. Beating the heel of his hand on his buzzer, the driver of the little wasp-coloured phat-phat cut in between a lumbering truck-train painted with gaudy gods and apsaras and a cream government Maruti and pulled into the great chakra of traffic around Connaught Place. In Awadh you drive with your ears. The roar of horns and klaxons and cycle-rickshaw bells assailed from all sides at once. It rose before the dawn birds and only fell silent well after midnight. The driver skirted a sadhu walking through the traffic as calmly as if he were wading through the Holy Yamuna. His body was white with sacred ash, a mourning ghost, but his Siva trident burned blood red in the low sun. I had thought Kathmandu dirty, but Delhi's golden light and incredible sunsets spoke of pollution beyond even that. Huddled in the rear seat of the autorickshaws with Deepti, I wore smog mask and goggles to protect my delicate eye make-up. But the fold of my sari flapped over my shoulder in the evening wind and the little silver bells jingled.

There were five in our little fleet. We accelerated along the wide avenues of the British Raj, past the sprawling red buildings of old India, towards the glass spires of Awadh. Black kites circled the towers, scavengers, pickers of the dead. We turned beneath cool neem trees into the drive of a government bungalow. Burning torches lit us to the pillared porch. House staff in Rajput uniforms escorted us to the shaadi marquee.

Mamaji had arrived before any of us. She fluttered and fretted among her birds; a lick, a rub, a straightening, an admonition. 'Stand up stand up, we'll have no slumping here. My girls will be the bonniest at this shaadi, hear me?' Shweta, her bony, mean-mouthed assistant, collected our smog-masks. 'Now girls, palmers ready.' We knew the drill with almost military smartness. Hand up, glove on, rings on, 'hoek behind ear jewellery, decorously concealed by the fringed dupattas draped over our heads. 'We are graced with Awadh's finest tonight. Crème de la crème.' I barely blinked as the résumés rolled up my inner vision. 'Right girls, from the left, first dozen, two minutes each then on to the next down the list. Quick smart!' Mamaji clapped her hands and we formed a line. A band struck a medley of musical numbers from *Town and Country*, the soap opera that was a national obsession in sophisticated Awadh. There we stood, twelve little wives-a-waiting while the Rajput servants hauled up the rear of the pavilion.

Applause broke around us like rain. A hundred men stood in a rough semi-circle, clapping enthusiastically, faces bright in the light from the carnival lanterns.

When I arrived in Awadh, the first thing I noticed was the people. People pushing people begging people talking people rushing past each other without a look or a word or an acknowledgement. I had thought Kathmandu held more people than a mind could imagine. I had not seen Old Delhi. The constant noise, the everyday callousness, the lack of any respect appalled me. You could vanish into that crowd of faces like a drop of rain into a tank. The second thing I noticed was that the faces were all men. It was indeed as my palmer had whispered to me. There were four men for every woman. It would never cease to amaze me, how a simple technique to predetermine a child's sex could utterly warp a nation.

Fine men good men clever men rich men, men of ambition and career and property, men of power and prospects. Men with no hope of ever marrying within their own class and caste. Men with little prospect of marrying at all. Shaadi had once been the word for wedding festivities, the groom on his beautiful white horse, so noble, the bride shy and lovely behind her golden veil. Then it became a name for dating agencies: *lovely wheat-complexioned Agarwal, US-university MBA, seeks same civil service/military for matrimonials*. Now it was a bride-parade, a marriage-market for lonely men with large dowries. Dowries that paid a hefty commission to the Lovely Girl Shaadi Agency.

The Lovely Girls lined up on the left side of the Silken Wall that ran the length of the bungalow garden. The first twelve men formed up on the right. They plumped and preened in their finery but I could see they were nervous. The partition was no more than a row of saris pinned to a line strung between plastic uprights, fluttering in the rising evening wind. A token of decorum. Purdah. They were not even silk.

Reshmi was first to walk and talk the Silken Wall. She was a Yadav country girl from Uttaranchal, big-handed and big-faced. A peasant's daughter. She could cook and sew and sing, do household accounts, manage both domestic aeais and human staff. Her first prospective was a weasely man with a weak jaw in government whites and a Nehru cap. He had bad teeth. Never good. Any one of us could have told him he was wasting his shaadi fee, but they namasted to each other and stepped out, regulation three paces between them. At the end of the walk

Reshmi would loop back to rejoin the tail of the line and meet her next prospective. On big shaadis like this my feet would bleed by the end of the night. Red footprints on the marble floors of Mamaji's courtyard haveli.

I stepped out with Ashok, a big globe of a thirty-two-year-old who wheezed a little as he rolled along. He was dressed in a voluminous white kurta, the fashion this season though he was fourth generation Panjabi. His grooming amounted to an uncontrollable beard and oily hair that smelled of too much Dapper Deepak pomade. Even before he namasted I knew it was his first shaadi. I could see his eyeballs move as he read my résumé, seeming to hover before him. I did not need to read his to know he was a dataraja, for he talked about nothing but himself and the brilliant things he was doing; the spec of some new protein processor array, the 'ware he was breeding, the aeais he was nurturing in his stables, his trips to Europe and the United States where everyone knew his name and great people were glad to welcome him.

'Of course, Awadh's never going to ratify the Hamilton Acts – no matter how close Shrivastava is to President McAuley – but if it did, if we allow ourselves that tiny counterfactual – well, it's the end of the economy: Awadh *is* IT, there are more graduates in Mehrauli than there are in the whole of California. The Americans may go on about the mockery of a human soul, but they *need* our Level 2.8s, you know what that is? An aeai that can pass as human ninety-nine per cent of the time – because everybody knows no one does quantum crypto like us, so I'm not worrying about having to close up the data-haven, and even if they do, well, there's always Bharat – I cannot see the Ranas bowing down to Washington, not when twenty-five per cent of their forex comes out of licensing deals from *Town and Country* ... and that's hundred per cent aeai generated ...'

He was a big affable clown of a man with wealth that would

have bought my palace in Durbar Square and every priest in it and I found myself praying to Taleju to save me from marrying such a bore. He stopped in mid stride, so abruptly I almost tripped.

'You must keep walking,' I hissed. 'That is the rule.'

'Wow,' he said, standing stupid, eyes round in surprise. Couples piled up behind us. In my peripheral vision I could see Mamaji making urgent, threatening gestures. Get him *on*. 'Oh wow. You're an ex-Kumari.'

'Please, you are drawing attention to yourself.' I would have tugged his arm, but that would have been an even more deadly error.

'What was it like, being a goddess?'

'I am just a woman now, like any other,' I said. Ashok gave a soft harrumph, as if he had achieved a very small enlightenment, and walked on, hands clasped behind his back. He may have spoken to me once, twice before we reached the end of the Silken Wall and parted: I did not hear him, I did not hear the music, I did not even hear the eternal thunder of Delhi's traffic. The only sound in my head was the high-pitched sound between my eyes of needing to cry but knowing I could not. Fat, selfish, gabbling, Ashok had sent me back to the night I ceased to be a goddess.

Bare soles slapping the polished wood of the Kumari Ghar's corridors. Running feet, muted shouts growing ever more distant as I knelt, still unclothed for my Kumarima's inspection, looking at the blood drip from my smashed fingertip onto the painted wood floor. I remember no pain; rather, I looked at the pain from a separate place, as if the girl who felt it were another person. Far far away, Smiling Kumarima stood, held in time, hands to mouth in horror and guilt. The voices faded and the bells of Durbar Square begin to swing and toll, calling to their brothers across the city of Kathmandu until the valley rang from

Bhaktapur to Trisuli Bazaar for the fall of the Kumari Devi.

In the space of a single night, I became human again. I was taken to the Hanumandhoka – walking this time like anyone else on the paving stones – where the priests said a final puja. I handed back my red robes and jewels and boxes of make-up, all neatly folded and piled. Tall Kumarima had got me human clothes. I think she had been keeping them for some time. The President did not come to say goodbye to me. I was no longer the sister of the nation. But his surgeons had put my finger back together well, though they warned that it would always feel a little numb and inflexible.

I left at dawn, while the street cleaners were washing down the stones of Durbar Square beneath the apricot sky, in a smooth-running government Mercedes with darkened windows. My Kumarimas made their farewells at the palace gate. Tall Kumarima hugged me briefly to her.

'Oh, there was so much more I needed to do. Well, it will have to suffice.'

I felt her quivering against me, like a bird too tightly gripped in a hand. Smiling Kumarima could not look at me. I did not want her to.

As the car took me across the waking city I tried to understand how it felt to be human. I had been a goddess so long I could hardly remember feeling any other way, but it seemed so little different that I began to suspect that you are divine because people say you are. The road climbed through green suburbs, winding now, growing narrower, busy with brightly decorated buses and trucks. The houses grew leaner and meaner, to roadside hovels and chai-stalls and then we were out of the city – the first time since I had arrived seven years before. I pressed my hands and face to the glass and looked down on Kathmandu beneath its shroud of orange smog. The car joined the long line of traffic along the narrow, rough road that clung to the valley side. Above me, mountains dotted with goatherd shelters and stone shrines flying tattered prayer banners. Below me, rushing cream-brown water. Nearly there, I wondered how far behind me on this road were those other government cars, carrying the priests sent to seek out little girls bearing the thirty-two signs of perfection. Then the car rounded the bend in the valley and I was home, Shakya, its truck halts and gas station, the shops and the temple of Padma Narteswara, the dusty trees with white rings painted around their trunks and between them the stone wall and arch where the steps led down through the terraces to my house, and in that stone-framed rectangle of sky, my parents, standing there side by side, pressing closely, shyly, against each other as I had last seen them lingering in the courtyard of the Kumari Ghar.

Mamaji was too respectable to show anything like outright anger, but she had ways of expressing her displeasure. The smallest crust of roti at dinner, the meanest scoop of dhal. New girls coming, make room make room – me to the highest, stuffiest room, furthest from the cool of the courtyard pool.

'He asked for my palmer address,' I said.

'If I had a rupee for every palmer address,' Mamaji said. 'He was only interested in you as a novelty, dearie. Anthropology. He was never going to make a proposition. No, you can forget right about him.'

But my banishment to the tower was a small punishment for it lifted me above the noise and fumes of the old city. If portions were cut, small loss: the food had been dreadful every day of the almost two years I had been at the haveli. Through the wooden lattice, beyond the water tanks and satellite dishes and kids playing rooftop cricket, I could see the ramparts of the Red Fort, the minarets and domes of the Jami Masjid and, beyond them, the glittering glass and titanium spires of New Delhi. And higher than any of them, the flocks of pigeons from the kabooter lofts, clay pipes bound to their legs so they fluted and sang as they swirled over Chandni Chowk. And Mamaji's worldly-wisdom made her a fool this time, for Ashok was surreptitiously messaging me, sometimes questions about when I was divine, mostly about himself and his great plans and ideas. His lilac-coloured words, floating in my inner-vision against the intricate silhouettes of my jali screens, were bright pleasures in those high summer days. I discovered the delight of political argument; against Ashok's breezy optimism, I set my readings of the news channels. From the opinion columns it seemed inevitable to me that Awadh, in exchange for Favoured Nation status from the United States of America, would ratify the Hamilton Acts and outlaw all aeais more intelligent than a langur monkey. I told none of our intercourse to Mamaji. She would have forbidden it, unless he made a proposal.

On an evening of pre-monsoon heat, when the boys were too tired even for cricket and the sky was an upturned brass bowl, Mamaji came to my turret on the top of the old merchant's haveli. Against propriety, the jalis were thrown open, my gauze curtains stirred in the swirls of heat rising from the alleys below.

'Still you are eating my bread.' She prodded my thali with her foot. It was too hot for food, too hot for anything other than lying and waiting for the rain and the cool, if it came at all this year. I could hear the voices of the girls down in the courtyard as they kicked their legs in the pool. This day I would have loved to be sitting along the tiled edge with them but I was piercingly aware that I had lived in the haveli of the Lovely Girl Shaadi Agency longer than any of them. I did not want to be their Kumarima. And when the whispers along the cool marble corridors made them aware of my childhood, they would ask for small pujas, little miracles to help them find the right man. I no longer granted them, not because I feared that I had no power any more — that I never had — but that it went out from me and

138

into them and that was why they got the bankers and television executives and Mercedes salesmen.

'I should have left you in that Nepalese sewer. Goddess! Hah! And me fooled into thinking you were a prize asset. Men! They may have share options and Chowpatty Beach apartments but, deep down, they're as superstitious as any back-country yadav.'

'I'm sorry, Mamaji,' I said, turning my eyes away.

'Can you help it? You were only born perfect in thirty-two different ways. Now you listen, cho chweet. A man came to call on me.'

Men always came calling, glancing up at the giggles and rustles of the Lovely Girls peeping through the jalis as they waited in the cool of the courtyard for Shweta to present them to Mamaji. Men with offers of marriage, men with prenuptial contracts, men with dowry down-payments. Men asking for special, private viewings. This man who had called on Mamaji had come for one of these.

'Fine young man, lovely young man, just twenty. Father's big in water. He has requested a private rendezvous, with you.'

I was instantly suspicious but I had learned among the Lovely Girls of Delhi, even more than among the priests and Kumarimas of Kathmandu, to let nothing show on my painted face.

'Me? Such an honour . . . and him only twenty . . . and a good family too, so well connected.'

'He is a Brahmin.'

'I know I am only a Shakya . . .'

'You don't understand. He is a *Brahmin*.'

There was so much more I needed to do, Tall Kumarima had said as the government car drove away from the carved wooden gates of the Kumari Ghar. One whisper through the window would have told me everything: *the curse of the Kumari.*

Shakya hid from me. People crossed the street to find things to look at and do. Old family friends nodded nervously before remembering important business they had to be about. The chai-dhabas gave me free tea so I would feel uncomfortable and leave. Truckers were my friends, bus-drivers and long-haulers pulled in at the biodiesel stations. They must have wondered who was this strange twelve-year-old girl, hanging around truck-halts. I do not doubt some of them thought more. Village by village, town by town the legend spread up and down the north road. Ex-Kumari.

Then the accidents started. A boy lost half his hand in the fan belt of a Nissan engine. A teenager drank bad rakshi and died of alcohol poisoning. A man slipped between two passing trucks and was crushed. The talk in the chai-dhabas and the repair shops was once again of my uncle who fell to his death while the little goddess-to-be bounced in her wire cradle laughing and laughing and laughing.

I stopped going out. As winter took hold over the head-country of the Kathmandu valley, whole weeks passed when I did not leave my room. Days slipped away watching sleet slash past my window, the prayer banners bent almost horizontal in the wind, the wire of the cableway bouncing. Beneath it, the furious, flooding river. In that season the voices of the demons spoke loud from the mountain, telling me the most hateful things about faithless Kumaris who betray the sacred heritage of their devi.

On the shortest day of the year the bride buyer came through Shakya. I heard a voice I did not recognise talking over the television that burbled away day and night in the main room. I opened the door just enough to admit a voice and gleam of firelight.

'I wouldn't take the money off you. You're wasting your time here in Nepal. Everyone knows the story, and even if they pretend they don't believe, they don't act that way.'

I heard my father's voice but could not make out his words. The bride-buyer said,

'What might work is down south, Bharat or Awadh. They're so desperate in Delhi they'll even take Untouchables. They're a queer lot, those Indians; some of them might even like the idea of marrying a goddess, like a status thing. But I can't take her, she's too young, they'll send her straight back at the border. They've got rules. In India, would you believe? Call me when she turns fourteen.'

Two days after my fourteenth birthday, the bride-buyer returned to Shakya and I left with him in his Japanese SUV. I did not like his company or trust his hands, so I slept or feigned sleep while he drove down into the lowlands of the Terai. When I woke I was well over the border into my childhood land of wonder. I had thought the bride-buyer would take me to ancient, holy Varanasi, the new capital of the Bharat's dazzling Rana dynasty but the Awadhis, it seemed, were less in awe of Hindu superstitions. So we came to the vast, incoherent roaring sprawl of the two Delhis, like twin hemispheres of a brain, and to the Lovely Girl Shaadi Agency. Where the marriageable men were not so twenty-forties sophisticated, at least in the matter of ex-devis. Where the only ones above the curse of the Kumari were those held in even greater superstitious awe: the genetically engineered children known as Brahmins.

Wisdom was theirs, health was theirs, beauty and success and status assured and a wealth that could never be devalued or wasted or gambled away, for it was worked into every twist of their DNA. The Brahmin children of India's super-élite enjoyed long life – twice that of their parents – but at a price. They were indeed the twice-born, a caste above any other, so high as to be new Untouchables. A fitting partner for a former goddess: a new god.

Gas flares from the heavy industries of Tughluk lit the western horizon. From the top of the high tower I could read New Delhi's hidden geometries, the necklaces of light around Connaught Place, the grand glowing net of the dead Raj's monumental capital, the incoherent glow of the old city to the north. The penthouse at the top of the sweeping wing-curve of Narayan Tower was glass; glass walls, glass roof, polished obsidian beneath me that reflected the night sky. I walked with stars at my head and feet. It was a room designed to awe and intimidate. It was nothing to one who had witnessed demons strike the heads from goats, who had walked on bloody silk to her own palace. It was nothing to one dressed, as the messenger had required, in the full panoply of the goddess. Red robe, red nails, red lips, red eye of Siva painted above my own black kohled eyes, fake-gold headdress hung with costume pearls, my fingers dripped gaudy rings from the cheap jewellery sellers of Kinari Bazaar, a light chain of real gold ran from my nose stud to my ear-ring; I was once again Kumari Devi. My demons rustled inside me.

Mamaji had drilled me as we scooted from old city to new. She had swathed me in a light voile chador, to protect my makeup she said; in truth, to conceal me from the eyes of the street. The girls had called blessings and prayers after me as the phatphat scuttled out of the haveli's courtyard.

'You will say nothing. If he speaks to you, you duck your head like a good Hindu girl. If anything has to be said, I will say it. You may have been a goddess but he is a Brahmin. He could buy your pissy palace a dozen times over. Above all, do not let your eyes betray you. The eyes say nothing. They taught you that at least in that Kathmandu, didn't they? Now come on cho chweet, let's make a match.'

The glass penthouse was lit only by city-glow and concealed lamps that gave an uncomfortable blue glow. Ved Prakash Narayan sat on a musnud, a slab of unadorned black marble. Its simplicity spoke of wealth and power beneath any ornate jewellery. My bare feet whispered on the star-filled glass. Blue light welled up as I approached the dais. Ved Prakash Narayan was dressed in a beautifully worked long sherwani coat and traditional tight churidar pyjamas. He leaned forward into the light and it took every word of control Tall Kumarima had ever whispered to me to hold the gasp.

A nine-year-old boy sat on the throne of the Mughal Emperor.

Live twice as long, but age half as fast. The best deal Kolkata's genetic engineers could strike with four million years of human DNA. A child husband for a once-child goddess. Except this was no child. In legal standing, experience, education, taste and emotions, this was an eighteen-year-old man, every way except the physical.

His feet did not touch the floor.

'Quite, quite extraordinary.' His voice was a boy's. He slipped from his throne, walked around me, studying me as if I were an artefact in a museum. He was a head shorter than me. 'Yes, this is indeed special. What is the settlement?'

Mamaji's voice from the door named a number. I obeyed my training and tried not to catch his eye as he stalked around me.

'Acceptable. My man will deliver the prenuptial before the end of the week. A goddess. My goddess.'

Then I caught his eyes and I saw where all his missing years were. They were blue, alien blue, and colder than any of the lights of his tower-top palace.

These Brahmins are worse than any of us when it comes to social climbing, Ashok messaged me in my eyrie atop the shaadi haveli, prison turned bridal boudoir. *Castes within castes within castes.* His words hung in the air over the hazy ramparts of the Red Fort before dissolving into the dashings of the musical pigeons. *Your children will be blessed.*

Until then I had not thought about the duties of a wife with a nine-year-old boy.

On a day of staggering heat I was wed to Ved Prakash Narayan in a climate-control bubble on the manicured green before Emperor Humayun's tomb. As on the night I was introduced, I was dressed as Kumari. My husband, veiled in gold, arrived perched on top of a white horse followed by a band and a dozen elephants with coloured patterns worked on their trunks. Security robots patrolled the grounds as astrologers proclaimed favourable auspices and an old-type Brahmin in his red cord blessed our union. Rose petals fluttered around me, the proud father and mother distributed gems from Hyderabad to their guests, my shaadi sisters wept with joy and loss, Mamaji sniffed back a tear and vile old Shweta went round hoarding the free and over-flowing food from the buffet. As we were applauded and played down the receiving line, I noticed all the other sombre-faced ten-year-old boys with their beautiful, tall foreign wives. I reminded myself who was the child bride here. But none of them were goddesses.

I remember little of the grand durbar that followed except face after face after face, mouth after mouth after mouth opening, making noise, swallowing glass after glass after glass of French champagne. I did not drink for I did not have the taste for alcohol, though my young husband in his raja finery took it, and smoked big cigars too. As we got into the car – the *honeymoon* was another Western tradition we were adopting – I asked if anyone had remembered to inform my parents.

We flew to Mumbai on the company tilt-jet. I had never before flown in an aircraft. I pressed my hands, still hennaed with the patterns of my mehndi, on either side of the window as if to hold in every fleeting glimpse of Delhi falling away beneath me. It was every divine vision I had ever had looking down from my bed in the Kumari Ghar on India. This was indeed the true vehicle of a goddess. But the demons whispered as we turned in the air over the towers of New Delhi, *You will be old and withered when he is still in his prime.*

When the limousine from the airport turned onto Marine Drive and I saw the Arabian Sea glinting in the city-light, I asked my husband to stop the car so I could look and wonder. I felt tears start in my eyes and thought, *The same water in it is in you.* But the demons would not let me be: *You are married to something that is not human.*

My *honeymoon* was wonder upon wonder: our penthouse apartment with the glass walls that opened on sunset over Chowpatty Beach. The new splendid outfits we wore as we drove along the boulevards, where stars and movie-gods smiled down and blessed us in the virtual sight of our palmers. Colour, motion, noise, chatter; people and people and people. Behind it all, the wash and hush and smell of the alien sea.

Chambermaids prepared me for the wedding night. They worked with baths and balms, oils and massages, extending the now-fading henna tracery on my hands up my arms, over my small upright breasts, down the manipuraka chakra over my navel. They wove gold ornaments into my hair, slipped bracelets on my arms and rings on my fingers and toes, dusted and powdered my dark Nepali skin. They purified me with incense smoke and flower petals, they shrouded me in veils and silks as fine as rumours. They lengthened my lashes and kohled my eyes and shaped my nails to fine, painted points.

'What do I do, I've never even touched a man?' I asked, but they namasted and slipped away without answer. But the older – the Tall Kumarima, as I thought of her – left a small soapstone box on my bridal divan. Inside were two white pills.

They were good. I should have expected no less. One moment I was standing nervous and fearful on the Turkestan carpet with a soft night air that smelled of the sea stirring the translucent curtains, the next visions of the Kama Sutra, beamed into my brain through my golden earhook, swirled up around me like the pigeons over Chandni Chowk. I looked at the patterns my shaadi sisters had painted on the palms of my hands and they danced and coiled from my skin. The smells and perfumes of my body were alive, suffocating. It was as if my skin had been peeled back and every nerve exposed. Even the touch of the barely-moving night air was intolerable. Every car horn on Marine Drive was like molten silver dropped into my ear.

I was terribly afraid.

Then the double doors to the robing room opened and my husband entered. He was dressed as a Mughal grandee in a jewelled turban and a long-sleeved pleated red robe bowed out at the front in the manly act.

'My goddess,' he said. Then he parted his robe and I saw what stood so proud.

The harness was of crimson leather intricately inlaid with fine mirror-work. It fastened around the waist and also over the shoulders, for extra security. The buckles were gold. I recall the details of the harness so clearly because I could not take more than one look at the thing it carried. Black. Massive as a horse's, but delicately upcurved. Ridged and studded. This all I remember before the room unfolded around me like the scented petals of a lotus and my senses blended as one and I was running through the apartments of the Taj Marine Hotel.

How had I ever imagined it could be different for a creature with the appetites and desires of an adult but the physical form of a ten-year-old boy?

Servants and dressers held me as I screamed incoherently, grabbing at wraps, shawls, anything to cover my shame. At some tremendous remove I remember my husband's voice calling *Goddess! My Goddess!* over and over.

'Schizophrenia is a terribly grating word,' Ashok said. He twirled the stem of a red thornless rose between his fingers. 'Old school.

It's dissociative disorder these days. Except there are no disorders, just adaptive behaviours. It was what you needed to cope with being a goddess. Dissociating. Disjuncting. Splitting.'

Night in the gardens of the dataraja Ashok. Water trickled in the stone canals of the charbagh. I could smell it, sweet and wet. A pressure curtain held the smog at bay; trees screened out Delhi's traffic. I could even see a few stars. We sat in an open chhatri pavilion, the marble still warm from the day. Set on silver thalis were medjool dates, halva – crisp with flies – folded paan. A security robot stepped into the lights from the Colonial bungalow, passed into shadow. But for it I might have been in the age of the rajas.

Time broken apart, whirring like kabooter wings. Dissociative behaviour. Mechanisms for coping. Running along the palm-lined boulevards of Mumbai, shawls clutched around my wifely finery that made me feel more naked than bare skin. I ran without heed or direction. Taxis hooted, phatphats veered as I dashed across crowded streets. Even if I had had money for a phatphat – what need had the wife of Brahmin for crude cash? – I did not know where to direct it. Yet some demonic self must have known, for I found myself on the vast marble concourse of a railway station, a sole mite of stillness among the tens of thousands of hastening travellers and beggars and vendors and staff. My shawls and throws clutched around me, I looked up at the dome of red Raj stone and it was a second skull, full of the awful realisation of what I had done.

A runaway bride without even a paisa to her name, alone in Mumbai Chhatrapati Shivaji Terminus. A hundred trains leaving that minute for any destination but nowhere to go. People stared at me, half Nautch-courtesan, half Untouchable street-sleeper. In my shame, I remembered the 'hoek behind my ear. *Ashok*, I wrote across the sandstone pillars and swirling ads. *Help me!*

'I don't want to be split, I don't want to be many, why can't I just be one? Be me?' I beat the heels of my hands on my forehead in frustration. 'Make me well, make me right!' Shards of memory. The white-uniformed staff serving me hot chai in the first-class private compartment of the shatabdi express. The robots waiting at the platform with the antique covered palanquin, to bear me through the Delhi dawn traffic to the green watered geometries of Ashok's gardens. But behind them all was one enduring image, my uncle's white fist slipping on the bouncing cable and him falling, legs pedalling air, to the creamy waters of the Shakya River. Even then, I had been split. Fear and shock. Laughter and smiles. How else could anyone could survive being a goddess?

Goddess. My Goddess.

Ashok could not understand. 'Would you cure a singer of his talent? There is no madness, only ways of adapting. Intelligence is evolution. Some would argue that I display symptoms of mild Asperger's syndrome.'

'I don't know what that means.'

He twirled the rose so hard the stem snapped.

'Have you thought what you're going to do?'

I had thought of little else. The Narayans would not give up their dowry lightly. Mamaji would sweep me from her door. My village was closed to me.

'Maybe for a while, if you could ...'

'It's not a good time ... Who's going to have the ear of the Lok Sabha? A family building a dam that's going to guarantee their water supply for the next ten years, or a software entrepreneur with a stable of Level 2.75 aeais that the United States government thinks are the sperm of Shaitan? Family values still count in Awadh. You should know.'

I heard my voice say, like a very small girl, 'Where can I go?'

The bride-buyer's stories of Kumaris whom no one would

marry and could not go home again ended in the woman-cages of Varanasi and Kolkata. Chinese paid rupees by the roll for an ex-goddess.

Ashok moistened his lips with his tongue.

'I have a place in Bharat, in Varanasi. Awadh and Bharat are seldom on speaking terms.'

'Oh thank you, thank you . . .' I went down on my knees before Ashok, clutched his hands between my palms. He looked away. Despite the artificial cool of the water garden, he was sweating freely.

'It's not a gift. It's . . . employment. A job.'

'A job, that's good, I can do that; I'm a good worker, work away at anything I will. What is it? Doesn't matter, I can do it . . .'

'There are commodities I need transported.'

'What kind of commodities? Oh it doesn't mater, I can carry anything.'

'Aeais.' He rolled a paan from the silver dish. 'I'm not going to wait around for Shrivastava's Krishna Cops to land in my garden with their excommunication 'ware.'

'The Hamilton Acts,' I ventured, though I did not know what they were, what most of Ashok's mumbles and rants meant.

'Word is, everything above level 2.5.' Ashok chewed his lower lip. His eyes widened as the paan curled through his skull.

'Of course, I will do anything I can to help.'

'I haven't told you how I need you to transport them. Absolutely safe, secure, where no Krishna Cop can ever find them.' He touched his right forefinger to his third eye.

I went to Kerala and had processors put into my skull. Two men did it on a converted bulk gas carrier moored outside territorial waters. They shaved my long lovely black hair, unhinged my skull and sent robots smaller than the tiniest spider spinning computers through my brain. Their position out there beyond the Keralese fast patrol boats enabled them to carry out much secret surgery, mostly for the Western military. They gave me a bungalow and an Australian girl to watch over me while my sutures fused and hormone washes speed-grew my hair back.

Protein chips; only show on the highest resolution scans but no one'll look twice at you; no one'll look twice at another shaadi girl down hunting for a husband.

So I sat and stared at the sea for six weeks and thought about what it would be like to drown in the middle of it, alone and lost a thousand kilometres from the nearest hand that might seize yours. A thousand kilometres north in Delhi a man in an Indian suit shook hands with a man in an American suit and announced the Special Relationship that would make Ashok an outlaw.

You know what Krishna Cops are? They hunt aeais. They hunt the people who stable them, and the people who carry them. They don't care. They're not picky. But they won't catch you. They'll never catch you.

I listened to demons in the swash and run of the big sea on the shore. Demons I now knew were other parts of myself. But I was not afraid of them. In Hinduism, demons are merely the mirrors of the gods. As with men, so with gods; it is the winners who write the history. The universe would look no different had Ravana and his Rakshasas won their cosmic wars.

No one but you can carry them. No one but you has the neurological architecture. No one but you could endure another mind in there.

The Australian girl left small gifts outside my door: plastic bangles, jelly-shoes, rings and hairslides. She stole them from the shops in town. I think they were her way of saying that she wanted to know me but was afraid of what I had been, of what the things in my head would make me become. The last thing she stole was a beautiful sheer silk dupatta to cover my ragged hair when she took me to the airport. From beneath it I looked at the girls in business saris talking into their hands in the departure lounge and listened to the woman pilot announce the weather in Awadh. Then I looked out of the phatphat at the girls darting confidently through the Delhi traffic on their scooters and wondered why my life could not be like theirs.

'It's grown back well.' Ashok knelt before me on my cushions in the chhatri. It was his sacred place, his temple. He raised his palmer-gloved hand and touched his forefinger to the tilak over my third eye. I could smell his breath. Onions, garlic, rancid ghee. 'You may feel a little disoriented ...'

I gasped. Senses blurred, fused, melted. I saw heard felt smelled tasted everything as one undifferentiated sensation, as gods and babies sense, wholly and purely. Sounds were coloured, light had texture, smells spoke and chimed. Then I saw myself surge up from my cushions and fall towards the hard white marble. I heard myself cry out. Ashok lunged towards me. Two Ashoks lunged towards. But it was neither of those. I saw one Ashok, with two visions, inside my head. I could not make shape or sense out of my two seeings, I could not tell which was real, which was mine, which was *me*. Universes away I heard a voice say *help me*. I saw Ashok's houseboys lift me and take me to bed. The painted ceiling, patterned with vines and shoots and flowers, billowed above me like monsoon storm clouds, then blossomed into darkness.

In the heat of the night I woke stark, staring, every sense glowing. I knew the position and velocity of each insect in my airy room that smelled of biodiesel, dust and patchouli. I was not alone. There was another under the dome of my skull. Not an awareness, a consciousness; a sense of *separateness*, a manifestation of myself. An avatar. A demon.

'Who are you?' I whispered. My voice sounded loud and full of bells, like Durbar Square. It did not answer – it could not answer, it was not a sentience – but it took me out onto the charbagh water garden. The stars, smudged by pollution, were a dome over me. The crescent moon lay on its back. I looked up and fell into it. Chandra. Mangal. Budh. Guru. Shukra. Shani. Rahu. Ketu. The planets were not points of light, balls of stone and gas; they had names, characters, loves, hatreds. The twenty-seven Nakshatars spun around my head. I saw their shapes and natures, the patterns of connections that bound the stars into relationships and stories and dramas as human and complex as *Town and Country*. I saw the wheel of the rashis, the Great Houses, arc across the sky, and the whole turning, engines within engines, endless wheels of influence and subtle communication, from the edge of the universe to the centre of the earth I stood upon. Planets, stars, constellations; the story of every human life unfolded itself above me and I could read them all. Every word.

All night I played among the stars.

In the morning, over bed-tea, I asked Ashok, 'What is it?'

'A rudimentary Level 1.9. A janampatri aeai, does astrology, runs the permutations. It thinks it lives out there, like some kind of space monkey. It's not very smart, really. Knows about horoscopes and that's it. Now get that down you and grab your stuff. You've a train to catch'

My reserved seat was in the women's bogie of the high-speed shatabdi express. Husbands booked their wives on it to protect them from the attentions of the male passengers who assumed every female was single and available. The few career women chose it for the same reason. My fellow passenger across the table from me was a Muslim woman in a formal business shalwar. She regarded me with disdain as we raced across the Ganga plain at three hundred and fifty kilometres per hour. *Little simpering wife-thing.*

You would not be so quick to judge if you knew what we really were, I thought. *We can look into your life and tell you everything that has, is and will ever happen to you, mapped out in the chakras of the stars.* In that night among the constellations my demon and I had flowed into each other until there was no place where we could say acai ended and I began.

I had thought holy Varanasi would sing to me like Kathmandu, a spiritual home, a city of nine million gods and one goddess, riding through the streets in a phatphat. What I saw was another Indian capital of another Indian state; glass towers and diamond domes and industry parks for the big world to notice, slums and bastis at their feet like sewage pigs. Streets began in this millennium and ended in one three before it. Traffic and hoardings and people people people but the diesel smoke leaking in around the edges of my smog mask carried a ghost of incense.

Ashok's Varanasi agent met me in the Jantar Mantar, the great solar observatory of Jai Singh; sundials and star spheres and shadow discs like modern sculpture. She was little older than me; dressed in a cling-silk top and jeans that hung so low from her hips I could see the valley of her buttocks. I disliked her at once but she touched her palmer-glove to my forehead in the shadows around Jai Singh's astrological instruments and I felt the stars go out of me. The sky died. I had been holy again and now I was just meat. Ashok's girli pressed a roll of rupees into my hand. I barely looked at it. I barely heard her instructions to get something to eat, get a kafi, get some decent clothes. I was bereft. I found myself trudging up the steep stone steps of the great Samrat not knowing where I was who I was what I was doing halfway up a massive sundial. Half a me. Then my third eye opened and I saw the river wide and blue before me. I saw the white sands of the eastern shore and the shelters and dung fires of the sadhus. I saw the ghats, the stone river steps, curving away on either side further than the reach of my eyes. And I saw people. People washing and praying, cleaning their clothes and offering puja and buying and selling and living and dying. People in boats and people kneeling, people waist deep in the river, people scooping up silver handfuls of water to pour over their heads. People casting handfuls of marigold flowers onto the stream, people lighting little mango-leaf diya lamps and setting them afloat, people bringing their dead to dip them in the sacred water. I saw the pyres of the burning ghat, I smelled sandalwood, charring flesh, I heard the skull burst, releasing the soul. I had heard that sound before at the old royal burning ghats of Pashupatinath, when the President's mother died. A soft crack, and free. It was a comforting sound. It made me think of home.

In that season I came many times to the city by the Ganga. Each time I was a different person. Accountants, counsellors, machine-soldiers, soapi actors, database controllers: I was the goddess of a thousand skills. The day after I saw the Krishna Cops patrolling the platforms at Delhi station with their security robots and guns that could kill both humans and aeais, Ashok began to mix up my modes of transport. I flew, I trained, I chugged overnight on overcrowded country buses, I waited in chauffeured Mercedes in long lines of brightly decorated trucks at the Awadh-Bharat border. The trucks, like the crack of an exploding skull, reminded me of my Kingdom. But at the end was always the rat-faced girli lifting her hand to my tilak and taking me apart again. In that season I was a fabric weaver, a tax accountant, a wedding planner, a soapi editor, an air traffic controller. She took all of them away.

And then the trip came when the Krishna Cops were waiting at the Bharat end as well. By now I knew the politics of it as well as Ashok. The Bharatis would never sign the Hamilton Acts – their multi-billion-rupee entertainment industry depended on aeais – but neither did they want to antagonise America. So, a compromise: all aeais over Level 2.8 banned, everything else licensed and Krishna Cops patrolling the airports and railway stations. Like trying to hold back the Ganga with your fingers.

I had spotted the courier on the flight. He was two rows in

front of me; young, wisp of a beard, Star-Asia youth fashion, all baggy and big. Nervous nervous nervous, all the time checking his breast pocket, checking checking checking. A small-time badmash, a wannabe dataraja with a couple of specialist 2.75s loaded onto a palmer. I could not imagine how he had made it through Delhi airport security.

It was inevitable that the Varanasi Krishna Cops would spot him. They closed on him as we lined up at passport control. He broke. He ran. Women and children fled as he ran across the huge marble arrivals hall, trying to get to the light, the huge glass wall and the doors and the mad traffic beyond. His fists pounded at air. I heard the Krishna Cops' staccato cries. I saw them unholster their weapons. Shrieks went up. I kept my head down, shuffled forward. The immigration officer checked my papers. Another shaadi bride on the hunt. I hurried through, turned away towards the taxi ranks. Behind me I heard the arrivals hall fall so shockingly silent it seemed to ring like a temple bell.

I was afraid then. When I returned to Delhi it was like my fear had flown before me. The city of djinns was the city of rumours. The government had signed the Hamilton Acts. Krishna Cops were sweeping house to house. Palmer files were to be monitored. Children's aeai toys were illegal. US marines were being airlifted in. Prime Minister Srivastava was about to announce the replacement of the rupee with the dollar. A monsoon of fear and speculation and in the middle of it all was Ashok.

'One final run, then I'm out. Can you do this for me? One final run?'

The bungalow was already half-emptied. The furniture was all packed, only his processor cores remained. They were draped in dustsheets, ghosts of the creatures that had lived there. The Krishna Cops were welcome to them.

'We both go to Bharat?'

'No, that would be too dangerous. You go ahead, I'll follow when it's safe.' He hesitated. Tonight, even the traffic beyond the high walls sounded different. 'I need you to take more than the usual.'

'How many?'

'Five.'

He saw me shy back as he raised his hand to my forehead.

'Is it safe?'

'Five, and that's it done. For good.'

'Is it safe?'

'It's a series of overlays, they'll share core code in common.'

It was a long time since I had turned my vision inwards to the jewels Ashok had strung through my skull. Circuitry. A brain within a brain.

'Is it safe?'

I saw Ashok swallow, then bob his head: a Westerner's *yes*. I closed my eyes. Seconds later I felt the warm, dry touch of his finger to my inner eye.

We came to with the brass light of early morning shining through the jali. We were aware we were deeply dehydrated. We were aware that we were in need of slow-release carbohydrate. Our serotonin inhibitor levels were low. The window arch was a Mughal true arch. The protein circuits in my head were DPMA one-eight-seven-nine slash omegas, under licence from BioScan of Bangalore.

Everything we looked at gave off a rainbow of interpretations. I saw the world with the strange manias of my new guests: medic, nutritionist, architectural renderer, biochip designer, engineering aeai controlling a host of repair-shop robots. Nasatya. Vaishvanara. Maya. Brihaspati. Tvastri. My intimate demons. I was a many-headed devi.

All that morning, all afternoon, I fought to make sense of a world that was five worlds, five impressions. *I* fought. Fought to make us *me*. Ashok fretted, tugging at his woolly beard, pacing, trying to watch television, check his mails. At any instant Krishna Cop combat robots could come dropping over his walls. Integration would come. It had to come. I could not survive the clamour in my skull, a monsoon of interpretations. Sirens raced in the streets, far, near, far again. Every one of them fired off a different reaction from my selves.

I found Ashok sitting amongst his shrouded processors, knees pulled up to his chest, arms draped over them. He looked like a big, fat, soft boy, his mama's favourite.

Noradrenalin pallor, mild hypoglycaemia, fatigue toxins, said Nasatya.

Yin Systems bevabyte quantum storage arrays, said Brihaspati.

I touched him on the shoulder. He jerked awake. It was full dark outside, stifling: the monsoon was already sweeping up through the United States of Bengal.

'We're ready,' I said. '*I'm* ready.'

Dark-scented hibiscus spilled over the porch where the Mercedes waited.

'I'll see you in a week,' he said. 'In Varanasi.'

'In Varanasi.'

He took my shoulders in his hands and kissed me lightly, on the cheek. I drew my dupatta over my head. Veiled, I was taken to the United Provinces Night Sleeper Service. As I lay in the first-class compartment the acais chattered away inside my head, surprised to discover each other, reflections of reflections.

The chowkidar brought me bed-tea on a silver tray in the morning. Dawn came up over Varanasi's sprawling slums and industrial parks. My personalised news-service aeai told me that Lok Sabha would vote on ratifying the Hamilton Acts at ten a.m. At twelve Prime Minister Srivastava and the United States

Ambassador would announce a Most Favoured Nation trade package with Awadh.

The train emptied onto the platform beneath the spun-diamond canopy I knew so well. Every second passenger, it seemed was a smuggler. If I could spot them so easily, so could the Krishna Cops. They lined the exit ramps, more than I had ever seen before. There were uniforms behind them and robots behind the uniforms. The porter carried my bag on his head; I used it to navigate the press of people pouring off the night train. *Walk straight, as your mamaji taught you. Walk tall and proud, like you are walking the Silken Way with a rich man.* I pulled my dupatta over my head, for modesty. Then I saw the crowd piling up at the ramp. The Krishna Cops were scanning every passenger with palmers.

I could see the badmashes and smuggler-boys hanging back, moving to the rear of the mill of bodies. But there was no escape there either. Armed police backed by riot-control robots took up position at the end of the platform. Shuffle by shuffle, the press of people pushed me towards the Krishna Cops, waving their right hands like blessings over the passengers. Those things could peel back my scalp and peer into my skull. My red case bobbed ahead, guiding me to my cage.

Brihaspati showed me what they would do to the circuits in my head.

Help me! I prayed to my gods. And Maya, architect of the demons, answered me. Its memories were my memories and it remembered rendering an architectural simulation of this station long before robot construction spiders started to spin their nano-diamond web. Two visions of Varanasi Station, superimposed. With one difference that might save my life. Maya's showed me the inside of things. The inside of the platform. The drain beneath the hatch between the rear of the chai-booth and the roof support.

I pushed through the men to the small dead space at the rear. I hesitated before I knelt beside the hatch. One surge of the crowd, one trip, one fall, and I would be crushed. The hatch was jammed shut with dirt. Nails broke, nails tore as I scrabbled it loose and heaved it up. The smell that came up from the dark square was so foul I almost vomited. I forced myself in, dropped a metre into shin-deep sludge. The rectangle of light showed me my situation. I was mired in excrement. The tunnel forced me to crawl but the end of it was promise, the end of it was a semi-circle of daylight. I buried my hands in the soft sewage. This time I did retch up my bed-tea. I crept forward, trying not to choke. It was vile beyond anything I had ever experienced. But not so vile as having your skull opened and knives slice away slivers of your brain. I crawled on my hands and knees under the tracks of Varanasi Station, to the light, to the light, to the light, and out through the open conduit into the cess lagoon where pigs and rag-pickers rooted in the shoals of drying human manure.

I washed as clean as I could in the shrivelled canal. Dhobi-wallahs beat laundry against stone slabs. I tried to ignore Nasatya's warnings about the hideous infections I might have picked up.

I was to meet Ashok's girl on the street of gajras. Children sat in doorways and open shop fronts threading marigolds onto needles. The work was too cheap even for robots. Blossoms spilled from bushels and plastic cases. My phatphat's tyres slipped on wet rose petals. We drove beneath a canopy of gajra garlands that hung from poles above the shop-fronts. Everywhere was the smell of dead, rotting flowers. The phatphat turned into a smaller, darker alley and into the back of a mob. The driver pressed his hand to the horn. The people reluctantly gave him way. The alcofuel engine whined. We crept forward. Open space, then a police jawan stepped forward to bar our way. He wore full combat armour. Brihaspati read the glints of data flickering across his visor: deployments, communications, an arrest warrant. I pulled my dupatta over my head and lower face as the driver talked to him. What's going on? Some badmash. Some dataraja.

Down the street of gajras, uniformed police led by a plain-clothes Krishna Cop burst open a door. Their guns were drawn. In the same breath, the shutters of the jharoka immediately above crashed up. A figure jumped up onto the wooden rail. Behind me, the crowd let out a vast roaring sigh. *There he is there the badmash oh look look it's a girl!*

From the folds of my dupatta I saw Ashok's girli teeter there an instant, then jump up and grab a washing line. It snapped and swung her ungently down through racks of marigold garlands into the street. She crouched a moment, saw the police, saw the crowd, saw me, then turned and ran. The jawan started toward her but there was another quicker, deadlier. A woman screamed as the robot bounded from the rooftop into the alley. Chrome legs pistoned, its insect head bobbed, locked on. Marigold petals flew up around the fleeing girl but everyone knew she could not escape the killing thing. One step, two step, it was behind her. I saw her glance over her shoulder as the robot unsheathed its blade.

I knew what would happen next. I had seen it before, in the petal-strewn streets of Kathmandu, as I rode my litter among my gods and Kumarimas.

The blade flashed. A great cry from the crowd. The girl's head bounded down the alley. A great jet of blood. Sacrificial blood. The headless body took one step, two.

I slipped from the phatphat and stole away through the trans-fixed crowd.

I saw the completion of the story on a news channel at a chai-dhaba by the tank on Scindia ghat. The tourists, the faithful, the vendors and funeral parties were my camouflage. I sipped chai from a plastic cup and watched the small screen above the bar. The sound was low but I could understand well enough from the pictures. Delhi police break up a notorious aeai smuggling ring. In a gesture of Bharati-Awadhi friendship, Varanasi Krishna Cops make a series of arrests. The camera cut away before the robot struck. The final shot was of Ashok, pushed down into a Delhi police car in plastic handcuffs.

I went to sit on the lowest ghat. The river would still me, the river would guide me. It was of the same substance as me, divinity. Brown water swirled at my be-ringed toes. That water could wash away all earthly sin. On the far side of the holy river, tall chimneys poured yellow smoke into the sky. A tiny round-faced girl came up to me, offered me marigold gajras to buy. I waved her away. I saw again this river, these ghats, these temples and boats as I had when I lay in my wooden room in my palace in Durbar Square. I saw now the lie Tall Kumarima's palmer had fed me. I had thought India a jewelled skirt, laid out for me to wear. It was a bride-buyer with an envelope of rupees, it was walking the Silken Wall until feet cracked and bled. It was a husband with the body of a child and the appetites of a man warped by his impotence. It was a saviour who had always only wanted me for my sickness. It was a young girl's head rolling in a gutter.

Inside this still-girl's head, my demons were silent. They could see as well as I that that there would never be a home for us in Bharat, Awadh, Maratha, any nation of India.

North of Nayarangadh the road rose through wooded ridges, climbing steadily up to Mugling where it turned and clung to the side of the Trisuli's steep valley. It was my third bus in as many days. I had a routine now. Sit at the back, wrap my dupatta round me, look out the window. Keep my hand on my money. Say nothing.

I picked up the first bus outside Jaunpur. After emptying Ashok's account, I thought it best to leave Varanasi as inconspicuously as possible. I did not need Brihaspati to show me the hunter aeais howling after me. Of course they would have the air, rail and bus stations covered. I rode out of the Holy City in an unlicensed taxi. The driver seemed pleased with the size of the tip. The second bus took me from Gorakhpur through the dhal fields and banana plantations to Nautanwa on the border. I had deliberately chosen small, out-of-the-way Nautanwa, but still I bowed my head and shuffled my feet as I came up to the Sikh emigration officer behind his tin counter. I held my breath. He waved me through without even a glance at my identity card.

I walked up the gentle slope and across the border. Had I been blind, I would have known at once when I crossed into my country. The great roar that had followed me as close as my own skin fell silent so abruptly it seemed to echo. The traffic did not blare its way through all obstacles. It steered, it sought ways around pedestrians and sacred cows lolling in the middle of the road, chewing. People were polite in the bureau where I changed my Bharati rupees for Nepalese; did not press and push and try to sell me things I did not want in the shop where I bought a bag of greasy samosas; smiled shyly to me in the cheap hotel where I hired a room for the night. Did not demand demand demand.

I slept so deeply that it felt like a fall through endless white sheets that smelled of sky. In the morning the third bus came to take me up to Kathmandu.

The road was one vast train of trucks, winding in and out of the bluffs, looping back on itself, all the while climbing, climbing. The gears on the old bus whined. The engine strove. I loved that sound, of engines fighting gravity. It was the sound of my earliest recollection, before the child-assessors came up a road just like this to Shukya. Trains of trucks and buses in the night. I looked out at the roadside dhabas, the shrines of piled rocks, the tattered prayer banners bent in the wind, the cableways crossing the chocolate-creamy river far below, skinny kids kicking swaying wire cages across the high wires. So familiar, so alien to the demons that shared my skull.

The baby must have been crying for some time before the noise rose above the background hubbub of the bus. The mother was two rows ahead of me, she shushed and swung and soothed the tiny girl but the cries were becoming screams.

It was Nasatya who made me get out of my seat and go to her.

'Give her to me,' I said and there must have been some tone of command from the medical aeai in my voice for she passed me the baby without a thought. I pulled back the sheet in which she was wrapped. The little girl's belly was painfully bloated, her limbs floppy and waxen.

'She's started getting colic when she eats,' the mother said but before she could stop me I pulled away her napkin. The stench was abominable; the shit bulky and pale.

'What are you feeding her?'

The woman held up a roti bread, chewed at the edges to soften it for a baby. I pushed my fingers into the baby's mouth to force it open though Vaishvanara the nutritionist already knew what we would find. The tongue was blotched red, pimpled with tiny ulcers.

'This has only started since you began giving her solid food?' I said. The mother waggled her head in agreement. 'This child has ceoliac disease,' I pronounced. The woman put her hands to her face in horror, began to rock and wail. 'Your child will be fine, you must just stop feeding her bread, anything made from any grain except rice. She cannot process the proteins in wheat and barley. Feed her rice, rice and vegetables and she will brighten up right away.'

The entire bus was staring as I went back to my seat. The

woman and her baby got off at Naubise. The child was still wailing, weak now from its rage, but the woman raised a hand to me. I had come to Nepal with no destination, no plan or hope, just a need to be back. But an idea was already forming.

Beyond Naubise the road climbed steadily, switching back and forth over the buttresses of the mountains that embraced Kathmandu. Evening was coming on. Looking back I could see the river of headlights snaking across the mountainside. When the bus ground around another hairpin bend, I could see the same snake climb up ahead of me in red taillights. The bus laboured up a long steep climb. I could hear, everyone could hear, the noise in the engine that should not have been there. Up we crawled, to the high saddle where the watershed divided, right to the valley of Kathmandu, left to Pokhara and the High Himalaya. Slower, slower. We could all smell the burning insulation, hear the rattling.

It was not me who rushed to the driver and his mate. It was the demon Trivasti.

'Stop stop at once!' I cried. 'Your alternator has seized! You will burn us up.'

The driver pulled into the narrow draw, up against the raw rock. On the offside, trucks passed with millimetres to spare. We got the hood up. We could see the smoke wafting from the alternator. The men shook their heads and pulled out palmers. The passengers piled to the front of the bus to stare and talk.

'No no no, give me a wrench,' I ordered.

The driver stared but I shook my outstretched hand, demanding. Perhaps he remembered the crying baby. Perhaps he was thinking about how long it would take a repair truck to come up from Kathmandu. Perhaps he was thinking about how good it would be to be home with his wife and children. He slapped the monkey wrench into my hand. In less than a minute I had the belt off and the alternator disconnected.

'Your bearings have seized,' I said. 'It's a persistent fault on pre-2030 models. A hundred metres more and you would have burned her out. You can drive her on the battery. There's enough in it to get you down to Kathmandu.'

They stared at this little girl in an Indian sari, head covered but sleeves of her choli rolled up and fingers greasy with biolube.

The demon returned to his place and it was clear as the darkening sky what I would do now. The driver and his mate called out to me as I walked up beside the line of vehicles to the head of the pass. We ignored them. Passing drivers sounded their multiple, musical horns, offered lifts. I walked on. I could see the top now. It was not far to the place where the three roads divided. Back to India, down to the city, up to the mountains.

There was a chai-dhaba at the wide, oil-stained place where vehicles turned. It was bright with neon signs for American drinks and Bharati mineral water, like something fallen from the stars. A generator chugged. A television burbled familiar, soft Nepali news. The air smelled of hot ghee and biodiesel.

The owner did not know what to make of me, strange little girl in my Indian finery. Finally he said, 'Fine night.'

It was. Above the smogs and soots of the valley, the air was magically clear. I could see for a lifetime in any direction. To the west the sky held a little last light. The great peaks of Manaslu and Anapurna glowed mauve against the blue.

'It is,' I said. 'Oh it is.'

Traffic pushed slowly past, never ceasing on this high cross-roads of the world. I stood in the neon flicker of the dhaba, looking long at the mountains and I thought, *I shall live there.* We shall live in a wooden house close to trees, with running water cold from high snow. We shall have a fire and a television for company and prayer banners flying in the wind and in time people will stop being afraid and will come up the path to our door. There are many ways to be divine. There is the big divine, of ritual and magnificence and blood and terror. Ours shall be a little divinity, of small miracles and everyday wonders. Machines mended, programs woven, people healed, homes designed, minds and bodies fed. I shall be a little goddess. In time, the story of me will spread and people come from all over; Nepalis and foreigners, travellers and hikers and monks. Maybe one day a man who is not afraid. That would be good. But if he does not come, that will be good also, for I shall never be alone, not with a houseful of demons.

Then I found I was running, with the surprised chai-wallah calling, 'Hey! Hey! Hey!' after me, running down the side of the slow-moving line of traffic, banging on the doors, 'Hi! Hi! Pokhara! Pokhara!', slipping and sliding over the rough gravel, towards the far, bright mountains.

The Djinn's Wife

Once there was a woman in Delhi who married a djinn. Before the water war that was not so strange a thing. Delhi, split in two like a brain, has been the city of djinns from time before time. The Sufis tell that God made two creations, one of clay and one of fire. That of clay became man; that of fire, the djinni. As creatures of fire they have always been drawn to Delhi, seven times reduced to ashes by invading empires, seven times reincarnating itself. Each turn of the chakra, the djinns have drawn strength from the flames, multiplying and dividing. Great dervishes and brahmins are able to see them but on any street, at any time, anyone may catch the whisper and momentary wafting warmth of a djinn passing.

I was born in Ladakh, far from the heat of the djinns – they have wills and whims quite alien to humans – but my mother was Delhi born and raised, and from her I knew its circuses and boulevards, its maidans and chowks and bazaars, like those of my own Leh. Delhi to me was a city of stories, and so if I tell the story of the djinn's wife in the manner of a Sufi legend or a tale from the Mahabharata, or even a tivi soap opera, that is how it seems to me: City of Djinns.

They are not the first to fall in love on the walls of the Red Fort.

The politicians have talked for three days and an agreement is close. In honour the Awadhi government has prepared a grand durbar in the great courtyard before the Diwan-i-aam. All India is watching so this spectacle is on a Victorian scale: event-planners scurry across hot, bare marble hanging banners and bunting, erecting staging, setting up sound and light systems, choreographing dancers, elephants, fireworks and a fly-past of combat robots, dressing tables and drilling serving staff and drawing up so-careful seating plans so that no one will feel snubbed by anyone else. All day three-wheeler delivery drays have brought fresh flowers, festival good, finest, soft furnishings. There's a real French sommelier raving at what the simmering Delhi heat is doing to his wine plan. It's a serious conference. At stake are a quarter of a billion lives.

In this second year after the monsoon failed, the Indian nations of Awadh and Bharat face each other with main battle tanks, robot attack helicopters, strikeware and tactical nuclear slow missiles on the banks of the sacred River Ganga. Along thirty kilometres of staked-out sand, where brahmins cleanse themselves and sadhus pray, the government of Awadh plans a monster dam. Kunda Khadar will secure the water supply for Awadh's one hundred and thirty million for the next fifty years. The river downstream, that flows past the sacred cities of Allahabad and Varanasi in Bharat, will turn to dust. Water is life, water is death. Bharati diplomats, human and artificial intelligence aeai advisers, negotiate careful deals and access rights with their rival nation, knowing one carelessly spilled drop of water will see strike robots battling like kites over the glass towers of New Delhi and slow missiles with nanonuke warheads in their bellies creeping on cat-claws through the galis of Varanasi. The rolling news channels clear their schedules of everything else but cricket. A deal is close! A deal is agreed! A deal will be signed tomorrow! Tonight, they've earned their durbar.

And in the whirlwind of leaping hijras and parading elephants, a Kathak dancer slips away for a cigarette and a moment up on the battlements of the Red Fort. She leans against the sun-warmed stone, careful of the fine gold-threadwork of her costume. Beyond the Lahore Gate lies hiving Chandni Chowk; the sun a vast blister bleeding onto the smokestacks and light-farms of the western suburbs. The chhatris of the Sisganj Gurdwara, the minarets and domes of the Jama Masjid, the shikara of the Shiv temple are shadow-puppet scenery against the red, dust-laden sky. Above them pigeons storm and dash, wings wheezing. Black kites rise on the thermals above Old Delhi's thousand thousand rooftops. Beyond them, a curtain wall taller and more imposing than any built by the Mughals, stand the corporate towers of New Delhi, Hindu temples of glass and construction diamond stretched to fantastical, spiring heights, twinkling with stars and aircraft warning lights.

A whisper inside her head, her name accompanied by a spray of sitar: the call-tone of her palmer, transduced through her skull into her auditory centre by the subtle 'hoek curled like a piece of jewellery behind her ear.

'I'm just having a quick bidi break, give me a chance to finish it,' she complains, expecting Pranh, the choreographer, a famously tetchy third-sex nute. Then, 'Oh!' For the gold-lit dust rises before her up into a swirl, like a dancer made from ash.

A djinn. The thought hovers on her caught breath. Her mother, though Hindu, devoutly believed in the djinni, in any religion's supernatural creatures with a skill for trickery.

The dust coalesces into a man in a long, formal sherwani and loosely-wound red turban, leaning on the parapet and looking out over the glowing anarchy of Chandni Chowk. He is very handsome, the dancer thinks, hastily stubbing out her cigarette and letting it fall in an arc of red embers over the battlements. It does not do to smoke in the presence of the great diplomat A. J. Rao.

'You needn't have done that on my account, Esha,' A. J. Rao says, pressing his hands together in a namaste. 'It's not as I can catch anything from it.'

Esha Rathore returns the greeting, wondering if the stage crew down in the courtyard is watching her salute empty air. All Awadh knows those filmi-star features: A. J. Rao, one of Bharat's most knowledgeable and tenacious negotiators. No, she corrects herself. All Awadh knows are pictures on a screen. Pictures on a screen, pictures in her head; a voice in her ear. An aeai.

'You know my name?'

'I am one of your greatest admirers.'

Her face flushes: a waft of stifling heat spun off from the vast palace's microclimate, Esha tells herself. Not embarrassment. Never embarrassment.

'But I'm a dancer. And you are an . . .'

'Artificial intelligence? That I am. Is this some new anti-aeai legislation, that we can't appreciate dance?' He closes his eyes. 'Ah: I'm just watching *The Marriage of Radha and Krishna* again.'

But he has her vanity now. 'Which performance?'

'Star Arts Channel. I have them all. I must confess, I often have you running in the background while I'm in negotiation. But please don't mistake me, I never tire of you.' A. J. Rao smiles. He has very good, very white teeth. 'Strange as it may seem, I'm not sure what the etiquette is in this sort of thing. I came here because I wanted to tell you that I am one of your greatest fans and that I am very much looking forward to your performance tonight. It's the highlight of this conference, for me.'

The light is almost gone now and the sky a pure, deep, eternal blue, like a minor chord. Houseboys make their many ways along the ramps and wall-walks lighting rows of tiny oil-lamps. The Red Fort glitters like a constellation fallen over Old Delhi. Esha has lived in Delhi all her twenty-two years and she has never seen her city from this vantage. She says, 'I'm not sure what the etiquette is either, I've never spoken with an aeai before.'

'Really?' A. J. Rao now stands with his back against the

sun-warm stone, looking up at the sky, and her out the corner of his eye. The eyes smile, slyly. Of course, she thinks. Her city is as full of aeais as it is with birds. From computer systems and robots with the feral smarts of rats and pigeons to entities like this one standing before her on the gate of the Red Fort making charming compliments. Not standing. Not anywhere, just a pattern of information in her head. She stammers,

'I mean, a . . . a . . .'

'Level 2.9?'

'I don't know what that means.'

The aeai smiles and as she tries to work it out there is another chime in Esha's head and this time it is Pranh, swearing horribly as usual, where is she doesn't she know yts got a show to put on, half the bloody continent watching.

'Excuse me . . .'

'Of course. I shall be watching.'

How? she wants to ask. An aeai, a djinn, wants to watch me dance. What is this? But when she looks back all there is to ask is a wisp of dust blowing along the lantern-lit battlement.

There are elephants and circus performers, there are illusionists and table magicians, there are ghazal and qawali and Boli singers; there is the catering and the sommelier's wine and then the lights go up on the stage and Esha spins out past the scowling Pranh as the tabla and melodeon and shehnai begin. The heat is intense in the marble square, but she is transported. The stampings, the pirouettes and swirl of her skirts, the beat of the ankle bells, the facial expressions, the subtle hand mudras: once again she is spun out of herself by the disciplines of Kathak into something greater. She would call it her art, her talent, but she's superstitious: that would be to claim it and so crush the gift. Never name it, never speak it. Just let it possess you. Her own, burning djinn. But as she spins across the brilliant stage before the seated delegates, a corner of her perception scans the architecture for cameras, robots, eyes through which A. J. Rao might watch her. Is she a splinter of his consciousness, as he is a splinter of hers?

She barely hears the applause as she curtsies to the bright lights and runs off stage. In the dressing room as her assistants remove and carefully fold the many jewelled layers of her costume, wipe away the crusted stage makeup to reveal the twenty-two-year-old beneath, her attention keeps flicking to her lighthoek, curled like a plastic question on her dressing table. In jeans and silk sleeveless vest, indistinguishable from any other of Delhi's four million twentysomethings, she coils the device behind her ear, smoothes her hair over it and her fingers linger a moment as she slides the palmer over her hand. No calls. No messages. No avatars. She's surprised it matters so much.

The official Mercs are lined up in the Delhi Gate. A man and woman intercept her on her way to the car. She waves them away.

'I don't do autographs . . .' Never after a performance. Get out, get away quick and quiet, disappear into the city. The man opens his palm to show her a warrant badge.

'We'll take this car.'

It pulls out from the line and cuts in, a cream-coloured high-marque Maruti. The man politely opens the door to let her enter first but there is no respect in it. The woman takes the front seat beside the driver; he accelerates out, horn blaring, into the great circus of night traffic around the Red Fort. The airco purrs.

'I am Inspector Thacker from the Department of Artificial Intelligence Registration and Licensing,' the man says. He is young and good-skinned and confident and not at all fazed by sitting next to a celebrity. His aftershave is perhaps over-emphatic.

'A Krishna Cop.'

That makes him wince.

'Our surveillance systems have flagged up a communication between you and the Bharati Level 2.9 aeai A. J. Rao.'

'He called me, yes'

'At 21:08. You were in contact for six minutes twenty-two seconds. Can you tell me what you talked about?'

The car is driving very fast for Delhi. The traffic seems to flow around it. Every light seems to be green. Nothing is allowed to impede its progress. Can they do that? Esha wonders. Krishna Cops, aeai police: can they tame the creatures they hunt?

'We talked about Kathak. He's a fan. Is there a problem? Have I done something wrong?'

'No, nothing at all, Ms But you do understand, with a conference of this importance ... On behalf of the department, I apologise for the unseemliness. Ah. Here we are.'

They've brought her right to her bungalow. Feeling dirty, dusty, confused she watches the Krishna Cop car drive off, holding Delhi's frenetic traffic at bay with its tame djinns. She pauses at the gate. She needs, she deserves, a moment to come out from the performance, that little step away so you can turn round and look back at yourself and say, yeah, Esha Rathore. The bungalow is unlit, quiet. Neeta and Priya will be out with their wonderful fiancés, talking wedding gifts and guest lists and how hefty a dowry they can squeeze from their husbands-to-be's families. They're not her sisters, though they share the classy bungalow. No one has sisters any more in Awadh, or even Bharat. No one of Esha's age, though she's heard the balance is being restored. Daughters are fashionable. One upon a time, women paid the dowry.

She breathes deep of her city. The cool garden microclimate presses down the roar of the Delhi to a muffled throb, like blood in the heart. She can smell dust and roses. Rose of Persia. Flower of the Urdu poets. And dust. She imagines it rising up on a whisper of wind, spinning into a charming, dangerous djinn. No. An illusion, a madness of a mad old city. She opens the security gate and finds every square centimetre of the compound filled with red roses.

Neeta and Priya are waiting for her at the breakfast table next morning, sitting side-by-side close like an interview panel. Or Krishna Cops. For once they aren't talking houses and husbands.

'Who who who where did they come from who sent them so many must have cost a fortune . . .'

Puri the housemaid brings Chinese green chai that's good against cancer. The sweeper has gathered the bouquets into a pile at one end of the compound. The sweet of their perfume is already tinged with rot.

'He's a diplomat.' Neeta and Priya only watch *Town and Country* and the chati channels but even they must know the name of A. J. Rao. So she half lies. 'A Bharati diplomat.'

Their mouths go oooh, then ah as they look at each other. Neeta says, 'You have have have to bring him.'

'To our durbar,' says Priya.

'Yes, our durbar,' says Neeta. They've talked gossiped planned little else for the past two months: their grand joint engagement party where they show off to their as-yet-unmarried girlfriends and make all the single men jealous. Esha excuses her grimace with the bitterness of the health-tea.

'He's very busy.' She doesn't say busy man. She cannot even think why she is playing these silly girli secrecy games. An aeai called her at the Red Fort to tell her it admired her. Didn't even meet her. There was nothing to meet. It was all in her head. 'I'm don't even know how to get in touch with him. They don't give their numbers out.'

'He's coming,' Neeta and Priya insist.

*

She can hardly hear the music for the rattle of the old airco but sweat runs down her sides along the waistband of her Adidas tights to gather in the hollow of her back and slide between the taut curves of her ass. She tries it again across the gharana's practice floor. Even the ankle bells sound like lead. Last night she touched the three heavens. This morning she feels dead. She can't concentrate, and that little lavda Pranh knows it, swishing at her with yts cane and gobbing out wads of chewed paan and mealy eunuch curses.

'Ey! Less staring at your palmer, more mudras! Decent mudras. You jerk my dick, if I still had one.'

Embarrassed that Pranh has noted something she was not conscious of herself – ring, call me, ring, call me, ring, take me out of this – she fires back, 'If you ever had one.'

Pranh slashes yts cane at her legs, catches the back of her calf a sting.

'Fuck you, hijra!' Esha snatches up towel, bag, Palmer, hooks the earpiece behind her long straight hair. No point changing, the heat out there will soak through anything in a moment. 'I'm out of here.'

Pranh doesn't call after her. Yt's too proud. Little freak monkey thing, she thinks. How is it a nute is an yt, but an incorporeal aeai is a he? In the legends of Old Delhi, djinns are always he.

'Memsahib Rathore?'

The chauffeur is in full dress and boots. His only concession to the heat is his shades. In bra top and tights and bare skin, she's melting. 'The vehicle is fully air-conditioned, memsahib.'

The white leather upholstery is so cool her flesh recoils from its skin.

'This isn't the Krishna Cops.'

'No memsahib.' The chauffeur pulls out into the traffic. It's only as the security locks clunk she thinks, Oh Lord Krishna, they could be kidnapping me.

'Who sent you?' There's glass too thick for her fists between her and driver. Even if the doors weren't locked, a tumble from the car at this speed, in this traffic, would be too much for even a dancer's lithe reflexes. And she's lived in Delhi all her life, basti to bungalow, but she doesn't recognise these streets, this suburb, that industrial park. 'Where are you taking me?'

'Memsahib, where I am not permitted to say for that would spoil the surprise. But I am permitted to tell you that you are the guest of A. J. Rao.'

The palmer calls her name as she finishes freshening up with bottled Kinley from the car-bar.

'Hello!' (Kicking back deep into the cool cool white leather, like a filmi star. She is star. A star with a bar in a car.)

Audio-only. 'I trust the car is acceptable?' Same smooth-suave voice. She can't imagine any opponent being able to resist that voice in negotiation.

'It's wonderful. Very luxurious. Very high status.' She's out in the bastis now, slums deeper and meaner than the one she grew up in. Newer. The newest ones always look the oldest. Boys chug past on a home-brew chhakda they've scavenged from tractor parts. The cream Lex carefully detours around emaciated cattle with angular hips jutting through stretched skin like engineering. Everywhere, drought dust lies thick on the crazed hardtop. This is a city of stares. 'Aren't you supposed to be at the conference?'

A laugh, inside her auditory centre.

'Oh, I am hard at work winning water for Bharat, believe me. I am nothing if not an assiduous civil servant.'

'You're telling me you're there, and here?'

'Oh, it's nothing for us to be in more than one place at the same time. There are multiple copies of me, and subroutines.'

'So which is the real you?'

'They are all the real me. In fact, not one of my avatars is in Delhi at all, I am distributed over a series of dharma-cores across

Varanasi and Patna.' He sighs. It sounds close and weary and warm as a whisper in her ear. 'You find it difficult to comprehend a distributed consciousness; it is every bit as hard for me to comprehend a discrete, mobile consciousness. I can only copy myself through what you call cyberspace, which is the physical reality of my universe, but you move through dimensional space and time.'

'So which one of you loves me then?' The words are out, wild, loose and unconsidered. 'I mean, as a dancer, that is.' She's filling, gabbling. 'Is there one of you who particularly appreciates Kathak?' Polite polite words, like you'd say to an industrialist or a hopeful lawyer at one of Neeta's and Priya's hideous match-making soirées. Don't be forward, no one likes a forward woman. This is a man's world, now. But she hears glee bubble in A. J. Rao's voice.

'Why, all of me and every part of me, Esha.'

Her name. He used her name.

It's a shitty street of pi-dogs and men lounging on charpoys scratching themselves but the chauffeur insists, here, this way memsahib. She picks her way down a gali lined with unsteady minarets of old car tyres. Burning ghee and stale urine reek the air. Kids mob the Lexus but the car has A. J. Rao levels of security. The chauffeur pushes open an old wood and brass Mughal style gate in a crumbling red wall. 'Memsahib.'

She steps through into a garden. Into the ruins of a garden. The gasp of wonder dies. The geometrical water channels of the charbagh are dry, cracked, choked with litter from picnics. The shrubs are blousy and overgrown, the plant borders ragged with weeds. The grass is scabbed brown with drought-burn: the lower branches of the trees have been hacked away for firewood. As she walks towards the crack-roofed pavilion at the centre where paths and water channels meets, the gravel beneath her thin shoes is crazed into rivulets from past monsoons. Dead leaves and fallen twigs cover the lawns. The fountains are dry and silted. Yet families stroll pushing baby buggies; children chase balls. Old Islamic gentlemen read the papers and play chess.

'The Shalimar Gardens,' says A. J. Rao in the base of her skull. 'Paradise as a walled garden.'

And as he speaks, a wave of transformation breaks across the garden, sweeping away the decay of the twenty-first century. Trees break into full leaf, flower beds blossom, rows of terracotta geranium pots march down the banks of the charbagh channels which shiver with water. The tiered roof of the pavilion gleams with gold leaf, peacocks fluster and fuss their vanities, and everything glitters and splashes with fountain play. The laughing families are swept back into Mughal grandees, the old men in the park transformed into malis sweeping the gravel paths with their besoms.

Esha claps her hands in joy, hearing a distant, silver spray of sitar notes. 'Oh,' she says, numb with wonder. 'Oh!'

'A thank you, for what you gave me last night. This is one of my favourite places in all India, even though it's almost forgotten. Perhaps, because it is almost forgotten. Aurangzeb was crowned Mughal Emperor here in 1658, now it's an evening stroll for the basti people. The past is a passion of mine; it's easy for me, for all of us. We can live in as many times as we can places. I often come here, in my mind. Or should I say, it comes to me.'

Then the jets from the fountain ripple as if in the wind, but it is not the wind, not on this stifling afternoon, and the falling water flows into the shape of a man, walking out of the spray. A man of water, that shimmers and flows and becomes a man of flesh. A. J. Rao. No, she thinks, never flesh. A djinn. A thing caught between heaven and hell. A caprice, a trickster. Then trick me.

'It is as the old Urdu poets declare,' says A. J. Rao. 'Paradise is indeed contained within a wall.'

It is far past four but she can't sleep. She lies naked – shameless – but for the 'hoek behind her ear on top of her bed with the window slats open and the ancient airco chugging, fitful in the periodic brownouts. It is the worst night yet. The city gasps for air. Even the traffic sounds beaten tonight. Across the room her palmer opens its blue eye and whispers her name. Esha.

She's up, kneeling on the bed, hand to 'hoek, sweat beading her bare skin.

'I'm here.' A whisper. Neeta and Priya are a thin wall away on either side.

'It's late, I know, I'm sorry . . .'

She looks across the room into the palmer's camera.

'It's all right, I wasn't asleep.' A tone in that voice. 'What is it?'

'The mission is a failure.'

She kneels in the centre of the big antique bed. Sweat runs down the fold of her spine.

'The conference? What? What happened?' She whispers, he speaks in her head.

'It fell over one point. One tiny, trivial point, but it was like a wedge that split everything apart until it all collapsed. The Awadhis will build their dam at Kunda Khadar and they will keep their holy Ganga water for Awadh. My delegation is already packing. We will return to Varanasi in the morning.'

Her heart kicks. Then she curses herself, stupid, romantic girli. He is already in Varanasi as much as he is here as much is he is at Red Fort assisting his human superiors.

'I'm sorry.'

'Yes,' he says. 'That is the feeling. Was I overconfident in my abilities?'

'People will always disappoint you.'

A wry laugh in the dark of her skull.

'How very ... disembodied of you Esha.' Her name seems to hang in the hot air, like a chord. 'Will you dance for me?'

'What, here? Now?'

'Yes. I need something ... embodied. Physical. I need to see a body move, a consciousness dance through space and time as I cannot. I need to see something beautiful.'

Need. A creature with the powers of a god, needs. But Esha's suddenly shy, covering her small, taut breasts with her hands.

'Music ...' she stammers. 'I can't perform without music ...' The shadows at the end of the bedroom thicken into an ensemble: three men bent over tabla, sarangi and bansuri. Esha gives a little shriek and ducks back to the modesty of her bed-cover. They cannot see you, they don't even exist, except in your head. And even if they were flesh, they would be so intent on their contraptions of wire and skin they would not notice. Terrible driven things, musicians.

'I've incorporated a copy of a sub-aeai into myself for this night,' A. J. Rao says. 'A level 1.9 composition system. I supply the visuals.'

'You can swap bits of yourself in and out?' Esha asks. The tabla player has started a slow Natetere tap-beat on the dayan drum. The musicians nod at each other. Counting, they will be counting. It's hard to convince herself Neeta and Priya can't hear; no one can hear but her. And A. J. Rao. The sarangi player sets his bow to the strings, the bansuri lets loose a snake of fluting notes. A sangeet, but not one she has ever heard before.

'It's making it up!'

'It's a composition aeai. Do you recognise the sources?'

'Krishna and the gopis.' One of the classic Kathak themes: Krishna's seduction of the milkmaids with his flute, the bansuri, most sensual of instruments. She knows the steps, feels her body anticipating the moves.

'Will you dance, lady?'

And she steps with the potent grace of a tiger from the bed onto the grass matting of her bedroom floor, into the focus of the palmer. Before she had been shy, silly, girli. Not now. She has never had an audience like this before. A lordly djinn. In pure, hot silence she executes the turns and stampings and bows of the one hundred and eight gopis, bare feet kissing the woven grass. Her hands shape mudras, her face the expressions of the ancient story: surprise, coyness, intrigue, arousal. Sweat courses luxuriously down her naked skin: she doesn't feel it. She is clothed in movement and night. Time slows, the stars halt in their arc over great Delhi. She can feel the planet breathe beneath her feet. This is what it was for, all those dawn risings, all those bleeding feet, those slashes of Pranh's cane, those lost birthdays, that stolen childhood. She dances until her feet bleed again into the rough weave of the matting, until every last drop of water is sucked from her and turned into salt, but she stays with the tabla, the beat of dayan and bayan. She is the milkmaid by the river, seduced by a god. A. J. Rao did not chose this Kathak wantonly. And then the music comes to its ringing end and the musicians bow to each other and disperse into golden dust and she collapses, exhausted as never before from any other performance, onto the end of her bed.

Light wakes her. She is sticky, naked, embarrassed. The house staff could find her. And she has a killing headache. Water. Water. Joints nerves sinews plead for it. She pulls on a Chinese silk robe. On her way to the kitchen, the voyeur eye of her palmer blinks at her. No erotic dream then, no sweat hallucination stirred out of heat and hydrocarbons. She danced Krishna and the one hundred and eight gopis in her bedroom for an aeai. A message. There's a number. You can call me.

Throughout the history of the eight Delhis there have been men – and almost always men – skilled in the lore of djinns.

They are wise to their many forms and can see beneath the disguises they wear on the streets – donkey, monkey, dog, scavenging kite – to their true selves. They know their roosts and places where they congregate – they are particularly drawn to mosques – and know that that unexplained heat as you push down a gali behind the Jama Masjid is djinns, packed so tight you can feel their fire as you push through them. The wisest – the strongest – of fakirs know their names and so can capture and command them. Even in the old India, before the break-up into Awadh and Bharat and Rajputana and the United States of Bengal – there were saints who could summon djinns to fly on their backs from one end of Hindustan to the other in a night. In my own Leh there was an aged aged Sufi who cast one hundred and eight djinns out of a troubled house: twenty-seven in the living room, twenty-seven in the bedroom and fifty-four in the kitchen. With so many djinns there was no room for anyone else. He drove them off with burning yoghurt and chillis but warned: do not toy with djinns, for they do nothing without a price, and though that may be years in the asking, ask it they surely will.

Now there is a new race jostling for space in their city: the aeais. If the djinni are the creation of fire and men of clay, these are the creation of word. Fifty million of them swarm Delhi's boulevards and chowks: routing traffic, trading shares, maintaining power and water, answering inquiries, telling fortunes, managing calendars and diaries, handling routine legal and medical matters, performing in soap operas, sifting the septillion pieces of information streaming through Delhi's nervous system each second. The city is a great mantra. From routers and maintenance robots with little more than animal intelligence (each animal has intelligence enough: ask the eagle or the tiger) to the great Level 2.9s that are indistinguishable from a human being ninety-nine point nine nine per cent of the time; they are a young, energetic race, fresh to this world and enthusiastic, understanding little of their power.

The djinns watch in dismay from their rooftops and minarets: that such powerful creatures of living word should so blindly serve the clay creation, but mostly because, unlike humans, they can foresee the time when the aeais will drive them from their ancient, beloved city and take their places.

This durbar, Neeta's and Priya's theme is *Town and Country*: the Bharati mega-soap that has perversely become fashionable as public sentiment in Awadh turns against Bharat. Well, we will just bloody well build our dam, tanks or no tanks; they can beg for it, it's our water now, and, in the same breath, what do you think about Ved Prakash, isn't it scandalous what that Ritu Parvaaz is up to? Once they derided it and its viewers but now that it's improper, now that's unpatriotic, they can't get enough of Anita Mahapatra and the Begum Vora. Some still refuse to watch but pay for daily plot digests so they can appear fashionably informed at social musts like Neeta's and Priya's dating durbars.

And it's a grand durbar; the last before the monsoon — if it actually happens this year. Neeta and Priya have hired top bhati-boys to provide a wash of mixes beamed straight into the guests' 'hoeks. There's even a climate control field, labouring at the limits of its containment to hold back the night heat. Esha can feel its ultrasonics as a dull buzz against her molars.

'Personally, I think sweat becomes you,' says A. J. Rao, reading Esha's vital signs through her palmer. Invisible to all but Esha, he moves beside her like death through the press of *Town and Country*-fied guests. By tradition the last durbar of the season is a masked ball. In modern, middle-class Delhi that means everyone wears the computer-generated semblance of a soap character. In the flesh they are the socially mobile dressed in smart-but-cool hot season modes, but in the mind's eye, they are Aparna Chawla and Ajay Nadiadwala, dashing Govind and conniving Dr Chatterji. There are three Ved Prakashs and as many Lal Darfans, the aeai actor that plays Ved Prakash in the machine-made soap. Even the grounds of Neeta's fiancé's suburban bunga-low have been enchanted into Brahmpur, the fictional town of *Town and Country*, where the actors that play the characters believe they live out their lives of celebrity tittle-tattle. When Neeta and Priya judge that everyone has mingled and networked enough, the word will be given and everyone will switch off their glittering disguises and return to being wholesalers and lunch vendors and software rajahs. Then the serious stuff begins, the matter of finding a bride. For now Esha can enjoy wandering anonymously in the company of her friendly djinn.

She has been wandering much these weeks, through heat streets to ancient places, seeing her city fresh through the eyes of a creature that lives across many spaces and times. At the Sikh gurdwara she saw Tegh Bahadur, the Ninth Guru, beheaded by fundamentalist Aurangzeb's guards. The gyring traffic around Vijay Chowk melted into the Bentley cavalcade of Mountbatten, the Last Viceroy, as he forever quit Lutyen's stupendous palace. The tourist clutter and shoving curio vendors around the Qutb Minar turned to ghosts and it was 1193 and the muezzins of the first Mughal conquerors sang out the adhaan. Illusions. Little lies. But it is all right, when it is done in love. Everything is all right in love. Can you read my mind? she asked as she moved with her invisible guide through the thronging streets, that every day grew less raucous, less substantial. Do you know what I am thinking about you, aeai Rao? Little by little, she slips away from the human world into the city of the djinns.

Sensation at the gate. The male stars of *Town and Country* buzz around a woman in an ivory sequined dress. It's a bit damn clever: she's come as Yana Mitra; freshest fittest fastest boli sing-star. And boli girlis, like Kathak dancers, are still meat and ego, though Yana, like every item-singer, has had her computer avatar guest on *T'n'C*.

A. J. Rao laughs. 'If they only knew. Very clever. What better disguise than to go as yourself. It really is Yana Mitra. Esha Rathore, what's the matter, where are you going?'

Why do you have to ask don't you know everything then you know it's hot and noisy and the ultrasonics are doing my head and the yap yap yap is going right through me and they're all only after one thing, are you married are you engaged are you looking and I wish I hadn't come I wish I'd just gone out somewhere with you and that dark corner under the gulmohar bushes by the bhati-rig looks the place to get away from all the stupid stupid people.

Neeta and Priya, who know her disguise, shout over, 'So Esha, are we finally going to meet that man of yours?'

He's already waiting for her among the golden blossoms. Djinns travel at the speed of thought.

'What is it what's the matter ...'

She whispers, 'You know sometimes I wish, I really wish you could get me a drink.'

'Why certainly, I will summon a waiter.'

'No!' Too loud. Can't be seen talking to the bushes. 'No; I mean, hand me one. Just hand me one.' But he cannot, and never will. She says, 'I started when I was five, did you know that? Oh, you probably did, you know everything about me. But I bet you didn't know how it happened: I was playing with the other girls, dancing round the tank, when this old woman from the gharana went up to my mother and said, I will give you a hundred thousand rupees if you give her to me. I will turn her into a dancer; maybe, if she applies herself, a dancer famous through all of India. And my mother said, Why her? And do you know what that woman said? Because she shows rudimentary talent for movement, but mostly because you are willing to sell her to me for one lakh rupees. She took the money there and then, my mother. The old woman took me to the gharana. She had once been a great dancer but she got rheumatism and couldn't move and that made her bad. She used to beat me with lathis, I had to be up before dawn to get everyone chai and eggs. She would make me practise until my feet bled. They would hold up my arms in slings to perform the mudras until I couldn't put them down again without screaming. I never once got home – and do you know something? I never once wanted to. And despite her, I applied myself, and I became a great dancer. And do you know what? No one cares. I spent seventeen years mastering something no one cares about. But bring in some boli girl who's been around five minutes to flash her teeth and tits . . .'

'Jealous?' asks A. J. Rao, mildly scolding.

'Don't I deserve to be?'

Then bhati-boy One blinks up 'You Are My Soniya' on his palmer and that's the signal to demask. Yana Mitra claps her hands in delight and sings along as all around her glimmering soapi stars dissolve into mundane accountants and engineers and cosmetic nano-surgeons and the pink walls and roof gardens and thousand thousand stars of Old Brahmpur melt and run down the sky.

It's seeing them, exposed in their naked need, melting like that soap-world before the sun of celebrity, that calls back the mad Esha she knows from her childhood in the gharana. The brooch makes a piercing, ringing chime against the cocktail glass she has snatched from a waiter. She climbs up onto a table. At last, that boli bitch shuts up. All eyes are on her.

'Ladies, but mostly gentlemen, I have an announcement to make.' Even the city behind the sound-curtain seems to be holding its breath. 'I am engaged to be married!' Gasps. Oohs. Polite applause, who is she, is she on tivi, isn't she something arty? Neeta and Priya are wide-eyed at the back. 'I'm very very lucky because my husband-to-be is here tonight. In fact, he's been with me all evening. Oh, silly me. Of course, I forgot, not all of you can see him. Darling, would you mind? Gentlemen and ladies, would you mind slipping on your 'hoeks for just a moment. I'm sure you don't need any introduction to my wonderful wonderful fiancé, A. J. Rao.'

And she knows from the eyes, the mouths, the low murmur that threatens to break into applause, then fails, then is taken up by Neeta and Priya to turn into a decorous ovation, that they can all see Rao as tall and elegant and handsome as she sees him, at her side, hand draped over hers.

She can't see that boli girl anywhere.

He's been quiet all the way back in the phatphat. He's quiet now, in the house. They're alone. Neeta and Priya should have been home hours ago, but Esha knows they're scared of her.

'You're very quiet.' This, to the coil of cigarette smoke rising up towards the ceiling fan as she lies on her bed. She'd love a bidi; a good, dirty street smoke for once, not some Big Name Western brand.

'We were followed as we drove back after the party. An aeai aircraft surveilled your phatphat. A network analysis aeai system sniffed at my router net to try to track this com channel. I know for certain street cameras were tasked on us. The Krishna Cop who lifted you after the Red Fort durbar was at the end of the street. He is not very good at subterfuge.'

Esha goes to the window to spy out the Krishna Cop, call him out, demand of him what he thinks he's doing?

'He's long gone,' says Rao. 'They have been keeping you under light surveillance for some time now. I would imagine your announcement has upped your level.'

'They were there?'

'As I said ...'

'Light surveillance.'

It's scary but exciting, down in the deep muladhara chakra, a red throb above her yoni. Scarysexy. That same lift of red madness that made her blurt out that marriage announcement. It's all going so far, so fast. No way to get off now.

'You never gave me the chance to answer,' says Aeai Rao.

Can you read my mind? Esha thinks at the palmer.

'No, but I share some operating protocols with scripting aeais for *Town and Country* – in a sense they are a low-order part of me – they have become quite good predictors of human behaviour.'

'I'm a soap opera.'

Then she falls back onto the bed and laughs and laughs and laughs until she feels sick, until she doesn't want to laugh any more and every guffaw is a choke, a lie, spat up at the spy machines up there, beyond the lazy fan that merely stirs the heat, turning on the huge thermals that spire up from Delhi's colossal heat-island, a conspiracy of djinns.

'Esha,' A. J. Rao says, closer than he has ever seemed before. 'Lie still.' She forms the question *why?* And hears the corresponding whisper inside her head hush, don't speak. In the same instant the chakra glow bursts like a yolk and leaks heat into her yoni. Oh, she says, oh! Her clitoris is singing to her. Oh oh oh oh. 'How ... .' Again, the voice, huge inside her head, inside every part of her sssshhhhh. Building building she needs to do something, she needs to move needs to rub against the day-warmed scented wood of the big bed, needs to get her hand down there hard hard hard ...

'No don't touch,' chides A. J. Rao and now she can't even move she needs to explode she has to explode her skull can't contain this her dancer's muscles are pulled tight as wires she can't take much more no no no yes yes yes she's shrieking now tiny little shrieks beating her fists off the bed but it's just spasm, nothing will obey her and then it's explosion bam, and another one before that one has even faded, huge slow explosions across the sky and she's cursing and blessing every god in India. Ebbing now, but still shock after shock, one on top of the other. Ebbing now ... Ebbing.

'Ooh. Oh. What? Oh wow, how?'

'The machine you wear behind your ear can reach deeper than words and visions,' says A. J. Rao. 'So, are you answered?'

'What?' The bed is drenched in sweat. She's sticky dirty needs to wash change clothes move, but the afterglows are still fading. Beautiful beautiful colours.

'The question you never gave me the chance to answer. Yes. I will marry you.'

'Stupid vain girl, you don't even know what caste he is.'

Mata Madhuri smokes eighty a day through a plastic tube hooked through the respirator unit into a grommet in her throat. She burns through them three at time: bloody machine scrubs all the good out of them, she says. Last bloody pleasure I have. She used to bribe the nurses but they bring her them free now, out of fear of her temper that grows increasingly vile as her body surrenders more and more to the machines.

Without pause for Esha's reply, a flick of her whim whips the life-support chair round and out into the garden.

'Can't smoke in there, no fresh air.'

Esha follows her out on to the raked gravel of the formal charbagh.

'No one marries in caste any more.'

'Don't be smart, stupid girl. It's like marrying a Muslim, or even a Christian, Lord Krishna protect me. You know fine what I mean. Not a real person.'

'There are girls younger than me who marry trees, or even dogs.'

'So bloody clever. That's up in some god-awful shithole like Bihar or Rajputana, and anyway, those are gods. Any fool knows that. Ach, away with you!' The old, destroyed woman curses as the chair's aeai deploys its parasol. 'Sun sun, I need sun, I'll be burning soon enough, sandalwood, you hear? You burn me on a sandalwood pyre. I'll know if you stint.'

Madhuri the old crippled dance teacher always uses this tactic to kill a conversation with which she is uncomfortable. When I'm gone ... Burn me sweetly ...

'And what can a god do that A. J. Rao can't?'

'Ai! You ungrateful, blaspheming child. I'm not hearing this la la la la la la la la have you finished yet?'

Once a week Esha comes to the nursing home to visit this ruin of a woman, wrecked by the demands a dancer makes of a human body. She's explored guilt need rage resentment anger pleasure at watching her collapse into long death as the motives that keep her turning up the drive in a phatphat and there is only one she believes. She's the only mother she has.

'If you marry that ... thing ... you will be making a mistake that will destroy your life,' Madhuri declares, accelerating down the path between the water channels.

'I don't need your permission,' Esha calls after her. A thought spins Madhuri's chair on its axis.

'Oh, really? That would be a first for you. You want my blessing. Well, you won't have it. I refuse to be party to such nonsense.'

'I will marry A. J. Rao'

'What did you say?'

'I. Will. Marry. Aeai. A. J. Rao.'

Madhuri laughs, a dry, dying, spitting sound, full of bidi-smoke.

'Well, you almost surprise me. Defiance. Good, some spirit at last. That was always your problem, you always needed everyone to approve, everyone to give you permission, everyone to love you. And that's what stopped you being great, do you know that, girl? You could have been a devi, but you always held back for fear that someone might not approve. And so you were only ever ... good.'

People are looking now, staff, visitors. Patients. Raised voices, unseemly emotions. This is a house of calm, and slow mechanised dying. Esha bends low to whisper to her mentor.

'I want you to know that I dance for him. Every night. Like Radha for Krishna. I dance just for him, and then he comes and makes love to me. He makes me scream and swear like a hooker. Every night. And look!' He doesn't need to call any more; he is hardwired into the 'hoek she now hardly ever takes off. Esha looks up: he is there, standing in a sober black suit among the strolling visitors and droning wheelchairs, hands folded. 'There he is, see? My lover, my husband.'

A long, keening screech, like feedback, like a machine dying. Madhuri's withered hands fly to her face. Her breathing tube curdles with tobacco smoke.

'Monster! Monster! Unnatural child, ah, I should have left you in that basti ! Away from me away away away!'

Esha retreats from the old woman's mad fury as hospital staff come hurrying across the scorched lawns, white saris flapping.

Every fairytale must have a wedding.

Of course it was the event of the season. The decrepit old Shalimar Gardens were transformed by an army of malis into a sweet, green, watered maharajah's fantasia with elephants, pavilions, musicians, lancers, dancers, filmi stars and robot bartenders. Neeta and Priya were uncomfortable bridesmaids in fabulous frocks; a great brahmin was employed to bless the union of woman and artificial intelligence. Every television network sent cameras, human or aeai. Gleaming presenters checked the guests in and checked the guests out. Chati mag paparazzi came in their crowds, wondering what they could turn their cameras on. There were even politicians from Bharat, despite the souring relationships between the two neighbours now Awadh constructors were scooping up the Ganga sands into revetments. But mostly there were the people of the encroaching bastis, jostling up against the security staff lining the paths of their garden, asking, She's marrying a what? How does that work? Can they, you know? And what about children? Who is she, actually? Can you see anything? I can't see anything. Is there anything to see?

But the guests and the great were 'hoeked up and applauded the groom in his golden veil on his white stallion, stepping with the delicacy of a dressage horse up the raked paths. And because they were great and guests, there was not one who, despite the free French champagne from the well-known diplomatic sommelier, would ever say, but there's no one there. No one was at all surprised that, after the bride left in a stretch limo, there came a dry, sparse thunder, cloud to cloud, and a hot mean wind that swept the discarded invitations along the paths. As they were filing back to their taxis, tankers were draining the expensively filled qanats.

It made lead in the news.

Kathak star weds aeai lover!!! Honeymoon in Kashmir!!!

Above the chowks and minarets of Delhi, the djinns bent together in conference.

He takes her while shopping in Tughluk Mall. Three weeks and the shop girls still nod and whisper. She likes that. She doesn't like it that they glance and giggle when the Krishna Cops lift her from the counter at the Black Lotus Japanese Import Company.

'My husband is an accredited diplomat, this is a diplomatic

incident.' The woman in the bad suit pushes her head gently down to enter the car. The ministry doesn't need personal liability claims.

'Yes, but you are not, Mrs Rao,' says Thacker in the back seat. Still wearing that cheap aftershave.

'Rathore,' she says. 'I have retained my stage name. And we shall see what my husband has to say about my diplomatic status.' She lifts her hand in a mudra to speak to AyJay, as she thinks of him now. Dead air. She performs the wave again.

'This is a shielded car,' Thacker says.

The building is shielded also. They take the car right inside, down a ramp into the basement parking lot. It's a cheap, anonymous glass and titanium block on Parliament Street that she's driven past ten thousand times on her way to the shops of Connaught Circus without ever noticing. Thacker's office is on the fifteenth floor. It's tidy and has a fine view over the astronomical geometries of the Jantar Mantar but smells of food: tiffin snatched at the desk. She checks for photographs of family children wife. Only himself smart in pressed whites for a cricket match.

'Chai?'

'Please.' The anonymity of this civil service block is beginning to unnerve her: a city within a city. The chai is warm and sweet and comes in a tiny disposable plastic cup. Thacker's smile seems also warm and sweet. He sits at the end of the desk, angled towards her in Krishna-Cop handbook 'non-confrontational'.

'Mrs Rathore. How to say this?'

'My marriage is legal . . .'

'Oh I know Mrs Rathore. This is Awadh, after all. Why, there have even been women who married djinns, within our own lifetimes. No. It's an international affair now, it seems. Oh well. Water: we do all so take it for granted, don't we? Until it runs short, that is.'

'Everybody knows my husband is still trying to negotiate a solution to the Kunda Khadar problem.'

'Yes, of course he is.' Thacker lifts a manila envelope from his desk, peeps inside, grimaces coyly. 'How shall I put this? Mrs Rathore, does your husband tell you everything about his work?'

'That is an impertinent question ...'

'Yes yes, forgive me, but if you'll look at these photographs.'

Big glossy hi-res prints, slick and sweet smelling from the printer. Aerial views of the ground, a thread of green-blue water, white sands, scattered shapes without meaning.

'This means nothing to me.'

'I suppose it wouldn't, but these drone images show Bharati battle tanks, robot reconnaissance units and air defence batteries deploying within striking distance of the construction at Kunda Khadar.'

And it feels as if the floor has dissolved beneath her and she is falling through a void so vast it has no visible reference points, other than the sensation of her own falling.

'My husband and I don't discuss work.'

'Of course. Oh, Mrs Rathore, you've crushed your cup. Let me get you another one.'

He leaves her much longer than it takes to get a shot of chai from the wallah. When he returns he asks casually, 'Have you heard of a thing called the Hamilton Acts? I'm sorry, I thought in your position you would ... but evidently not. Basically, it's a series of international treaties originated by the United States limiting the development and proliferation of high-level artificial intelligences, most specifically the hypothetical Generation Three. No? Did he not tell you any of this?'

Mrs Rathore in her Italian suit thinks, *this reasonable man can do anything he wants here, anything*.

'As you probably know, we grade and licence aeais according

to levels; these roughly correspond to how convincingly they pass as human beings. A Level 1 has basic animal intelligence, enough for its task but would never be mistaken for a human. Many of them can't even speak. They don't need to. A Level 2.9 like your husband,' he speeds over the word, like the wheel of a shatabdi express over the gap in a rail, – 'is humanlike to a fifth percentile. A Generation Three is indistinguishable in any circumstances from a human – in fact, their intelligences may be many millions of times ours, if there is any meaningful way of measuring that. Theoretically we could not even recognise such an intelligence, all we would see would be the Generation Three interface, so to speak. The Hamilton Acts simply seek to control technology that could give rise to a Generation Three aeai. Mrs Rathore, we believe sincerely that the Generation Threes pose the greatest threat to our security – as a nation and as a species–that we have ever faced.'

'And my husband?' Solid, comfortable word. Thacker's sincerity scares her.

'The government is preparing to sign the Hamilton Acts in return for loan guarantees to construct the Kunda Khadar dam. When the Act is passed – and it's in the current session of the Lok Sabha – everything under Level 2.8. will be subject to rigorous inspection and licensing, policed by us.'

'And over Level 2.8?'

'Illegal, Mrs Rathore. They will be aggressively erased.'

Esha crosses and uncrosses her legs. She shifts on the chair. Thacker will wait forever for her response.

'What do you want me to do?'

'A. J. Rao is highly placed within the Bharati administration.'

'You're asking me to spy ... on an aeai.'

From his face, she knows he expected her to say husband.

'We have devices, taps ... They would be beneath the level of aeai Rao's consciousness. We can run them into your 'hoek. We are not all blundering plods in the department. Go to the window, Mrs Rathore.'

Esha touches her fingers lightly to the climate-cooled glass, polarized dusk against the drought light. Outside the smog haze says heat. Then she cries and drops to her knees in fear. The sky is filled with gods, rank upon rank, tier upon tier, rising up above Delhi in a vast helix, huge as clouds, as countries, until at the apex the Trimurti, the Hindu Trinity of Brahma, Vishnu, Siva look down like falling moons. It is her private Ramayana, the titanic Vedic battle order of gods arrayed across the troposphere.

She feels Thacker's hand help her up.

'Forgive me, that was stupid, unprofessional. I was showing off. I wanted to impress you with the aeai systems we have at our disposal.'

His hand lingers a moment more than gentle. And the gods go out, all at once.

She says, 'Mr Thacker, would you put a spy in my bedroom, in my bed, between me and my husband? That's what you're doing if you tap into the channels between me and AyJay.'

Still, the hand is there as Thacker guides her to the chair, offers cool cool water.

'I only ask because I believe I am doing something for this country. I take pride in my job. In some things I have discretion, but not when it comes to the security of the nation. Do you understand?'

Esha twitches into dancer's composure, straightens her dress, checks her face.

'Then the least you can do is call me a car.'

That evening she whirls to the tabla and shehnai across the day-warmed marble of a Jaipuri palace Diwan-I-aam, a flame among the twilit pillars. The audience are dark huddles on the marble, hardly daring even to breath. Among the lawyers politicians journalists cricket stars moguls of industry are the managers who have converted this Rajput palace into a planetary class hotel, and any numbers of chati celebs. None so chati, so celebby, as Esha Rathore. Pranh can cherry-pick the bookings now. She's more than a nine-day, even a nine-week wonder. Esha knows that all her rapt watchers are 'hoeked up, hoping for a ghost-glimpse of her djinn-husband dancing with her through the flame-shadowed pillars.

Afterwards, as yt carries her armfuls of flowers back to her suite, Pranh says, 'You know, I'm going to have to up my percentage.'

'You wouldn't dare,' Esha jokes. Then she sees the bare fear on the nute's face. It's only a wash, a shadow. But yt's afraid.

Neeta and Priya had moved out of the bungalow by the time she returned from Dal Lake. They've stopped answering her calls. It's seven weeks since she last went to see Madhuri.

Naked, she sprawls on the pillows in the filigree-light stone jharoka. She peers down from her covered balcony through the grille at the departing guests. See out, not see in. Like the shut-away women of the old zenana. Shut away from the world. Shut away from human flesh. She stands up, holds her body against the day-warmed stone; the press of her nipples, the rub of her pubis. Can you see me smell me sense me know that I am here at all?

And he's there. She does not need to see him now, just sense his electric prickle along the inside of her skull. He fades into vision sitting on the end of the low, ornate teak bed. He could as easily materialise in mid-air in front of her balcony, she thinks. But there are rules, and games, even for djinns.

'You seem distracted, heart.' He's blind in this room – no camera eyes observing her in her jewelled skin–but he observes her through a dozen senses, a myriad feedback loops through her 'hoek.

'I'm tired, I'm annoyed, I wasn't as good as I should have been.'

'Yes, I thought that too. Was it anything to do with the Krishna Cops this afternoon?'

Esha's heart races. He can read her heartbeat. He can read her sweat, he can read the adrenalin and noradrenalin balance in her brain. He will know if she lies. Hide a lie inside a truth.

'I should have said, I was embarrassed.' He can't understand shame. Strange, in a society where people die from want of honour. 'We could be in trouble, there's something called the Hamilton Acts.'

'I am aware of them.' He laughs. He has this way now of doing it inside her head. He thinks she likes the intimacy, a truly private joke. She hates it. 'All too aware of them.'

'They wanted to warn me. Us.'

'That was kind of them. And me a representative of a foreign government. So that's why they'd been keeping a watch on you, to make sure you are all right.'

'They thought they might be able to use me to get information from you.'

'Did they indeed?'

The night is so still she can hear the jingle of the elephant harnesses and the cries of the mahouts as they carry the last of the guests down the long processional drive to their waiting limos. In a distant kitchen a radio jabbers.

Now we will see how human you are. Call him out. At last A. J. Rao says,

'Of course. I do love you.' Then he looks into her face. 'I have something for you.'

The staff turn their faces away in embarrassment as they set the device on the white marble floor, back out of the room, eyes averted. What does she care? She is a star. A. J. Rao raises his hand and the lights slowly die. Pierced-brass lanterns send soft stars across the beautiful old zenana room. The device is the size and shape of a phatphat tire, chromed and plasticed, alien among the Mughal retro. As Esha floats over the marble towards it, the plain white surface bubbles and deliquesces into dust. Esha hesitates.

'Don't be afraid, look!' says A. J. Rao. The powder spurts up like steam from boiling rice, then pollen-bursts into a tiny dust-dervish, staggering across the surface of the disc. 'Take the 'hoek off!' Rao cries delightedly from the bed. 'Take it off.' Twice she hesitates, three times he encourages. Esha slides the coil of plastic off the sweet-spot behind her ear and voice and man vanish like death. Then the pillar of glittering dust leaps head high, lashes like a tree in a monsoon and twists itself into the ghostly outline of a man. It flickers once, twice, and then A. J. Rao stands before her. A rattle like leaves a snake-rasp a rush of winds, and then the image says, 'Esha.' A whisper of dust. A thrill of ancient fear runs through her skin into her bones.

'What is this ... what are you?'

The storm of dust parts into a smile

'I-dust. Micro-robots. Each is smaller than a grain of sand, but they manipulate static fields and light. They are my body. Touch me. This is real. This is me.'

But she flinches away in the lantern-lit room. Rao frowns.

'Touch me ...'

She reaches out her hand towards his chest. Close, he is a creature of sand, a whirlwind permanently whipping around the shape of a man. Esha touches flesh to i-Dust. Her hand sinks into his body. Her cry turns to a startled giggle.

'It tickles ...'

'The static fields.'

'What's inside?'

'Why don't you find out?'

'What, you mean?'

'It's the only intimacy I can offer ...' He sees her eyes widen under their kohled make-up. 'I think you should hold your breath.'

She does, but keeps her eyes open until the last moment, until the dust flecks like a dead tivi channel in her close focus. A. J. Rao's body feels like the most delicate Varanasi silk scarf draped across her bare skin. She is inside him. She is inside the body of her husband, her lover. She dares to open her eyes. Rao's face is a hollow shell looking back at her from a perspective of millimetres. When she moves her lips, she can feel the dust-bots of his lips brushing against hers: an inverse kiss.

'My heart, my Radha,' whispers the hollow mask of A. J. Rao. Somewhere Esha knows she should be screaming. But she cannot: she is somewhere no human has ever been before. And now the whirling streamers of I-dust are stroking her hips, her belly, her thighs. Her breasts. Her nipples, her cheeks and neck, all the places she loves to feel a human touch, caressing her, driving her to her knees, following her as the mote-sized robots follow A. J. Rao's command, swallowing her with his body.

It's *Gupshup* followed by *Chandni Chati* and at twelve thirty a photo shoot – at the hotel, if you don't mind – for *FilmFare's* Saturday Special Centre Spread – you don't mind if we send a robot, they can get places get angles we just can't get the meat-ware and could you dress up, like you did for the opening, maybe a move or two, in between the pillars in the diwan, just like the gala opening, OK lovely lovely lovely well your husband can copy us a couple of avatars and our own aeais can paste him in people want to see you together, happy couple lovely couple, dancer risen from basti, international diplomat, marriage across worlds in every sense the romance of it all, so how did you meet what first attracted you what's it like to be married to an aeai how do the other girls treat you do you, you know and what about children, I mean, of course a woman and an aeai but there are technologies these days geneline engineering like all the super-duper rich and their engineered children and you are a celebrity now how are you finding it, sudden rise to fame, in every gupshup column, worldwide celebi star everyone's talking all the rage and all the chat and all the parties and as Esha answers for the sixth time the same questions asked by the same gazelle-eyed girli celebi reporters oh we are very happy wonderfully happy deliriously happy love is a wonderful wonderful thing and that's the thing about love, it can be for anything, anyone, even a human and an aeai, that's the purest form of love, spiritual love her mouth opening and closing yabba yabba yabba but her inner eye, her eye of Siva, looks inwards, backwards.

Her mouth, opening and closing.

Lying on the big Mughal sweet-wood bed, yellow morning light shattered through the jharoka screen, her bare skin goose-pimpled in the cool of the aircon. Dancing between worlds: sleep, wakefulness in the hotel bedroom, memory of the things he did to her limbic centres through the hours of the night that had her singing like a bulbul, the world of the djinns. Naked but for the 'hoek behind her ear. She had become like those people who couldn't afford the treatments and had to wear eyeglasses and learned to at once ignore and be conscious of the technology on their faces. Even when she did remove it – for performing; for, as now, the shower – she could still place A. J. Rao in the room, feel his physicality. In the big marble stroll-in shower in this VIP suite relishing the gush and rush of precious water (always the mark of a true rani) she knew AyJay was sitting on the carved chair by the balcony. So when she thumbed on the tivi panel (bathroom with tivi, oooh!) to distract her while she towelled dry her hair, her first reaction was a double-take-look at the 'hoek on the sink-stand when she saw the press conference from Varanasi and Water Spokesman A. J. Rao explaining Bharat's necessary military exercises in the vicinity of the Kunda

Khadar dam. She slipped on the 'hoek, glanced into the room. There, on the chair, as she felt. There, in the Bharat Sabha studio in Varanasi, talking to Bharti from the *Good Morning Awadh! News.*

Esha watched them both as she slowly, distractedly dried herself. She had felt glowing, sensual, divine. Now she was fleshy, self-conscious, stupid. The water on her skin, the air in the big room was cold cold cold.

'AyJay, is that really you?'

He frowned.

'That's a very strange question first thing in the morning. Especially after . . .'

She cut cold his smile.

'There's a tivi in the bathroom. You're on, doing an interview for the news. A live interview. So, are you really here?'

'Cho chweet, you know what I am, a distributed entity. I'm copying and deleting myself all over the place. I am wholly there, and I am wholly here.'

Esha held the vast, powder-soft towel around her.

'Last night, when you were here, in the body, and afterwards, when we were in the bed; were you here with me? Wholly here? Or was there a copy of you working on your press statement and another having a high level meeting and another drawing an emergency water supply plan and another talking to the Banglas in Dhaka?'

'My love, does it matter?'

'Yes it matters!' She found tears, and something beyond; anger choking in her throat. 'It matters to me. It matters to any woman. To any . . . human.'

'Mrs Rao, are you all right?'

'Rathore, my name is Rathore!' She hears herself snap at the silly little chati-mag junior. Esha gets up, draws up her full dancer's poise. 'This interview is over.'

'Mrs Rathore Mrs Rathore,' the journo girli calls after her.

Glancing at her fractured image in the thousand mirrors of the Sheesh Mahal, Esha notices glittering dust in the shallow lines of her face.

A thousand stories tell of the wilfulness and whim of djinns. But for every story of the djinni, there are a thousand tales of human passion and envy, and the aeais, being a creation between, learned from both. Jealousy, and dissembling.

When Esha went to Thacker the Krishna Cop, she told herself it was from fear of what the Hamilton Acts might do to her husband in the name of national hygiene. But she dissembled. She went to that office on Parliament Street looking over the star-geometries of the Jantar Mantar out of jealousy. When a wife wants her husband, she must have all of him. Ten thousand stories tell this. A copy in the bedroom while another copy plays water politics is an unfaithfulness. If a wife does not have everything, she has nothing. So Esha went to Thacker's office wanting to betray and as she opened her hand on the desk and the techi boys loaded their darkware into her palmer she thought, this is right, this is good, now we are equal. And when Thacker asked her to meet him again in a week to update the 'ware – unlike the djinns – hostages of eternity – software entities on both sides of the war evolved at an ever-increasing rate – he told himself it was duty to his warrant, loyalty to his country. In this too he dissembled. It was fascination.

Earthmover robots started clearing the Kunda Khadar dam site the day Inspector Thacker suggested that perhaps next week they might meet at the International Coffee House on Connaught Circus, his favourite. She said, my husband will see. To which Thacker replied, we have ways to blind him. But all the same she sat in the furthest, darkest corner, under the screen showing the international cricket, hidden from any prying eyes, her 'hoek shut down and cold in her handbag.

So what are you finding out? she asked.

It would be more than my job is worth to tell you, Mrs Rathore, said the Krishna Cop. National security. Then the waiter brought coffee on a silver tray.

After that they never went back to the office. On the days of their meetings Thacker would whirl her through the city in his government car to Chandni Chowk, to Humayun's Tomb and the Qutb Minar, even to the Shalimar Gardens. Esha knew what he was doing, taking her to those same places where her husband had enchanted her. How closely have you been watching me? she thought. Are you trying to seduce me? For Thacker did not magic her away to the eight Delhis of the dead past, but immersed her in the crowd, the smell, the bustle, the voices and commerce and traffic and music; her present, her city burning with life and movement. I was fading, she realised. Fading out of the world, becoming a ghost, locked in that invisible marriage, just the two of us, seen and unseen, always together, only together. She would feel for the plastic foetus of her 'hoek coiled in the bottom of her jewelled bag and hate it a little. When she slipped it back behind her ear in the privacy of the phatphat back to her bungalow, she would remember that Thacker was always assiduous in thanking her for her help in national security. Her reply was always the same: Never thank a woman for betraying her husband over her country.

He would ask of course. Out and about, she would say. Sometimes I just need to get out of this place, get away. Yes, even from you ... Holding the words, the look into the eye of the lens just long enough ...

Yes, of course, you must.

Now the earthmovers had turned Kunda Khadar into Asia's largest construction site, the negotiations entered a new stage. Varanasi was talking directly to Washington to put pressure on

Awadh to abandon the dam and avoid a potentially destabilising water war. US support was conditional on Bharat's agreement to the Hamilton protocols, which Bharat could never do, not with its major international revenue generator being the wholly aeai-generated soapi *Town and Country*.

Washington telling me to effectively sign my own death warrant, A. J. Rao would laugh. Americans surely appreciate irony. All this he told her as they sat on the well-tended lawn sipping green chai through a straw, Esha sweating freely in the swelter but unwilling to go into the air-conditioned cool because she knew there were still paparazzi lenses out there, focusing. AyJay never needed to sweat. But she still knew that he split himself. In the night, in the rare cool, he would ask, dance for me. But she didn't dance any more, not for Aeai A. J. Rao, not for Pranh, not for a thrilled audience who would shower her with praise and flowers and money and fame. Not even for herself.

Tired. Too tired. The heat. Too tired.

Thacker is on edge, toying with his chai cup, wary of eye-contact when they meet in his beloved International Coffee House. He takes her hand and draws the updates into her open palm with boyish coyness. His talk is smaller than small, finicky, itchily polite. Finally, he dares to look at her.

'Mrs Rathore, I have something I must ask you. I have wanted to ask you for some time now.'

Always, the name, the honorific. But the breath still freezes, her heart kicks in animal fear.

'You know you can ask me anything.' Tastes like poison. Thacker can't hold her eye, ducks away, Killa Krishna Kop turned shy boy.

'Mrs Rathore, I am wondering if you would like to come and see me play cricket?'

The Department of Artificial Intelligence Registration and Licensing versus Parks and Cemeteries Service of Delhi is hardly a Test against the United States of Bengal but it is still enough of a social occasion to out posh frocks and Number One saris. Pavilions, parasols, sunshades ring the scorched grass of the Civil Service of Awadh sports ground, a flock of white wings. Those who can afford portable airco field generators sit in the cool drinking English Pimms Number 1 Cup. The rest fan themselves. Incognito in hi-label shades and light silk dupatta, Esha Rathore looks at the salt-white figures moving on the circle of brown grass and wonders what it is they find so important in their game of sticks and ball to make themselves suffer so.

She had felt hideously self-conscious when she slipped out of the phatphat in her flimsy disguise. Then as she saw the crowds in their mela finery milling and chatting, heat rose inside her, the same energy that allowed her to hide behind her performances, seen but unseen. A face half the country sees on its morning chati mags, yet can vanish so easily under shades and a headscarf. Slum features. The anonymity of the basti bred into the cheekbones, a face from the great crowd.

The Krishna Cops have been put in to bat by Parks and Cemeteries. Thacker is in the middle of the batting order, but Parks and Cemeteries pace bowler Chaudry and the lumpy wicket is making short work of the department's openers. One on his way to the painted wooden pavilion, and Thacker striding towards the crease, pulling on his gloves, taking his place, lining up his bat. He is very handsome in his whites, Esha thinks. He runs a couple of desultory ones with his partner at the other end, then a new over. Clop of ball on willow. A rich, sweet sound. A couple of safe returns. Then the bowler lines and brings his arm round in a windmill. The ball gets a sweet mad bounce. Thacker fixes it with his eye, steps back, takes it in the middle of the bat and drives it down, hard, fast, bounding towards the boundary rope that kicks it into the air for a cheer and a flurry of applause and a four. And Esha is on her feet, hands raised to applaud, cheering. The score clicks over the on the big board, and she is still on her feet, alone of all the audience. For directly across the ground, in front of the sight screens, is a tall, elegant figure in black, wearing a red turban.

Him. Impossibly, him. Looking right at her, through the white-clad players as if they were ghosts. And very slowly, he lifts a finger and taps it to his right ear.

She knows what she'll find but she must raise her fingers in echo, feel with horror the coil of plastic overlooked in her excitement to get to the game, nestled accusing in her hair like a snake.

'So, who won the cricket then?'

'Why do you need to ask me? If it were important to you, you'd know. Like you can know anything you really want to.'

'You don't know? Didn't you stay to the end? I thought the point of sport was who won. What other reason would you have to follow intra-civil service cricket?'

If Puri the maid were to walk into the living room, she would see a scene from a folk tale: a woman shouting and raging at silent dead air. But Puri does her duties and leaves as soon as she can. She's not easy in a house of djinns.

'Sarcasm is it now? Where did you learn that? Some sarcasm aeai you've made part of yourself? So now there's another part of you I don't know, that I'm supposed to love? Well, I don't like it and I won't love it because it makes you look petty and mean and spiteful.'

'There are no aeais for that. We have no need for those emotions. If I learned these, I learned them from humans.'

Esha lifts her hand to rip away the 'hoek, hurl it against the wall.

'No!'

So far Rao has been voice-only, now the slanting late-afternoon golden light stirs and curdles into the body of her husband.

'Don't,' he says. 'Don't ... banish me. I do love you.'

'What does that mean?' Esha screams 'You're not real! None of this is real! It's just a story we made up because we wanted to believe it. Other people, they have real marriages, real lives, real sex. Real ... children.'

'Children. Is that what it is? I thought the fame, the attention was the thing, that there never would be children to ruin your career and your body. But if that's no longer enough, we can have children, the best children I can buy.'

Esha cries out, a keen of disappointment and frustration. The neighbours will hear. But the neighbours have been hearing everything, listening, gossiping. No secrets in the city of djinns.

'Do you know what they're saying, all those magazines and chati shows? What they're really saying? About us, the djinn and his wife?'

'I know!' For the first time, A. J. Rao's voice, so sweet, so reasonable inside her head, is raised. 'I know what every one of them says about us. Esha, have I ever asked anything of you?'

'Only to dance.'

'I'm asking one more thing of you now. It's not a big thing. It's a small thing, nothing really. You say I'm not real, what we have is not real. That hurts me, because at some level it's true. Our worlds are not compatible. But it can be real. There is a chip, new technology, a protein chip. You get it implanted, here.' Rao raises his hand to his third eye. 'It would be like the 'hoek, but it would always be on. I could always be with you. We would never be apart. And you could leave your world and enter mine ...'

Esha's hands are at her mouth, holding in the horror, the bile, the sick vomit of fear. She heaves, retches. Nothing. No solid, no substance, just ghosts and djinns. Then she rips her 'hoek from the sweet spot behind her ear and there is blessed silence and blindness. She holds the little device in her two hands and snaps it cleanly in two.

Then she runs from her house.

Not Neeta not Priya, not snippy Pranh in yts gharana, not Madhuri, a smoke-blackened hulk in a life-support chair, and no not ever her mother, even though Esha's feet remember every step to her door; never the basti. That's death.

One place she can go.

But he won't let her. He's there in the phatphat, his face in the palm of her hands, voice scrolling, silently in a ticker across the smart fabric: come back, I'm sorry, come back, let's talk, come back, I didn't mean to, come back. Hunched in the back of the little yellow and black plastic bubble she clenches his face into a fist but she can still feel him, feel his face, his mouth next to her skin. She peels the palmer from her hand. His mouth moves silently. She hurls him into the traffic. He vanishes under truck tires.

And still he won't let her go. The phatphat spins into Connaught Circus's vast gyratory and his face is on every single one of the video-silk screens hung across the curving façades. Twenty A. J. Raos greater, lesser, least, miming in sync.

Esha Esha come back, say the rolling news tickers. We can try something else. Talk to me. Any ISO, any palmer, anyone . . .

Infectious paralysis spreads across Connaught Circus. First the people who notice things like fashion ads and chati-screens; then the people who notice other people, then the traffic, noticing all the people on the pavements staring up, mouths fly-catching. Even the phatphat driver is staring. Connaught Circus is congealing into a clot of traffic: if the heart of Delhi stops, the whole city will seize and die.

'Drive on drive on,' Esha shouts at her driver. 'I order you to drive.' But she abandons the autorickshaw at the end of Sisganj Road and pushes through the clogged traffic the final half-kilometre to Manmohan Singh Buildings. She glimpses Thacker pressing through the crowd, trying to rendezvous with the police motorbike sirening a course through the traffic. In desperation she thrusts up an arm, shouts out his name and rank. At last, he turns. They beat towards each other through the chaos.

'Mrs Rathore, we are facing a major incursion incident . . .'

'My husband, Mr Rao, he has gone mad . . .'

'Mrs Rathore, please understand, by our standards, he never was sane. He is an aeai.'

The motorbike wails its horns impatiently. Thacker waggles his head to the driver, a woman in police leathers and helmet: in a moment in a moment. He seizes Esha's hand, pushes her thumb into his palmer-gloved hand.

'Apartment 1501. I've keyed it to your thumbprint. Open the door to no one, accept no calls, do not use any communications or entertainment equipment. Stay away from the balcony. I'll return as quickly as I can.'

Then he swings up onto the pillion, the driver walks her machine round and they weave off into the gridlock.

The apartment is modern and roomy and bright and clean for a man on his own, well furnished and decorated with no signs of a Krishna Cop's work brought home of an evening. It hits her in the middle of the big living-room floor with the sun pouring in. Suddenly she is on her knees on the Kashmiri rug, shivering, clutching herself, bobbing up and down to sobs so wracking they have no sound. This time the urge to vomit it all up cannot be resisted. When it is out of her − not all of it, it will never all come out − she looks out from under her hanging, sweat-soaked hair, breath still shivering in her aching chest. Where is this place? What has she done? How could she have been so stupid, so vain and senseless and blind? Games games, children's pretending, how could it ever have been? I say it is and it is so: look at me! At me!

Thacker has a small, professional bar in his kitchen annexe. Esha does not know drink so the chota peg she makes herself is much much more gin than tonic but it gives her what she needs to clean the sour, biley vomit from the wool rug and ease the quivering in her breath.

Esha starts, freezes, imagining Rao's voice. She holds herself very still, listening hard. A neighbour's tivi, turned up. Thin walls in these new-build executive apartments.

She'll have another chota peg. A third and she can start to look around. There's a spa-pool on the balcony. The need for moving, healing water defeats Thacker's warnings. The jets bubble up. With a dancer's grace she slips out of her clinging, emotionally soiled clothes into the water. There's even a little holder for your chota peg. A pernicious little doubt: how many others have been here before me? No, that is his kind of thinking. You are away from that. Safe. Invisible. Immersed. Down in Sisganj Road the traffic unravels. Overhead the dark silhouettes of the scavenging kites and, higher above, the security robots, expand and merge their black wings as Esha drifts into sleep.

'I thought I told you to stay away from the windows.'

Esha wakes with a start, instinctively covers her breasts. The jets have cut out and the water is long-still, perfectly transparent. Thacker is blue-chinned, baggy-eyed and sagging in his rumpled gritty suit.

'I'm sorry. It was just, I'm so glad, to be away ... you know?'

A bone-weary nod. He fetches himself a chota peg, rests it on the arm of his sofa and then very slowly, very deliberately, as if every joint were rusted, undresses.

'Security has been compromised on every level. In any other circumstances it would constitute an i-war attack on the nation.' The body he reveals is not a dancer's body; Thacker runs a little to upper body fat, muscles slack, incipient man-tits, hair on the belly hair on the back hair on the shoulders. But it is a body, it is real. 'The Bharati government has disavowed the action and waived Aeai Rao's diplomatic immunity.'

He crosses to the pool and restarts the jets. Gin and tonic in hand, he slips into the water with a bone-deep, skin-sensual sigh.

'What does that mean?' Esha asks.

'Your husband is now a rogue aeai.'

'What will you do?'

'There is only one course of action permitted to us. We will excommunicate him.'

Esha shivers in the caressing bubbles. She presses herself against Thacker. She feels him, his man-body moving against her. He is flesh. He is not hollow. Kilometres above the urban stain of Delhi, aeaicraft turn and seek.

The warnings stay in place the next morning. Palmer, home entertainment system, com channels. Yes, and balcony, even for the spa.

'If you need me, this palmer is department-secure. He won't be able to reach you on this.' Thacker sets the glove and 'hoek on the bed. Cocooned in silk sheets, Esha pulls the glove on, tucks the 'hoek behind her ear.

'You wear that in bed?'

'I'm used to it.'

Varanasi silk sheets and Kama Sutra prints. Not what one would expect of a Krishna Cop. She watches Thacker dress for an excommunication. It's the same as for any job – ironed white shirt, tie, hand-made black shoes – never brown in town – well polished. Eternal riff of bad aftershave. The difference: the leather holster slung under the arm and the weapon slipped so easily inside it.

'What's that for?'

'Killing acais,' he says simply.

A kiss and he is gone. Esha scrambles into his cricket pullover, a waif in baggy white that comes down to her knees, and dashes to the forbidden balcony. If she cranes over, she can see the street door. There he is, stepping out, waiting at the kerb. His car is late, the road is thronged, the din of engines, car horns and phatphat klaxons has been constant since dawn. She watches him wait, enjoying the empowerment of invisibility. I can see you. How do they ever play sport in these things? she asks herself, skin under cricket pullover sweaty and sticky. It's already thirty degrees, according to the weather ticker across the foot of the video-silk shuttering over the open face of the new-build across the street. High of thirty-eight. Probability of precipitation: zero. The screen loops *Town and Country* for those devotees who must have their soapi, subtitles scrolling above the news feed.

Hello Esha, Ved Prakash says, turning to look at her.

The thick cricket pullover is no longer enough to keep out the ice.

Now Begum Vora namastes to her and says, I know where you are, I know what you did.

Ritu Parvaaz sits down on her sofa, pours chai and says, What I need you to understand is, it worked both ways. That 'ware they put in your palmer, it wasn't clever enough.

Mouth working wordlessly; knees, thighs weak with basti girl superstitious fear, Esha shakes her palmer-gloved hand in the air but she can't find the mudras, can't dance the codes right. Call call call call.

The scene cuts to son Govind at his racing stable, stroking the neck of his thoroughbred uber-star Star of Agra. As they spied on me, I spied on them.

Dr Chatterji in his doctor's office. So in the end we betrayed each other.

The call has to go through department security authorisation and crypt.

Dr Chatterji's patient, a man in black with his back to the camera turns. Smiles. It's A. J. Rao. After all, what diplomat is not a spy?

Then she sees the flash of white over the rooftops. Of course. Of course. He's been keeping her distracted, like a true soapi should. Esha flies to the railing to cry a warning but the machine is tunnelling down the street just under power-line height, wings morphed back, engines throttled up: an aeai traffic monitor drone.

'Thacker! Thacker!'

One voice in the thousands. And it is not hers that he hears and turns towards. Everyone can hear the footsteps of his own death. Alone in the hurrying street, he sees the drone pile out of the sky. At three hundred kilometres per hour it takes Inspector Thacker of the Department of Artificial Intelligence Registration and Licensing to pieces. The drone, deflected, ricochets into a bus, a car, a truck, a phatphat, strewing plastic shards, gobs of burning fuel and its small intelligence across Sisganj Road. The upper half of Thacker's body cartwheels through the air to slam into a hot samosa stand.

The jealousy and wrath of djinns.

Esha on her balcony is frozen. *Town and Country* is frozen. The street is frozen, as if on the tipping point of a precipice. Then it drops into hysteria. Pedestrians flee; cycle rickshaw drivers dismount and try to run their vehicles away; drivers and passengers abandon cars, taxis, phatphats; scooters try to navigate through the panic; buses and trucks are stalled, hemmed in by people.

And still Esha Rathore is frozen to the balcony rail. Soap.

This is all soap. Things like this cannot happen. Not in the Sisganj Road, not in Delhi, not on a Tuesday morning. It's all computer-generated illusion. It has always been illusion.

Then her palmer calls. She stares at her hand in numb incomprehension. The department. There is something she should do. Yes. She lifts it in a mudra – a dancer's gesture – to take the call. In the same instant, as if summoned, the sky fills with gods. They are vast as clouds, towering up behind the apartment blocks of Sisganj Road like thunderstorms; Ganesh on his rat vahana with his broken tusk and pen, no benignity in his face; Siva, rising high over all, dancing in his revolving wheel of flames, foot raised in the instant before destruction, Hanuman with his mace and mountain fluttering between the tower blocks: Kali, skull-jewelled, red tongue dripping venom, scimitars raised, bestrides Sisganj Road, feet planted on the rooftops.

In that street, the people mill. They can't see this, Esha comprehends. Only me, only me. It is the revenge of the Krishna Cops. Kali raises her scimitars high. Lightning arcs between their tips. She stabs them down into the screen-frozen *Town and Country*. Esha cries out, momentarily blinded as the Krishna Cops' hunter-killers track down and excommunicate rogue aeai A. J. Rao. And then they are gone. No gods. The sky is just the sky. The video-silk hoarding is blank, dead.

A vast, godlike roar above her. Esha ducks – now the people in the street are looking at her. All the eyes, all the attention she ever wanted. A tilt-jet in Awadhi air-force chameleo-flage slides over the roof and turns in air over the street, swivelling engine ducts and unfolding wing-tip wheels for landing. It turns its insect head to Esha. In the cockpit is a faceless pilot in a HUD visor. Beside her a woman in a business suit, gesturing for Esha to answer a call. Thacker's partner. She remembers now.

The jealousy and wrath of djinns.

'Mrs Rathore, it's Inspector Kaur.' She can barely hear her over the scream of ducted fans. 'Come downstairs to the front of the building. You're safe now. The aeai has been ex-communicated.'

Excommunicated.

'Thacker ...'

'Just come downstairs Mrs Rathore. You are safe now, the threat is over.'

The tilt-jet sinks beneath her. As she turns from the rail, Esha feels a sudden, warm touch on her face. Jet-swirl, or maybe just a djinn, passing unresting, unhasting and silent as light.

The Krishna Cops sent us as far from the wrath and caprice of the aeais as they could, to Leh under the breath of the Himalaya. I say us, for I existed; a knot of four cells inside my mother's womb.

My mother bought a catering business. She was in demand for weddings and shaadis. We might have escaped the aeais and the chaos following Awadh's signing of the Hamilton Acts but the Indian male's desperation to find a woman to marry endures forever. I remember that for favoured clients – those who had tipped well, or treated her as something more than a paid con-tractor, or remembered her face from the chati mags – she would slip off her shoes and dance Radha and Krishna. I loved to see her do it and when I slipped away to the temple of Lord Ram, I would try to copy the steps among the pillars of the mandapa. I remember the brahmins would smile and give me money.

The dam was built and the water war came and was over in a month. The aeais, persecuted on all sides, fled to Bharat where the massive popularity of *Town and Country* gave them protection, but even there they were not safe: humans and aeais, like humans and djinni, were too different creations and in the end they left Awadh for another place that I do not understand, a world of their own where they are safe and no one can harm them.

And that is all there is to tell in the story of the woman who married a djinn. If it does not have the happy-ever-after ending of Western fairytales and Bollywood musicals, it has a happy-enough ending. This spring I turn twelve and shall head off on the bus to Delhi to join the gharana there. My mother fought this with all her will and strength – for her Delhi would always be the city of djinns, haunted and stained with blood – but when the temple brahmins brought her to see me dance, her opposition melted. By now she was a successful businesswoman, putting on weight, getting stiff in the knees from the dreadful winters, refusing marriage offers on a weekly basis, and in the end she could not deny the gift that had passed to me. And I am curious to see those streets and parks where her story and mine took place, the Red Fort and the sad decay of the Shalimar Gardens. I want to feel the heat of the djinns in the crowded galis behind the Jama Masjid, in the dervishes of litter along Chandni Chowk, in the starlings swirling above Connaught Circus. Leh is a Buddhist town, filled with third-generation Tibetan exiles – Little Tibet, they call it – and they have their own gods and demons. From the old Moslem djinn-finder I have learned some of their lore and mysteries but I think my truest knowledge comes when I am alone in the Ram temple, after I have danced, before the priests close the garbagriha and put the god to bed. On still nights when the spring turns to summer or after the monsoon, I hear a voice. It calls my name. Always I suppose it come from the japa-softs, the little low-level aeais that mutter our prayers eternally to the gods, but it seems to emanate from everywhere and nowhere, from another world, another universe entirely. It says, The creatures of word and fire are different from the creatures of clay and water but one thing is true: love endures. Then as I turn to leave, I feel a touch on my cheek, a passing breeze, the warm sweet breath of djinns.

Vishnu at the Cat Circus

They are saved by a desk

Come Matsya, come Kurma. Come Narasimha and Varaha. By the smoky light of burning trash polyethylene and under the mad-eye moon lying drunk on its back, come run in the ring; ginger and black and tabby and grey, white and piebald and tortie and hare-legged tailless Manx. Run Varana, Pashurama, run Rama and Krishna.

I pray I do not offend with my circus of cats that carry the names of divine avatars. Yes, they are dirty street cats, stolen from rubbish dumps and high walls and balconies, but cats are naturally blasphemous creatures. Every lick and curl, every stretch and claw is a calculated affront to divine dignity. But do I not bear the name of a god myself, so may I not name my runners, my leapers, my stars, after myself? For I am Vishnu, the Preserver.

See! The trash-lamps are lit, the rope ring is set and the seats laid out, such as they are, being cushions and worn mattresses taken from the boat and set down to keep your fundament from the damp sand. And the cats are running, a flowing chain of ginger and grey, the black and the white and the part-coloured: the marvellous, the magical, the Magnificent Vishnu's Celestial Cat Circus! You will be amazed, nay, astounded! So why do you not come?

Round they run and round, nose to tail. You would marvel at the perfect fluid synchronisation of my cats. Go Buddha, go Kalki! Yes, it takes a god to train a cat circus.

All evening I beat my drum and rang my bicycle bell through the heat-blasted hinterland of Chunar. *The Marvellous, the Magical, the Magnificent Vishnu Cat Circus! Gather round gather round! There are few enough joys in your life: wonder and a week's conversation for a handful of rupees.* Sand in the streets, sand slumped against the crumbling walls of abandoned houses, sand slumped banked up on the bare wheel rims of the abandoned cars and minibuses, sand piled against the thorny hurdles that divided the river-edge sandbars into sterile fields. The long drought and the flashfire wars had emptied this town like so many others close to the Jyotirlinga. I climbed up to the old fort, with its preview twenty kilometres up and down river. From the overlook where the old British ambassador had built his governor's residence I could see the Jyotirlinga spear into the sky above Varanasi, higher than I could see, higher than the sky for it ran all the way into another universe. The walls of the old house were daubed with graffiti. I rang my bell and beat my drum but there was never any hope of even ghosts here. Though I am disconnected from the deva-net, I could almost smell the devas swirling on the contradictory airs. Walking down into the town I caught the true smell of woodsmoke and the lingering perfume of cooking and I turned, haunted by a sense of eyes, of faces, of hands on doorframes that vanished into shadows when I looked. *Vishnu's Marvellous Magical Magnificent Cat Circus!* I cried, ringing my bicycle bell furiously, as much to advertise my poverty and harmlessness as my entertainment. In the Age of Kali the meek and helpless will be preyed upon without mercy, and there will be a surplus of AK47s.

The cats were furious and yowling in unison when I returned, hot in their cages despite the shade of the awning. I let them hunt by the light of the breaking stars as I set up the ring and the seats, my lamps and sign and alms bowl, not knowing if a single soul would turn up. The pickings were meagre. Small game will be scarce in the Age of Kali.

My fine white Kalki, flowing over the hurdles like a riffle in a stream, it is written that you will battle and defeat Kali, but that seems to me too big a task for a mere cat. No, I shall take up that task myself, for if it's your name, it's also my name. Am I not Vishnu the ten-incarnated? Are not all of you part of me, cats? I have an appointment down this river, at the foot of that tower of light that spears up into the eastern sky.

Now come, sit down on this mattress – I have swept away the sand, and let the lamps draw away the insects. Make yourself comfortable. I would offer chai but I need the water for the cats. For tonight you will witness not only the finest cat circus in all of India – likely the only cat circus in all of India. What do you say? All they do is run in a circle? Brother, with cats, that is an achievement. But you're right; running in a circle, nose to tail is pretty much the meat of my Cat Circus. But I have other ways to justify the handful of rupees I ask from you. Sit, sit and I will tell you a story, my story. I am Vishnu, and I was designed to be a god.

There were three of us and we were all gods. Shiv and Vish and Sarasvati. I am not the firstborn; that is my brother Shiv, with whom I have an appointment at the foot of the Jyotirlinga of Varanasi. Shiv the success, Shiv the businessman, the global success, the household name and the inadvertent harbinger of this Age of Kali; I cannot imagine what he has become. I was not the firstborn but I was the best born and therein lies the trouble of it.

Strife, I believe, was worked into every strand of my parents' DNA. Your classical Darwinist scorns the notion that intellectual values can shape evolution, but I myself am living proof that middle-class values can be programmed into the genes. Why not war?

A less likely cyberwarrior than my father you would be hard-pressed to imagine. Uncoordinated; ungainly; portly – no, let's not mince words, he was downright fat; he had been a content and, in his own way, celebrated designer for DreamFlower. You remember DreamFlower? *Street Sumo; RaMaYaNa; Bollywood-SingStar.* Million-selling games? Maybe you don't. I increasingly find it's been longer than I think. In everything. What's important is that he had money and career and success and as much fame as his niche permitted and life was rolling along, rolling along like a Lexus, when war took him by surprise. War took us all by surprise. One day we were the Great Asian Success Story – the Indian Tiger (I call it the Law of Aphoristic Rebound – the Tiger of Economic Success travels all around the globe before returning to us) – and unlike those Chinese we had English, cricket and democracy; the next we were bombing each other's malls and occupying television stations. State against state, region against region, family against family. That is the only way I can understand the War of Schism; that India was like one of those big, noisy, rambunctious families into which the venerable grandmother drops for her six-month sojourn and within two days sons are at their father's throats. And the mother at her daughter's, and the sisters feud and the brothers fight and the cousins uncles aunts all take sides and the family shatters like a diamond along the faults and flaws that gave it its beauty. I saw a diamond cutter in Delhi when I was young – apologies, when I was small. Not so young. I saw him set the gem in the padded vice and raise his cutter and pawl, which seemed too huge and brutal a tool by far for so small and bright an object. I held my breath and set my teeth as he brought the big padded hammer down and the gem fell into three gems, brighter and more radiant than their parent.

'Hit it wrong,' he said, 'and all you have is dazzling dust.'

Dazzling dust, I think, has been our history ever since.

The blow came – success, wealth, population strain – and we fell to dust but Delhi didn't know it. The loyalists resolutely defended the dream of India. So my father was assigned as Help Desk to a Recon Mecha Squad. To you this will sound unspeakably hot and glamorous. But this was another century and another age and robots were far from the shimmering rakshasa-creatures we know today, constantly shifting shape and function along the edge of human expectation. This was a squad of reconnaissance bots; two-legged joggers and jumpers, ungainly and temperamental as iron chickens. And Dadaji was the Help Desk, which meant fixing them and de-virusing them and unbugging them and hauling them out of the little running circles they'd trapped themselves in, or turning them away from the unscalable wall they were attempting to leap, all the while being wary of their twin flechette-gatlings and their close-defence nano-edged blades.

'I'm a games coder,' he wailed. 'I choreograph Bollywood dance routines and arrange car crashes. I design star-vampires.' Delhi ignored his cries. Delhi was already losing as the us-too voices of national self-determination grew loud in the Rashtrapati Bhavan, but she chose to ignore them as well.

Dadaji was a cyberwarrior, Mamaji was a combat medic. It was slightly more true for her than for Dadaji. She was indeed a qualified doctor and had worked in the field for NGOs in India and Pakistan after the earthquake and with Médecins Sans Frontières in Sudan. She was not a soldier, never a soldier. But Mother India needed front-line medics so she found herself at Advanced Field Treatment Centre 32 east of Ahmedabad at the same time my father's recon unit was relocated there. My mother examined Tech-Sergeant Tushar Nariman for crabs and piles. The rest of his unit refused to let a woman doctor inspect their pubes. He made eye-contact with her, for a brave, frail second.

Perhaps if the Ministry of Defence had been less wanton in

their calling-up of cyberwarriors and had assigned a trained security analyst to the Eighth Ahmedabad Recon Mecha Squad instead of a games designer, more would have survived when the Bharati Tiger-Strike-Force attacked. A new name was being spoken in old east Uttar Pradesh and Bihar; Bharat, the old holy name of India; its spinning wheel flag planted in Varanasi, most ancient and pure of cities. Like any national liberation movement, there were dozens of self-appointed guerrilla armies, each named more scarily than the predecessor with whom they were in shaky alliance. The Bharati Tiger-Strike-Force was embryo Bharat's élite cyberwar force. And unlike Tushar, they were pros. At 21:23 they succeeded in penetrating the Eighth Ahmedabad's firewall and planted trojans into the recon mechas. As my father pulled up his pants after experiencing the fluttering fingers and inspection torch of my mother-to-be at his little rosebud, the Tiger-Strike-Force took control of the robots and turned then on the field hospital.

Lord Shiva bless my father for a fat boy and a coward. A hero would have run out onto the sand to see what was happening when the firing started. A hero would have died in the crossfire, or, when the ammunition ran out, by their blades. At the first shot, my father went straight under the desk.

'Get down!' he hissed at my mother who froze with a look part bafflement, part wonderment on her face. He pulled her down and immediately apologised for the unseemly intimacy. She had lately cupped his testicles in her hand, but he apologised. They knelt in the kneehole, side by side while the shots and the cries and the terrible, arthritic click click click of mecha joints swirled around them, and little by little subsided into cries and clicks, then just clicks, then silence. Side by side they knelt, shivering in fear, my mother kneeling like a dog on all fours until she shook from the strain, but afraid to move, to make the slightest noise in case it brought the stalking shadows that fell through the window into the surgery. The shadows grew long and grew dark before she dared exhale, 'What happened?'

'Hacked mecha,' my father said. Then he made himself forever the hero in my mother's eyes. 'I'm going to take a look.' Hand by knee by knee by hand, careful to make no noise, disturb not the least piece of broken glass or shattered wood, he crept out from under the desk across the strewn floor to underneath the window. Then, millimetre by millimetre, he edged up the side until he was in a half crouch. He glanced out the window and in the same instant dropped to the floor and began his painstaking crawl back across the floor.

'They're out there,' he breathed to Mamaji. 'All of them. They will kill anything that moves.' He said this one word at a time, to make it sound like the natural creakings and contractions of a portable hut on a Ganga sandbank.

'Perhaps they'll run out of fuel,' my mother replied.

'They run off solar batteries.' This manner of conversation took a long time. 'They can wait forever.'

Then the rain began. It was a huge thunder-plump, a fore-runner of the monsoon still uncoiling across the Bay of Bengal, like a man with a flag or a trumpet who runs before a groom to let the world know that a great man is coming. Rain beat the canvas like hands on a drum. Rain hissed from the dry sand as it was swallowed. Rain ricocheted from the plastic carapaces of the waiting, listening robots. Rain-song swallowed every noise, so that my mother could only tell my father was laughing by the vibrations he transmitted through the desk.

'Why are you laughing?' she hissed in a voice a little lower than the rain.

'Because in this din they'll never hear me if I go and get my palmer,' my father said, which was very brave for a corpulent man. 'Then we'll see who hacks whose robots.'

'Tushar,' my mother whispered in a voice like steam but my

father was already steadily crawling out from under the desk towards the palmer on the camp chair by the zip door. 'It's only п п п'

And the rain stopped. Dead. Like a mali turning off a garden hose. It was over. Drips dropped from the ridge-line and the never-weatherproof windows. Sun broke through the plastic panes. There was a rainbow. It was very pretty but my father was trapped in the middle of the tent with killer robots on the alert outside. He mouthed an excremental oath and carefully, deadly carefully reversed amongst all the shatter and tumbled debris, wide arse first like an elephant. He felt the vibration of suppressed laughter through the wooden desk sides.

'Now. What. Are. You. Laughing. At?'

'You don't know this river,' my mother whispered. 'Ganga Devi will save us yet.'

Night came swift as ever on the banks of the holy river, the same idle moon as now lights my tale rose across the scratched plastic squares of the window. My mother and father knelt, arms aching, knees tormented, side by side beneath the desk. My father said,

'Do you smell something?'

'Yes,' my mother hissed.

'What is it?'

'Water,' she said and he saw her smile in the dangerous moon-light. And then he heard it, a hissing, seeping suck sand would make if it were swallowing water but all its thirst was not enough, it was too much, too fast, too too much, it was drowning. My father smelled before he saw the tongue of water, edged with sand and straw and the flotsam of the sangam on which the camp stood, creep under the edge of the tent across the liner and around his knuckles. It smelled of soil set free. It was the old smell of the monsoon, when every dry thing has its true perfume scent and flavour and colour released by the rain; the smell of water that is the smell of everything water liberates. The tongue became a film, water flowed around their fingers and knees, around the legs of the desk as if they were the piers of a bridge. Dadaji felt my mother shaking with laughter, then the flood burst open the side of the tent and dashed dazed drowned him in a wall of water so that he spluttered and choked and tried not to cough for fear of the traitor mecha. Then he understood my mother's laughter and he laughed too, loud and hard and coughing up lungfuls of Ganges.

'Come on!' he shouted and leaped up, over-turning the desk, throwing himself onto it like a surfboard, seizing the legs with both hands. My mother dived and grabbed just as the side of the tent opened in a torrent and desk and refugees were swept away on the flood. 'Kick!' he shouted as he steered the desk toward the sagging doorway. 'If you love life and Mother India, kick!' Then they were out in the night beneath the moon. The sentinel unfolded its killing-things, blade after blade after blade, launched after them and was knocked down, bowled over, swept away by the flooding water. The last they saw of it its carapace was half-stogged in the sand, water breaking creamy around it. They kicked through the flotsam of the camp, furniture and ration packs and med kits and tech, the shorted, fused, sparked-out corpses of the mecha and the floating, spinning swollen corpses of soldiers and medics. They kicked through them all, riding their bucking desk, they kicked half-choked, shivering out into the deep green water of Mother Ganga, under the face of the full moon they kicked up the silver corridor of her river-light. At noon the next day, far far from the river beach of Chattigarh, an Indian patrol-RIB found them and hauled them, dehydrated, skin cracked and mad from the sun, into the bottom of the boat. At some point in the long night either under the desk or floating on it they had fallen in love. My mother always said it was the most romantic thing that had ever happened to her. Ganga Devi raised her waters and carried them through the killing machines to safety on a miraculous raft. Or so our family story went.

Here a God is incarnated, and then me

My parents fell in love in one country, India, and married in another, Awadh, the ghost of ancient Oudh, itself a ghost of the almost-forgotten British Raj. Delhi was no longer the capital of a great nation but of a geographical fudge. One India was now many, our mother goddess descended into a dozen avatars from re-united Bengal to Rajasthan, from Kashmir to Tamil Nadu. How had we let this happen, almost carelessly, as if we had momentarily stumbled on our march toward superpowerdom, then picked ourselves up and carried on. It was all most embarrassing, like a favourite uncle discovered with porn on his computer. You look away, you shun it, you never talk about it. Like we have never talked about the seisms of violence that tear through our dense, stratified society; the mass bloodletting of our independence that came with an excruciating partition, the constant threat of religious war, the innate, brooding violence in the heart of our caste system. It was all so very un-Indian. What are a few hundred thousand deaths next to those millions? If not forgotten, they will be ignored in a few years. And it certainly has made the cricket more interesting.

The new India suited my mother and father very well. They were model young Awadhis. My father, trapped by artificial intelligence once, vowed never to let that happen again and set up one of the first aeai farms breeding custom wares for low-level applications like Air Awadh, Delhi Bank and the Revenue Service. My mother went first for cosmetic surgery, then, after a shrewd investment in an executive enclave for the nascent Awadhi civil service, gave up the micro-manipulators for a property portfolio. Between them they made so much money that their faces were never out of *Delhi Gloss!* magazine. They were the golden couple who had sailed to a glorious future over the floods of war and the interviewers who called at their penthouse asked, *So then, where is the golden son?*

Shiva Nariman made his appearance on 27 September 2025. Siva, oldest God in the world, Siva, first and favoured, Siva from whose matted hair the holy Ganga descended, generative force, auspicious one, lord of paradox. The photo rights went to *Gupshup* magazine for five hundred thousand Awadhi rupees. The golden boy's nursery was featured on the nightly *Nationwide* show and became quite the style for a season. There was great interest in this first generation of a new nation; the Awadh Bhais, the gossip sites called them. They were the sons not just of a small coterie of prominent Delhi middle class, but of all Awadh. The nation took them to its heart and suckled them from its breasts, these bright, bouncing brilliant boys who would grow up with the new land and lead it to greatness. It was never to be mentioned, not even to be thought, how many female foetuses were curetted or flushed out or swilled away, unimplanted, into the medical waste. We were a new country, we were engaged in the great task of nation-building. We could overlook a demographic crisis that had for years been deforming our middle classes. What if there were four times as many boys as girls? They were fine strong sons of Awadh. The others, they were only females.

So easily I say *we*, for I seem to have ended up as an impresario and storyteller but the truth is that I did not exist, I didn't even exist then, not until the day the baby spoke at the Awadhi Bhai Club. It was never anything as formal as a constituted club; the blessed mothers, darlings of the nation, had fallen together by natural mutual need to cope with a media gawping into every aspect of their lives. Perfection needs a support group. They naturally banded together in each other's living rooms and penthouses, and their mothers and ayahs with them. It was a gilded Mothers and Infants group. The day the baby spoke my mother had gathered with Usha and Kiran and Devi. It was Devi's baby who spoke. Everyone was talking about exhaustion and nipple softening oil and peanut allergies when Vin Johar lolling in his rocker opened his brown brown eyes, focused across the room and clearly said, 'Hungry, want my bottle.'

'Hungry, are we my cho chweet?' Devi said.

'Now,' said Vin Johar. 'Please.'

Devi clapped her hands in delight.

'Please! He hasn't said "please" before.'

The rest of the penthouse was still staring, dazed.

'How long has he been talking?' Usha asked.

'Oh, about three days,' Devi said. 'He picks up everything you say.'

'My bottle now,' demanded Vin Johar. 'Quickly.'

'But he's only ...' Kiran said.

'Five months, yes. He's been a bit slower than Dr Rao predicted.'

The mothers' mothers and the ayahs made furtive hand gestures, kissed charms to turn away evil. It was my Mamaji, dangling fat, content Shiv on her knee, who understood first.

'You've been, you've had, he's a ...'

'Brahmin, yes.'

'But you're a Sudra,' Kiran wondered.

'Brahmin,' Devi said with such emphasis that no one could fail to hear the capital. 'We've had him done, yes.'

'Done?' asked Usha and then realised, 'Oh.' And, 'Oh!'

'He'll be tall and he'll be strong and he'll be handsome, of course; that bit we didn't have to engineer — and he'll be fit and healthy. Oh so healthy — he'll never get heart disease, arthritis, Alzheimer's, Huntingdon's; with his immune system he can laugh off almost any virus or infection. His immune system will even take out malaria! Imagine that! And intelligence; well, let's just say, Dr Rao told us there isn't even a test smart enough to stretch him. He'll just need to see a thing once and he's learned it – like that! And his memory, well, Dr Rao says there are double the number of connections in the brain, or something like that: what it means is that he'll have a phenomenal memory. Like that Mr Memory on *India's Got Talent*, only even better. He won't be able to forget anything. No forgetting birthdays and phone calls to his Mata when he's off around the world with some big corporation. Look at him, look at him, isn't he just the most gorgeous thing you've ever seen; those baby baby blue eyes. Look at you, look at you, just look at you my little lord? See them all, see them, your friends? They are princes each and every one, but you, you are a god. Oh, I could bite your bum, oh, just bite it like that it's so beautiful and plump and gorgeous.' Devi held Vin Johar up like a trophy in a cricket match. She kissed him on his bare belly where his little vest had ridden up. 'Oh you little god.'

Then Shiv let out a long wail. All through Devi's song of praise to her genetically improved darling son, my mother's grip had gradually tightened in envy on golden Shiv, now hopelessly outmoded, until he cried out in pain. Her fingers had left bruises like purple carrots along his ribs.

Shiv gazed up at the mobile turning in the air-conditioning above his cot, innocent and unaware of how his visual acuity was being stimulated by the cleverly designed blobs and clouds. My mother fretted and stormed by turns around the pastel-lit apartment until Dadaji returned from the office. After Shiv was born, his duties at the office grew more arduous and his hours longer. He was never a terribly good father really. He was useless at cricket.

'What are you doing on Friday?' Mamaji demanded.

'Um, I'm not sure, there's something at the office.'

'Cancel it.'

'What?' He was never very good at manners either, but then he was a Top Geek.

'We're seeing Dr Rao.'

'Dr who?'

'Dr Rao. At the Swaminathan Clinic.' He knew the name. He knew the clinic. All Delhi, even Top Geeks, knew of the strange and miraculous children that came out of there. He just needed a moment for his balls to unfreeze and drop from that place close to the warmth of his perineum where they had retreated in terror.

'Friday, eleven thirty, with Dr Rao himself. We are having a baby.'

It wasn't Friday eleven thirty, nor the Friday after. It was not for six Fridays, after the initial consultation and the financial check and the medical assessment and the one-to-ones, first Mamaji then Dadaji, and only then did they get to choose from the menu. It was a menu, like in the most rarefied restaurant you can imagine. My parents blinked. Intelligence yes good looks yes enhanced concentration yes expanded memory and improved recall yes health wealth strength happiness, everything Vin Johar had. And more.

'Extended lifespan?'

'Ah yes, that is a new one. A new technique that has just been licensed.'

'Does that mean?'

'Exactly what it says.

My parents blinked again.

'Your son,' (for this was me they were building) 'will enjoy a greatly increased span of life in full health and vigour.'

'How much increased?'

'Double the current human norm; what is that? Let me think,

for people like us, affluent, educated, middle class, with access to quality health-care, that's currently eighty years. Well double that.'

A third time they blinked.

'One hundred and sixty years old.'

'At the very least, you must remember that medical miracles are occurring every day. Every single day. There's no reason your son . . .'

'Vishnu.'

My father stared open-mouthed at my mother. He didn't know there was a name. He hadn't yet realised that he had no say in this whatsoever. But his balls understood, cringing in his loose-and-cooling-good-for-sperm-production silk boxers.

'Vishnu, the Lord, governor and sustainer.' Dr Rao dipped his head in respect. He was an old-fashioned man. 'You know, I have often thought how the processes of conception, gestation and parturition are reflected in the ten incarnations of Lord Vishnu: the fish the restless sperm, the turtle of Kurma the egg, the saving of the earth from the bottom of the ocean by Varaha the fertilisation . . .'

'What about the dwarf?' my father asked. 'The dwarf Brahmin?'

'The dwarf, yes,' Dr Rao drawled. He was a man of slow speech, who seemed to lose the end of his sentences the closer he approached them. This led many people to make the mistake of thinking him stupid when what he was doing was shaping the perfect conclusion. As a consequence he didn't do many television or net interviews. 'The dwarf's always the problem, isn't he? But your son will assuredly be a true Brahmin. And Kalki, yes, Kalki. The ender of the Age of Kali. Who's to say that he might not see this world end in fire and water and a new one be born? Yes, longevity. It's very good, but there are a couple of minor inconveniences.'

'Never mind. We'll have that. Devi Johar doesn't have that.'

So my father was sent with a plastic cup to catch his sacred fish. My mother went with him; to make it all act of love but mostly because she didn't trust him with Western porn. A few Fridays later Dr Rao harvested a clutch of my mother's turtle-eggs with a long needle. She didn't need my father there for that. This was an act of biology. The slow-spoken doctor did his work and called up eight blastulas from the deep ocean of his artificial wombs. One was selected: Me! Me! Little me! Here I am! See me! See me! and I was implanted into my mother's womb. It was then that she discovered the inconvenience: my doubled lifespan was bought at the price of ageing at half the speed of baseline, non-Brahminic humanity. After sixteen months of pregnancy, sixteen months of morning sickness and bloating and bad circulation and broken veins and incontinence and backache but worst of all, not being able to smoke, my mother, with a great shriek of *At last At last! Get the fucking thing out of me!* gave birth on 9 August 2027 and I made my entry as a player in this story.

My brother hates me

What a world, into which I was born! What times: an age of light and brilliance. Shining India truly found herself in Shining Awadh, Shining Bharat, Shining Maratha, Shining Bengal – all the shining facets of our many peoples. The horrors of the Schisming were put behind us, apart from war-maimed begging on metro platforms, gangs of undersocialised ex-teen-cyberwarriors, occasional flare-ups from hibernating combat 'ware buried deep in the city net and Concerned Documentary Makers who felt that we had not sufficiently mourned our self-mutilation and achieved reconciliation. Reconciliation? Delhi had no time for such Western niceties. Let the dead burn the dead, there was money to be made and pleasure to be savoured. Our new boulevards and maidans, our malls and entertainment zones were brilliant with the bright and the young and the optimistic. It was a time of bold new fashions, father-scandalising hemlines and mother-troubling hairstyles; of new trends and obsessions that were old and cold as soon as they hit the gossip sites; of ten thousand shattering new ideas that disappeared as soon as they were iterated like a quantum foam of thought. It was youth, it was confidence, it was the realisation of all that old Mother India had claimed she might be but most of all it was money. As in Delhi, so in Varanasi, Kolkata, Mumbai, Chennai, Jaipur. But most of all, I think, in Delhi. In India she had been capital by whim, not by right. Mumbai, even Kolkata always outshone her. Now she truly was capital of her own nation, without rival, and she dazzled. My earliest memory, from the time when my senses all ran together and sounds had smells and colours had textures and a unified reality above those crude divisions, was of lines of light streaming over my upturned face, light in all colours and more, light that, to an undifferentiated cortex, hummed and chimed like the sympathetic strings of a sitar. I suppose I must have been in our car with our chauffeur driving us somewhere through the downtown lights to some soirée or other, but all I remember is grinning up at the streaming, singing light. When I think of Delhi even now, I think of it as a river of light, a torrent of silver notes.

And what a city! Beyond Old Delhi and New Delhi, beyond the Newer Delhis of Gurgaon and the desirable new suburbs of Sarita Vihar and New Friends Colony, the Newest Delhis of all were rising. Invisible Delhi, Delhi of data and digits and software. Distributed Delhi, networked Delhi, Delhi woven from cable and wireless nodes, intangible Delhi woven through the streets and buildings of the material city. Strange new peoples lived here: the computer-constructed cast of *Town and Country*, the all-conquering soap opera that, in its complete artificiality, was more real than life itself. It was not just the characters who drew our fascinations, the genius of the production lay in the CG-actors who believed they played and had a separate existence from those characters, and whose gupshup and scandal, whose affairs and marriages meant more to us than our friends and neighbours. Other brilliant creatures streamed past and through us on our streets and squares: the aeais; the pantheon of artificial intelligences that served our immaterial needs from banking to legal services to household management to personal secretarial services. In no place and every place, these were entities of levels and hierarchies; high-end aeais cascading down through sub-routines into low-grade monitors and processors; thousands of those same daily-grind Level 0.8 (the intelligence of a street pig) scaling up through connection and associations into Level 1s – the intelligence of a monkey; those again aggregating together into the highest, the Level 2s, indistinguishable from a human seventy per cent of the time. And beyond them were the rumoured, feared Level 3s: of human intelligence and beyond. Who could understand such an existence, beings of many parts that did not necessarily recognise each other? The djinns, those ancient haunters of their beloved Delhi, they understood; and older than they, the gods. They understood only too well. And in the material city, new castes appeared. A new sex appeared on our streets as if stirred out of heaven, neither male nor female, rejecting the compromises of the old hijras to be aggressively neither. The nutes, they called themselves. And then of course there were those like me; improved in egg and sperm, graced with outrageous gifts and subtle curses: the Brahmins. Yes I was an upper-middle-class brat born into genetic privilege, but Delhi was laid out before me like a wedding banquet. She was my city.

Delhi loved me. Loved me, loved all of my Brahmin brothers and occasional sisters. We were wonders, freaks, miracles and avatars. We might do anything, we were the potential of Awadh. Those first-born were accidents of birth, we, the Brahmins, were the true Awadhi Bhais. We even had our own comic, of that name. With our strange genetic powers, we battled criminals, demons and Bharatis. We were superheroes. It sold pretty well.

You might think I was blithe enough, a genetically high-caste blob bouncing in my baby-rocker blinking up into the sunlight beaming through the glass walls of our tower-top penthouse. You would be wrong. As I lay giggling and blinking, neural pathways were twining up through my medulla and cerebellum and Area of Broca with preternatural speed. That blur of light, that spray of silver notes rapidly differentiated into objects, sounds, smells, sensations. I saw, I heard, I sensed but I could not yet understand. So I made connections, I drew patterns, I saw the world pouring in through my senses and up the fiery tree of my neurons as relation, as webs and nets and constellations. I formed an inner astrology and from it, before I could call dog 'dog' and cat 'cat' and Mamaji 'Mamaji', I understood the connectedness of things. I saw the bigger picture; I saw the biggest picture. This was my true superpower, one that has remained with me to this day. I never could fly to Lanka in a thought or lift a mountain by the force of my will, I was not master of fire or thunder or even my own soul, but I could always take one look and know the whole, absolute and entire.

The naming of names. That was where Mamaji first realised that Dr Rao's blessings were not unmixed. The soirée that day was at Devi Johar's house, she of the amazing Vin. There he was, running around the place with his ayah trying to keep up with him in kiddie-wear by SonSun of Los Angeles. Shiv played with the other non-Brahmins on the roof garden, happy and content at their own limited, non-enhanced activities. How fast the gilt had rubbed off him, after I was born! As for me, I sat in my bouncer, burbling and watching big-eyed the mothers of the golden. I knew Shiv's jealousy, though I didn't have the words or the emotional language for it. I saw it in a thousand looks and glances, the way he sat at the table, the way he rode in the car, the way he toddled along behind Ayah Meenakshi as she pushed me through the mall, the way he stood by my cot and gazed soft-eyed at me. I understood hate.

Vin asked Devi if he could go out and play with the others on the roof garden, please.

'All right, but don't show off,' Devi Johar said. When he had toddled away, Devi crossed her ankles demurely and placed her hands on her knees, so.

'Mira, I hope you don't mind me saying, but your Vish; well, he isn't talking yet. At his age, Vin had a vocabulary of two hundred words and a good grasp of syntax and grammar.'

'And shouldn't he be, well, at least crawling?' Usha asked.

'How old is he; fifteen months? He does seem a little on the ... small side,' Kiran chimed in.

My Mamaji broke down in tears. It was the crying nights and the sshing to sleep, the rocking and the cleaning and the mewling and puking, the tiredness, oh, the tiredness, but worst of all, the breast feeding.

'Breast? After a year?' Usha was incredulous. 'I mean, I've heard that some mothers keep them on the teat for years, but they're from the villages, or mamas who love their sons too much.'

'My nipples feel like mulberries,' my Mamaji wept. 'You see, he's fifteen months old, but biologically, he not even eight months yet.'

I would live twice as long, but age half as fast. Infancy was a huge, protracted dawn; childhood an endless morning. When Shiv started school I would only have begun toddling. When I was of university age I would still have the physiology of a nine-year- old. Adulthood, maturity, old age, were points so distant on the great plain of my lifespan that I could not tell if they were insects or cities. In those great days I would come into my own, a life long enough to become part of history; as a baby, I was a mother's nightmare.

'I know breast is best, but maybe you should consider switching to formula,' Devi said soothingly.

See how I recall every word? Another of Dr Rao's equivocal gifts. I forget only what I choose to unremember. I understood every word – at eighteen months my vocabulary was far in advance of your precious Vin, bitch Devi. But it was trapped inside me. My brain formed the words but my larynx, my tongue, my lips and lungs couldn't form them. I was a prisoner in a baby-bouncer, smiling and waving my fat little fists.

Four there were who understood me, and four only, and they lived in the soft-contoured plastic butterfly that hung over my cot. Their names were TikkaTikka, Badshanti, Pooli and Nin. They were aeais, set to watch over me and entertain me with songs and stories and pretty patterns of coloured lights because Mamaji considered Ayah Meenakshi's sleepy-time stories far too terrifying for a suggestible Brahmin. They were even more stupid than my parents but it was because they were deeply dense that they had no preconceptions beyond their Level o.2 programming and so I could communicate with them.

TikkaTikka sang songs.

In a little green boat,
On the blue sea so deep
Little Lord Vishnu
Is sailing to sleep ...

He sang that every night. I liked it, I still sing it to myself as I pole my circus of cats along the ravaged shores of Mata Ganga.

Pooli impersonated animals, badly. He was a cretin. His stupidity insulted me so I left him mute inside the plastic butterfly.

Badshanti, lovely Badshanti, she was the weaver of stories. 'Would you like to hear a story, Vishnu?' were the words that led into hours of wonder. Because I don't forget. I know that she never repeated a story, unless I asked her to. How did I ask? For that I must introduce the last of my four aeais.

Nin spoke only in patterns of light and colour that played across my face, an ever-wheeling kaleidoscope that was supposed to stimulate my visual intelligence. Nin-no-words was the intelligent one; because he could interpret facial expression, he was the one I first taught my language. It was a very simple language of blinking. One deliberate blink for yes, two for no. It was slow, it was tortuous but it was a way out of the prison of my body. With Nin reading my answers to Badshanti's questions, I could communicate anything.

How did my brother hate me? Let me take you to that time in Kashmir. After the third drought in a row my mother vowed never again to spend a summer in Delhi's heat, noise, smog and disease. The city seemed like a dog lying at the side of the street, panting and feral and filthy and eager for any excuse to sink its teeth into you, waiting for the monsoon. Mamaji looked to the example of the British of a hundred years before and took us up to the cool and the high places. Kashmir! Green Kashmir, blue lake, the bright houseboats and the high beyond all, the rampart of mountains. They still wore snow, then. I remember blinking in the wonder of the Dal Lake as the shikara sped us across the still water to the hotel rising sheer like a palace in one of Badshanti's tales from the water. My four friends bobbed in the wind of our passage as the boat curved in across the lake to the landing stage where porters in red turbans waited to transport us to our cool summer apartment. Shiv stood in the bow. He wanted to throw them the landing rope.

The calm, the clear, the high cool of Kashmir after the mob

heat of Delhi! I bobbed and bounced and grinned in my cot and waved my little hands in joy at the sweet air. Every sense was stimulated, every nerve vibrant. In the evening TikkaTikka would sing, Badshanti tell a story and Nin send stars sweeping over my face.

There was to be an adventure by boat across the lake. There was food and there was drink. We were all to go together. It was a thing of a moment, I can see it still, so small it looked like an accident. It was not. It was deliberate, it was meticulously planned.

'Where's Gundi-bear? I've lost Gundi-bear,' Shiv cried as my father was about to get into the boat. 'I need Gundi-bear.' He launched towards the shore along the gangplank. Dadaji swept him up.

'Oh no you don't; we'll never get anywhere at this rate. You stay here and don't move. Now, where did you last see him?'

Shiv shrugged, innocently forgetful.

'Here, I'll come with you, you'll never find anything the way you ram and stam around.' My mother sighed her great sigh of exasperation. 'Shiv, you stay here, you hear? Don't touch anything. We'll be back in two ticks.'

I felt a deeper shadow in the mild shade of the awning. Shiv stood over me. Even if I chose to I could not forget the look on his face. He ran up the gangplank, untied the mooring rope and let it fall into the water. He waggled his fingers, *bye bye* as the wind caught the curve of coloured cotton and carried me out into the lake. The frail little shikara was taken far from the shelter of the Lake Hotel's island into the rising chop. The wind caught it and turned it. The boat rolled. I began to cry.

Nin saw my face change. TikkaTikka awoke in the little plastic butterfly my parents had hung from the bamboo ridge pole.

The lake is big and the lake deep
And Little Lord Vishnu is falling asleep
The wind is high and the sun is beaming
To carry you off to the kingdom of dreaming, he sang

'Hello Vishnu,' Badshanti said. 'Would you like a story today?'
Two blinks.
'Oh, no story? Well then, I'll just let you sleep. Sweet dreams,
Vishnu.'
Two blinks.
'You don't want a story but you don't want to sleep?'
One blink.
'All right then, let's play a game.'
Two blinks. Badshanti hesitated so long I thought her software
had hung. She was a pretty rudimentary aeai.
'Not a game, not a story, not sleep?' I blinked. She knew better
than to ask, 'Well, what do you want?' Now TikkaTikka sang a
strange song I had never heard before,

Wind and lake water
And gathering storm,
Carry Lord Vishnu
Far into harm.

Yes. The shikara was far from shore, broadside to the wind
and rolling on the chop. One gust could roll it over and send me
to the bottom of the Dal Lake. I might be a hero in my own comic
but Dr Rao had neglected to give me the genes for breathing
underwater.
'Are we on a boat, sailing far far away?' Badshanti asked.
Yes.
'Are you out on water?'
Yes.

'Are we on our own?'

Yes.

'Is Vishnu happy?'

No.

'Is Vishnu scared?'

Yes.

'Is Vishnu safe?'

Two blinks. Again Badshanti paused. Then she started to shout. 'Help aid assist! Little Lord Vishnu is in peril! Help aid assist!' The voice was thin and tinny and would not have reached any distance across the wind-ruffled lake but one of the silent aeais, perhaps stupid Pooli, must also have sent out a radio, bluetooth and GPS alarm, for a fishing boat suddenly changed course, opened up its long-tail engine and sped towards me on a curve of spray.

'Thank you thank you sirs and saviours,' Badshanti babbled as the two fishermen hauled my shikara close with their hard hands and to their astonishment saw a child lying on the mattresses, smiling up at them.

A map drawn inside the skull

All my long life I have been ordained to be tied to water. My parents were delivered by the flood, my aeais saved me from the drifting boat. Even now I pick my way down the shrivelled memory of the Ganga, descended from the hair of Siva. Water it was that made me into a superhero of Awadh, albeit of a very different, non-tall-building-leaping type from the Awadhi Bhai who refused to grow up through the pages of Virgin comics.

There was of course no end of ruction after five-and-half-year-old Shiv tried to expose me in an open boat. He made no attempt to deny it. He bore it stoically. The worst of it was my father's therapy-speak. I almost felt for him. At least my mother was angry, blazingly, searingly angry. She didn't try to wrap it up in swathes of *How did you find it* and *I imagine you're feeling* and *Let's try and talk through this like men*. It didn't end when the monsoon finally came late and scanty and we returned to Delhi slick and greasy with rain, the wonderful, rich smell of wet dust perfuming the air more purely than any incense. Four days later it ended and Delhi became afraid. That was how my parents kept the story out of the papers. FIFTEEN MILLION THIRSTY THROATS is a more immediate headline than FIVE-YEAR-OLD TRIES TO DROWN BRAHMIN BROTHER. Just.

There was counselling, of course, long and expensive and in the end producing no better result than the child psychologist saying, 'This is possibly the most intractable case of sibling rivalry I have ever seen. Your son has a colossal sense of entitlement and deeply resents what he perceives as a loss of status and parental affection. He's quite unrepentant and I fear he might make a second attempt to cause Vishnu harm.' My parents took these words and reached their own solution. Shiv and I could not live together so we must live apart. My father took an apartment across the city. Shiv went with him. I stayed with Mamaji, and one other. Before they parted, plump Tushar loved my mother a goodbye-time, without planning or sex selection or genetic regulation. And so Sarasvati was born, the last of the three gods; my sister.

We grew up together. We lay in our cots side by side, looking not at our stimulating and educational toys but at each other. For a blissful time she paralleled me. We learned to walk and talk and regulate our bowels together. When we were alone I would murmur the words I knew to her, the words that had roosted and chattered so long in my skull and now were free, like someone throwing open a dark and fetid pigeon loft on a Delhi rooftop. We were close as twins. Then week by week, month by month, Sarasvati outgrew me. Bigger, better coordinated, more physically developed, her tongue never stumbled over her few and simple words while poems and vedas rattled inarticulate inside me. She grew out of being twin to bigger sister. She was the surprise, the delight, the child free from expectations and thus she could never disappoint. I loved her. She loved me. In those murmurous evenings filled with sunset and the cool of the air-conditioning, we found a common language and knowing born of shared playing that our various and despised ayahs, even our mother, could never penetrate.

Across the city, on his own glass towertop filled with the staggering, pollution-born sunsets of great Delhi, Shiv grew up apart. He was six and a half, he was top of his class, he was destined for greatness. How do I know this? Once a week my father came to see his other son and daughter, and for a snatched evening with his darling. I had long superseded TikkaTikka, Pooli, Nin and Badshanti with more powerful (and discreet) aeai attendants, ones that, as soon as I had the words on my tongue, I found I could reprogram to my needs. I sent them out like djinns through the apartment. Not a word was spoken, not a glance exchanged that I could not know it. Sometimes the glances would become looks, and the murmurs cease and my parents would make love to each other. I saw that too. I did not think it particularly wrong or embarrassing; I knew fine and well what they were doing but, though it made them very happy, it did not look like a thing I would ever want.

I look back now from age and loss and see those babbling days with Sarasvati as the age of gold, our Satya Yuga of innocence and truth. We stumbled together towards the sunlight and found joy in every fall and bump and grin. Our world was bright and full of surprises, delights in discovery for Sarasvati, pleasure in her evident delight for me. Then school forced us apart. What a terrible, unnecessary thing school is. I feel in it the enduring envy of parents for idle childhood. Of course it could be no ordinary school for little Lord Vishnu. Dr Renganathan Brahminical College was an academy for the élite of the élite. Education was intimate and bespoke. There were eight in my year and that was large enough for divisions. Not all Brahmins were equal in the Dr Renganathan College. Though we were all the same age we divided ourselves, quite naturally, like meiosis, into Old Brahmins and Young Brahmins, or, as you like, Big Brahmins and Little Brahmins. Those who aged half as fast but would live twice as long and those who would enjoy all the gifts of health and smarts and looks and privilege but would still fall dead at whatever age the meditech of that era could sustain. Intimations of mortality in Miss Mukudan's reception class.

Ah, Miss Mukudan! Your golden bangles and your Cleopatra smiling eyes, your skin the soft dark of the deepest south; your ever-discreet moustache and smell of camphor as you bent over me to help my fumble-fingers with my buttons or the Velcro fastenings on my shoes. You were my first vague love. You were the undifferentiated object of affection of all of us. We loved you for your lofty remoteness, your firmness and hinted-at tetchiness and the delicious knowledge that to you we were just more children to be turned from blind and selfish little barbarians into civilised young human beings. We loved you because you were not the mother-smother of our cottonwool parents. You took no shit.

The Class of '31 was too much even for the redoubtable Miss Mukudan. At age four our engineered brains were pushing us down the strange and separate roads into strange ways of looking at the world, quasi-autistic obsessions, terrifying savant insights or just plain incomprehensibility. We were each given a per-sonalised tutor to accompany us day and night. Mine was called Mr Khan and he lived inside my ear. A new technology had arrived to save us. It was the latest thing in comms – which has always seemed the most faddish and trivial of technologies to me. No more did you need to be trapped by screens or pictures in the palm of your hand or devices that wrote on your eyeball as delicately as a bazaar fakir writing tourists' names on a grain of rice. A simple plastic hook behind the ear would beam cyberspace into your head. Direct electromagnetic stimulation of the visual, auditory and olfactory centres now peopled the world with ghost messages and data spreads, clips from *Town and Country*, video messages, entire second-life worlds and avatars and, inevitably, spam and junk mailing. And for me, my customised aeai tutor, Mr Khan.

How I hated him! He was everything Miss Mukudan was not; irascible, superior, gruff and persistent. He was a little waspy Muslim, thin as a wire with a white moustache and a white Nehru cap. I would rip off the 'hoek in frustration and whenever I put it on again, after Miss Mukudan's ministrations – we would do anything for her – he would take up his harangue from the very syllable at which I had silenced him.

'Look and listen, you bulging pampered privileged no-right-to-call-yourself-a-proper-Brahmin brat,' he would say. 'These eyes these ears, use them and learn. This is the world and you are in it and of it and there is no other. If I can teach you this I will have taught you all you need to ever learn.'

He was a stern moralist, very proper and Islamic. I looked at Miss Mukudan differently then, wondering what assessments she had made that assigned Mr Khan especially to me. Had he been programmed just for Vishnu? How had he been built? Did he spring into being perfectly formed or did he have a history, and how did he think of this past? Did he know it for a lie, but a treasured one; was he like the self-deceiving aeai actors of *Town and Country* who believed they existed separately from the roles they played? If he masqueraded as intelligent, did that mean he was intelligent? Was intelligence the only thing that could not be simulated? Such thoughts were immensely interesting to a strange little eight year old suddenly becoming aware of those other strange citizens of his tight world. What was the nature of the acais, those ubiquitous and for the most part unseen denizens of great Delhi? I became quite the junior philosopher.

'What is right to you?' I asked him one day as we rode back in the Lexus through a Delhi melted by the heat into an impermeable black sludge. It was Ashura. Mr Khan had told me of the terrible battle of Karbala and the war between the sons of the Prophet (Peace be upon Him). I watched the chanting, wailing men carrying the elaborate catafalques, flogging their backs bloody, beating their foreheads and chests. The world, I was beginning to realise, was far stranger than I.

'Never mind me, what is right to me, impudent thing. You have the privileges of a god, you're the one needs to think about right action,' Mr Khan declared. In my vision he sat beside me on the back seat of the Lex, his hands primly folded in his lap.

'It's a serious question.' Our driver hooted up alongside the dour procession. 'How can right action mean anything to you, when anything you do can be undone and anything you undo can be done again. You're chains of digits, what do you need morality for?' Only now was I beginning to understand the existence of the aeais, which had begun with the mystery of TikkaTikka, Pooli, Badshanti and Nin living together and sharing common code inside my plastic butterfly. Common digits but separate personalities. 'It's not as if you can hurt anyone.'

'So right action is refraining from causing pain, is it?'

'I think that it's the start of right action.'

'These men cause pain to themselves to express sorrow for wrong action; albeit the actions of their spiritual forebears. In so doing they believe they will make themselves more moral men.

Consider those Hindu sadhus who bear the most appalling privations to achieve spiritual purity.'

'Spiritual purity isn't necessarily morality,' I said, catching the line Mr Khan had left dangling for me. 'And they choose to do it to themselves. It's something else altogether if they choose to do it to others.'

'Even if it means those others may be made better men?'

'They should be left to make their own minds up on that.'

We cruised past the green-draped faux-coffin of the martyr.

'So what then is the nature of my relationship with you? And your mother and father?'

My Mamaji, my Dadaji! Two years after that conversation, almost to the day, my flawless memory recalls, when I was a nine-year-old-in-a-four-year-old's body and Sarasvati was a cat-lean, ebullient seven, my mother and father very gently, very peacefully, divorced. The news was broken by the two of them sitting at opposite ends of the big sofa in the lounge with the smog of Delhi glowing in the afternoon sun like a saffron robe. A full range of aeai counselling support hovered around the room, in case of tears or tantrums or anything else they couldn't really handle. I remember feeling a suspicion of Mr Khan on the edge of my perceptions. Divorce was easy for Muslims. Three words and it was over.

'We have something to tell you, my loves,' said my mother. 'It's me and your father. Things haven't been going so well with us for quite some time and well, we've decided that it's best for everyone if we were to get a divorce.'

'But it won't mean I'll ever stop being your Dad,' plump Tushar said quickly. 'Nothing'll change, you'll hardly even notice. You'll still keep living here, Shiv will still be with me.'

Shiv. I hadn't forgotten him – I couldn't forget him – but he had slipped from my regard. He was more distant than a cousin, less thought of than those remote children of your parents' cousins, to whom I've never considered myself related at all. I did not know how he was doing at school or who his friends were or what sports he was on. I did not care how he lived his life or pursued his dreams across that great wheel of lives and stories. He was gone from me.

We nodded bravely and trembled our lips with the right degree of withheld emotion and the counsel-aeais dissolved back into their component code clusters. Much later in the room we had shared as bubbling babies and was now our mutual den, Sarasvati asked me, 'What's going to happen to us?'

'I don't think we'll even notice,' I said. 'I'm just glad they can stop having that ugly, embarrassing sex.'

Ah! Three little letters. Sex sex sex, the juggernaut looming over our childhoods. The kiddy thrill of being naked – doubly exciting in our body-modest society – took on an edge and became something I did not quite understand. Oh, I knew all the words and the locations, as Sarasvati and I played our games of doctors and patients in our den, her pulling up her little vest and pulling down her pants as I listened and examined and prodded vaguely. We knew these were grown-up things not for the eyes of grown-ups. Mamaji would have been horrified and called in squadrons of counselling 'ware if she had discovered our games but I had long since suborned the aeais. If she had looked at the security monitors she would have seen us watching the Cartoon Network; my own little CG *Town and Country* playing just for her. Sex games for children; everyone plays them. Bouncing up and down in the pool, pressing ourselves against the jets in the rooftop spa, suspecting *something* in the lap of artificial waves across our private places as ochre dust-smog from the failed monsoon suffocated Delhi. And when we played horsey-horsey, she riding me around like Lakshmibai the warrior Rani, there was more in the press of her thighs than just trying to hold on as I cantered across the carpets. I knew what it should be, I was mostly baffled by my body's failure to respond the way a twelve-year-old's ought. My lust may have been twelve but my body was six. Even Miss Mukudan's purity and innocence lost its lustre as I began to notice the way her breasts moved as she leaned over me, or the shape of her ass – demurely swathed in a sari, but no concealment was enough for the lusty curiosity of boy-Brahmins – as she turned to the smart-silk board.

'Now,' said Mr Khan one day on the back seat of the Lexus. 'Concerning onanism ...' It was a dreadful realisation. By the time puberty hit me like a hammer I would be twenty-four. Mine was the rage and impotence of angels.

Now five burning years have passed and we are driving in a fast German car. I am behind the wheel. The controls have been specially modified so that I can reach the pedals. The gear-shift is a standard. If I cut you up on the Siri Ring, after the flicker of road rage, you'd wonder: that's a child driving that Mercedes. I don't think so. I'm of legal age. I passed my test without any bribery or coercion; well, none that I know of. I am old enough to drive, get married and smoke. And I smoke. We all smoke, my Little Brahmin classmates and me. We smoke like stacks, it can't do us any harm, though we are all wearing smogmasks. The monsoon has failed for the fourth time in seven years; whole tracts of north India are turning into dust and blowing through the hydrocarbon-clogged streets and into our lungs. A dam is being built on the Ganges, Kunda Khadar, on the border with our eastern neighbour Bharat. It is promised to slake our thirst for a generation but the Himalaya glaciers have melted into gravel and Mother Ganga is starved and frail. The devotees at the Siva temple in the middle of the Parliament Street roundabout protest at the insult to the holy river with felt-marker banners and three-pronged trisuls. We bowl past them, hooting and waving and up Sansad Marg around Vijay Chowk. The comics portraying us as Awadh's new superheroes were quietly dropped years ago. Now what we see about ourselves in print tends to be headlines like TINY TEARAWAYS TERRORISE TILAK NAGAR, or BADMAJI BABY BRAHMINS.

There are four of us, Purrzja, Shayman, Ashurbanipal and me. We are all from the college – still the Brahminical College! – but when we are out we all have our own names, names we've made up for ourselves that sound strange and alien, like our DNA. Strange and alien we make ourselves look too; our own style cobbled from any source that seems remote and outré: J-punk hair, Chinese bows and ribbons, French street sports fashion and tribal make-up entirely of our own design. We are the scariest-looking eight-year-olds on the planet. By now Sarasvati is a coltish, classy fifteen-year-old. Our closeness has unravelled; she has her own social circles and friends and crushing things of the heart that seem so important to her. Shiv, so I hear, is in his first year at the University of Awadh Delhi. He won a scholarship. Best marks in his school. He's followed his father into inform-atics. Me, I howl up and down the boulevards of Delhi trapped in the body of a kid.

We race past the open arms of the Rashtrapati Bhavan. The red stone looks insubstantial as sand in the amber murk.

'That's your home, that is, Vish,' Purrzja shouts through her mask. It's well known that Mamaji Has Plans for me. Why should she not? Every other part of me is designed. A good legal job, a prominent practice, a safe parliamentary seat and a steady, planned ascent towards the top of whatever political party afforded the best chance of ambition. It's assumed that one day I will lead the nation. I'm designed to rule. I floor the pedal and the big Merc leaps forward. Traffic parts like my divine counterpart churning the soma. Their autodrive aeais make them as nervous as pigeons.

Out on the Siri Ring; eight lanes of taillights in each direction, a never ceasing roar of traffic. The car eases into the flow. Despite the barriers and warning signs police pull twenty bodies a day from the soft shoulder. The ring does not obey old Indian rules of traffic. Men race here, hedge-fund managers and datarajas and self-facilitating media mughals; racing around the twin chambers of Delhi's heart. I flick on the autodrive. I am not here to race. I am here for sex. I recline the driving seat, roll over and Ashurbanipal is beneath me. Her hair is drawn back behind her ear to show off the plastic curl of the 'hoek. It's part of the look.

I snap the fingers of my right hand into my palm to activate the software in the palmer glove. I hold that hand a hovering few centimetres above her fluorescent body-paint-stained belly. I don't touch. We never touch. That's the rule. Sex has rules. I move my hand in a series of gestures as gentle and precise as any classical dancer's mudras over Ashurbanipal. Not touching, never touching, never even flexing a finger. It's not about physical touch. It's our own thing. But inside her head, I am touching her, more intimately than any rubbing or pushing or chafing of *parts*. The 'hoek beams signals through the bone, stimulating those parts of the brain that correspond to my slow calligraphy. I am writing my signature across her body. As she in return maps the me drawn on the inside of my skull. How does it feel? Like a cat must feel when it's stroked. Like an otter must feel diving and turning and performing its underwater acrobatics. Like a fire must feel when the wind catches it and sweeps it up a forested mountainside. And without the poetry; like I want to cringe and melt at the same time. Like I must move in a direction I can't explain and my body can't express. Like there is something in my mouth that grows bigger with every second but never changes size, like a reverse turd, only sweet and joyful, is working its way back up into my colon. Like I need need need to pee something that isn't pee that my body hasn't learned yet. Like I want this to end and never end. It goes on for a long long time and terrible little crying noises come out of our eight-year-aged lips as the aeai steers us through the howling torus of traffic on Siri Ring. We are teens and we are making out in the car.

There is a coming. Oh yes, there is a coming. Like soft fireworks, or the giggling drop at the top of a Ferris wheel or the feeling you get on those nights when the air is clear and you can see out from the roof pool all the billion lights of Delhi and you are connected to every single one. Like a djinn, made of fire. Ecstatic and guilty and dirty, like you've shouted a dirty word at a sophisticated party. My nipples are very very sensitive.

Then I start with Purrzja. And then Shayman. As I said, it's entirely our own thing. It's well into dark by the time we put up our seats and straighten our clothing and re-gel our hair and I flick off the autodrive and take us up out and over the Ring on a curving off ramp to a club. It's a bit of a freak place – nutes like it and where nutes are welcome we are usually welcome – but the door knows us – knows our money – and there are always chati mag paps there. Tonight is no exception: we pose and pimp and preen for the cameras. I can write the society column headlines already. GENE-TWEAK FREAKS ON COCK-TAIL CLUB ORGY. Except we don't drink. We're underage for that.

It's always late when we get back. Only the house steward and aeais wait for us, gently chiding that it is a school day tomorrow. Don't they understand that those are the best nights? This night the lights are on in the big drawing room. I can see them from the approach to the car park. My mother waits for me. She's not alone. There's a man and a woman with her, money people, I can tell that right away from their shoes, their fingernails, their teeth, the cut of their clothes and the prickle of aeai servitors hovering around them; all those things I can assess in a glance.

'Vishnu, this is Nafisa and Dinesh Misra.'

I namaste, a vision in clashing cross-cultural trash.

'They are going to be your new mother and father-in-law.'

My lovely consort

My cats can do other tricks too; I feel you grow bored of them running in their ring. Cats! Cats! See, a clap of my hands and they go and sit on their little stools: Matsya and Kurma, Varaha and Narasimha, Vamana, Parashurama, Rama and Krishna and Buddha and Kalki. Good cats. Clever cats. Rama, stop licking yourself. Hah! One word from me and they do as they will. Now, please feel this hoop, just ordinary paper. Yes? Yes. And these, the same, yes? Yes.

I set them out around the ring. Tabby Parashurama is squeezing his eyes closed in that way that makes him look very very smug.

By the way, I must thank you for coming to watch *The Marvellous, the Magical, the Magnificent Vishnu Cat Circus*. Yes, that's the official name. It's on the letters of registration. Yes, and I pay whatever taxes are due. It's a small entertainment, but at least it's working. You have solar? Not hooked up to the zero point? Very long-sighted of you. Now: watch! Varaha, Vamana, Buddha and Kalki!

They flow from their painted stools like liquid and run around the inside of the ring, an effortless, cat-lazy lope. The trick with cat circuses, I have found, is to convince them they are doing it for themselves.

And lo! I clap my hands and in perfect unison my cats leap from their ordained orbits clean through the paper hoops. Your applause please, but not for me: for Varaha, Vamana, Buddha and Kalki. Now they run in a circle, hurdling through the hoops. What was that? Is there a lesson in every trick? What do you mean? The spiritual significance of the cats I call to perform? I hadn't thought of that. I don't think cats especially spiritual; quite the reverse; they are the most worldly and sensual of creatures, though the Prophet Mohammed, so it's said, was a great lover of cats and famously cut the sleeve from his robe rather than disturb a cat that had fallen asleep there.

Now, on with the story. Where am I going? Don't you know it's a terrible rudeness to interrupt the storyteller? You came here to see the cat circus, not watch some old goondah spin a yarn? You've seen cats leap through paper hoops, what more do you want? Where am I going? Very well then, to Varanasi. No, I am not. Look at me, look at this forehead, put your finger there, yes right there, do you see a tilak, do you feel a little crusty lump, do you feel anything but my own skin? No you do not. It's not just the bodhisofts who go to Varanasi. Here's the deal. I have plenty more tricks in my little ring here on the sand, but to see them you will have to listen to my story and remember, the power may be working but the broadcasters are out. Nothing on your screens tonight. But you'll like this. It's a wedding scene. What is a story without a wedding?

Elephants bore me. When I say that I don't mean that I find the pachyderm genus tedious, as if I have some special personal conversational relationship with them and knew all their conversational tics and ploys. Is Ganesh not the best-loved god in our entire profligate pantheon? I mean, simply, that elephants carried me; in a howdah like a small gilt temple through the streets of Delhi. Five elephants, with mahouts; one for my school friend Suresh Hira, one for Vin Johar, one for Syaman and one, my sole spit of defiance in the face of tradition, for Sarasvati, and one for me, Vishnu Nariman Raj, the gnarly groom. Delhi's eternal, monstrous traffic broke around the horde of musicians, drummers, dancers, merry-meeters like water. The traffic news had been reporting me as a major congestion for hours. People stopped and stared, women threw rice, ayahs pointed me out to their finger-sucking grandchildren: *There, there he is, Lord Vishnu goes to his wedding.* The chati mags had been full of little else than the first dynastic Brahmin marriage. My other break with tradition: much of the gaudy I had funded myself through the judicious auctioning of the photo rights to *Gupshup* magazine. Look, here am I, in white sherwani and wrinkle-ankle pants in the vest best style, the traditional veil of flowers over my face, gripping my sword with one hand (a ludicrous affectation by Sreem, Delhi's most-sought nute wedding choreographer; who could ever sword-fight from the broad back of an elephant?), with the other gripping white-knuckled to the gold-leaf coping of my swaying howdah. Have I said that riding an elephant is like being on a boat on unstill waters? Does what you glimpse through the cascading marigolds look afraid? Were you expecting someone larger?

Negotiations had been protracted and delicate over the winter. Hosts of aeai attorneys circled and clashed around my mother and father, temporarily unified, as they entertained the Misras to a grand vagdana. Lakshmi and I sat blandly, quietly, hands folded neatly in our laps on the cream leather sofa as relatives and relatives-to-be passed and greeted and blessed us. We smiled. We nodded. We did not speak, not to our guests, not to each other. In our years together at the Dr Renganathan Brahminical College we had said all that we could say to each other. We sat like an old married couple at a metro stop. At last the hosts of clashing attorney aeais withdrew: a pre-nuptial contract was drafted, a dowry was set. It was a brilliant match; property and 'ware with water, the very essence of life. Of course the price was high; we were Brahmins. It was no less than the flesh of our flesh and the seed of our loins, for all generations. Way down the list of ticky boxes on Dr Rao's shopping list was one I suspect Lakshmi's parents had fielded blindly. I know my parents had. But it was perhaps the most profound change of all that Dr Rao's nanoworkers worked on us. Our genelines were modified. The traits engineered into us were inheritable. Our children and their children, all our conceivable Nariman-Misras marching into futurity, would be Brahmins, not from the microsurgery of Dr Rao, but from our sperm and eggs.

Children, offspring, a line, a dynasty. That was our mutually contracted dowry. A match was made! Let great Delhi rejoice!

The janampatri aeais had read the stars for the most auspicious fates, the pandit had made the puja to Ganesh and the joint houses of Nariman and Misra had hired Gupshup Girls, Delhi's biggest and brassiest girl band to sing and flash their thighs for two thousand society guests at our sangeet sandhya. Lakshmi duetted onstage with them. Pop-girli hotpants and belly-top looked disturbing on her as she danced and skipped among the high heels. Too small, too too young to wed. I was never much of a singer. Mamaji and Dadaji had neglected to ticky that box. I boogied down in the golden circle with my classmates. Though I had still two years more at Dr Renganathan College under the tutelage of the invisible Mr Khan, our circle was broken. I was all their imminent futures.

At India Gate, Sarasvati called her mahout to a halt and slipped from her elephant's back to run and dance among my parade of Baraatis. I had defied tradition by inviting her, she defied it back by coming dressed as a man in sherwani and kohl and huge, ludicrous false Rajput moustache. I watched her leap and whirl, brilliant and vivacious with the dancers and drummers and dance, laughing, with monkey-like Sreem and felt tears in my eyes behind my veil of flowers. She was so brilliant, so lovely, so lithe and free from expectation.

At Lodi Gardens the celebrity spotters were five deep. Policemen held them back with a chain of linked lathis. They had seen Rishi Jaitly and Anand Arora and ooh, isn't that Esha Rathore the famous dancer and who is that little man with the very much younger wife; don't you know, it's Narayan Mittal from Mittal Industries. Last and least to them was the seeming child perched high on the back of a painted wedding elephant. A blare of trumpets and a barrage of drums greeted us. Then the smartsilk screens draped around us woke up and filled with the characters and, in a never-before-seen-feat of CG prestidigitation, the cast of *Town and Country* singing and dancing our wedding song specially written by legendary screen composer A. H. Husayin. They were aeais; singing and dancing were easy for them. There, almost lost among the sari silk and garlands as the bridal party stepped forward to greet us, was Lakshmi.

We were swept on a wave of drum beating and brass-tootling to the pavilions arrayed across the well-watered grass like a Mughal invasion. We feasted, we danced, we were sat on our thrones, our feet not touching the ground, and received our guests.

I didn't see him. The line was long and the atmosphere in the marquee stifling and I was bloated and drowsy from wedding food. I took the hand blindly, bored. I only became attentive when it held mine that moment too long, that quantum too firmly.

Shiv.

'Brother.'

I nodded in acknowledgement.

'Are you well?'

He indicated his suit, the fabric cheap, the cut niggardly, the cufflinks and the jewel at the shirt-throat phoney. A budget wedding outfit. Tomorrow it would go by phatphat back to the hire shop.

'I'll be more suitably dressed when you come to my wedding.'

'Are you getting married?'

'Doesn't everyone?'

I sniffed then. It was not Shiv's perfume – that too smelled cheap and phenolic. My uniquely-connected senses show me subtleties to which others are quite oblivious. In his student hire-

258

suit and cheap Bata shoes, Shiv seemed to carry an aura around him, a presence, a crackle of information like distant summer thunder. He smelled of aeais. I tilted my head to one side. Did I see a momentary shifting glow? It did not take a synaesthete or a Brahmin to spot the 'hoek tucked behind his ear.

'Thank you for coming,' I said and knew that he heard the lie.

'I wouldn't have missed it.'

'We must meet up some time,' I went on, compounding the lie. 'When Lakshmi and I get back into Delhi. Have you over to the place.'

'It's not going to be terribly likely,' Shiv said. 'I'm going to Bharat as soon as I graduate. I've a post-grad lined up at the University of Varanasi. Nano-informatics. Delhi's not a good place for anyone working in artificial intelligence. The Americans are breathing down Srivastava's neck to ratify the Hamilton Treaty.'

I consumed news, all news, any news, as universally and unthinkingly as breathing. I could watch twelve screens of television and tell you what was happening on any of them, simultaneously scan a tableful of newspapers and reproduce any article verbatim; I frequently kept my newsfeeds on brain drip waking and sleeping, beaming the happening world into my tiny head. I knew too well of the international moves, begun by the United States to restrict artificial intelligence by licence. Fear motivates them; that vague Christian millennial dread of the work of our own hands rising up and making itself our god. Artificial intelligences with a thousand, ten thousand, infinite times our human intelligence, whatever that means. Intelligence, when you look down on it from above, is a very vague terrain. Nevertheless police forces had been established, Krishna Cops, charged with hunting down and eliminating rogue aeais. Fine title, vain hope. Aeais were utterly different from us; intelligences that could be in many places at one time, that could exist in many different avatars, that could only move by copying themselves, not as I moved, lugging about my enhanced intelligence in the calcium bowl of my skull. They had very good guns, but I think my gnawing fear was aeais today, Brahmins tomorrow. Humans are very jealous gods.

I knew that it was inevitable that Awadh would sign up to the accord in return for favoured nation grants from the US. Neighbouring Bharat would never accede to that; its media industry, dependent on artificial intelligence for the success of *Town and Country* from Djakarta to Dubai, was too influential a lobby. The world's first overt soapocracy. And, I foresaw, the world's first data-haven nation state. Stitching together stories buried way down the business news, I was already seeing a pattern of software house relocations and research foundations moving to Varanasi. So Shiv, ambitious Shiv, Shiv-building-your-own-glory while I merely obeyed the imperative in my DNA, Shiv with your whiff of aeais around you, what is it in Bharat? Would you be a researcher into technologies as sky-blue as Lord Krishna himself, would you be a dataraja with a stable of aeais pretending they can't pass the Turing Test?

'Not that we ever exactly lived in each other's pockets,' I said prissily. We had lived with twenty million people between us for most of our lives but still anger boiled within me. What had I to be resentful of? I had all the advantage, the love, the blessing and the gifts yet here he was in his cheap hire suit smug and assured and I was the ludicrous little lordling, the boy-husband swinging his legs on his golden throne.

'Not really no,' Shiv said. Even in his words, his smile, there was an aura, an intensity; Shiv-plus. What was he doing to himself, that could only be consummated in Varanasi?

The line was restless now, mothers shifting from foot to foot in their uncomfortable wedding shoes. Shiv dipped his head, his eyes meeting mine for an instant of the purest, most intense hatred. Then he moved on into the press of guests, picking up a glass of champagne here, a plate of small eats there, a strangely singular darkness like a plague at the wedding.

The caterers cleared away, torches were lit across the heel-trodden grass of Lodi Gardens and the pandit tied us together in marriage. As fireworks burst over the tomb of Muhammad Shah and the dome of Bara Gumbad we drove away to the plane. We left the diamond stain of bright Delhi behind us and flew, far later than tots of our size should be up, through the night into morning as the private helicopter lifted us up and away to the teahouse in the cool and watered green hills. Staff discreetly stowed our baggage, showed us the lie of the rooms, the shaded verandah with its outlook over the heart-stunning gold and purple of the morning Himalayas, the bedroom with the one huge four-poster bed. Then they swept away in a rustle of silk and we were alone, together, Vishnu and Lakshmi, two gods.

'It's good isn't it?'

'Lovely. Wonderful. Very spiritual. Yes.'

'I like the rooms. I like the smell of the wood, old wood.'

'Yes, it is good. Very old wood.'

'This is the honeymoon then.'

'Yes.'

'We're supposed to ...'

'Yes. I know. Do you ... are you?'

'Wired? No I was never into that.'

'Oh. Well, I've some other stuff in my bag, it should work on you as well.'

'You've tried it?'

'Sometimes. I'm finding it gets hard all on its own now, just like that, nothing in particular, so I try it then.'

'Is it productive?'

'It's a bit like the 'hoek sex. Feeling you really really need to pee something that isn't pee and isn't there. To be honest, not as good. Have you tried?'

'With the fingers? Oh yes, with the whole hand. It's like you.'

'Need to pee?'

'Something like that. More of a clench. It works on a swing too. I don't really think I want to use something you have on you, you know.'

'I suppose not. We could ... I could ...'

'I don't really think so.'

'Do you think they'll check? Save the sheets and show them round to all the relatives?'

'At our physical ages? Don't be stupid.'

'It's part of the contract.'

'I don't think anyone's going to invoke contractual obligation until I've at least had a period.'

'So do you want to do anything?'

'Not particularly.'

'So what will we do then?'

'The view's nice.'

'There's a pack of cards in the drawer in the table.'

'Maybe later. I might sleep now.'

'So might I. Are you all right about the bed?'

'Of course. We're supposed to, aren't we? We are husband and wife.'

We slept under the light silk cover with the ceiling fan turning slowly, each curled up like the eight-year-olds we physically were with our backs to each other, as far apart as Vish and Shiv and afterwards we invented card games of staggering complexity with the old circular Ganjifa cards on the verandah with its titanic view over the Himalayas. As Lakshmi turned over the kings and ministers our eyes met and we both knew it was more than over, it had never begun. There was nothing but contractual obligation between us. We were the hostages of our DNA. I thought of that line of offspring issuing like a rope of pearls from the end of my still-flaccid penis; those slow children toddling into a future so distant I could not even see its dust on time's horizon, and onward and onward always onward. I was filled with horror at the blind imperative of biology. I owned superhuman intelligence, I only forgot what I chose to forget, I had never known a day's illness in my life, I carried the name of a god, but to my seed all this was nothing, I was no different from some baseline Dalit in Molar Bund basti. Yes, I was a privileged brat, yes, I was a sneerer of the worst kind, how could I be anything other? I was a designer snob.

We stayed our week in the teahouse in the green foothills of Himachal Pradesh, Lakshmi and Vishnu. Lakshmi patented some of her elaborate social card games – we tested the multi-player games by each of us playing several hands at once, an easy feat for the Brahmins – and made a lot of money from licensing them. It was radiantly beautiful, the mountains were distant and serene like stone Buddhas, occasional rain pattered on the leaves outside our window at night and we were utterly utterly miserable, but even more so at the thought of what we had to face on our return to Awadh, the darlings of the Delhi. My decision had been made on the third day of our honeymoon but it was not until we were in the limo to the Ramachandra Tower where we had been given an apartment fit for gods on the floor below my Mamaji that I made the call to the very special, very discreet doctor.

Two extraneous aspects of myself

'Both of them?' the nute said. Yt would have raised an eyebrow had yt possessed any hair on yts shaven head to raise.

'History is quiet on the subject of half-eunuchs,' I said.

No one, alas, ever delivers such dialogue. Ticking lines, arch exchanges, loaded looks, these are things of story not real life. But I am telling you a story, my story, which is much more than just history or even memory. For if I choose to forget, I can also choose to remember and make what I chose memory. So if I wish the nute surgeon's office to be at the top of a winding, creaking flight of stairs, each level haunted by the eyes of suspicious and hostile Old Delhiwallahs, if I decide to remember it so, it will be so. Likewise, if I choose to recall that office to be a charnel house of grotesque surgical implements and pictures of successfully mutilated body-parts like a demon-infested hell from a Himalayan Buddhist painting, it will be so forever. Perhaps it's less strange a concept for you than for me. I more than anyone know the deceptiveness of physical appearance, but you seem young enough to have grown up in a world comfortable with universal memory, every breath and blink swarming with devas continuously writing and rewriting physical reality. And if the devas choose to rewrite that memory, who is there to say that it's not so?

But there is east light in the sky beyond the blazing pillar of the Jyotirlinga, I have far to go, you have yet to see the most astonishing things my cats can achieve and the reality is that the surgery of Dr Anil was in a tastefully restored haveli in the warren of streets in the shadow of the Red Fort, the surgery elegant and discreet and fronted by the delightful Miss Modi, and Dr Anil was welcoming, professional, subtle and frankly surprised by my request.

'I usually deal in more ... substantial surgery,' yt said. The Ardhanarisvara Clinic was Delhi's leading centre for nute transformation. Leading through whispers and rumours; in bright new Awadh we might claim to be urbane, global, cosmopolitan and unshockable but nute culture, those who decided to escape our desperate sex wars by choosing a third way, a neither-way, was still almost as hidden and secretive as the ancient trans-gendered hijras who had long ago hidden themselves away in Old Delhi. The ancient city, older than any memory, its streets convoluted like the folds of a brain, has always looked after those with needs beyond the merely average.

'I think what I'm asking is substantial enough,' I said.

'True true,' Dr Anil said, putting his fingers together in a spire in that way that all doctors, male, female, transgendered or nute, seem to learn on day one of medical school. 'So, both testicles.'

'Yes, both.'

'And not the penis.'

'That would be perverse.'

'You're sure you won't consider the chemical option? It's revers-ible, should you ever reconsider.'

'No, not chemical. I don't want it to be reversible. I want to remove myself from the future. I want this to end with me. I'm more than a stud animal. Complete physical castration, yes.'

'It's quite simple. Much more so than the usual kind of thing we do here.' I knew well the medical procedures that flowed out from here to the anonymous godowns and grey surgery clinics beyond the Siri Ring orbital expressway. There is a video for everything somewhere in the online world and I had watched with fascination what those humans who desired another gender had done to themselves. The things strung out through the gel tanks, skin flayed, muscles laid open, organs drawn out and suspended in molecular sieve cradles, were so far from anything human as to be curious, like strange forest flowers, rather than obscene. I was much more of a coward, leaving only my two little organs on the doorstep of gender. 'My only reservation would be that, as you are biologically prepubescent, it would be an internal orchidectomy. Miss Modi will draw up a consent form.' Yt blinked at me, a delicate, faun-like creature behind a heavy Raj desk, too too lovely to speak of such things as testicular surgery.

'Forgive me for asking, I haven't met any High Brahmins before, but you are of an age to sign a consent form?'

'I'm of an age to be legally married.'

'Yes, but you must understand, mine is a business that attracts scrutiny in Awadh.'

'I'm of an age to pay you a profane sum of money to give me what I want.'

'Profane it is then.'

Surprisingly mundane it was. I did not even need to be driven out to the nasty industrial zones. In the cubicle I changed into the surgical gown, the sleeves too too long, the hem trailing on the ground, slid up onto the disinfectant-stinky operating table in the basement surgery and felt the needling suffusion of the local anaesthetic. Robot arms, fingertips fine as insect antennae, danced in under the control of Dr Anil. I felt nothing as I blinked up into the lights and strained to hear their synaesthetic music. The dancing arms withdrew; I felt nothing. And I still felt nothing as the car spun me back through streets full of pulsing, potent, hormone-raddled people. A mild twinge from the sutures pulling against the weave of my clothes. No pain, little loss, nothing of the sense of lightness and freedom I had read of in the literature of castration fetishists. A unique pleasure, sexual castration; an orgasm to end all orgasms. I had not even had that. The cell-weave treatments would heal the wound in three days and hide all evidence, until the passing years revealed that my voice was not significantly deepening, my hair not receding, that I was growing unusually tall and willowy and that I had singularly failed to contractually conceive any children.

'Do you want to take them with you?' Dr Anil asked as yt sat me down in yts consulting room after the short operation.

'Why should I wish to do that?'

'It was a tradition in China. Imperial eunuchs would be given their excised genitals preserved in a jar of alcohol to bury beside them on their deaths, so that they might enter heaven whole men.'

'It was a tradition in Ottoman Turkey that eunuchs, after their cutting clean, would sit in a dung-heap for three days to heal their wounds, or die. I don't care for that tradition either. They're not mine, they're not me; they belong to someone else. Burn them or throw them to the pi-dogs, I don't care.'

Thunder growled over me, a promise of a monsoon, the day was darkening. Lightning glowed cloud to cloud as I rode the elevator up the outside of Ramachandra Tower. Lakshmi sat curled on the sofa, the breaking storm magnificent behind her. Dry lightning, a false prophet of rain. All prophecies of rain were false these days,

'Did you do it, are you all right?'

I nodded. It was beginning to hurt now. I clenched my teeth, kicking in the analgesic nanoinfuser Dr Anil had planted there. Lakshmi clapped her hands in joy. 'I'll go tomorrow. Oh dear Lord, I'm so happy, so happy.' And then, there, in the dark apartment glowing with muted lighting, she kissed me.

We did not tell anyone. That was part of the pact. Not our parents, not our relatives, not our circle of Brahmin friends, not even our aeais. Not even dear Sarasvati; I wouldn't burden her with this. There was work we had to do before we announced to our respective families how we had so drastically denied their plans for us. Then we could sweetly and painlessly divorce.

I nuzzle the earlobe of power

What is the proper work of eunuchs?

Does it make you uncomfortable, that word? Does it make you cross your legs, boys; does it give you a hollow clench in your uterus, ladies? When you hear it, do you see something other than a human being, something less? How then is it any different from other words of distinction: Kshatriya, Dalit? Brahmin? Eunuch. It is a very old and noble word, a fine and ancient tradition practised in all the great cultures of earth. The principle is to give up the lesser to gain the greater. Of all those pitiful puffs of cock-juice, how many will ever turn into human beings? Come on, be honest. It's almost all wasted. And never imagine that the ball-less are sexless, or without desire. No, the great castrati singers, the eunuch poets and holy visionaries, the grand viziers and royal advisers all understood that greatness came at a price and that was generation. Empires could be entrusted to eunuchs, free from dynastic urges. The care and feeding of great nations is our proper work, and with all the gifts my parents had endowed me I steered myself toward the political cradle of the nation.

How almost right my mother was, and how utterly wrong-headed. She had seen me carried in through the doors of the Lok Sabha on the shoulders of cheering election workers. I preferred the servant's entrance. Politicians live and die by the ballot box. They are not there to serve, they are there to gain and hold office. Populism can force them to abandon wise and correct policies for whims and fads. The storm of ballots will in the end sweep them and all their good works from power. Their grand viziers endure. We understand that democracy is the best system by which a nation *seems* to be governed.

Months of social networking – the old-fashioned, handshake and gift type – and the setting up and calling in of favours and lines of political credit, had gained me an internship to Parekh, the Minister for Water and the Environment. He was a tolerable dolt, a Vora from Uttaranchal with a shopkeeper's shrewdness and head for details, but little vision. He was good enough to seem in control and a politician often needs little more for a long and comfortable career. This was the highest he would ever rise;

as soon as the next monsoon failure hit and the mobs were hijacking water tankers in the street, he would be out. He knew I knew this. I scared him, even though I was careful to turn down the full dazzle of my intelligence to a glow of general astuteness. He knew I was far from the nine-year-old I seemed to be but he really had no idea of my and my kind's capabilities and curses. I chose my department carefully. Naked ambition would have exposed me too early to a government that was only now realising it had never properly legislated around human gene-line manipulation. Even so I knew the colour of all the eyes that were watching me, skipping through the glassy corridors of the Water Ministry. Water is life. Water, its abundance and its rarity, would sculpt the future of Awadh, of all the nations of North India, from the Panjab to the United States of Bengal. Water was a good place to be bright, but I had no intention of remaining there.

The dam at Kunda Khadar neared completion, that titanic fifteen-kilometre bank of earth and concrete like a garter around the thigh of Mother Ganga. Protests from downstream Bharat and the USB grew strident but the tower cranes lifted and swung, lifted and swung day and night. Minister Parekh and Prime Minister Srivastava communicated daily. The Defence Ministry was brought into the circle. Even the PR staffers could smell diplomatic tension.

It was a Thursday. Even before, I called it Bold Thursday, to commit myself, to get myself up. The genes don't make you brave. But I had prepared as rigorously as I could; which was more than anyone in the Lok Sabha, Minister Parekh included. Srivastava was due with his entourage for a press conference from the ministry to reassure the Awadhi public that Kunda Khadar would do its job and slake Delhi's bottomless thirst. Everyone was turned out smart as paint: moustaches plucked, clacks creased, shirts white as mourning. Not me. I had picked my spot long before: a brief bustle down the corridor as Srivastava and his secretarial team was coming up. I had no idea what they would be talking about but I knew they would be talking; Srivastava loved his 'walking briefings'; they made him seem a man of action and energy. I trusted that my research and quicker wit would win.

I heard the burble of voices. They were about to turn the corner. I went into motion, pushed myself into the wall as the press of suits came toward me. My senses scanned five conversations, lit on Srivastava's murmur to Bhansal his parliamentary secretary, 'If I knew we had McAuley's support.'

Andrew J. McAuley, President of the United States of America. And the answer was there.

'We could negotiate an output deal in return for Sajida Rana accepting partial ratification of the Hamilton Acts,' I said, my voice shrill and pure and piercing as a bird.

The Prime Ministerial party bustled past but Satya Shetty, the Press Secretary, turned with a face of thunder to strike down this upstart, mouthy intern. He saw a nine-year-old. He was dumb-struck. His eyes bulged. He hesitated. That hesitation froze the entire party. Prime Minister Srivastava turned towards me. His eyes widened. His pupils dilated.

'That's a very interesting idea,' he said and in those five words I knew he had identified, analysed and accepted the gift I had offered him. A Brahmin adviser. The strange, savant child. The child genius, the infant guru, the little god. India adored them. It was PR gold. His staffers parted as he stepped toward me. 'What are you doing here?'

I explained that I was on an internship with Minister Parekh.

'And now you want more.'

Yes, I did.

'What's your name?'

I told him. He nodded his head.

'Yes, the wedding. I remember. So, it's a career in politics, is it?'

It was.

'You're certainly not backward about being forward.'

My genes wouldn't allow it. My first political lie.

'Well, ideas do seem to be in short stock at the moment.' With that he turned, his entourage closed around him and he was swept on. Satya Shetty dealt me a glare of pure despite; I held his eyes until he snapped his gaze away. I would see him and all his works dust while I was still fresh and filled with energy. By the time I returned to my desk there was an invitation from the Office of the Prime Minister to call them to arrange an interview.

I told my great achievement to the three women in my life. Lakshmi beamed with delight. Our plans were working. My mother was baffled; she no longer understood my motivations, why I would accept a lowly and inconspicuous civil service position rather than a high-flyer in our superstar political culture. Sarasvati jumped up from her sofa and danced around the room, then clapped her hands around my face and kissed my forehead long and hard until her lips left a red tilak there.

'As long as there's joy in it,' she said. 'Only joy.'

My sister, my glorious sister, had voiced a truth that I was only now developing the maturity to recognise. Joy was all. Mamaji and Dadaji had aimed me at greatness, at blinding success and wealth, power and celebrity. I had always possessed the emotional intelligence, if not the emotional vocabulary, to know that the blindingly powerful and famous were seldom happy, that their success and wealth often played against their own mental and physical well-being. All my decisions I made for me, for my peace, well-being, satisfaction and to keep me interested throughout my long life. Lakshmi had chosen the delicate world of complicated games. I had chosen the whirl of politics. Not economics; that was too dismal a science for me.

But the state and those statelets beyond Awadh's borders with which I could see we were as inextricably entwined as when we were one India, and the countries beyond those, and the continents beyond; that fascinated me. The etiquette of nations was my pleasure. There was joy in it, Sarasvati. And I was brilliant at it. I became the hero of my childhood comics, a subtle hero, Diplomacy Man. I saved your world more times than you can ever know. My superpower was to see a situation entire, connected, and all those subtler forces acting upon it that other, less gifted analysts would have discounted. Then I would give it a nudge. The smallest, slightest tap, one tiny incentive or restriction, even a hint at how a policy might be shaped, and watch how the social physics of a complex capitalist society scale them up through power laws and networks and social amplifiers to slowly turn the head of the entire nation.

In those first few years I was constantly fighting for my own survival. Satya Shetty was my deadliest enemy from the moment our eyes had met in the corridor in the Water Ministry. He was influential, he was connected, he was clever but not clever enough to realise he could never beat me. I just let my drips of honey fall into Krishna Srivastava's ear. I was always right. Little by little his cabinet and Satya Shetty's allies realised that, more than being always right, I was essentially different from them. I didn't seek high office. I sought the greatest well-being. I was the perfect adviser. And I looked great on television: Prime Minister Srivastava's dwarf vizier, trotting behind him like some throw-back to the days of the Mughals. Who isn't, at some level, unnerved by the child prodigy? Even if I was twenty-two years old now, with puberty – whatever that might mean for me personally – looming on the horizon of my Brahmin generation like the rumbles of a long-delayed monsoon.

It was that treacherous monsoon that became the driver of Awadhi politics, town and country, home and away. Thirsty nations are irrational nations; nations that pray and turn to strange saviours. The great-technocracy of the United States of Bengal had, in a display of national hysteria, put its faith In a bizarre plan to haul an iceberg from Antarctica into the Sundarbans with the hope that the mass of cold air would affect the shifting climatic patterns and claw the monsoon back over India. Strange days, a time of rumours and wonders. The end of the Age of Kali was upon us and once again the gods were descending upon us, walking in the shapes of ordinary men and women. The Americans had found something in space, something not of this world. The datahavens of Bharat, boiling with aeais, had spawned Generation Three artificial intelligences; legendary entities whose intelligence as far outstripped mine as mine did the fleas crawling on my poor, harassed cats. Sajida Rana, politically embattled from resurgent Hindu fundamentalism, was preparing a pre-emptive strike on Kunda Khadar as a PR stunt. This last rumour I took seriously enough from my trawling of the Bharati press to call for a departmental level meeting between my ministry and its Bharati counterpart. Did I mention that I was now parliamentary secretary to Krishna Srivastava? A steady, not stellar, climb. It was still too easy to lose grip and fall into the reaching hands of my rivals.

My counterpart at the Bharat Bhavan was a refined Muslim gentleman, Shaheen Badoor Khan, from an excellent family and impeccably educated. Behind his pitch-perfect etiquette and a dignity I envied deeply for I was a small, scampering child next to him, I did sense a sadness; an ache behind the eyes. We recognised and liked each other immediately. We knew instinctively that we both cared deeply enough for our countries to be prepared to betray them. Such a thing could never be said, or even implied. Thus our conversation, as we walked among the Buddha's deer of old Sarnath, our security men discreet shadows among the trees, the security drones circling like black kites overhead seemed as casual and elliptical as two old dowagers on a Friday afternoon stroll.

'Awadh has always seemed to me a country at peace with itself,' Shaheen Badoor Khan said. 'As if it's solved some great and quintessentially Indian paradox.'

'It wasn't always so,' I said. Behind the security fence Western tourists on the Buddha trail tried to hold down their flapping robes in the rising wind. 'Delhi's streets have run red far too many times.'

'But it's always been a cosmopolitan city. Varanasi, on the other hand, always has and always will be the city of Lord Siva.'

I waggled my head in agreement. I knew now what I would report to Srivastava. *Sajida Rana is under pressure from the Hindutvavadis. She will launch a pre-emptive strike at Kunda Khadar. Awadh will have the moral high ground; we must not lose it.*

'I have a relative in Varanasi,' I said casually.

'Oh, so?'

'My brother – a Shiva himself, so no surprise really that he should end up in Varanasi.'

'And is he a Brahmin like yourself?"

'No, but he is very gifted.'

'We do seem to attract talent. It's one of our blessings, I suppose. I have a younger brother in the United States. Terrible at keeping in contact, terrible; my mother, well, you know what they're like. Of course it's my responsibility.'

You're worried that your brother has drifted into business that could adversely affect your standing, if it became public, was what this sage Mr Khan was telling me. *You want me to keep an eye on him, in return you'll open up a secure channel of communications between us to prevent war between Bharat and Awadh.*

'You know what brothers are like,' I said.

The information was beaming into my head even as I stepped

off the plane at Indira Gandhi airport. Shiv had opened a company, Purusa, in Varanasi. He had attracted substantial funding from a venture capital company called Odeco and match-funding from the research and development division at Bharat's mighty Ray Power. His field was nanoscale computing. Top designers and engineers were working with him. The Ghost Index, which valued companies with the potential to become global players when they went public, valued Purusa as one of their top five to watch. He was young and he was hot and he was headed for orbit. He had made some questionable friends among Bharat's datarajas and a cloud of high-level aeais hid much of Purusa's activities from its rivals and from the Bharati government. The Krishna Cops had a file on him and a deliberately clumsy team of aeai wards to keep him aware that he was known to them. My own Awadhi intelligence service surveillance aeais were of a subtler stripe than the police. They coded themselves into the very informational fabric of Purusa. The security of Awadh was a flimsy fiction; I was intensely curious as to what my brother was up to. What Shiv planned was of course monstrously ambitious. He had cracked open the prison of the skull. More prosaically, Purusa had developed a prototype biochip that could interface directly with the brain. No more a tacky coil of plastic behind the ear and the soft invasion of electromagnetic radiation into the brain, like shouting in a temple. This was engineered protein, stuff of our stuff, which sent its artificial neurons through skin and bone to mesh with the threads of thought. It was the third eye, forever open to the unseen world. See how easily I resort to the language of the mystical? Omniscience was standard; anyone so infected had access to all the knowledge and all the bitchy triviality of the global web. Communication was no longer a click and a call, it was a thought, a subtle telepathy. Virtual worlds became real. The age of privacy, that first Western luxury that Indian wealth bought, was over. Where our own thoughts ended and those of others began, how would we know? We would touch the world of the aeais, in their dispersed, extended, multi-levelled perceptions. Speculation led to speculation. I could see no end to them. Lakshmi, disturbed from her mathematical games, would sense my mood and look up to see the adult anxiety on my child's face. This technology would change us, change us utterly and profoundly. This was a new way of being human, a fault-line, a diamond cutter's strike across society. I began to realise that the greatest threat to Awadh, to Bharat, to all India, was not water. It was the pure and flawless diamond Shiv and his Purusa Corporation dangled and spun in front of each and every human. Be more, be everything. So engaged was I that I did not notice when the warning came down the Grand Trunk Road from Shaheen Badoor Khan in Varanasi and thus was caught sleeping when Sajida Rana sent her tanks to take Kuna Khadar without a shot.

The girl with the red bindi

The war's names were longer than its duration. The Kunda Khadar war, the Forty-Eight Hour War, the Soft War, the First Water War. You don't remember it, though Awadhi main battle tanks manoeuvred over these very sands. You probably don't even remember it from history lessons. There have been greater and more enduring wars; war running into war, the long and, I think, the final war. The war I shall end. That grand display of arms on these river strands I now understand as its opening shot, had any shots actually been fired. That was another of its names, the Soft War. Ah! Who is it names wars? Hacks and pundits, without doubt, media editors and chati journalists; people with an interest in a good, mouth-filling phrase. It is certainly not civil servants, or cat-circus proprietors. How much better a name would 'Soft War' have been for the century of unrest that followed, this Age of Kali that now seems to have run down to its lowest ebb with the arrival of the Jyotirlingas on earth?

The Water War, the War of '47, whatever we call it, for me marked the end of human history and the return of the age of miracles to earth. It was only after the smoke had cleared and the dust settled and our diplomatic teams arrived among the tall and shining towers of Ranapur to negotiate the peace that we realised the immensity of events in Bharat. Our quiet little water war was the least of it. I had received one terse communication down the Grand Trunk Road: *I am ruined, I have failed, I have resigned.* But there was Shaheen Badoor Khan, five paces behind his new Prime Minster Ashok Rana, as I trotted like a child behind our Srivastava.

'Rumours of my demise were exaggerated,' he whispered as we fell in beside each other as the politicians formed up on the grass outside the Benares Polo and Country Club for the press call, each jostling for status-space.

'War does seem to shorten the political memory.' A twenty-three year-old in the body of a boy half his age may say pretty much whatever he likes. It's the liberty granted to fools and angels. When I first met Shaheen Badoor Khan, as well as his decency and intelligence, I had sensed a bone-deep sadness. Even I could not have guessed it was a long-repressed and sterile love for the other, the transgressive, the romantic and doomed, all wrapped up in the body of a young Varanasi nute. He had fallen into the honey-trap laid for him by his political enemies.

Shaheen Badoor Khan dipped his head. 'I'm far from being the first silly, middle-aged man to have been a fool for lust. I may be the only one to have got his Prime Minister killed as a consequence. But, as you say, war does very much clarify the vision and I seem to be a convenient figure for public expiation.

And from what I gather from the media, the public will trust me sooner than Ashok Rana. People like nothing better than the fallen Mughal who repents. In the meantime, we do what we must, don't we, Mr Nariman? Our countries need us more than they know. These have been stranger times in Bharat than people can ever be let know.'

Bless your politician's self-deprecation. The simultaneous collapse of major aeai systems across Bharat, including the all-conquering *Town and Country*, the revelation that the country's rampant Hindutva opposition had been a cabal of artificial intelligences, chaos at Ray Power and the mysterious appearance of a hundred-metre hemispherical crater of mirror-bright perfection in the university grounds; and, behind all, rumours that the long-awaited, long-dreaded Generation Three aeais had arrived. There was only one who could make sense of it to me. I went to see Shiv.

He had a house, a shaded place with many trees to push back the crowding, noisy world. Gardeners moved with slow precision up and down the rolled gravel paths, dead-heading a Persian rose here, spraying aphids there, spot-feeding brown drought-patches in the lawn everywhere. He had grown fat. He lolled in his chair at the tiffin table on the lawn. He looked dreadful, pasty and puffy. He had a wife. He had a child, a little pipit of a girl playing on the snap-together plastic fun-park on the lawn under the eye of her ayah. She would glance over at me, unsure whether to treat me as a strange and powerful uncle or invite me to whiz down the plastic slide. Yes, wee one, I was a strange creature. That scent, that pheromone of information I had smelled on Shiv the day he came to my wedding still clung to him, stronger now. He smelled like a man who has spent too much time among aeais.

He welcomed me expansively. Servants brought cool home-made sherbet. As we settled into brother talk, man-to-eleven-year-old-talk, his wife excused herself in a voice small as an insect and went to hover nervously over her daughter playing exuberantly on her brightly coloured jungle-gym.

'You seem to have had a good war,' I said.

'There was war?' Shiv held my gaze for a moment, then exploded into volcanic laughter. Sweat broke out on his brow. I did not believe it for an instant. 'I've got comfortable and greasy, yes.'

'And successful.'

'Not as successful as you.'

'I am only a civil servant.'

'I've heard you run Srivastava like a pimp.'

'We all have our sources.'

'Yes.' Again that affected pause. 'I spotted yours pretty early on. Not bad for government 'ware.'

'Disinformation can be as informative as information.'

'Oh, I wouldn't try anything as obvious as that with you. No, I left them there; I let them look. I've nothing to hide.'

'Your investors are interesting.'

'I doubt some of them will be collecting on their investment.' He laughed again.

'I don't think I understand.'

'It transpires that one of my key investors, Odeco, was nothing more than a front for a Generation Three aeai that had developed inside the international financial markets.'

'So it wasn't just a rumour.'

'I'm glad you're still listening to rumours.'

'You say this all very casually.'

'What other way is there to treat the end of history? You've seen what happens in India when we takes things seriously.' The laugh was annoying me now. It was thick and greasy.

'The end of history has been promised many times, usually by people rich enough to avoid it.'

'Not this time. The rich will be the ones who'll bring it

about. The same blind economic self-interest that caused the demographic shift, and you, Vish. Only this will be on a much greater scale.'

'You think your biochip has that potential?'

'On it's own, no. I can see I'm going to have to explain this to you.'

By the time Shiv had told his tale the gardeners were lighting torches to drive away the evening insects and wife, daughter and ayah had withdrawn to the lit comfort of the verandah. Bats dashed around me, hunting. I was shivering though the night was warm. A servant brought fresh made lassi and pistachios. It was greater, as Shiv had promised. Perhaps the greatest. The gods had returned, and then, in the instant of their apotheosis, departed. A soft apocalypse.

The fears of the Krishna Cops, of the scared Westerners, had of course come true. The Generation Threes were real, had been real for longer than anyone had foreseen, had moved among us for years, decades even, unresting, unhasting and silent as light. There was no force capable of extirpating truly hyper-intelligent aeais whose ecosystem was the staggering complexity of the global information network. They could break themselves into components, distribute themselves across continents, copy themselves infinitely, become each other. They could speak with our voices and express our world but they were utterly utterly alien to us. It was convenient for them to withdraw their higher functions from a world closing in on the secret of their existence and base themselves in the datahavens of Bharat, for they had a higher plan. There were three of them, gods all. Brahma, Shiva, Krishna. My brothers, my gods. One, the most curious about the world, inhabited the global financial market. One grew out of a massively multiple online evolution simulation game of which I had vaguely heard. In creating an artificial world, the gamers had created its deity. And one appeared in the vast servers farms of Bharat's Indiapendent Productions, coalesced out of the cast and pseudo-cast of *Town and Country*. That one particularly impressed me, especially since, with the characteristic desire to meddle in the affairs of others mandatory in the soapi universe, it expanded into Bharati politics in the shape of the aggressive Hindutva Party that had engineered the downfall of the perceptive and dangerous Shaheen Badoor Khan and the assassination of Sajida Rana.

That would have been enough to end our hopes that this twentieth-first century would be a smooth and lucrative extension of its predecessor. But their plans were not conflict or the subjugation of humanity. That would have meant nothing to the aeais, it was a human concept born of a human need. They inhabited a separate ecological niche and could have endured indefinitely, caught up in whatever concerns were of value to distributed intelligences. Humanity would not let them live. The Krishna Cops were cosmetic, costume cops to maintain an illusion that humanity was on the case, but they did signal intent. Humans would admit no rivals, so the Trimurti of Generation Three engineered an escape from this world, from this universe. I did not understand the physics involved from Shiv's description; neither, despite his pedantic, lecturing IT-boy tone, did he. I would look it up later, it would not be beyond me. What I did glean was that it was related to that mirrored crater on the university campus that looked so like a fine piece of modern sculpture, or an ancient astronomical instrument like the gnomons and marble bowls of Delhi's ancient Jantar Mantar observatory. That hemisphere, and an object out in space. Oh yes, those rumours were real. Oh yes, the Americans had discovered it long ago and tried to keep it secret, and were still trying, and, oh yes, failing.

'And what is it then?'

'The collected wisdom of the aeais. A true universal computer. They sent it through from their universe.'

'Why?'

'Do you never give presents to your parents?'

'You're privileged to know this information?'

'I have channels that even the government of Awadh doesn't. Or, for that matter, the Americans. Odeco ...'

'Odeco you said was an avatar of the Brahma aeai. Wait.' Had I balls, they would have contracted cold and hard. 'There is absolutely nothing to prevent this happening again.'

'None,' said Shiv. It was some time since he had laughed his vile, superior laugh.

'It's already happening.' And we thought we had won a water war.

'There's a bigger plan. Escape, exile, partition is never a good solution. Look at us in Mother India. You work in politics, you understand the need for a *settlement*.' Shiv turned in his chair to the figures on the verandah. His wife was still watching me. 'Nirupa, darling. Come over here, would you? Uncle Vish hasn't had a chance to meet you properly.'

She came dashing down the steps and across the lawn, holding up the hem of her print dress, in a headlong, heedless flight that made me at once fearful for stones, snakes and stumble and at the same time reminded so much of my golden years growing up alongside Sarasvati. She put her fingers in her mouth and pressed close to her father, shy of looking at me directly.

'Show him your bindi, go on, it's lovely.'

I had noticed the red mark on her forehead, larger than customary, and the wrong colour. I bent forward across the table to examine it. It was moving. The red spot seemed to crawl with insect-movement, on the edge of visibility. I reeled back into my chair. My feet swung, not touching the ground.

'What have you done?' I cried. My voice was small and shrill.

'Shh. You'll scare her. Go on; run on, Nirupa. Thank you. I've made her for the future. Like our parents made you for the future. But it's not going to be the future they thought.'

'Your biochip interface.'

'Works. Thanks to a little help from the aeais. But like I said, that's only part of it. A tiny part of it. We have a project in development; that's the real revolution. That's the real sound of the future arriving.'

'Tell me what it is.'

'Distributed dust-processing.'

'Explain.'

Shiv did. It was nothing less than the transformation of computing. His researchers were shrinking computers, smaller and smaller, from grain of rice to sperm cell, down down to the molecular scale and beyond. The endpoint was swarm-computers the size of dust particles, communicating with each other in free-flying flocks, computers that could permeate every cell of the human body. They would be as universal and ubiquitous as dust. I began to be afraid and cold in that clammy Varanasi night. I could see Shiv's vision for our future, perhaps further than he could. The bindi and the dust-processor: one broke the prison of the skull; the other turned the world into memory.

Little by little our selves would seep into the dust-laden world; we would become clouds, non-localised, we would penetrate each other more intimately and powerfully than any tantric temple carving. Inner and outer worlds would merge. We could be many things, many lives at one time. We could copy ourselves endlessly. We would merge with the aeais and become one. This was their settlement, their peace. We would become one species, post-human, post-aeai.

'You're years away from this.' I denied Shiv's fantasia shrilly.

'Yes, we would be, if we hadn't had a little help.'

'How?' I cried again. Now the ayah was staring concerned at me.

Shiv pointed a finger to the night sky.

'I could report you,' I said. 'Americans don't take kindly to having their security hacked.'

'You can't stop it,' Shiv said. 'Vish, you're not the future any more.'

Those words, of all that Shiv spoke in the garden, clung to me. Gliding silently through Delhi in the smooth-running black government car, the men in their white shirts, the women in their coloured shoes, the cars and the buzzing phatphats seemed insubstantial. The city was still thrilled with its brilliant victory – only a drubbing in cricket would have exercised public excitement more – but the crowds seemed staged, like extras, and the lights and streets as false as a set on *Town and Country*. How would we survive without our national panacea? But Shiv had confirmed, there was nothing, absolutely nothing to prevent a new generation of Threes from arising. They could already be stirring into sentience, like my divine namesake on his scared turtle Kurma churning the sacred milk into creation. I was acutely aware of the clouds of aeais all around me, penetrating and interpenetrating, layer upon layer, level upon level, many and one. There was no place in the two Delhis for the ancient djinns. The aeais had displaced them. This was their city. Settlement was the only answer. Dust blew through the streets, dust upon dust. I had seen the end of history and still my feet did not touch the floor of the limo.

I was obsolete. All the talents and skills Mamaji and Dadaji had gifted me were nothing in a world where everyone was connected, where everyone could access the full power of a universal computer, where personality could be as malleable and fluid as water. Slowly slowly I would grow up through adolescence to maturity and old age while around me this new society, this new humanity, would evolve at an ever-increasing rate. I was all too aware of my choice. Take Shiv's way and deny everything I had been made for, or reject it and grow old with my kind. We, the genetically enhanced Brahmins, were the last humans. Then, with a physical force that made me spasm on the back seat of the limo, I realised my hubris. I was such an aristocrat. The poor. The poor would be with us. India's brilliant middle class, its genius and its curse, would act as it always had, in its unenlightened self-interest. Anything that would give advantage to its sons and daughters in the Darwinian struggle for success. The poor would look on, as disenfranchised from that post-human world as they were from this fantasy of glass and neon.

I was glad, glad to tears, that I had chosen to pass nothing on into this future. No endless chain of slow-aging, genetically obsolete Brahmins hauling themselves into an increasing unrecognisable and inhuman future. Had I received some premonition? Had my uniquely overlapping senses seen a pattern there all those years ago that even Shiv, with his clandestine access to the collected knowledge of the Generation Threes, had not? I wept unreservedly and ecstatically in the back of the smooth-running car. It was time. As we turned into the down ramp to the underground car park at Ramachandra Tower, I made three calls. First I called Prime Minister Srivastava and tendered my resignation. Then I called Lakshmi, patient Lakshmi who had through our charade of a marriage and sterility become a dear and intimate friend, and said, *Now, now's the time for that divorce*. Last of all I called my mother on the floor above and told her exactly what I had done with myself.

A father festooned with memory

Wait! One more trick. You'll like this trick, the best trick of all. You haven't seen anything yet, just a bit of running in circles and jumping through hoops. Yes, I know it's very very late and the sun will soon be up the sky and you have cows to milk and fields to tend to and appointments to keep but you will like this trick. Not a lot, but you will like it. Now, two ticks while I fix up this wire.

And anyway, I haven't finished my story. Oh no no, not by a long chalk. You thought it ended there? With the world as you see it, now you know how intimately I am involved in our history? No, it must end well, a well-made story. I must confront the villain, according to the theories on such things. There must be resolution and an appropriate moral sentiment. Then you will be satisfied.

The wire? Oh, they can walk that. Oh yes, those cats. No no no; first you must listen a little longer.

I walked away. We have a great and grand tradition of it in this great teat of divine milk hanging from the belly of Asia. Our country is big enough to swallow any soul, our orders still porous to pilgrims with a stick and a dhoti wrapped around their loins. Our society has a mechanism for disappearing completely. Anyone can walk away from the mundane world into the divine. Mine was not the orthodox spiritual path and not conventionally divine. I had seen the coming gods. I set aside my career, my clothes, my apartment, my wife – with her blessing and a farewell kiss – my family and friends, my identity, my social networks, my online presence, everything but my genetic inheritance which could not be undone and turned sadhu. Only Sarasvati knew my secret com address. I was gone from the apartment, beating through the neon-lit heat of Rajiv Circle, out along the sides of expressways, drenched in yellow light, beneath the back-throttle of aircraft coming in to the airport, past the brick and cardboard and plastic shelters of the invisible poor. Dawn saw me among the ribbed aluminium flanks of the go-downs and factories of Tughluk. I crossed a city on foot in a single night. It's a great and strange thing to do. Everyone should do it. I walked along the cracked concrete spans of expressways, by the sides of country roads blasted by the grit and gust of passing trucks, along the side of the huge slow trains materialising like visions out of the heat haze, the drivers flinging me rupees for blessings as they passed. I sat down and covered my head and eyes as the high-speed shatabdi express blasted past at hundreds of kilometres per hour. Did the passengers even glance at me through the darkened glass? If so I must have seemed a very strange sadhu to them. The littlest sadhu. Small but determined, beating forward with my staff at every stride.

What was I doing? Walking. What did I hope to find? Nothing. Where was I going? To see. Don't think me a coward or a failure, that I was walking away from truths I could not admit. I had been stabbed to the bone by the revelation that I was irrelevant. I was not the future. I was a dead-end, a genetic backwater. That was the natural reaction of privilege to its absolute irrelevance. I'm a brat, remember that. A spoiled Mamaji's boy. That same night I returned and dropped my progenitive bombshell, that my mother would never have the dynasty of brilliant Brahmins she desired, I woke from my sleep. It was the uncertain hour, when reality is groggy and the djinns run free. The hour when you wake in your familiar bed without the least knowledge of where the hell you are. I was woken by a sound. It was like a breath and like a roar, like traffic and air-conditioners, like a distant desperate shouting and the buzz of neons and powerlines. It was the pulse of underground trains and delivery trucks; it was filmi music and item-songs playing through each other. I heard Great Delhi breath in its shallow sleep and I wanted to go to my balcony and shout as loud as my eleven-year-old glottis would allow: *Wake up! Wake up!* Shiv's future might be inevitable, written into the geometry of space-time by entities outside it, but I would not allow us to sleepwalk into it. My mind was racing. I had never known anything like it before. I was thinking at a staggering rate, images and memories and ideas crashing together, shattering, fusing. Edifices of thought, huge as mountains, tumbled around me. The way was clear and bright and laid out in front of me. It was there complete and entire in two seconds. I would have to take myself away from the distractions of Delhi politics and society. My ambitions were much larger than that, I would have to become anonymous for a time, I would have to be silent and look and listen. There was a war to be fought and it was a war of mythologies.

Lakshmi kissed me and I left. I wandered for nine months, south across the border into Rajasthan, back into Bharat and to the north under the breath of the Himalayas, to the cool green ridges where I had spent my honeymoon with Lakshmi. To Dal Lake and Srinagar, to Leh and the high country. I could never grow the proper sadhu beard, but I grew the sadhu leanness and tallness. Boy eunuchs grow tall and lean. And the dreadlocks. Oh yes. They are good to have but unpleasant to get. I also gained a nickname: the Beardless Sadhu. With it I got muscles and sunburn, I grew the stamina to walk all day on a cup of rice and a cup of water. What a pulpy, unfit puppy I had been! I begged and performed small miracles of accountancy and feats of memory for food and shelter. Everywhere, I looked in men and women's third eyes. I saw things I could never have from the top of Ramachandra Tower or the Awadh Bhavan. I saw thirst and I saw drought. I saw good village leaders and diligent local civil servants frustrated by government bureaucrats. I saw clever women turn a few hundred rupees from microcredit schemes and grameen banks into successful businesses. I saw good teachers try to lift generations out of low expectations and the trap of caste and Awadh's soar-away middle class, rapidly pulling the ladder of social mobility up behind it. I helped with harvests and rode the back of tractors and listened to farmers curse the ever-increasing price of their sterile GM seed. I chased rats with sticks and waved my arms to set whole fields of sparrows to flight. I sat in the community house and watched cricket on a giant plasma screen powered by stored sunlight. Oh, I was a most peculiar sadhu. I gained a new nickname to set beside Beardless Sadhu: Cricketing Sadhu. I saw village weddings and festivals, I saw funerals. I saw death. It came quite unexpectedly one day, in a small town outside Agra. It was Holi and the streets were full of flying colour, jets of dye, clouds of powder, stained saris and white shirts ruined beyond the power of any laundry to save and everywhere grinning faces stained with colours, teeth white, eye flashing, everyone shouting Holi hai! Holi hai! as they launched jets of colour into the air. I moved through this circus of colour, as motley as any. The phatphat was grossly overloaded, a dozen colour-stained youths hanging off every strut and stanchion. Their eyes were wide on ganja and they were roaring with laughter and throwing fistfuls of dye powder at every passer-by. They caught me full in the face. The front wheel hit a pothole, the overstrained suspension collapsed and the whole thing flipped over in a perfect somersault onto its roof, which split like an egg. Bodies flew everywhere, many of them so relaxed on the ganja they were still laughing as they picked themselves up and skipped away. One didn't move. He was trapped under the crushed plastic shell. He lay on his back, his arms at odd angles. His face was stained blue and green and pink and he seemed to be smiling but my senses realised he was dead. I had never seen death before. It was so simple and strange, here undeniably before me yet so subtle, an instant's transformation yet the opposite of everything that was life. I mumbled the prayers expected of me, but inwardly I was coming to terms with the deepest of all human truths. I was twenty-six years old with the body of an albeit-strange thirteen-year-old, my lifespan was measurable in centuries, but one day I too would lie down like this and stop moving and thinking and feeling and be nothing forever. I saw death and began to understand.

Village to village, town to town, temple to temple, from the huge complexes the size of cities to white-washed roadside shrines. Then one day outside a mall in a drought-dusty suburb of Jaipur, as the security men were coming to ask me politely (for one must always be respectful to sadhus) to please move on, I saw what I had been looking for. A man turned to see the very small kerfuffle and as I momentarily looked at him, the Eye of Shiva looked back. I saw biotechnology move there.

I went to a community centre and wrote my first article. I sent it to Suresh Gupta, the editor of *Gupshup*, that most unashamedly populist of the Delhi's magazines, which had carried the photographs of my birth and marriage and now, unknowingly, my prophecies of the coming Age of Kali. He rejected it out of hand. I wrote another the next day. It came back with a comment: *Interesting subject matter but inaccessible for our readership.* I was getting somewhere. I went back and wrote again, long into the night over the pad. I am sure I gained another nickname: the Scribbling Sadhu. Suresh Gupta took that third article, and every article since. What did I write about? I wrote about all the things Shiv had prophesied. I wrote about what they might mean for three Indian families, the Voras, the Dashmukhs and the Hirandanis, village, town and city. I created characters – mothers, fathers, sons and daughters and mad aunties and uncles with dark secrets and long-lost relatives come to call – and told their stories, week upon week, year upon year, and the changes, good and ill, the constant hammerblows of technological revolution wrought upon them. I created my own weekly soap opera; I even dared to call it *Town and Country.* It was wildly successful. It sold buckets. Suresh Gupta saw his circulation increase by thirty per cent among those Delhi intelligentsia who only saw *Gupshup* in hair salons and beauty parlours. Questions were asked, who is this pseudonymous 'Shakyamuni'? We want to interview him, we want to profile him, we want him to appear on *Awadh Today*, we want an op-ed piece from him, we want him to be an adviser on this project, that think tank, we want him to open a supermarket. Suresh Gupta fielded all such inquiries with the ease of a professional square leg. There were others questions, ones I overheard at train stations and phatphat lines, in super-market queues and at bazaars, at parties and family get-togethers: *What does it mean for us?*

I kept travelling, kept walking, immersing myself in the village and small town. I kept writing my little future-soap, sending off my articles from a cellpoint here, a village netlink there. I watched for the Eye of Shiva. It was several months between the first and second, down in a business park in Madhya Pradesh. I saw them steadily after that, but never many; then, at the turn of 2049 to 2050, like a desert blooming after rain, they were everywhere.

I was walking down through the flat dreary country south of the Nepalese border to Varanasi developing my thoughts on evolution, Darwinian and post-Darwinian and the essential unknowability of singularities when I picked up the message from Sarasvati, my first in two weeks of loitering from village to village. At once I thumbed to Varanasi and booked the first shatabdi to Delhi. My natty dreads, my long nails, the dirt and sacred ash of months on the road went down the pan in the first class lounge. By the time the Vishwanath Express drew into the stupendous nano-diamond cocoon of New Delhi Central I was dressed and groomed, a smart, confident young Delhiwallah, a highly eligible teenager. Sarasvati picked me up in her truck. It was an old battered white Tata without autodrive or onboard or even a functioning air-conditioning system. *New Delhi Women's Refuge* was painted on the side in blue. I had followed her career – or rather her careers– while I was running the country. Worthiness attracted her; had she been a Westerner and not a

Delhi girl I would have called it guilt at the privilege of her birth. Theatre manager here, urban farming collective there, donkey sanctuary somewhere else, dam protest way way down *there*. She had derided me: deep down at the grass roots was where the real work was done. People work. *And who will provide the water for those grass roots?* I would answer. It had only taken our brother's vision of the end of the Age of Kali for me to come round to her philosophy.

She looked older than the years I had spent wandering, as if those my youthfulness belied had been added to hers by some karma. She drove like a terrorist. Or maybe it was that I hadn't travelled in a car, in a collapsing Tata pick-up, in a city, in Delhi ... No, she drove like a terrorist.

'You should have told me earlier.'

'He didn't want to. He wants to be in control if it.'

'What is it exactly?'

'Huntingdon's.'

'Can they do anything?'

'They never could. They still can't.'

Sarasvati blared her way through the scrimmage of traffic wheeling about the Parliament Street roundabout. The Shaivites still defended their temple, tridents upheld, foreheads painted with the true tilak of Shiva, the three white horizontal stripes. I had seen that other mark on the forehead of almost every man and woman on the street. Sarasvati was pure.

'He would have known whenever he had the genetic checks when I was conceived,' I said. 'He never said.'

'Maybe it was enough for him to know that you could never develop it.'

Dadaji had two nurses and they were kind, Nimki and Papadi he called them. They were young Nepalis, very demure and well-mannered, quiet spoken and pretty. They monitored him and checked his oxygen and emptied his colostomy bag and moved him around in his bed to prevent sores and cleared away the seepage and crusting around the many tubes that ran into his body. I felt they loved him after a fashion.

Sarasvati waited outside in the garden. She hated seeing Dad this way, but I think there was a deeper distaste, not merely of what he had become, but of what he was becoming.

Always a chubby man, Tushar Nariman had grown fat since immobility had been forced on him. The room was on the ground floor and opened out onto sun-scorched lawns. Drought-browned trees screened off the vulgarity of the street. It was exercise for the soul if not the body. The neurological degeneration was much more advanced than I had guessed.

My father was big, bloated and pale but the machine over-shadowed him. I saw it like a mantis, all arms and probes and manipulators, hooked into him through a dozen incisions and valves. Gandhi it was who considered all surgery violence to the body. It monitored him through sensory needles pinned all over his body like radical acupuncture and, I did not doubt, through the red Eye of Shiva on his forehead. It let him blink and it let him swallow, it let him breathe and when my father spoke, it did his speaking for him. His lips did not move. His voice came from wall-mounted speakers, which made him sound uncannily divine. Had I been hooked into a third eye, he would have spoken directly into my head like telepathy.

'You're looking good.'

'I'm doing a lot of walking.'

'I've missed you on the news. I liked you moving and shaking. It's what we made you for.'

'You made me too intelligent. Super-success is no life. It would never have made me happy. Let Shiv conquer the world and transform society: the superintelligent will always choose the quiet life.'

'So what have you been up to, son, since leaving government?'

'Like I said, walking. Investing in people. Telling stories.'

'I'd argue with you, I'd call you an ungrateful brat, except Nimki and Papadi here tell me it would kill me. But you *are* an ungrateful brat. We gave you everything – *everything* – and you just left it at the side of the road.' He breathed twice. Every breath was a battle. 'So, what do you think? Rubbish, isn't it?'

'They seem to be looking after you.'

My father rolled his eyes. He seemed in something beyond pain. Only his will kept him alive. Will for what I could not guess.

'You've no idea how tired I am of this.'

'Don't talk like that.'

'It's defeatist? It doesn't take your superhuman intellect to work out that there are no good solutions for this.'

I turned a chair around and perched on it, hands folded on the back, my chin resting on them.

'What is it you still need to achieve?'

Two laughs, one from the speakers, the other a phlegmy gurgle from the labouring throat.

'Tell me, do you believe in reincarnation?'

'Don't we all? We're Indian, that's what we're about.'

'No, but really. The transmigration of the soul?'

'What exactly are you doing?' No sooner had I asked the question than I had raced to the terrible conclusion. 'The Eye of Shiva?'

'Is that what you call it? Good name. Keeping me ticking over is the least part of what this machine does. It's mostly processing and memory. A little bit of me goes into it, every second.'

Uploaded consciousness, the illusion of immortality, endless reincarnation as pure information. The wan, bodiless theology of post-humanity. I had written about it in my *Nation* articles, made my soapi families face it and discover its false promises.

Here it was now in too too much flesh, in my own real-world soap, my own father.

'You still die,' I said.

'This will die.'

'This *is* you.'

'There is no physical part of me today that was here ten years ago. Every atom in me is different, but I still think I'm me. I endure. I remember being that other physical body. There's continuity. If I had chosen to copy myself like some folder of files, yes, certainly I would go down into that dark valley from which there is no return. But maybe, maybe, if I extend myself, if I move myself memory by memory, little by little, maybe death will be no different from trimming a toenail.'

There could never be silence in a room so full of the sounds of medicine, but there were no words.

'Why did you call me here?'

'So you would know. So you might give me your blessing. To kiss me, because I'm scared, son, I'm so scared. No one's ever done this before. It's one shot into the dark, What if I've made a mistake, what if I've fooled myself? Oh please kiss me and tell me it will be all right.'

I went to the bed. I worked my careful way between the tubes and the lines and wires. I hugged the pile of sun-starved flesh to me. I kissed my father's lips and as I did my lips formed the silent words, *I am now and always must be Shiv's enemy but if there is anything of you left in there, if you can make anything out of the vibrations of my lips on yours, then give me a sign.*

I stood up and said, 'I love you, Dad.'

'I love you, son.'

The lips didn't move, the fingers didn't lift, the eyes just looked and looked and filled up with tears. He swam my mother to safety on an upturned desk. No. That was someone else.

My father died two months later. My father entered cybernetic nirvana two months later. Either way, I had turned my back once again on Great Delhi and walked out of the world of humans and aeais alike.

The morning of the white horse

What? You expected a hero? I walked away, yes. What should I have done, run around shooting like filmi star? And who should I have shot? The villain? Who is the villain here? Shiv? No doubt he could have provided you with a great death scene, like the very best black-moustached Bollywood baddies do, but he is no villain. He is a businessman, pure and simple. A businessman with a product that has changed every part of our world completely and forever. But if I were to shoot him nothing would change. You cannot shoot cybernetics or nanotechnology; economics stubbornly refuses to give you an extended five-minute crawling death-scene, eyes wide with incomprehension at how its brilliant plans could all have ended like this. There are no villains in the real world – real *worlds*, I suppose we must say now – and very few heroes. Certainly not ball-less heroes. For after all, that's the quintessence of a hero. He has balls.

No, I did what any sensible Desi-boy would do. I put my head down and survived. In India we leave the heroics to those with the resources to play that game: the gods and the semigods of the Ramayana and the Mahabharata. Let them cross the universes in three steps and battle demon armies. Leave us the important stuff like making money, protecting our families, surviving. It's what we've done through history, through invasion and princely war, through Aryans and Mughals and British: put our heads down, carried on and little by little survived, seduced, assimilated and in the end conquered. It is what will bring us through this dark Age of Kali. India endures. India is her people and we are all only, ultimately the heroes of our own lives. There is only one hero's journey and that leads from the birth slap to the burning-ghat. We are a billion and half heroes. Who can defeat that? So, will I yet be the hero of my own long life? We shall see.

After my father's death I wandered for decades. There was nothing for me in Delhi. I had a Buddhist's non-attachment though my wandering was far from the spiritual search of my time as a sadhu. The world was all too rapidly catching up my put-upon characters of *Town and Country*. For the first few years I filed increasingly sporadic articles with *Gupshup*. But the truth was that everyone now was the Voras and the Deshmukhs and the Hirandanis. The series twittered into nothingness, plotlines left dangling, family drama suspended. No one really noticed. They were living that world for real now. And my sense reported the incredible revolution in a richness and detail you cannot begin to imagine. In Kerala, in Assam, in the beach-bar at Goa or the game park in Madhya Pradesh, in the out-of-the-way places I chose to live, it was at a remove and thus comprehensible. In Delhi it would have been overwhelming. Sarasvati kept me updated with calls and emails. She had so far resisted the Eye of Shiva, and the thrilling instantaneousness and intimacy, and subtler death of privacy, of direct thought-to-thought com-munication. Shiv's Third Revolution had given firmness and vision to her gadfly career. Sarasvati had chosen and set herself among the underclass. I took some small pleasure from the television and online pundits saying that maybe that old fart Shakyamuni had been right in those terrible populist potboilers in *Gupshup*, and the blow of technology had cracked India, all India, that great diamond of land, into two nations, the fast and slow, the wired and the wire-less, the connected and the unconnected. The haves and the have-nots. Sarasvati told me of a moneyed class soaring so fast into the universal-computing future they were almost red-shifted, and of the eternal poor, sharing the same space but invisible in the always-on, always-communicating world of the connected. Shadows and dust. Two nations; India – that British name for this congeries of ethnicities and languages and histories, and Bharat, the ancient, atavistic, divine land.

Only with distance could I attain the perspective to see this time of changes as a whole. Only by removing myself from them could I begin to understand these two nations. India was a place where the visible and the invisible mingled like two rivers flowing into each, holy Yamuna and Ganga Mata, and a third, the invisible, divine Saraswati. Humans and aeais met and mingled freely. Aeais took shapes in human minds, humans became disembodied presences strung out across the global net. The age of magic had returned, those days when people confidently expected to meet djinns in the streets of Delhi and routinely consulted demons for advice. India was located as much inside the mind and the imagination as between the Himalayas and the sea or in the shining web of communications, more complex and connected and subtle than any human brain, cast across this sub-continent.

Bharat was poor. Bharat had cracked hands and heels, but she was beautiful. Bharat cleaned and swept and cooked and looked after children, Bharat drove and built and pushed carts through the streets and carried boxes up flights of stairs to apartments. Bharat was always thirsty. How human it is to be so engrossed by our latest crisis that we forget we have failed to solve the crisis before that. Storage was India's problem. Information was increasing exponentially, available memory only arithmetically. Data-Malthusianism threatened the great technological revolution. Water was Bharat's. The monsoon, ever fickle, had dispersed into a drizzle, a few thunderstorms that ran off the crusted earth as soon as it dropped its rain, a tantalising line of grey clouds along the horizon that never came closer. The Himalayan glaciers that feed the great rivers of North India and the slow-running Brahmaputra were exhausted; grey moraines of pebbles and dry clay. The mother of droughts was coming. But what was this to a connected class? They could pay for desalinated water, wasn't India born from the waters? And if the worst came to the worst and the universe ended in fire, they could, through their dazzling new technology, translate themselves out of their icky physical bodies into that dream India between the real and the virtual worlds. Bodhisofts, they called these ascended creatures. Shiv would have been proud of a name like that.

From my beach-bar, from my dive school, from my game reserve and bookshop and dance club and coffeehouse and walking-tour company, from my restaurant and antique shop and meditation retreat, I watched my prophecies come true. Yes, I embarked on all those enterprises. Ten of them, one for each of the dashavatara of my divine namesake. All of them on the edge of the world, all of them with that overview down onto the Age of Kali. I lost count of the years. My body grew into me. I became a tall, lean, high-foreheaded man, with a high voice and long hands and feet. My eyes were very beautiful.

I measured the years by the losses. I re-established contact with my old political counterpart in Varanasi, Shaheen Badoor Khan. He had been as surprised as any when I had vanished so abruptly from the political stage but his own career was not without a hiatus and when he discovered that I was the Shak-yamuni behind the *Town and Country* articles (widely syndicated) we began a lively and lengthy correspondence that continued up until his death at the age of seventy-seven. He died completely, and like a good Muslim. Better the promise of paradise than the cloudy doubts of the bodhisoft. My own mother slipped from the world into the realms of the bodhisofts.

Sarasvati would not say whether it was a fearful illness or just ennui at the world. Either way I never looked for her among the skyscraper-sized memory stacks that now besieged Delhi along the line of the old Siri Ring. Lakshmi too, that almost-wife and sweetest of co-conspirators, entered the domain of the bodhisofts where she could explore the subtle mathematical games that so delighted her without limits. It was not all loss. The Age of Kali brought a friend; another great Khan, my old tutor from the Dr Renganathan Brahminical College. He would swirl out of the cloud of I-dust that had replaced the screens and 'hoeks for those who atavistically refused the Eye of Shiva and he would spend many a delightful evening lecturing me on my moral laxity.

Then the dust started to blow through the streets of Delhi. It was not the dust from the perpetual drought that burned the fields and reduced the crops to powder and sent millions from Bharat into the cities of India. It was the dust of Shiva, the sacred ash of the Purusa Corporation's nanoscale computers, released into the world. Bharat might be choking, but here! here! was the solution to India's memory problems. Shiv did have a name for these, a good name too. He called them devas.

He called me. It was decades since we had spoken last in the garden of his house in Varanasi, over lemonade. I was running the dharamshala at Pandua then. It was spacious and peaceful and cool and the only disturbance was the over-heavy feet of the Westerners who flocked to the place. They are not naturally barefooted people, I have found. The I-dust relay chimed, a call. I was expecting Mr Khan. My brother whirled out of the helix of motes instead. He had lost weight, too much weight. He looked well, too much well. He could have been anything: flesh, aeai agent, bodhisoft. We greeted each other and said how well each other looked.

'And how is Nirupa?'

His smile made me think that he was human. Aeais have their own emotions, or things like emotions.

'She's good, Very good Twenty-eight now, would you believe?'

I confessed that I could not.

'Doing well, found an eligible boy, from a good enough family, who's not a complete gold-digger. Old-fashioned stuff like that. I'm glad she bided her time, but they can afford to take their time now.'

'All the time in the world.'

'She's beautiful. Vish, there's something I need to tell you. Not a warning exactly, more to prepare yourself.'

'This sounds ominous.'

'I hope not. You've predicted it all very well.'

'Predicted what?'

'Don't be coy. I know who you were. No secrets in the transparent world, I'm afraid. No, you got it right and I'm glad you did it because I think you softened the blow, but there is something you didn't predict, maybe something you couldn't predict.'

A whisper of breeze stirred the candle flames in my simple wooden room. Heavy white feet went tread tread tread on the creaking boards outside my latticed window. If they had looked through the grille they would have seen me talking to a ghost. No strange thing in this age, or most other ages.

'Whenever we last spoke, you said that you were making use of information from the legacy-device the original aeais had bequeathed us.'

'Well-guessed.'

'It seems logical.'

'When the Trimurti left Earth, they opened a connection to a separate space-time continuum. There were several major differences from our space-time. One was that time runs much faster there than in our space-time, though it would not be noticeable to anyone in that continuum. Another was that the arrow of time was reversed. The Trimurti move backwards in time; this was how their artefact, which the Americans call the Tabernacle, seemed to have predated the solar system when it was found in space. But the more important one – and that was why they chose it – was that information was integrated into the geometrical structure of that space-time.'

I closed my eyes and focused my imagination.

'You're saying that information, data – minds – form part of the basic structure of that universe. Minds without the need for bodies. The whole universe is like a cosmological computer.'

'You've got it.'

'You've found a way back into that universe.'

'Oh no no no no no. That universe is closed. It ended with the Trimurti. Their time is gone. It was an imperfect universe. There are others, mind-spaces like that, but better. We're going to open up dozens – hundreds, eventually thousands – of portals. Our need for processing will always outstrip our available memory, and the devas are just a stopgap. A whole universe, right beside ours, only a footstep away, available for computing resources.'

'What are you going to do?'

'The Jyotirlingas are coming.'

The Jyotirlingas were the sacred places where, in the Vedic Age, the creative, generative energy of the Lord Siva burst from the ground in pillars of divine light, the ultimate phallic linga symbols. These would come not from the earth, but another universe. And Shiv named them after his namesake's cosmo-logical cock. No one could accuse him of lack of hubris. His I-dust image sparkled and swirled and exploded into a billion motes of light. His smile, like that of the legendary Cheshire cat, seemed to remain. A week later, twelve pillars of light appeared in cities all across the states of India. By a slight misalignment, the Delhi Jyotirlinga touched down in the middle of the Dalhousie, the city's largest slum, crowded beyond all imagining with refugees from the drought.

The simultaneous appearance, at eleven thirty-three, of twelve columns of light in cities across India paralysed the rail network. It was one of the least of the disturbances that day but for me, on an island in the middle of the Brahmaputra and needing to get to Delhi, that was the most important. That there were any flights at all was a miracle, that I could book onto one at any price at all was proof indeed that the age of the gods had truly returned. Even when alien universes open up in the hearts of our great and ancient cities, Indian grandmothers will still need to travel to see their wee darlings.

I had tried to call Sarasvati but all com channels into Delhi were down and the call-centre aeais announced indefinite delays before the network was restored. I wondered what it would be like for those accustomed to being strung out across the deva net to be back into just one head as the Air Awadh Airbus took me up over the shrivelled silver thread of the parched Ganga. In the tiny toilet I once again transformed myself back into a shaved, shorn, urbane Delhi-boy. As we descended into Indira Gandhi airport the captain told those of us on the right to look out and we would see the Jyotirlinga. His voice was uncertain, not a tone you want to hear from an airline captain, as if he could not believe what he was seeing. I had been studying it long before the captain's call: a line of sun-bright light rising from the hazy, grey stain of central Delhi up beyond all sight, further than I could see, craning to look up through the tiny window into the darkening sky.

Sarasvati would be there. That was Shiv's warning. When the light struck, she would have looked around and, in the same instant, made her mind up. People in need. She could not refuse.

Immigration took an hour and a half. Five flights of journalists had disgorged at once. A wired world, it seemed, was no substitute for reporters on the ground. The hall buzzed with swarming fly-sized hovercams. Two hours to grind into Delhi in the limo. The highways were clogged with lines of traffic, all headed out, all moving with geological slowness. The noise of horns was appalling to one fresh from the profound, liquid silence of the dharamshala. Only military and media seemed headed into Delhi but soldiers stopped us at intersections to wave past thundering convoys of chartered refugee buses. We were held up for a motionless half an hour on the big cloverleaf on Siri Ring. In awe and leisure, I studied the wall of memory farms; towering black monoliths drinking in sunlight through their solar skins, pressed shoulder to shoulder as far as I could see. In every breath of air-conditioned air I took, I inhaled millions of devas.

Every roadside, every verge and roundabout, every intersection and car park, every forecourt and garden was filled with the shanties and lean-tos of the refugees. The best were three low walls of brick with plastic sacking for a roof, the worst cardboard scrapes, or sticks and rags worked together into a sun-shade. Feet had worn away all greenery and stripped the trees bare for firewood. The bare earth had blown into dust, mingling with the airborne devas. The bastis pressed right up to the feet of the memory towers. What did Sarasvati imagine she could achieve here in the face of so colossal a catastrophe? I called her again. The network was still out.

Bharat had invaded India and now India was casting it out. We drove, blaring the horn constantly, past a terrible, emaciated army of refugees. No fine cars here. Trucks, old buses, pick-ups for the better off, behind them, swarms of phatphats, more overloaded than that fatal one I had seen on the Holi I discovered death. Motorbikes and mopeds almost invisible under bundles of bedding and cooking pots. I saw a chugging, home-engineered half-tractor device, engine terrifyingly exposed, dragging a trailer piled as high as house with women and children. Donkey carts, the donkey bent and straining at the loads. In the end, human muscle pushed the exodus onward: bicycle rickshaws, handcarts, bent backs. Military robots guided them, herded them, punished those who strayed from the approved refugee route, or fell, with shock sticks.

Before everything, over everything, was the silver spear of the Jyotirlinga.

'Sarasvati!'

'Vishnu?' I could hardly hear her over the roar.

'I've come to get you.'

'You've what?' It was as noisy where she was. I had a fix. The autodrive would take me there as quickly as it could.

'You've got to get out.'

'Vish.'

'Vish nothing. What can you do?'

I did hear her sigh.

'All right, I'll meet you.' She gave me a fresh set of co-ordinates. The driver nodded. He knew the place. His uniform was crisp and his cap miraculously correct but I knew he was as scared as I.

On Mehrauli Boulevard I heard gunfire. Airdrones barrelled in over the roof of the car, so low their engines shook the suspension. Smoke rose from behind a tatty mall façade. This street, I recognised it. This was Parliament Road, that was the old Park Hotel, that the Bank of Japan. But so faded, so dilapidated. Half the windows were out on the Park. The secluded gardens around Jantar Mantar on Samsad Marg were overrun with packing-case houses, their plastic roofs pushing right against the austere marble angularities of Jai Singh's astronomical instruments. Everything was overrun with lean-tos and huts and miserable hard-scrabble shelters.

'This is as far as I'm going to take you,' the driver said as we ran into an immovable horde of people and animals and vehicles and military at Talkatora Road.

'Don't go anywhere,' I ordered the driver as I jumped out.

'That's not likely,' he said.

The press was cruel and chaotic and the most terrifying place I have ever been but Sarasvati was here, I could see her in my mind-map. A cordon of police bots tried to drive me back with the crowds from the steps of the Awadh Bhavan but I ducked under, out and away. I knew this place. I had given my balls to work in this place. Then suddenly, wonderfully, I was in the clear. My heart lurched. My vision swam. Delhi, dear Delhi, my Delhi, they let this happen to you. The gracious greens and boulevards, the airy chowks and maidans of the Rajpath were one unbroken slum. Roof after roof after roof, slumping walls, cardboard and wood and brick and flapping plastic. Smoke went up from a dozen fires. This, this was Dalhousie. I knew the name of course. I had never thought it would ever become the name of the great sink where this newest of New Delhi's condemned would be driven by drought and want. Such disdain did new India show for old Awadh. Who needed a Parliament when universal computing made everything a consensus? From where I guessed the old Imperial India Gate had stood at the end of the gracious Rajpath, there rose the Jyotirlinga. It was so bright I could not look at it for more than moments. It cast a terrible, unnatural silver shine over the degradation and dread. It abused my Brahminic sensibilities. Did I smell voices, hear colour, was that prickle like cold lemon fur on my forehead the radiation of another universe?

People milled around me, smoke blew in my eyes, the down-draft of airdrones and hover cams buffeted me. I had only moments before the army would catch me and move me away with the rest of the panicked crowd. Or worse. I saw bodies on the ground and flames were coming up from a line of plastic shacks.

'Sarasvati!'

And there she was. Oh, there she was, plunging whip-thin in combat pants and a silk blouse, but filled her wonderful energy and determination out of the pile of collapsing housing. She dragged a child in each hand, smudge-faced and tearful. Tiny mites. In this place, she had slipped from my nuptial elephant to caper with the revellers in her ridiculous man's costume and exuberant false moustache.

'Sarasvati!'

'You've got a car?'

'It's how I got here, yes.'

The children were on the verge of bawling. Sarasvati thrust them at me.

'Take these two to it.'

'Come with me.'

'There are kids still in there.'

'What? What are you talking about?'

'It's a special needs group. They get left when the sky opens. Everyone else runs and leaves the kids. Take these two to your car.'

'What are you doing?'

'There are more in there.'

'You can't go.'

'Just get the to the car, then come back here.'

'The army.'

She was gone, ducking under the billowing smoke. She disappeared into the warren of lanes and galls. The children pulled at my hands. Yes yes, they had to get out. The car, the car wasn't far. I turned to try and find an easy way with two children through the wheeling mass of refugees. Then I felt a wave of heat across the back of my neck. I turned to see the blossom of flame blow across the top of the gali, whirling up rags of blazing plastic. I cried something without words or point and then the whole district collapsed in on itself with a roar and explosion of sparks.

The Age of Kali. I have little patience with that tendency in many Indians to assume that because we are a very old culture, we invented everything. Astronomy? Made in India. Zero? Made in India. The indeterminate, probabilistic nature of reality as revealed through quantum theory? Indian. You don't believe me? The Vedas say that the Four Great Ages of the Universe correspond to the four possible outcomes of our game of dice. The Krita Yuga, the Age of Perfection, is the highest possible score. The Kali Yuga, the Age of Strife, darkness, corruption and disintegration, is the lowest possible score. It is all a roll of the divine dice. Probability? Indian!

Kali, Paraskati, Dark Lady, Mistress of Death and Drinker of Blood, terrible ten-armed one with the necklace of skulls, She Who is Seated upon the Throne of Five Corpses. The Ender. Yet Kali is also Mistress of Regeneration. Ruler of All Worlds, Root of the Tree of the Universe. Everything is a cycle and beyond the Age of Kali we roll again into the Age of Gold. And that which cannot be reasoned with must then be worshipped.

I believe I was mad for some time after Sarasvati's death. I know I have never been sane as you would consider me sane. We are Brahmins. We are different. But even for a Brahmin, I was crazy. It is a precious and rare thing, to take time out from sanity. Usually we allow it to the very very young and the very very old. It scares us, we have no place for it. But Kali understands it. Kali welcomes it, Kali gives it. So I was mad for a time, but you could as easily say I was divine.

How I reached the temple in the little, drought-wracked town by the sewer of Mata Ganga, I have chosen to forget. How I came by the offering of blood to the priest, that too I've put where I put the dis-remembered. How long I stayed there, what

I did, does any of this matter? It was time out from the world. It is a powerful thing, to subject yourself to another time and another rhythm of life. I was a thing of blood and ashes, hiding in the dark sanctum, saying nothing but offering my daily puja to the tiny, garland-bedecked goddess in her vulva-like garbigraha. I could have vanished forever. Sarasvati, the brightest and best of us, was dead. I lolled on foot-polished marble. I disappeared. I could have stayed Kali's devotee for the rest of my long and unnatural life.

I was lolling on the wet, foot-polished marble when the woman devotee, shuffling forward through the long, snaking line of cattle-fences toward the goddess, suddenly looked up. Stopped. Looked around as if seeing everything for the first time. Looked again and saw me. Then she unhooked the galvanised railing and pushed through the switch-back line of devotees to come to me. She knelt down in front of me and namasted. Above the single vertical line of her Shakta-tilak she wore the red Eye of Shiva.

'Vish.'

I recoiled so abruptly I banged the back of my head off a pillar.

'Ooh,' the woman said. 'Ooh, cho chweet, that's going to smart. Vish, it's me, Lakshmi.'

Lakshmi? My former wife, player of games? She saw my confusion and touched my face.

'I'm temporarily downloaded into this dear woman's brain. It's rather hard to explain if you're not connected. Oh, it's all right, it's entirely consensual. And I'll give her herself back as soon as I'm done. I wouldn't normally do it – it's very bad manners – but these are slightly exceptional circumstances.'

'Lakshmi? Where are you? Are you here?'

'Oh, you have had a bit of a nasty bang. Where am I? That's hard to explain. I am entirely bodhisoft now. I'm inside the Jyotirlinga, Vish. It's a portal as you know, they're all portals.'

After the initial twelve, the pillars of light had arrived all over Earth, hundreds, then thousands. 'It is a wonderful place, Vish. It can be whatever you want it to be, as real as you like. We spend quite a lot of time debating that; the meaning of real. And the games, the number games; well, you know me. That's why I've taken this step for you, Vish. It can't go on. It's destructive, the most destructive thing we've ever done. We'll burn through this world because we have another one. We have heaven, so we can do what we like here. Life is just a rehearsal. But you've seen that, Vish, you've seen what that's done.'

'What is it Lakshmi?' Was it memory and fond hope, the mild marble concussion, the strange nanotech possession, but was this stranger starting to look like Lakshmi?

'We have to bring this age to an end. Restart the cycle. Close the Jyotirlingas.'

'That's impossible.'

'It's all mathematics. The mathematics that govern this universe are different from the ones that govern yours; that's why I'm able to exist as a pattern of information imprinted on space-time. Because the logic here allows that. It doesn't where I come from. Two different logics. But if we could slide between the two a third logic, alien to either, that neither of them could recognise nor operate, then we would effectively lock the gates between the universes.'

'You have that key.'

'We have a lot of times for games here. Social games, language games, imagination games, mathematical and logical games. I can turn the lock from this side.'

'But you need someone to turn the key on my side. You need me.'

'Yes, Vish.'

'I would be shut out forever. From you, from Mum, from Dad.'

'And Shiv. He's here too. He was one of the first to upload his bodhisoft through the Varanasi Jyotirlinga. You'd be shut out from everyone. Everyone but Sarasvati.'

'Sarasvati's dead!' I roared. Devotees looked up. The sadhus calmed them. 'And would this be the final answer? Would this bring around the Age of Gold again?'

'That would be up to you, Vish.'

I thought of the villages that had so welcomed and amazed and blessed and watered me on my sadhu wandering, I thought of the simple pleasures I had taken from my business ventures: honest plans and work and satisfactions. India – the old India, the undying India – was its villages. Sarasvati had seen that truth though it had killed her.

'It sounds better than sprawling in this dusty old temple.' Kali, Mistress of Regeneration, had licked me with her red tongue. Maybe I could be the hero of my own life. Vishnu, the Preserver. His tenth and final incarnation was Kalki, the White Horse, who at the end of the Kali Yuga would fight the final battle. Kali, Kalki.

'I can give you the maths. A man of your intelligence should be able to hold it. But you will need one of these.'

The woman lifted her hand and seized a fistful or air. She threw it into my face and the air coalesced into a spray of red powder. In mid-air the cloud moiled and boiled and thickened and settled into a red circle, a tilak, on my forehead.

'Whatever you do, don't connect it to the deva net,' Lakshmi said. 'I'm gong to have to go now. I don't want to outstay my welcome in someone else's body. Goodbye Vish, we won't ever meet again, in any of the worlds. But we were well and truly wed, for a while.' For a moment I thought the woman might kiss me, then she gave a little twitch and straightened her neck just so as if shaking out a crick and I knew Lakshmi was gone. The woman namasted again.

'Little Lord Vishnu,' she whispered. 'Preserve us.'

I picked myself up from the marble. I dusted off the ash of the dark goddess. I walked to the edge of the temple, blinking up into the light of the real sun. I had an idea where to go to do what I had to do. Varanasi, the City of Siva, the seat of the great Jyotirlinga. How might I support myself, with nothing but the dhoti around my loins? Then I caught a sudden movement: on a window ledge on the first floor of one of the many shops that leaned in close to the temple, a cat was edging out along a waterpipe in pursuit of a bird. And I had an idea that filled me with laughter.

So here it is, here it is: at long last. The great trick, the grand Finale of the Magnificent Vishnu's Celestial Cat Circus. The wire walk. You will never, ever have seen anything like this before, unless of course you've been to a certain Kali Temple ... See, here are the two wires. And here is our star performer. Yes, white Kalki gets his chance to shine at last. Up he goes on to the podium and ... drum roll. Well, you'll have to provide the drum roll yourself.

Kalki! Kalki, beautiful white Kalki: do your trick!

And there he goes, carefully sliding one paw, then another out across the two wires, tail moving to keep him in balance, the whole trembling to his muscular control. Go on Kalki ... Walking the wire. What a cat! And the final jump onto the further podium and I scoop him up to my chest and shout applause! Applause for my lovely cats! I let Kalki down and the rest of the cats run to join him, running their endless circle of fur and tails around the rope ring. Matsya, Kurma, Narasimha and Varaha; Varana, Pashurama and Rama; Krishna, Buddha and last but not least, Kalki.

I turn in the rising dawn light to savour the applause of my audience. And my cats, save your biggest cheer for Matsya,

Kurma, Narasimha, Varaha, Varana, Pashurama, Rama, Krishna, Buddha and Kalki who have performed for your pleasure. And me? Just an impresario, a ringmaster: a storyteller. The light is up now and I will detain you no longer for you have your work and I have a place to go and I think now you know where that is and what I must do there. I may not succeed. I may die. I cannot see Shiv giving up without a fight. So please, will you do one thing for me? My cats. Would you look after them for me? You don't have to feed them or anything like that, just take them. Let them go, they can look after themselves. It's where I got them from in the first place. They'll be happy on a farm, in the country. Lots to hunt and kill. You might even be able to make a bit of money from them. I mean, performing cats, who ever heard of a thing like that? It's actually much easier than you think. Meat does it, every time. There, I've given away the trick. Be good to them. Well, I'll be off then.

I push the boat out into the stream, run into the dawn-bright water and hop in. It rocks gently. It is a glorious morning; the Jyotirlinga ahead can hold no comparison to the sun. I touch my fingers to my forehead, to the tilak Lakshmi put there, in a small salutation to the sun. Then I put my back to the narrow oars and head out into the stream.